END TIMES: ALASKA

BOOKS ONE, TWO AND THREE
ENDURE, RUN, AND RETURN

D1715962

CRAIG MARTELLE

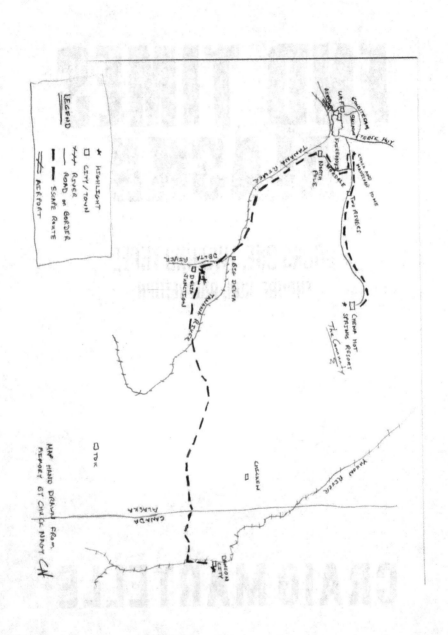

For Wendy Whitehead.
This book shows what my wife taught me about life.

A PERMUTED PRESS BOOK

ISBN: 978-1-68261-285-9

End Times Alaska:
Endure (Book One), Run (Book Two), Return (Book Three)
© 2017 by Craig Martelle
All Rights Reserved

Permuted Press, LLC
permutedpress.com

Published in the United States of America

ENDURE

Book One

WHY?

Smoke didn't billow from the barrel after I fired at the injured animal. I could see clearly the hole I'd blown through its chest. It had only been three days since the dog's humans had been home, but that was long enough.

The pair of dogs had fought viciously. One was dead and the other mortally wounded. I only put him out of his misery, at least that's what I told myself.

I'd broken through a window of a neighbor's home when I heard the pitiful wailing of the injured dog. I knew something was wrong when I heard it. A dog. Dying.

I couldn't leave it in pain, but that didn't make me feel any better.

It'd be best if I buried the two dogs, but temperatures were way too cold. What was it? Minus twenty Fahrenheit? Even the snow was frozen hard.

I left the dog where it lay, not far from its former house mate. I'd come back when it was warmer, before they started to decompose, and give them a proper burial.

I wondered how many times I'd tell myself that same story. I shoved the pistol, already cool after the shot, back into my pocket and put my glove on. I had the short walk home to think about how our lives had been a mere three days ago.

THE INSTANT

It was Tuesday morning. My wife, Madison, was a professor and started later in the day, so she was still home. Students in college couldn't be bothered to get out of bed early. Life began at the crack of noon. This was the best for us as it fit our lifestyle. I'd retired from the Marines quite a few years back, and filled the role of house husband, kept man, whatever you wanted to call it. I was too busy with the kids to work. In a previous life, I was gone from home two weeks out of every month.

It all happened in an instant. There was a bright flash from over the hills. The power went out. A massive thunderclap followed. The windows shook, but only one pane shattered. A strange sensation passed through the sky, like a heat wave one would see around the flames of a bonfire. Then calm returned. But not the power.

"What the hell was that?" I asked. It was a rhetorical question, the kind people ask when they are afraid. Neither my wife nor our dog attempted to answer.

Our two-year-old twins stopped playing, and both began to cry.

We looked toward the city, the direction of the flash, although there were ten miles, two hills, and a stand of trees between us and Fairbanks. It was late morning, but still mostly dark. This far north, Alaska in the winter was a different world. The sun both rises and sets in the south. It stays mostly on the horizon, visible for less than four hours on the solstice.

We expected to see the house next door burning. The explosion seemed that close.

But it wasn't. Nothing shone in the darkness nearby. Through the trees and above the hills, we could see the moonlight reflecting off a growing mushroom cloud.

"I think something blew up. The base? Maybe the power plant?" I didn't know what else to say. I was thinking out loud, and it didn't make sense, not even to me. Something had just happened, and it wasn't good.

"Do you think the power will come back on?" my wife asked.

"Not anytime soon. I'll set up the generator." It was the usual twenty-below-zero Fahrenheit outside. Snow covered everything. The trees sparkled with the cold frost, even in the near dark. It was pleasant. A few cars were on Chena Hot Springs Road. I wasn't sure where they'd be going. No one could have missed the explosion. Then again, there were always the curious and the obtuse.

Our cell phones showed no service. Our back-up battery power strips didn't even beep. A power surge must have preceded the outage. The surge protectors appeared to be dead.

I dug out our wind-up radio and gave it to Madison. She could spin it to life and see what the news said. "Why don't we just use your battery-powered radio?" she suggested. It had been ten minutes since we lost power and I already acted like we had nothing left.

We had everything left. I got the other radio for her.

Nothing. Static on static. This was an all-purpose radio, so it also had sideband. There wasn't anything anywhere. Nothing but noise. She set it aside. It was more important to take care of the twins. Two-year-olds require a great deal of attention, no matter what else is going on. No matter what other so-called priorities may exist.

And our dog Phyllis needed to go outside.

I bundled us both up, and we went outside. She did her thing while I set up the generator.

THE DOG MUSHER I

The power went out in an instant.

The Dog Musher looked around to see if it might be the line coming to his place. He couldn't see anything. Losing power was nothing new outside of Two Rivers, Alaska, and it was nothing to fear.

He had a small kennel, only twenty dogs, but it was all his. He wasn't young, but he wasn't old. He found solace in the dogs and peace in mushing. At one time, he had been somebody. Worked in a big city. Made lots of money.

Then he had a heart attack. His company foundered. His wife left him.

In Alaska, unless you live in a village, almost everyone comes from somewhere else. It's rude to ask about someone's past. Your past didn't matter here. What mattered was today and what you were doing to make it through the next winter.

In Alaska, dog mushers are revered. They were the first to break new trails. Long ago, they were the only ones who were mobile in winter. At one point they delivered the mail. They held communities together. Dog mushing wasn't a sport. It was a way of life.

It was a way of life that he had chosen when he abandoned the speed of the big city.

He had a shed full of dog food. He had two sleds. He had a huge pile of split firewood. He didn't need electricity. It was nice, but he didn't need it.

He hadn't planned to run the dogs today, but without power, he thought he would take them out. There is nothing sled dogs like more than running.

As usual, he took supplies to stay overnight, just in case something happened. He planned to return today, but one never knew. He would take it easy. He didn't have a destination in mind, so he'd let his lead dog follow his nose.

The Dog Musher took a full team – two lead dogs, two swing dogs, six team dogs, and then his two stalwart wheel dogs. The lead dogs were the smart ones. They picked out the trail and they set the pace. They led the dog team. The two swing dogs were trained to form an arc around a corner. If the dogs just followed the lead dogs, then they'd dive off the trail. Everything had to be done smoothly. A good team would flow behind the lead dogs, taking the weight of the sled with them, allowing the leaders to focus on the trail ahead. The team dogs were the work horses, pulling the majority of the weight. The wheel dogs were the strongest as they had to deal with the constant jerking of the sled. They were responsible for getting the sled moving. They would pick up the tension if the sled pulled back. The wheel dogs were calmer. They had to be.

The Dog Musher loved his team. "Line Out! Line Out!" he called to his lead dogs. They obediently pulled the rigging straight out from the sled. One at a time, he hooked up his dogs, giving them a pat on their haunches as he went to the next dog. After they were in position, he walked the line one more time to ensure the tug lines weren't tangled as they were attached to the tow line. The rigging was correct.

As the Dog Musher stepped behind the sled, the dogs were barely contained. They barked joyfully, ready to go. They wheel dogs pulled hard, trying to get the sled to move. This only resulted in them jumping into the air. The other dogs pranced. They couldn't stand still. The Dog Musher pulled up the snow hook and belted out a hearty, "Let's go!"

As one, the barking stopped and they pulled. The sled started to move and quickly picked up speed. The lead dogs jogged forward, then ran as the sled accelerated. They settled into a good pace, one they could maintain all day. Their booted paws made plastic sounds as they beat against the snow. This part of the trail was well-defined from frequent use. It was hard-packed and would be for the first few miles. After that, it was open range and who knew what they would encounter.

And the Dog Musher didn't care. For him, right now, this was heaven.

THE LOGISTICS

I was a pseudo-prepper. Living in Fairbanks, Alaska, one must understand that a polar vortex or an earthquake or a month straight of minus fifty degrees Fahrenheit weather could cut you off from the rest of the world. Since we lived about ten miles outside the city, even more so for us. We had one utility – electricity. Everything else was trucked in. Our internet was provided by a mifi slaved off a cell tower not too far away.

I believed in having enough of everything to get us to the next summer. It was more important now than ever.

I did a quick tally of what we had on hand. Gasoline, water, pellets for the stove, and so on. We had enough for one month of one thing, three of another.

My goal of being able to survive all winter was laudable, but this was the United States and the twenty-first century, so how long would we be without power? We thought maybe a week, but at this point, we'd wait for news and make it a big slumber party with the twins. We could cook on our stove top. It ran on propane, so we used a lighter and it worked great. We had a battery backup for our pellet stove. And we could use our generator to run the stove, as well as charge the battery and keep the refrigerator cold.

All in all, for the near term, we didn't have anything to worry about.

When the sun rose, it didn't shed any light on the situation. There was an unnatural haze in the direction of the city, but since prevailing winds blew toward the southeast, nothing was coming our way. Smoke billowed here and there. I thought, *Whatever happened started at least one heavy fire.*

THE FIRST DAY

Diapers. At two and a half years old, we were on the cusp of going diaper-free. We had diapers enough for ten days. We hoped our prediction of no power for seven days would pan out. If not, we'd have to run to the store. Would anything be open? I expected something would be. Somewhere anyway. Searching for diapers would probably be our first excursion.

The pellet stove stood in the great room of our one-story home and provided heat for a large, open area.

We took the mattress off the bed in the spare room and brought it into the great room, the only room heated when we were without power. We used the kerosene heater sparingly in the utility room to keep our water pump and heating system from freezing. Otherwise, fifty degrees inside the house would have to be considered balmy.

We dug out a few of our many blankets. We used some of them to make a tent off the couch. The twins were having a great time. They lived all of their short lives in Alaska, so the cold didn't bother them. It didn't take long for temperatures to drop in the house, a few degrees an hour. Our 5+ star energy rating served us well. It would keep the cold out while holding in the heat.

We took out extra winter clothes and brought those to the great room. No sense putting on a cold change of clothes if we didn't have to.

Toys. *We better bring some toys in from the kids' room*, I thought. *Who wants to play with a cold toy?*

It was still late morning. Lunch would be the same. The afternoon would be the same – playing outside, playing inside, reading to them, and naps. Then dinner would be the same. After dinner we would substitute reading for TV. All in all, not much changed. We would live in one room of the house for as long as it took to get the power back on.

We went outside a number of times so Phyllis could do her business. We put her heavy coat and boots on as we were outside for a while. The twins played in the snow. It was too cold to build a snowman, but plowing through the white stuff was always fun. Fairbanks has a dry climate so the snow was light. It can get deep, though, but for a two-year-old, anything is deep. They were buried to their waists. Phyllis would jump in behind them after they cleared a path.

It made the indoors seem that much warmer. There was a seventy-degree temperature difference between outside and in. We took off our coats, the twins their snowsuits, and we asked Mom to make us hot chocolate. Easy enough. Light the stove with a lighter. Heat the water. Make hot chocolate.

We were all together and we had what we needed. We would read by flashlight and we would all sleep in a pile, wearing sweats and whatever. We would share our warmth, especially from the dog. Phyllis would sleep in the middle – she'd be good with that. She loved her pack of humans!

The twins loved the attention from their parents. This day seemed to be all about them. They didn't care that the power was out. I couldn't be sure that they even noticed. It wasn't the first time we'd been without power.

The pellet stove ran well on the battery. We slept well. Power wasn't back on when I got up, though. Bummer.

THE SECOND DAY

Although Phyllis had short hair, her pit bull fur was dense, so she was comfortable in temperatures around freezing. She had different coats she wore depending upon how cold it was when she went outside. When it was really cold, she also wore boots.

She still went outside, so nothing changed for her either. Her dry dog food tasted good to her, whether it was sixty-eight or fifty inside.

For us, we could use the toilets for a bit, just until temperatures in the house dropped below freezing. At that point we risked backups from the line to the septic being frozen. Although the pump wouldn't run, we could manually refill the toilet tanks from one of numerous five-gallon jugs we kept in our garage.

The generator ran well enough. It started each time and was frugal on gas. In the first day, we only burned a gallon or so.

It was cold outside, but it was crystal clear. There wasn't any wind. It was always beautiful here in the winter. The stars filled the sky. The northern lights visited often, providing a magical scene over our home.

Traffic was intermittent on Chena Hot Springs Road. Cars and trucks came and went. We still had no cell phone signal. We decided to turn them off. No sense in wearing down the battery. Recharging was no longer easy. It had to be planned like anything else we wanted to run off the generator.

We took care of the refrigerator. I didn't want to lose my mustard collection! One needed to keep things in perspective. We also had cheese and meats and other things that needed to stay cool. Our time frame was a week. We could do the extension cord from the generator for that long.

The second day was about the inventory. What did we have? What did we need? What did we want?

Holy crap! I was going to run out of creamer for my coffee in the next day. At least I had plenty of coffee. Unfortunately, nearly all of it was for the Keurig. Which meant electricity. Which meant it would last a lot longer, because I would only get one, maybe two cups a day.

Fresh stuff – salad and whatever. We'd figure that out and not worry about it.

And of course, diapers.

Diapers and coffee. Those were the staples of my life.

So was routine.

We put the kids in their snowsuits and then positioned them on their sleds so Phyllis could get a good walk. We'd see what other people were doing in the neighborhood.

Since most people worked in the city, we expected that they came home early and would be staying home today, although there hadn't been any vehicles driving our road. A light dusting of snow from the previous day had not been disturbed.

Looking closely, it wasn't snow. It looked like ash. Maybe some people had panicked when they were without power and burned green wood. But then again, this is Alaska, and no one panics when the lights go out. They know what is okay to burn.

In our half-mile block with twelve homes, only one had a car in the driveway. No one had come or gone since the time of the accident.

That was odd. A number of people had dogs. One couple with small children left their Husky outside when they were gone. We went to that house. No answer at the door. No one home. I checked the back porch where they kept their dog when they weren't there. Madison stayed in the road with the kids, their breath making little clouds in front of their faces.

The Husky was curled up in her crate, trying to stay warm. She whimpered when she saw me. "You're coming with me," I told her. I would leave a note on the door to let the family know we had their dog. Whenever they returned, I'm sure they would appreciate the help. I know I would if Phyllis was trapped without us.

I had heard the Husky's name before, but couldn't remember what it was. We decided to call her Husky for now. There wasn't a leash, so I just held her collar. Phyllis seemed to welcome her. They sniffed each other as dogs do, and then we headed home.

The twins loved the new addition to the family. They loved dogs, man's best friend.

Except when we got home. Phyllis hadn't realized that her space was going to be invaded. So there was some growling and a brief throw-down, but after the yelling stopped, and the hierarchy established, we settled in. We put Husky in the garage by herself as we fed her a full bowl of dog food. She hadn't eaten in who knew how long. She drank thirstily from a separate bowl. Then we brought her back in the house. The dogs would have to learn to eat at the same time, in the same place, but not today.

We had one extra leash, the retractable kind. I didn't really like it, so I tied a carabiner to a length of rope, duct-taped over the knot, and declared it good.

Now I could take both dogs out. Around the house, Phyllis didn't need a leash, but I didn't want to risk her running in front of a vehicle during our walk around the neighborhood.

"It's strange that no one has come home. The roads must be blocked off." I wasn't sure what to think so I thought out loud. As a career Intelligence Officer, I had no problem speculating, but I liked data. With data, you could draw a conclusion. With more data, the chances improve that your conclusion will be correct. "I'm going to take your Jeep to town and see what's up." Madison's Jeep Wrangler was the better all-purpose vehicle than my Jeep Liberty.

"I'm not sure about that. Let's just stay home for a bit. I'm sure we'll find out something soon," she said.

"Turn on your cell phone and see if you can get a signal."

Madison powered up her new iPhone, holding it up to the windows as it searched. No signal.

"I'll just run to the gas station on Farmer's Loop and see if I can pick up some diapers."

"Okay, but don't be gone long. You can't call me if something happens."

I assured her that I would whip out and back. We hadn't heard traffic in a little while, so nothing would hold me up.

It wasn't too cold in the garage yet. We had been running the kerosene heater as needed to keep the utility room above freezing. We lived in some decadence, as our garage was heated by an in-floor system. The Jeep started right away. I turned its heater on full.

Without power, we had to unhook the garage door from the opening arm and lift it manually. Madison shut it after I pulled out. With nothing but static, I shut off the radio.

FIRST LOOK AT THE CITY

There are plenty of times when there is no traffic on Chena Hot Springs Road. The main roadway showed use, but the road was clear. I didn't think about it. I turned onto the road as I had done a thousand times before.

The intersection between Chena and the Steese Highway had claimed plenty of vehicles in its ditches. Today was no exception. Two vehicles were wedged against each other in the ditch of the on-ramp. I pulled past them and got out. The vehicles had been there for a while. Each was cold – frost filled the windshields. No one was inside. I didn't see any signs that someone had been hurt. Just another Steese fender bender.

I drove on.

A mile or so down the highway, it turns gently and you can see the western half of the city. I should say that you should be able to see the western half of the city. The entirety of what lay before me had been burned away, and smoke billowed into the sky from hundreds of fires that were burning themselves out. Nearly all of the buildings had been leveled. Much of the surrounding hillsides had also burned away. I sped up.

I pulled over at the Steese-Farmer's Loop intersection. My mind could not comprehend what I saw. It looked like the entire city was a junkyard. Very little stood. Nothing moved.

Most of the gas station at Farmer's Loop and Steese had collapsed and burned. It looked like the tanks had ruptured. This station had propane, fuel oil, and unleaded. Had.

I pulled to the side of the road and got out. The quiet surrounded me, pressed in on me. Nothing this side of the hill had been spared. My mind raced. The whole world had changed, at least our part of it.

It was clear. Help would not be coming.

The people. All gone.

Electricity would not come back on.

I looked at the ruins of the gas station. It was apparent that I wasn't the first to check things out. The cash register had been charred, but was mostly intact. It was open and empty. Of all the things people consider important, at this time, money was hardly one of them.

The good news was that other people were alive somewhere, as they'd raided the register after the destruction. But where were they?

Something about the enormity of the blast scratched at the back of my mind, but it didn't get my full attention. My list of concerns just grew by orders of magnitude.

I climbed back in the Jeep and raced home, ignoring stop signs and dead traffic signals. I drove the roads alone.

IT'S ALL GONE

"How can it all be gone," she replied. "The whole city? That's not possible."

"I should have taken my phone so I could get a picture, but yeah, it's all gone. I think there was a nuclear blast. I didn't think they had nukes at Wainwright. It's an Army post. I don't know about radiation, but toward the base, the scorching shows a massive explosion. I can't imagine what it was if it wasn't a nuke." I spoke in a stream of consciousness. It helped me think when I heard the arguments out loud. So I always talked to myself. Many times it was under the guise of talking with Phyllis or the twins.

"Either it was an accident or it wasn't. If it wasn't an accident, then it had to be an act of war – no civilians have anything that could cause that. Although the world isn't a great place right now, I haven't seen news that even hinted about us going to war. That tells me it was an accident. It was an accident with a nuke at the base. I don't know. The city is gone. Everybody who worked in the city is gone." I was speaking quickly, the words pouring out of me.

"What do we do?" Madison asked.

That was the question, wasn't it? What would we do indeed? Wait for help? Don't wait for help? I took deep breaths to calm myself.

"I don't think we can go anywhere. Even with all the gas we have in cans, would we make it someplace else? With the twins and now two dogs, we can't get there from here. We could try something later, but we should be seeing helicopters or airplanes or something. We have enough here for a while." I looked around as I held my wife's hand. "Let's wait and see what kind of help is on the way. I think we should hear something soon. We have to…" My mind rambled. There was so much to do.

"How can I let my mom know we are okay?" Madison asked.

"I don't know. Maybe we can get a message out through someone else. In any case, your mom won't know that we are okay, but we are. We'll get word to her sometime."

I didn't feel like we would hear anything. I was sick to my stomach.

We went outside to listen. We could hear a generator running somewhere in the distance. Dogs were barking on the other side of a stand of trees behind the house. A dog musher lived over there.

There wasn't any traffic on the road. There weren't the normal sounds of life happening. At minus twenty degrees Fahrenheit, birds don't sing, but there are always ravens. Not today though, which didn't bode well. Ravens are good luck in Alaska.

Maybe they were lamenting the loss of their brothers and sisters in town. Everything on the other side of the hills between us and town would have been affected. We didn't have any family in town, but we had plenty of friends. What happened to them? They could have been spared, couldn't they?

Where were the planes? There weren't any contrails in the sky. It had been more than a day since the explosion. Where was the governor? Wasn't he supposed to show up during a crisis and lead the people to salvation? Okay, that was a bit sarcastic, but it was hard to believe that the second largest city in Alaska could be wiped away and no one came to see it.

It was hard to take in. I kept asking myself, what happened and why?

The twins started crying. The dogs were enjoying their newfound friendship and there was a bit of chaos in the great room. That's the kind of crisis I prefer. One where we had some control in fixing it.

FAMILY MEETING

"What do we do?" my wife asked. We looked at each other. My wife was concerned. So was I as I tried to hide it. The twins were oblivious to it all. The dogs were asleep on our floor-bed.

"The city lost everything, but we lost nothing. We have what matters. Life isn't about what you can buy at the store. It's about living. Look at them." I pointed to the twins. "Fairbanks will come back. Sometime anyway. In the meantime, we do what we need to to make it until help arrives. Then we do what we need to do to make it to spring. Then there will be another step and another. We keep moving forward."

Madison snuggled next to me, burying her face in my chest. I closed my eyes and took a deep breath, smelling her hair, her clothes. I felt her next to me. I opened my eyes, looking at the twins. How blessed were we?

We didn't need much. I was a lifelong asthmatic. I needed my medications, but I always had about two months' supply on hand. Being a pseudo-prepper meant a certain amount of hoarding.

"Let's make a list of what we really need to get us to spring and maybe even into next summer. We'll keep a copy with us at all times, in case help comes. They can gather up people's needs and come back with the minimum to help people survive until the weather gets warmer."

Madison nodded. She was still in shock. Her mind was fully engaged, but she could not yet focus on just one thing.

I dug out a notepad and a pen and started to write.

"Asthma meds." I listed the three that were the most important. "Gasoline. What do you think? One hundred or more gallons can get us through the winter?"

Madison looked out the window. I put the list down and pulled her close. She rested her head on my chest, her shoulders slumped.

"What are you thinking?" I asked.

"What happened to the University?" It was almost a whisper.

I didn't know. I couldn't see it when I went to the city. Too much haze and smoke. Speculation is a horrible thing. We fill unknowns with ridiculous ideas. I suspected that the University had many buildings that survived. If buildings survived the blast, then people could have survived, too.

"Let's take a trip over there, tomorrow, at daylight. We have enough gas, although we could use more. I think the neighbors will be helping us, although they don't know it."

She nodded.

"Let's set ourselves up. If anyone else comes along, what can we share?" She looked at me, not understanding. "We're all in this together and I expect everyone will run short of something. It's minus twenty outside and it's probably going to get colder. People should be fine because everyone up here is used to certain trials and tribulations, but you never know. We all do better with a little help."

I wasn't suggesting the grand giveaway. I only proposed that we help others where we could. This might be a rough ride. When it was over, how would we see ourselves? I know that I wanted to see myself as one who helped. If I knew Madison, I expected she would be happier to see herself that way, too.

So, for the thirty-eighth time that day, I dressed to go outside. I took my flashlight and the dogs. Phyllis was wearing her coat and boots. Husky? I would have to figure out her tolerance for the cold. I didn't bother with leashes. No one was around. Plus, since we'd saved Husky's life, she was immediately loyal.

I took one of the kid's sleds. And my bolt cutter.

I went to our first neighbor's house. They both worked day jobs in the city. I knew they weren't coming home. They had gas cans outside their shed. One was almost empty, the other full. I put them both in the sled. There were two propane tanks. I took them, too. I used the bolt cutter on the shed's lock.

This was the first time I'd seen what was inside my neighbor's shed. A bad feeling came over me. I felt like a criminal rummaging. I vowed to keep track of what I had taken, should anyone ever question it. I would pay them back, whatever it took, if they returned.

The shed was filled with mostly summer stuff – mower, garden tools, summer tires, pesticides, potting soil. Interesting. I'd never seen them gardening. There was one more gas can, but it was labeled for a two-cycle. The only thing I had with a two-cycle engine was my chainsaw. I might need my chainsaw if we ran out of pellets, although you can't burn wood in a pellet stove. I took the can anyway.

We zipped back to the house. As I thought about it, I didn't want to store the gasoline cans in the garage, but leaving them out invited others to do what I had just done. I put the new gas cans and the ones from our shed in the garage, as far away from the kerosene stove as I could. The kerosene was going pretty fast. In another few days, we would be out of kerosene. We could burn fuel oil in it, but it would be smoky and give off noxious fumes. I wasn't sure that would be the best choice.

Husky was a big dog, so we would go through dog food quickly. We would need more, but not right now. I would go to Husky's house sometime in the next day or so, but that would mean breaking in, something I wasn't looking forward to. What would happen to me if it became easy to break into someone's house?

The house on the corner was owned by a working couple. They had a side-by-side quad, two snow machines, and a trailer. In the lower forty-eight, they called them snowmobiles, but not in Alaska. Here, they were snow machines. I didn't care what they were called. I cared that they worked.

These people were more traditional Alaskans than we were. They would have gasoline. After arranging our stash of gas cans, I headed back out. The dogs followed. They seemed happy to be outside, despite the growing darkness and perpetual cold.

A quarter-mile later found me knocking on the door. I waited. I knocked some more and then yelled, "Anyone home? Is anyone here?" A truck was in their driveway, but it hadn't been driven since before the explosion. I tried the door. It was locked. Today was not the day I would break in. I knew that day would come soon, unfortunately. Reality suggested we would need a snow machine or the quad.

I checked their shed. It smelled like gasoline. There was a fifty-five-gallon drum. With the flashlight on, I pulled the plug from the top. It was half full. Twenty-five or thirty gallons of gasoline. That would give us another month run time for our generator. The better part was that they had a hand pump. The barrel would be too much for a child's sled, but I filled two five-gallon gas cans he had on his snow machine trailer.

I looked around. They had everything, including a full winter's supply of split firewood.

When we made it back to the house, I dutifully recorded what I had taken and from where. I then added a second page of notes for future prospects. It was important to keep life and death information in context. With gas, we could run the generator, which recharged the battery backup while also directly running the pellet stove, which meant heat. At fifty degrees in the house, we could make it through the entire winter. If we didn't have power, we couldn't run the pellet stove. We could run the generator for two hours a day and that gave us all we needed to heat the house for the whole day. Two hours meant one gallon of gas. My rough math suggested that we now had enough to get us through three months of winter. *Help will arrive before then, won't it?* I wondered, especially since we hadn't seen anything that looked like the government. Someone should have shown the flag already. I worried, but wouldn't share my concerns with Madison. I needed to show her that we were in control and that we were fine.

This reminded me of my time in the Corps and a saying that a colonel once used. Amateurs talk tactics. Professionals talk logistics. I was thinking usage rates and supplies. I lived in my small world, lower on Maslow's hierarchy pyramid. My wife was more evolved.

Madison was thinking about what would happen to higher education. What would happen to her? She'd spent eight years in grad school earning her PhD. Now what?

DAY THREE BEGINS

I always woke up early. There's nothing like that first cup of coffee. No power. No problem. I would still have my coffee. As long as we had propane, I could boil water for rich joyousness.

Husky was a light sleeper. Phyllis slept like a rock. So Husky joined me in the kitchen while I heated water. She was soft. She was also a big bed hog. The twins didn't care as they were mini bed hogs. I found that I spent half the night barely on the mattress. Maybe we needed to put down a second and make a bigger bed.

The water reached boiling, so I shut off the stove. No sense heating it more than necessary. Waste not, want not, right? I still had to let my precious cup of joe cool a little before drinking. It didn't take long. It was only fifty degrees inside. Our indoor/outdoor thermometer was battery-powered. It showed the outside temperature at only minus five. It also predicted precipitation. If it was right (fifty/fifty chance), then hopefully it would hold off until we could get to the University for a look-see.

I enjoyed my coffee while reading a book on my iPhone. I turned it on to check for a signal. Nothing. I put it into Airplane mode, turned the screen down to a lower light level, and enjoyed my current book. I had downloaded a rather significant archive of books, so as long as I could keep my iPhone charged, I had reading material. I had both a solar charger, which didn't work very well in the Alaskan winter, and a Biolite stove. This small portable stove also charged electronics. All you needed was fine kindling to keep the fire burning. It burned fast, but it was small. I could use it to boil water for coffee and simultaneously charge my cell phone. At some point it would come in handy, but I didn't need it today.

We had plenty of batteries, especially if we took the ones in various remotes and other electronics throughout the house. It is surprising how many things we have with batteries. It is surprising how much electricity we use to make our lives convenient.

I bundled up and took Husky outside for a quick bathroom break. What about our bathrooms? We couldn't use our toilets anymore. I wasn't sure that fact had registered with Madison.

Peeing in the woods was how I grew up. Even in the cold it wasn't too bad. Madison would be more put out. Maybe we could use a bucket in the garage. Maybe I needed to move one of the Jeeps outside to make room for everything we needed to do in the garage.

I put Husky back inside. The Jeep started reluctantly. It was a bit sluggish, but at least it wasn't minus twenty. I popped the garage door and raised it by hand. I pulled the Jeep to the very edge of our parking pad, then backed it even further into a snowbank. It could be a long time before we needed it again. A very long time. I'd remove the battery and probably drain the gas tank, too. I'd have to do that in the light. Maybe it would get warmer outside. That would help me in my non-mechanic's approach to doing mechanical things.

I was an Intelligence Officer. Information. Theory. Thought. Not action. None of this was my forte. All I could do was the best I could do.

THE MORNING WALK

I was glad the rest of the family enjoyed their sleep. It made things easier when they woke up closer to late-morning sunrise. We were blessed with two happy babies. Charles and Aeryn would wake up giggling and happy with life. Diaper changes at fifty degrees took a little shine off, but after two and a half years, we were pretty efficient. Dirty diapers? In the garage. They were starting to pile up. I'd have to do something about that, too, along with the fact that no matter what, we would always be dangerously low on diapers. Maybe we needed a crash course on potty-training. They weren't quite ready, but need was probably going to make it non-negotiable.

I dressed again, putting a coat on Phyllis, but not her boots. Husky came along, too. While taking them for a walk around the neighborhood, my eyes were constantly drawn to things that could be important for our survival. My flashlight acted as a small window to our new world. *That thing there would be good. We could use that. I think we could find something useful there. What about the firewood? Maybe we can swap our pellet stove for their wood burner...*

The road was still clear as we hadn't had a snowstorm since the explosion. Would we need to keep it clear? We had a lawn tractor with a snow thrower on the front. If help arrived, a clean roadway would act as a beacon, bringing them to our home. Yes. I would keep the roadway clear, but only one lane worth, two passes with my tractor. Gasoline was at a premium, but worth the cost to welcome the arrival of any help and, as importantly, word of what happened and what our future looked like.

I lost sight of the dogs. I scanned the area with my flashlight, but didn't see anything. I stopped moving and listened. I heard a rustling by a house up ahead, then I heard the whimpering. I walked quickly that way. This was yet another house where no one had been home since the explosion. Husky was scratching at the door. I knocked and heard a sound inside. I knocked harder. Nothing. There was no heat, and frost covered the windows.

Using my elbow, I tried to break out a window pane. That wasn't as easy as I thought it would be. I looked around. There was a snow shovel. Using the handle as a ram, I broke through. Shining the flashlight in, there seemed to be dried blood on the floor. Had I really heard a sound from inside? I looked again before trying to climb through the window, and there, two eyes looked back at me. A dog. His fur was matted and there was a big gash in his side.

I heaved myself onto the window ledge. The dog inside growled at me. I pulled myself a little further over the window sill. He didn't get up. Maybe he couldn't. Behind him was the carcass of another dog. Without food, they had fought. The winner had been wounded. The loser was dead and partially eaten. It had been only three days.

Was this a sign of things to come?

I did not go inside. There was nothing I could do for the injured dog besides put him out of his misery. I hadn't thought before about arming myself. It was good that I had weapons. Once again, my mind had gone back to logistics while a dog was suffering. It was time to go.

We quickly returned home where I didn't bother to take off my coat while I dug out my pistol. "What's going on?" Madison was alarmed. Her eyes held mine. I didn't want to tell her. I didn't want to shock her.

"There's a badly injured dog. I'm sorry." I know she wanted to talk more, pleading for hope that the dog could be saved. We weren't in a position to do that, and not with this dog. We had two small children and this dog had killed out of necessity. Maybe the rest of my family would get to that point of understanding, but not today. I was already there.

I took care of it. And I felt horrible.

Back home, I didn't want to talk about it. I suggested that Madison take a hot shower, using our remaining hot water. The tank should still be warm and there was some pressure in the system. We might as well use it. Madison might as well use it. There's a lot to be said about a hot shower.

As it turned out, a lukewarm shower, as brief as it was, helped improve her mood a bit. It took most of the pressure in the system to bleed off the cold water, but when the warm water came, it was welcome.

CONTRAILS

As the sun finally climbed over the horizon, the hazy gray of a cloudy day hung all around us. We packed the twins into their car seats. And pulled the Jeep out. Madison shut the garage door and got in.

We were prepared for almost anything. We had cat litter to help us with traction if we got stuck. We had a shovel, an axe, and bolt cutters. We had a tow rope. We had extra blankets, food, and water. I had my pistol. A week ago, this trip would have taken about twenty minutes. I had no idea how long it would take today.

We took our cell phones and charger. No sense wasting recharging power while the engine was running. We also took a Bluetooth rechargeable speaker. It would be nice to play music at home.

We drove deliberately. If we got into an accident, there would be no help. It would make for a long walk home. Damn! I hadn't thought to bring the sleds for the twins. Without them, a walk home would be almost impossible.

On the Steese, there is a break in the trees where one can see the University's main buildings on the other side of the city. There were gaps in the smoke and haze that would probably hang over the city for weeks to come. Fires had burned the forests around the university, but the buildings appeared to be intact.

We made it to the gas station at Farmer's Loop and Steese without a problem. Once we turned onto Farmer's Loop, we realized how difficult things were going to be.

How many light poles had fallen across the road? How many power lines were in the road? How many vehicles had been on the road during the explosion? We slowed to a crawl. We had ten miles yet to go. We used the shoulder on the north side of the road often to get around the seemingly endless number of light and power poles. It was funny because we often complained about the lack of lighting on Farmer's Loop.

There was other debris in the road, too. From mailboxes to garbage cans to tarps. Anything that had been outside homes along the road had found its way into the open. Without other traffic, we were able to weave in and out, making some progress. Our biggest challenge appeared a couple miles in. Power lines were across the road. They were at all heights so we couldn't just crawl over them. I stopped and got out.

I tried pulling some cables down to the ground so we could drive over them. The lines were much heavier than I thought. Time for Plan B. "Get out the axe," I told Madison.

I couldn't cut the thick cable with my axe, but the power pole was made of wood. All I had to do was to break the support arm. I waded through the deep snow, setting myself up for a good angle to swing my axe. Madison watched me. She didn't want to be too close when I was swinging the axe. She knew me.

"Be careful."

Right on cue.

"Hey, look at that!" She pointed to the sky.

Contrails.

It looked like a commercial jet, maybe a 747 flying from Asia to the East Coast. That was a beautiful thing. To me, it meant that this interruption of our lives was temporary and not a whole new way of living. We cheered!

I set myself in and took a couple small swings with the axe. This wouldn't take long. I kept a wide stance, so just in case I missed, I wouldn't hit my foot. I angled the axe head slightly back and forth as it hit the beam. Cracks appeared. I pulled on the wood, then stomped on it. It broke and I fell into the snow.

"Are you all right?" Madison charged into the drift after me.

"I'm fine," I said as I brushed myself off. "We don't have too much daylight, so let's get going."

We continued to weave in and out of obstacles, but there were too many wires. We had only managed three miles, and we were stuck. It looked like a spider web ahead of us. We needed to turn around and try a different way.

"What do you think of College? Maybe Johansen and then University?" We had to try something else.

"How about Goldstream to Ballaine? That will keep us away from all of this," Madison offered.

We turned around and went back the way we had come. We had lost a great deal of time trying to navigate through the downed wires. Not much daylight remained.

The destruction along the roads was overwhelming. Farmer's Loop had houses on both sides. They weren't the newest homes, but I thought they would have been sturdier. The damage ranged from homes being leveled to just broken windows. None of them looked to be occupied. We scanned the hillside and saw what looked like smoke from a few fireplaces, but that was it. You could count the number on one hand.

Maybe others had pellet stoves like us. Those didn't smoke very much, but if you didn't have a generator or battery backup system, then your pellet stove wouldn't run. They were a convenient way to heat your house when electricity was available; otherwise, not so much.

We covered the five miles north on the Steese highway without any issues and turned west on Goldstream. This road seemed abandoned. There weren't many houses close to Steese, as the gravel piles that were gold dredge tailings lined both sides of the road. We saw one old lady outside with her dog and waved to her as we drove past. She waved back. It looked like she would have been happy had we stopped, but we were using up our daylight much quicker than I liked. We turned on Ballaine and followed its roller coaster approach as it headed to the eastern side of Farmer's Loop, close to the University.

The fires had ravaged the hillsides closer to the Loop. The cold and the intervening hills helped keep the fires from spreading, but the destruction was near complete. As we approached Farmer's Loop, the power lines were back, lying in the road. Numerous vehicles were scattered in and along the road. We purposefully didn't look inside them. Thank God we didn't have to get out to negotiate the obstacles. We made good time through this final carnage and to the University.

THE UNIVERSITY

First impressions were not bad. We drove onto the University campus using Tanana Loop. Trees had fallen and burned away. Debris was everywhere. Fires had burned through the area, taking out most of the family housing. Metal light poles remained standing, sentinels from a time when they had a purpose.

We didn't talk. The twins were asleep. Although she didn't say it, I knew Madison wanted to see her building, her office. So that's where we went. I couldn't go because of the twins, and we didn't want to haul them up three flights of stairs, so I offered her the pistol. She hesitated, and in the end, she wouldn't take it. We weren't supposed to have firearms on campus. I think the rules had changed, but that didn't matter anymore.

It only took her ten minutes before she returned. Somber.

"Was there anyone…?" I let the question hang. I hoped that no one had died in the building.

"No. There's no one there," she answered. "My office was fine. It's cold inside. A lot of windows are broken and some furniture fell over, but besides that, things look normal. Where are the people? Where are my friends?"

"And what happened?" I added.

A few professors whom we knew lived just off Farmer's Loop. We could stop by on our way back home. There was still daylight remaining, plus we had a trail to follow.

The twins woke up when Madison returned. We took the time to change them both. It was nice and warm in the Jeep, but we had to do it with the doors open. Their little bodies shivered when exposed to the elements, and they fussed. We bundled them back into their car seats.

We may come back to the university on another day, but for now, we'd check the homes of our friends.

Unfortunately, it was about to get worse. The snow finally started to fall.

SICKNESS

The first home, that of Patrice, was empty. Her mini-van was gone and no one was home. No sign of their dog, either. They had left. Without city utilities, they could not survive. Maybe leaving was the best thing for them.

We backtracked a bit from Patrice's home to get to Farmer's Loop, where our next stop was the home of Aidan, Sean, and their ten-year-old son. Smoke curled from their chimney. Someone was home!

We pulled in, and Madison jumped out and ran to the door. She beat on it, yelling for her friend and co-worker, Aidan. He opened the door and she jumped forward to give him a big hug. He pushed her away. "Don't touch me." He held his hands out, to fend her off. She was confused.

He looked sick. His skin was pale and splotchy. "Radiation." I'm not sure Madison understood. She was just happy he was alive. "We've all got it. You need to get out of here. Go back home and stay away from here," he pleaded.

"Are you all okay?" It hadn't hit her yet. The explosion was nuclear. An atom bomb had gone off in Fairbanks.

"No. We're not okay. We're dying from radiation poisoning."

Already?

"Do you need anything?" I asked, leaning out the Jeep window.

"No. Get out of here and get rid of those clothes. If you touched anything, get rid of that, too." Aidan's husband was an expert in the field of radiation, although he had focused more on atmospherics. He knew what was happening.

Madison started crying.

"Take care of yourselves and those kids of yours. Now please, go."

The snow fell lightly; small flakes hit the windshield. There wasn't any sound. Technology was loud. Without it, the world was a serene place, especially here, especially in the winter.

Madison sobbed in her seat.

"Don't touch your face with your gloves on. Take them off!"

She responded mechanically, letting them drop to the floor. How much had we touched at the University? How contaminated were we?

I drove probably faster than I should have, but our previous tracks in the ash were quickly disappearing. With our headlights on bright, I could see far enough ahead to stay in control. No traffic, but plenty of obstacles. We raced ahead at the front of the storm, maintaining a blistering pace of about fifteen miles an hour. We hit the end of a light pole and bounced into the air, but nothing broke. The Jeep kept rolling along.

"Be careful!" Madison shot at me. My family was here and I was putting them at risk.

"I'm sorry." I slowed to a crawl to get us back to Ballaine. I didn't want Madison outside any more. I didn't know what would cause us problems. I didn't know enough about radiation to feel comfortable that we weren't already sick.

Once on Ballaine, the roadway was mostly clear. We kept it in four-high and maintained a steady thirty-five mph.

I naturally slowed down as I came to the intersection of Ballaine and Goldstream. But I didn't stop. I kept it in four-wheel drive and headed up the hill toward home. This was the worst road in bad weather, but that was usually because people drove too fast. It was just us and we were only driving thirty-five.

The rest of the drive was uneventful, as much as a drive in the snow at dusk can be.

I didn't want to park the Jeep in the garage as it could be contaminated. We parked outside by the other Jeep, where we quickly took off our coats and wrestled the twins out of their car seats. We carried them to the garage, where we took off our boots, keeping them as close to the door as we could. The dogs were happy to see us. They had to wait.

When the twins were inside, we took off our pants. I pulled both pairs of jeans inside out so I didn't have to touch the outside. I put them by our contaminated boots. The dogs wanted to sniff everything they weren't supposed to, so I opened the door and shooed them outside. I put on my snow pants, a different pair of boots, and a heavy coat. I wrapped the boots in the inside-out jeans and carried everything outside. I didn't want to risk contaminating anything new, so I put them on the passenger floor of Madison's Jeep. I would move my Jeep back into the garage. It looked as if Madison's Jeep was down for the count, unless we found a Geiger counter somewhere. Maybe the Jeep wasn't contaminated, but we had no way of knowing for sure.

FALLOUT

Thank God for the prevailing winds and the hills, as they had saved us from the initial blast. They also saved us from the windblown radioactive dust. I felt guilty because I was happy that it wasn't us. Aidan had a bad case of radiation sickness, but he was in the bowl surrounding Fairbanks and had received what looked like a fatal dose.

One of the first symptoms of radiation sickness was nausea. I felt fine. Madison was upset, but that had nothing to do with being sick. We may have survived our trip to the city. I was worried about the twins. Their systems were not as well-developed. We needed to scrub down.

We heated a couple gallons of water, then went into the garage where there was a center drain. We cranked up the kerosene heater, then gave the twins a good scrub. They were none too pleased with any of it. We scrubbed our hands and faces, although we had been well covered when outside. We had taken our gloves off when we were in the Jeep. Madison had been inside the building, where she was more exposed than me. I didn't bring that up to her. I hoped that she hadn't kicked up too much dust and that she was okay. If not, there was nothing we could do.

I didn't want to lose her. I didn't want to have to carry on without her. I started to shake.

"What's wrong?" Madison was alarmed.

"Just had a cold chill. Brrr!" I ruffled the twins' hair. They still weren't pleased. "How is your stomach?" Nausea would have to be our measure. I didn't know what else to do, what else to look for.

"I'm not hungry, if that's what you mean. It was so horrible." I nodded. She wasn't ready to see what she had seen. Close friends were few and far between.

All the times when I didn't pay enough attention or wanted to watch some TV show. What had I taken for granted before? Here, in front of me now, was everything that mattered. And I was helpless to influence it. Why hadn't I checked further to see what the explosion was? I guessed a nuclear blast, but didn't think beyond that of what it meant. We would have never gone into town had we known. We took a great risk. Too much of a risk.

I turned off the kerosene heater. We hugged our twins, then went back inside. It was getting darker outside and there was plenty to do, but now was not the time. Tomorrow would be a better day.

"Who wants to hear Green Eggs and Ham!?" I yelled. We had one bag of Sam's Club popcorn in the cupboard. No sense trying to save it until it was no good. We even had some milk in the refrigerator. Time to make good hot chocolate, with milk. Who knew how long it would be before we could enjoy those delicacies again?

THE DOG MUSHER II

The Dog Musher went about his business as usual. The power still wasn't back on. A neighbor had driven by earlier and said that they were bugging out. The whole town was leaving, but he couldn't. He couldn't take all his dogs. He had a dog box for sixteen for his truck, but that wasn't enough.

He politely declined the invitation. The neighbor asked, since he was staying, if he could keep an eye on their place while they were gone. He nodded. They lived in the next house up the road. He didn't see what the big deal was. So there wasn't any power, that didn't mean you needed to be in a rush to leave.

"It's the end of the world! Bill drove down there yesterday and he said the whole city is gone! We're out here on our own!"

The city was gone? Maybe the world would be a better place with fewer cities, but Fairbanks needed to be there. It was big enough to support the needs of the community, but not so big that it sucked you in if you didn't want. Fairbanks was a good place with good people.

The Dog Musher thought it had to be an accident. No one could destroy a city deliberately, could they? No. It was an accident.

"There has to be some mistake. The city is gone?"

The neighbor nodded emphatically and threw his hands up in surrender. "I don't know. I'll see for myself when we drive through. My sister lives in Anchorage. We'll stay with her until things get sorted out. Then we'll be back."

"I'll watch your place for you. I'm sure you won't be gone long." As an afterthought, he added, "Be safe."

He needed to think. That meant it was time to take his dog team for a run.

THE CONVOY

About six inches of snow fell overnight. The plan was to have a cleared road for when help showed up.

I took the snow thrower out while it was still dark. It had good lights and there weren't any cars. I ran quickly, clearing a track around our parking pad, down the driveway, and down our dirt road all the way to Chena Hot Springs Road. One track down and one back. I made a loop around the neighborhood as well so we'd have a longer dog-walking trail. I ran in high gear. It took me a total of twenty minutes to clear what I wanted. At this rate, I could probably make it all winter with what was still in the gas tank. I would keep plowing a trail for as long as possible. We needed the normalcy of it.

It was late morning and the sun would be rising shortly. I was outside with the dogs, finishing up our morning generator run. We had two batteries charged and my Jeep was back in the garage. Madison's Jeep was now off limits.

With the generator shut down, the sound was obvious. Vehicles. And quite a few of them.

I put the dogs inside and raced to the road as quickly as my asthma would allow. I expected to see a convoy of military vehicles. That's not what it was.

It was a convoy of personal vehicles, mostly trucks, but also some motorhomes. They were coming from the Two Rivers side of us, heading toward the city. I got to the road by the time the first one was close. He stopped when he saw me waving.

"Grab your stuff and join us!" the scruffy old man yelled through the open window. A dog stuck its muzzle out and gave me a hearty sniff.

"Where are you going?" I asked as I scratched behind the dog's ears.

"Heading to Anchorage. We want to get out of here before we get trapped." The vehicles in the convoy slowed to a stop behind the old man. There were headlights for a good mile behind the first truck, and the vehicles were packed close together. A hundred vehicles? More? This could have been everyone left between here and Chena Hot Springs itself.

With him leading this many vehicles, there was no way he would be talked out of continuing. "There's radiation in the city. You might want to consider taking Goldstream and Ballaine, and don't stop or get out until you're on Parks Highway."

He nodded and furled his brow. "Thanks buddy – fall in at the end as soon as you can. We need to get moving. It's going to be a long drive." He rolled the window up and plowed forward. He was probably in the lead because of the over-sized tires on his truck. The truck bed was filled with gas cans.

I had no intention of trying to pack up and leave. I did not want to go back to the city. I didn't want to take my family back into the city.

I stood on the side of the road and waved at each truck as it passed. Mostly families. Lots of dogs. Some dog mushers with dog boxes full, sleds strapped on top. Lots and lots of stuff. The truck beds were loaded down with a variety of things. Some people looked like they were going camping. Others appeared to moving out, taking everything they owned with them.

A young couple pulled over. "Hey man! Time to blow this joint!"

Hippies. You have to love them. "Why do you think that?"

"There's nothing left, man. It's all fun and games until your stuff doesn't work. We were getting cold. We didn't have any firewood. Time to go. Come on, man! Join the party."

Party. How many people were dead? I felt guilty again. Why had we been chosen to survive? Why had these people been so lucky? I sighed.

"That's okay. We're fine. I think help will come before anything gets too bad. By the way, be careful in the city – keep your windows rolled up and don't stop. There's radiation in there. It was a nuke that took everything out." That didn't seem to resonate. I continued, "Thanks for checking in on me. Good luck and we'll see you again." They perked up, waving as they drove off.

I wasn't so sure they'd make it very far. Any of them.

WHAT TO DO

"Maybe we should join them…" Madison left it hanging, both a statement and a question. The pellet stove was running and we were huddled around it. The twins were trying to ride the dogs.

"I don't want to go back into the city. I don't think we can leave until the city is cleaned up. That means melting snow and the spring rain. Until then I don't think we can leave, not before next year anyway."

"What do we do?" she asked.

"We get them potty-trained. And we live." I hugged her tightly. "We live well." She looked at me with tears in her eyes. Our lives and our world had changed. We would talk about it the rest of the winter, but change was on us. The best thing we could do was to establish a routine. I needed order in my life. I needed little things like coffee. I needed my family around me. That included the dog, well, dogs.

"Let's put together a schedule. Something to accomplish each day. Something that will make tomorrow important. Every tomorrow." This was more than a suggestion. I needed it.

"I propose we have movie Friday. One day a week, we can watch a movie." This was convenient as today was Friday. "Who wants to watch a movie?" The twins hadn't ever watched that much TV, but it was still a treat. They were children of the twenty-first century. They nodded and ran to the couch. Oops. It wasn't quite movie time yet. The twins had one time reference and that was now. No other time existed for them.

We pulled them onto our laps. Not time yet for a movie, which would probably be Pinocchio or maybe Frozen. With two-year-olds, there was nothing else. It's what we signed up for when we decided to have kids. We had an extensive library of other movies, but I wasn't sure when we'd watch any of them. We had two discs from Netflix. I guess they wouldn't be getting those back anytime soon. I would continue to pay the monthly fee by direct deduction from the checking account. I'd get to pay Netflix in perpetuity for two discs. I'd cancel that stuff as soon as we could get online.

We penciled in the daily things we needed to do like run the generator, read to the twins. We needed to improve our scavenging. We could use more food, more dog food, pellets for the stove, and diapers. The never-ending search for diapers.

We weren't changing the twins as often as we should have, and they were developing rashes. We needed more baby powder, too. Potty-training might be a full-time job, but without diapers and with the rashes, what else was there to do?

Developing a scavenge plan was my way of getting some control back over our lives. The first house had to be the one on the corner where I had already drained their barrel of gas. They had a snow machine that we could use to pull a sleigh. They had a truck. And then there was Husky's house, where hopefully we'd find plenty of dog food. Both the dogs seemed to always be hungry. I was convinced they were using all their energy to grow hair. And then shed it in our great room.

We could stand to lose a little weight. I wasn't sure how long our supplies needed to hold out, but with radiation in the area, help might not come for a long time. We had to make everything last, so Madison and I had to ration what we ate. There must always be enough for the twins.

THE JOY OF SCAVENGING

It was hard to believe that it had only been three days since the explosion. We had more information now. It told me that we were on our own. Everything changed, but things remained the same. We still needed to go shopping, but we'd do it in a whole new way.

I put the bolt cutter, our axe, and a pry bar into one of the twin's sleds and pulled it behind me as I headed for the house on the corner. I took the dogs with me, even though temperatures were dropping. In Fairbanks, it warms up to snow, snows, then the snow acts as insulation, keeping temperatures steady for a little while afterwards. Then the sky clears up and temperatures plummet. It makes for a beautiful cold. Crystals form on the trees, making it look like Christmas all the time.

Speaking of Christmas, what kind of presents would I find in this house? I had a lock pick, but with the cold, there was no way I could work it with bare hands. I used the pry bar to break the lock on the door. Pine door frame. It came apart easily. I was looking for keys to the snow machine and the truck. This couple made it easy. There was a key rack by the front door. I took them all. I'd "borrow" the quad as well, just in case.

I turned to leave and then stopped. We needed food, too. I looked around their home. It was small, maybe a total of nine hundred square feet. They had a wood stove in the living room. The kitchen was open to the living room. They had a small table in the dining nook. The home looked well lived-in. It wasn't messy, and it wasn't dirty. They took good care of their home.

And I was standing in it like a thief. My stomach lurched. My conscience heaved. *But they aren't coming back,* I rationalized to myself. *I'm keeping a list of what I take.* But what about the damage I just did to their door? What about the violation of their space?

I would make a good scavenger, because it's what I needed to do. For my family. For survival. But I didn't like it.

They conveniently had plastic grocery bags. I took all their canned goods. They seemed to like potato chips. I took those, too. I didn't even eat potato chips. They gave me heartburn. They liked their beer. A case and a half of Miller Lite. It was frozen solid. Cans had burst. That was probably the proper fate for Miller Lite. I threw the two burst cans in their trash. No need for a mess when spring came.

I checked their freezer. They didn't have much. We could always get it later. It would be four or five months before it thawed.

Everything in the refrigerator was frozen. I left it. Maybe I would clean out their refrigerator, too. Or maybe not. I didn't think I would come back to their house. As the first one I "shopped" in, it would always bring back bad memories.

I put the groceries in the children's sled. That filled it up. I tried to start the truck, but it wouldn't even turn over. I put the key in the snow machine, choked it, and it fired up. It ran smoothly. I backed it out from beside their shed and headed it toward our house. I hooked up the rope from the little plastic sled and slowly drove home.

The snow machine would broaden my reach. I wanted to see who else was around. *Maybe we can have a circuit where people check in on each other, to make sure everyone was okay,* I thought. Or not. We had to take care of ourselves first.

But I didn't want to go to war with anyone over a few cans of Spam. Getting acquainted with the neighbors would reduce friction. We needed to look around, for our peace of mind, and because we had to. I couldn't turn my back on the rest of humanity, not when my family was in good shape. It would be selfish not to explore further.

I had a snow machine now (properly documented on my list of acquisitions, of course), so there was no excuse not to look for other survivors.

MORE SCAVENGING

Husky's house was the twin of the house on the corner. Small and efficient. The pine door frame gave easily. I looked for dog food. They had a small child. Maybe he was still in diapers.

When I opened the door, Husky pushed past me and raced through the house, her dog face anxious. Her body language was sad. She whimpered. I got down on a knee and pulled her in close, rubbing her ears and head. "I'm sorry, Husky. We'll take care of you. If your family ever comes back, they will see you happy and healthy." Her tail lifted a little and wagged reluctantly. "We owe that to them. We owe that to you. Come on, let's see what help your family has for us."

In the pantry was half of a fifty-pound bag of dog food and Milk Bone treats. That wasn't much, but it was all that was there.

Canned goods. Microwave popcorn. Moose meat in the freezer. That was the biggest score – moose made for good, healthy eating. I expected that hunting laws went out the window with the demise of the government agents in Fairbanks. A moose could give us nine hundred pounds of meat. That would be enough for us, the dogs, and any neighbors we might find. I'd dust off my Marlin 45-70. With the snow machine, I would be able to haul the meat home, no matter how far away I shot the moose.

Using my trusty bolt cutters, I cut the lock from their shed. I was rewarded with three five-gallon cans of gasoline. They also had a quad with a blade. That could come in handy and would be faster than the tractor. Then again, how much snow would I really need to move? I didn't bother with the quad.

I put everything in the plastic sled. I had to coax Husky from her former home. She was curled up on their couch. She knew. She mourned. I was happy to have her join our family. Maybe she realized that, as she reluctantly got up and left her home. Maybe we would visit the home on occasion so Husky could get a smell of her former humans and remember them. Remembering was important for us all to retain our humanity.

I pulled the sled back to our house and put everything away.

We had acquired almost one hundred gallons of gasoline. I didn't like the stacked gas cans in the garage. I took the sled and pulled it back to the house on the corner. I had emptied the barrel of gas, making the barrel easy to move. I made sure the cap was tight and put it on the sled, along with the good hand pump. The barrel was the best place for gasoline.

The light was beginning to fade. Time to pack in from today's shopping. Tomorrow, I'd take the snow machine to the gas station on Chena Hot Springs Road and see what there was to see. It was only a mile away. The snow machine would make short work of that. I needed to find a real snow machine sleigh, or fabricate one. The plastic sled needed to be attached with a stiff bar so that the sled didn't slam into the back of the snow machine when I stopped. If something broke, I wouldn't be able to fix it. I would try, but that wasn't my thing.

The world was there to help us make it through the harsh winter. We only had to ask in the right way.

CLASS IN SESSION

Madison was being a trooper. The twins weren't used to getting this much time with their mother. And they enjoyed it.

They were such good babies, it was inevitable that they would become good toddlers. From a dad's perspective, of course they were perfect. We understood that their attention span was ten to fifteen minutes. So we had to shape the classes for ten-minute blocks.

Madison accepted this new challenge as an academic would. She prepared lesson plans on topics with desired results. I thought the class schedule was humorous, but wouldn't laugh in front of the twins. I didn't want to jade their attitudes toward their new lives.

Topics were things like music appreciation, yoga, potty-training, drawing/coloring, dealing with the cold, Russian language, and so much more. Russian. I'd have to brush off my Cold War language skills if I was to participate or at least help reinforce the lessons. The classes were separated by play time, nap time, dog walks, and meals. She even worked in flexibility in case we needed to take the twins somewhere. (Another short road trip? But not to town.) She was a professional when it came to this.

I got to teach some of the classes. Cold weather was to be mine. I'd start with getting ready to go outside – what clothes were proper; how did you put them on; what if you don't have your snowsuit? We had classes for weeks. My classes would always get to end with playing outside.

And at the end of each day, we'd review as a family where we were, what we had accomplished, what we were going to do tomorrow.

It was important to have a plan. Even a loose one was better than no plan.

The twins were now in class. The absolute worst class ever was the potty-training. Since it was a little cold inside, as soon as their bare bottoms were exposed, they tightened up. Sitting on a cold training seat wasn't going to do it. So we would put the seats in front of the pellet stove and training would take place after everything was warm. It was miserable. Can't we just get flogged instead?

We kept pressing forward. Music appreciation was my favorite. We used my phone with 10 GB of music and a Bluetooth speaker. Music was the great equalizer. No matter what else was going on, if we could listen to music, things would be better. That is what we wanted to teach the twins. Music, meditation, yoga, dance. Everything that goes with being grounded as a human being. We all needed more of that. I think preparing for these classes and teaching them helped Madison to turn the corner very quickly in embracing our new lives. It helped me immensely. I was pragmatic, but not well-grounded.

My wife seemed happy, even though there was sadness when she thought about the magnitude of loss. It was so much more than just our loss, but we were the ones left to feel it. We had to remember. We had to honor the memory of our friends.

THE GAS STATION ON CHENA HOT SPRINGS ROAD

My next scavenge attempt was to the gas station. Surprisingly, it hadn't been cleaned out. A few things were missing, but it looked mostly intact. Maybe people thought that others had ransacked it so they left it alone. The expensive liquor was gone – maybe the employees had taken that on their way out. I didn't want or need the booze, but the high proof alcohol could be used in the engines as a last resort. I wondered what burned best – vodka or whiskey?

We had a great deal that was much higher on our list of priorities, like more diapers. And there they were!

I took all they had and checked the small storeroom in the back, where they had two full cases. It was the best find of all time. Especially since the potty-training with the twins was not progressing as we had hoped. Fine. It wasn't progressing at all and it was upsetting everyone. Even the dogs were miserable during the so-called training.

All kinds of snacks were available. I think this would be a multi-trip excursion. I needed to take everything they had, including toiletries. If needs be, we could provide this to the neighbors, should we run across any. With that same logic, however, we could leave it here so people like me could help themselves.

Who elected me the master keeper? I asked myself. *Who was I to be the honest broker?* My ego was getting in the way of common decency. I would take all the diapers. I would take some food. I would leave everything else. It wasn't mine to hoard.

The most significant find was behind the counter – the key to the underground gasoline storage tanks. Thousands of gallons of three different grades of fuel were at my fingerprints. My greed rushed back to the front. How much could I take back to the house?

First, how could I get it out of there? Hand pump. Garden hose. Duct tape. It would be time-consuming, but time was one thing we seemed to have plenty of. Daylight was at a premium, but this was worth running the generator for. With nearly unlimited gas, if I could find a big enough generator, I could power our whole house. We could do laundry! We could flush the toilets! We could have a great deal of our old lives back, if only for brief periods of time. How long would it be before the gasoline would go bad? I didn't know, but knew it would last through the winter. I could figure a way to take as much as I possibly could – maybe draining a neighbor's five-hundred-gallon fuel oil tank and filling it with gasoline. Only two of our neighbors had underground tanks.

That would work.

That was the plan. If everything turned out according to the plan, then our quality of life would vastly improve.

NO ONE'S COMING

We went about our routine through the first week. Then the second and the third.

If we had radiation sickness, we would have seen signs of it by now. It looked like we weren't going to die right away.

We didn't see any more contrails. We didn't hear any other airplanes. The last vehicle to drive by was in the convoy that passed weeks ago.

I dutifully kept the road in our neighborhood clear. We even shoveled a path into the forest so the dogs could have an expanded walk area.

Besides frequent trips to the gas station, I didn't venture out very far. If the snow machine broke down, I'd have to walk back to the house. The snow was too deep for casual walking and I still had not been able to find a sled built to be towed behind a snow machine. But then again, I had only looked around our immediate neighborhood.

The dogs that weren't far away hadn't barked since just after the event. I made a quick trip to that house to find that no one was home. The dogs were all gone. I'm glad I didn't find dead dogs. I should have checked earlier, but forgot about them when they hadn't barked. Their owner must have packed them up and joined the convoy or drove himself out early after the crisis. We had a great deal of time to think, yet things like this were easily forgotten. The focus I had for my family was all-consuming. Every fiber of my being was focused on providing in an environment that I was unfamiliar with. Maybe that discomfort I felt was fear. Real fear. If I failed, we'd all die. I wondered when help would come. I needed help.

Even with the threat of radiation, it seemed odd that the government had not made some attempt to contact survivors. That's what we were. That's what we would be. We would survive, with or without government help. In my mind, I drafted a very sternly worded letter to the governor and the President expressing my dismay at being left for dead. As a Marine, it was galling to think of being left behind. As a pragmatist, I expected that there were limited resources and competing priorities.

Alaskans were probably best suited to help themselves and endure. If I was in charge, I wouldn't be in a hurry to send assets to the interior if the big cities needed help. City people weren't able to have their own heat sources and private utilities. They would perish in droves without help from the outside. We never liked the confines of the city, so we lived where it was best for us.

And that saved our lives, for the time being anyway, while casting us into an unknown, harsh world.

Since outsiders were nowhere to be seen, the Intelligence Officer in me locked onto the need for competing priorities. If Fairbanks was the only place that had an accident, then we would see safety-suited responders. Maybe this was an attack, one of many, and there were no responders available.

We thought our world had changed completely. What if we were right and the change was forever?

A COW AND HER CALF

As part of our daily routine, I took the dogs around our neighborhood, making sure they got plenty of exercise. It was cold and dark and I wanted to wear them out while they were outside, so there was less chaos in the house. I owed my wife that much and, selfishly, I wanted peace for my own sanity.

I wore a AAA-battery powered head lamp. Between our stock and what was available from the gas station, we probably had years' worth of batteries. It was said that they had a ten-year shelf life. I hoped I never found out the truth of that claim. In the meantime, I was happy that I had a good headlamp to shine the light to keep the dogs out of trouble.

It started when both dogs started barking and ran ahead along the path around our neighborhood. I took a few steps after them, shining my flashlight to see why they were excited. The eyes of a small moose reflected in the distance.

A calf. That meant its mother was nearby. The golden rule is never get between a mother and her baby. That was doubly true in the wild. I started running and yelled for the dogs to come back. I ran out of air in about ten steps. I could either run or yell, but not both. I stopped, took a deep breath, and in my loudest Marine Corps voice, I called for Phyllis. She was trained to come on command, although sometimes it took the big voice.

She turned away from the calf and started coming. I yelled again. Husky had jumped into the snow and was now confused between chasing after the calf or following her Alpha back to her new family. While she stood there, deciding what to do, the cow appeared, none too pleased with the appearance of the dogs. I started running again, which was the wrong thing to do.

She wasn't afraid of any of us, neither the dogs nor me, and once I started running, Phyllis turned and headed back toward the big creatures. She didn't like moose, seeing them often from the comfort of our home. Her hackles go up and she gives the intruders her best growling bark. She started barking again as the cow ran toward them. Husky started barking. I tried to yell, but had no air left.

Finally, the dogs realized the predicament they'd put themselves in. As the cow barreled down on them, I shouted at it, but it wasn't fazed. The dogs danced out of the way as the cow tried to run them down.

Phyllis had her tail tucked tightly between her legs as the cow continued past and into the deep snow.

She slowed as she jogged after her calf.

My head swam. I dropped to a knee to try and get my breath back. My glasses fogged as I breathed quick shallow breaths, my mouth inside my coat. Breathing cold air doesn't help an asthmatic in distress.

Finally, my head cleared. The dogs barked at the trees into which the moose disappeared.

"Come on!" I yelled and the two happily jogged along our walking trail. "You two are going to be the death of me," I said as I followed the dogs back toward our home.

THE DOG MUSHER III

It was a clear day and I was doing what I always seemed to be doing, taking the dogs for a stroll around our neighborhood, when I heard a hearty "Ha" from up the road. I ran forward a few steps, then slowed to a fast walk. There was no running for me because I liked breathing.

My asthma would be a problem if I couldn't find replacement medications. It already was a problem, but at least not a debilitating one.

A musher and his dog team were headed this way. They moved along at a healthy clip and would be here in just a couple minutes.

I took the dogs to the house on the corner and put them inside, wedging the door closed behind me. I didn't want my dogs to be a distraction and maybe get into a fight with the sled dogs. Our pit bull would probably wreak havoc. Phyllis needed to be kept apart from the sled team. Husky would probably join them and run off.

I waited by the side of the road and waved as the Dog Musher approached. I thought of it as waving, but I was actually jumping up and down, doing things as if I was trying to call in a passing jetliner.

"Whoa. Whoa!" The dogs angled to a stop and the Dog Musher jammed his snow hook in. We both took off our right gloves as we approached.

"I'm Chuck. I have to say that you're the first person I've seen since a convoy passed almost three weeks ago." We put our gloves back on after shaking hands. Although it had warmed up, it was still a brisk fifteen degrees below zero.

"Yeah. They were from up by me. My neighbor was one of them. Do you know anything about them?"

"Radiation. I recommended that they bypass the city using Goldstream. Things are bad in there." I watched him nod. "Don't take your dogs any further down the road. You don't want to expose them. I'm not sure how far the contamination goes, but it can't be too far from here. There doesn't seem to be anyone left between here and the city."

"Radiation? What the hell is going on?" he asked.

"At one point in my life, I would have known," I lamented. "Not now. All I know is what I can see. The city is gone, and since the second day, we haven't seen any airplanes. Since the convoy, we haven't seen any vehicles. My wife, me, and our twins are the only ones around here. What about you?"

The Dog Musher looked at the early morning sky. He was probably answering in his head. Dog mushers tended to be very private people. We had gone to a number of Yukon Quest events and the dog mushers looked unhappy standing in a crowd of people. They spent so much time alone with their dogs that I wouldn't expect anything else. I knew the Dog Musher had been alone these past three weeks.

"There's no one left in Two Rivers either. Those who didn't work in the city left in that convoy. You wouldn't have any beef jerky, would you?"

An odd question, but not surprising. There were certain universals for those who lived in the wilderness.

"As a matter of fact…" I always kept one or two in my pocket when I was away from home. The calories could be lifesaving. I also had a Coast Guard nutrition pack, twenty-two hundred calories. It tasted like sawdust, but like the jerky, the calories were a survival tool. I handed a sealed Jacks Links beef steak to him. I had taken the last of the jerky from the gas station a few days ago. He removed his glove again and opened it up. He closed his eyes as he took small bites, enjoying the jerky to the utmost.

It was almost embarrassing as the time dragged on. His dog team was yapping and getting restless. When he finished the jerky, he seemed a changed man.

"I ran out of jerky two and a half weeks ago. At least I have enough dog food." The Dog Musher smiled. In the good tradition of Alaska, I didn't even ask his name. If he volunteered it, that was one thing. To me, he'd be the Dog Musher. I invited him to the house, but he declined. He needed to keep the dogs running as they were just warmed up. I asked him to stop by in the future, pointing down the road to where our house was. He replied that he would try. Perfect noncommittal response from what I expected was the typical dog musher. He was the only one I had ever talked with.

I was sure that we would meet again.

"It's almost time to restock dog food ourselves. I've seen some tracks. I think a lone cow is around here somewhere. Times are tough so she may be our first volunteer to be a food source. I'm sure we'll get more meat than we can use. I have a snow machine and a makeshift sleigh to tow behind it. I can bring some meat by if I can bag her, if you'd like?" I ended it as a question.

He was interested. Although he had passed a number on his way here today, butchering a moose by yourself is a monumental task. Maybe we could hunt one together. As long as the snow machine didn't get too close, his dog team would be fine.

He gave me directions to his place. I told him I would try to stop by sometime in the next week, whenever the weather was clear. It would be cold, but I didn't want to risk being out in a snowstorm. Although with the snow machine, I could cover the fifteen miles to his place in maybe twenty minutes. The road was fairly straight and had a nice base layer of snow. I had his sled track to follow as well.

We shook hands again, neither committing to anything. For a brief period of time, we shared the beauty of Alaska and some of the challenges living here. We did not live in fear. We just lived.

CHRISTMAS I

"You know, tomorrow is Christmas…" I left it at that. The twins had no idea, although they were at the age where they were supposed to be excited to see what Santa would bring. We had lost track of time. But not our phones. Even without service they knew the time and date. We dutifully checked the phone once or twice a day for service, and that's when I noticed the date.

The twins were down for their naps. They seemed to be asleep. We took our conversation to the other, colder side of the great room.

"I hadn't thought about it," Madison replied. "I'm not sure I like what Christmas has become. Too commercial."

I laughed. "I agree completely. This year, I refuse to go Christmas shopping! I will not buy anything in a store for them!"

As Madison thought about it, she giggled too. "This is our chance to make it what we think it should be."

I waited. "So, what do you think it should be?"

She knew that she had been set up. We had talked about this many times before the twins came along. At two years old, this was going to be a pivotal year for them. It was going to be Santa Claus bringing piles of presents, or a more traditional Christian celebration, or something of our own making. Although we didn't believe in the Seinfeld version called Festivus, we understood the point they were trying to make.

"Let's make it about giving and not getting." Of course. What did that look like? I made a hand gesture of 'tell me more.'

"We each give something out of the ordinary to each other. We have to be accountable, so we'll write things down if we give an act, like cleaning a room or doing dishes. We'll track it on a paper that we'll post on the wall." Madison believed that the most important gift you could give was your time. I saw the wisdom in it. Time is something that, once wasted, can never be gotten back. We have to make the most of our time.

That's why she was always so much better at parties than I was. Even though we are both introverts, she could flow through a party and leave everyone smiling. Her secret? Ask a question and give them your undivided attention as they answer. She then asked a short follow-up question to show that she'd listened to them. And then she moved on. She shared almost nothing of herself with strangers. As introverts do.

We thought our children were solid introverts. They were perfectly happy playing with each other. Weeks after the explosion, they remained unfazed. They didn't realize that tomorrow was Christmas. Time for another family meeting.

We gathered at our favorite place in front of the pellet stove. The dogs were easily worked up. We took some time to settle them down. Time in this case meant a couple of stale Milk Bones.

"Christmas is tomorrow. Do you know what that means?" I asked.

"Santa Claus!" our little girl Aeryn exclaimed. We hadn't used Santa Claus as an incentive for good behavior. I hadn't thought that we mentioned it at all in previous months and especially not in the past three weeks. Our daughter was a genius! That was one conclusion, or maybe last year's Christmas when the twins were one had made a good impression. A good commercialized impression. I think that I may have overdone it.

My wife looked at me. It was not pleasant.

"Well yes, sweetheart," she started, still giving me the hairy eyeball. "Santa Claus is a way for us to give to people we care about. Maybe tonight we will read you that story out of the Bible about the birth of Jesus Christ and what Christmas is supposed to be. Then we can talk more about what we want for each other."

"I want McDonald's fries," said Charles, our little man. This earned me a withering look from my wife.

"I don't even want to know why you would take them to McDonald's. You don't have a reason good enough." My retort of 'fine' died on my tongue. Of course I had taken them to McDonald's. It was between meals and they were hungry. It was quick, and they'd enjoyed them, it seemed. Maybe they'd enjoyed them a little too much. We wouldn't be going back anytime soon. Even if the McDonald's was resurrected, it appeared that we would not be going back.

I tried to recover some dignity. "Those aren't the kinds of things we ask for. Like right now, I want your mother to be happy that for a brief moment in time, you enjoyed the guilty pleasure of a French fry. But you are committing, from this moment forward, that you won't harm your body in the future with foods that are bad for you…" It didn't work. I was still in the dog house.

"What we were thinking is that we would do things for each other, things that we wouldn't normally do, like taking an extra turn cleaning the house. Your father will be digging our new outhouse very soon, for example."

But it's winter and the ground is like concrete…I left it unsaid.

"Come on everyone, time for chores," I said. I needed to escape and let things cool down a bit. It was Christmas Eve! And I still needed to run the generator, bring in more pellets, and maybe siphon a little water from someone's tank in our neighborhood.

ESCAPE

After the debacle of the family meeting, I hurried outside. I made sure everything was plugged in correctly, maximizing what we did with our power, and then started the generator. It ran smoothly. Even with the last three weeks, we still had not run it for one hundred total hours. It remained like new, our stalwart companion in crisis.

My newest best friend was the snow machine. I wanted to make a quick run to the gas station to see if maybe there was some treat I could get for the twins, something their mother would approve of. I needed her balance on these things otherwise I guarantee I would get them candy bars and Coke. I had been borderline diabetic. I liked my sweets, although after not having any for the past few years, my sweet tooth had disappeared. Honey as a sweetener worked just fine. I could no longer eat a piece of cake; it was too sweet. Not that there would be any cake.

The snow machine fired up on the first pull. I waved as I drove out. She was still giving me her mad look. Escape was my only recourse. Time was my friend, as in, I needed to give her some time to realize that there was no way I was digging a hole for an outhouse in the winter. Even with a pick axe it would have been brutal work.

I took it easy until I got to the open road. Following my own previous tracks, I gave it the gas and raced the short mile to the gas station. The snow machine slowed down quickly and I turned in. My tracks were the only ones in the past weeks. Only human ones, that is. It looked like a pack of dogs had been through here. With the door shut, they hadn't gone inside to cause any damage.

I looked more closely. These dogs had big paws. I put my gloved hand down to get a better frame of reference.

Wolves.

I jumped back on the sled and returned to the house. I came into our driveway a little quickly and was off the sled as it was winding down. I went inside to be certain that our dogs were still there. They were.

"No one goes outside without me. Dogs on a leash and we don't stray beyond our own yard. We stay away from the woods," I said firmly.

"What's going on?" Madison asked.

"Wolves." I always carried my .45 when 'shopping.' I grabbed my .45-70 rifle and headed back outside.

"Where are you going?" Madison asked.

"I want to see where they went. I want to see that they keep going. And if they don't, I have to make sure they can't bother us," I said in the voice of the Marine that I had been.

WOLVES

I jumped back on the sled and gunned it out of our neighborhood. I slowed to take the corner onto Chena Hot Springs Road and then opened it up.

I almost fell off. My rifle, slung across my back, didn't allow me to lean forward as much as I needed to. I slowed, adjusted things, then sped back up.

The wolf tracks went from the gas station straight out onto the road. They were on top of the Dog Musher's tracks. And the tracks started getting further apart. The wolves were running after the Dog Musher.

I maintained my speed at fifty mph, staying on the dog sled tracks. The wolf tracks marred the smoothness of the sled's passing. After ten miles, the tracks remained unchanged. The wolves continued to chase the dog sled. I didn't know how I could tell if the Dog Musher had been aware he was being followed. Maybe he was making a bee line for his kennel so he could secure his team and fight off the wolves.

At mile eleven, the wolf tracks left the road and headed down a driveway. I raced past where they had turned. I looked around at the woods to make sure I wasn't going to get ambushed, then turned and went slowly down the driveway. I could see where the wolf tracks intersected with moose tracks. The wolf pack had changed prey. I followed them a short way until a spot where I could see the moose had jumped a fence. It looked like the wolves didn't follow. Their tracks circled, then went left toward a break in the trees – the power line.

Once up the powerline, they picked up their pace and were running again. Up ahead, the power line intercepted the road. There was an embankment and I wasn't good enough with the snow machine yet. I went too slowly, going straight up and lost traction. I tried to turn and take it along the side. It started to roll.

I gunned it, but too late. It jumped a little forward, enough to unseat me. And it still rolled. Right over the top of me and down the bank, settling on its side at the bottom. The windscreen was broken and it was no longer running. I hoped that was because of the kill switch wristband I always used. I was more than eleven miles away from home with less than an hour of light remaining while on the trail of a wolf pack.

If I swore, now was perfect for it. But I didn't, and I didn't have the time. My rifle had dug into my back. My pistol dug into the ribs under my arm. The sled had slammed into my chest. I sat in the snow and took off my helmet. I listened for any sounds. It was quiet. I don't know what a wolf pack sounded like while hunting, but I expected to hear something. Maybe not.

I cleaned off the face shield and looked at my rifle. There was snow in the scabbard, but after wiping off the rifle action and shaking the snow out, I was back in business. I made sure there was a round in the chamber and that the safety was on.

My sled needed some love. I wiped it off enough. The broken windscreen wouldn't be a problem. I crossed my fingers and tried to start it.

It came to life on the first pull. My heart raced. I was out here hoping to help the Dog Musher while at the same time putting my family at risk. I should head straight back home.

But that wasn't who I was. The Dog Musher needed help right now. If I went home, who's to say that the wolves wouldn't follow me back?

I drove the snow machine at a crawl along the bottom of the embankment until I came to another driveway where a ramp had been created over the years. The sled smoothly negotiated it and I was back on the road, where I found the wolves had resumed following the Dog Musher.

FAILURE

Two Rivers was close by. I opened up the snow machine on the straightaways and was quickly at the Dog Musher's turn-off. The trail was far too easy to follow.

I slowed. Even with the engine still running, I could hear the sounds of battle – growls and yips of pain. Some barking. Some howling.

The Dog Musher had not known that he was being followed. It looked like he had arrived shortly before the wolves. Half his team had been unhooked and chained back to their dog houses. This is how the wolves found them. Easy prey.

The chained dogs had no chance. The Dog Musher had been in the open and was still fighting valiantly against three wolves. The other members of the pack were efficiently killing the sled dogs. I ripped the rifle off my back and took aim. The shot took one of the wolves in the flank. His back legs were almost ripped off – a 405-grain round fired from fifty feet away didn't need to hit the center of the target to be effective.

That left two attacking the Dog Musher. The shot had not startled the wolves at all. I expected them to run off, but they were in killing mode.

They were too close to the Dog Musher. Both had bitten deeply, and more than once. The Dog Musher's thick clothes helped, but he was still too exposed. One hand was a bloody stump. I angled in close with the snow machine, driving with one hand while holding the rifle in the other.

I stopped about twenty feet away and jumped off. A big male took notice and came at me. I shot him in the chest as he jumped. I fell backwards into the snow. I scrambled to get back up, but didn't make it all the way.

Another came at me. I shot him from a sitting position. My 45-70 had two rounds left. There were more wolves than that.

I took aim at a wolf ripping into the Dog Musher's leg. The man screamed in pain. I fired. I missed! I chambered the last round and fired again. This one hit home and the wolf exploded in fur and blood.

I struggled quickly to get my .45 out from inside my jacket. The cries from the sled dogs had stopped. Only the growls of the wolves remained. The Dog Musher was losing his fight for consciousness.

One of the five remaining wolves came at me, but not straight. It started to circle, keeping its gleaming eyes focused on me. I clicked the safety off with my thumb and drove the first round from the .45 right through its forehead. It went down while the shot rang loudly in my ears.

The other four were not so keen to engage. It looked like they were deciding what to do. Maybe I had killed the Alphas of the pack. I didn't care. At this point, I was in control. I walked toward the closest wolf, a female, and dropped her with a shot behind her shoulder.

The others started to run toward the nearest woods as if their pelts were on fire. I fired a couple times, but missed.

I followed them a short way to make sure they were still running. They were.

This battle was over.

I ran over to the Dog Musher, who was lying in his own blood, sobbing.

"My dogs…"

I looked back. All his dogs were dead or dying. There was blood everywhere.

I ripped off a piece of his coat and started to tighten it around his mangled hand. He convulsed in pain. He kept trying to get something out of his jacket, but it was on his left side. His right hand was of no use. I pulled his jacket open for him. He had a .38 caliber pistol. He hadn't been able to get it out in time to fight off the wolves.

The cold would keep his wounds from bleeding too much, but I needed bandages. I ran inside his cabin. There was a dresser and I hurriedly opened the drawers until I found t-shirts. I grabbed a handful and turned to run back outside. The retort of a gunshot shook the windows.

The wolves! I dropped the shirts and pulled my pistol out of my shoulder holster, levering off the safety as I burst out the door.

No wolves. No threat. Only the Dog Musher with the top of his head blown off. And his pistol on the ground nearby where it had jumped from his dead fingers.

My ears were still ringing from the earlier gunfire, but I couldn't hear any other sounds. The world returned to its normal state of peace. I looked around. Carnage. The smell of blood tainted the air. Gunpowder lingered.

I got behind the Dog Musher and lifted him off the ground. His head dripped gore onto the front of my jacket as I dragged him to his cabin. I put him on his bed and covered him up. After breakup (spring melt), I would return and bury him. He deserved better than this.

The wolves hadn't cared. We'd lived in Alaska for only four years, but in all that time, I had never heard of wolves attacking people. "Is this going to happen more often in our new world?" I asked myself.

If so, that meant things had changed dramatically for my family. We had to always be on the lookout. We had to always be armed. We had lived such sheltered lives before and never fully appreciated it.

Putting my feelings aside, I checked for supplies. The shed had two pallets of dog food. We could put that to good use. I took two as that was all that would fit on the back of the snow machine. I started it and, without looking back, headed for home.

THE UNHAPPY RETURN

I pulled in by our garage just after sunset. Madison bolted outside wearing just her hoodie and sweatpants when she saw me. I looked a mess. My coat would probably have to be burned. My snow pants weren't in much better condition.

"I'm fine." I said as she stared at the blood and gore frozen to the front of my jacket. "Not mine. They got the Dog Musher."

She mouthed the words, 'Oh my God.'

I pulled her inside the garage, where it was still cold, but not like being outside. "And all his dogs, too." I tore off the coat and threw it on the ground and pulled her in close for a hug.

I had broken into people's homes. I had stolen their goods. And I'd watched people die. Was I ready for this? I didn't think so.

I started crying. For the dogs. For the Dog Musher. For us. Madison cried softly, her head buried in my chest.

The day had started so promising with the visit of the Dog Musher. It ended horrifically, but oddly, we were safer because of it.

If I hadn't rolled the snow machine, I might have gotten there in time. If I hadn't gone off track to see where the wolf pack had gone, I might have gotten there in time.

And then they might have attacked me instead. All of them at once when they weren't distracted and I wasn't ready for them. Survivor's guilt. The Dog Musher did not have to take his own life. He was hurt, but he would have survived. But he didn't want to, not without his dogs.

Karma. Fate. It would have to do. One thing for sure – there were only three wolves left and they were probably still running. Then I got mad.

"I should have taken a pelt from one of them. Mess with us and we'll wear your skin." It had been a while since I'd served in the Corps, but Marines didn't lose their will to fight, their commitment to total victory.

CHRISTMAS EVE

It was still Christmas Eve. We needed to get back to the business of being a family. I stripped out of my nasty clothes, shivering as I raced inside in my underwear. I put on sweats, our favorite attire in our fifty-degree house.

First order of business? Give everyone a hug. Even the dogs. The twins hugged back, but the dogs had a tendency to get rather rambunctious. The dogs liked the first second of a hug, but then took it as the precursor for full contact play. They ran around and would have knocked things over if we had anything left that could be knocked over. We had learned since the explosion what it was like to live in a smaller space with four humans and two very happy dogs.

"What's for dinner?" We reveled in the mundane of preparing to eat. We put a stool in the kitchen for the twins to stand on so they could better see as we prepared our meals. What and how we prepared things didn't matter as much as being able to do it together.

We hadn't done this before the event, the explosion, the attack. It didn't matter what title we put on it. It was the before time. Now things like preparing dinner were the highlight of each day. We took too much for granted before in our day to day bustle. We were busy, but were we busy with the right things? Our perspective had improved.

Much seemed wrong with the world, but for our small part, there was a great deal right. We were comfortable enough. The great room stayed around fifty degrees. We had food, albeit a conglomeration of things we had on hand and found while 'shopping.' Comfort items were just that.

It doesn't matter what we made – some mix of canned vegetables, something rehydrated, and moose meat seasoned with something. All of it cooked on our stove, powered by the slow-moving propane in the candlelight. We waited until everyone was seated and served, and we expressed our thanks for each other and the food that we had.

The mundane. The little things that make life worth living.

I had seen death that day. I expected that it wouldn't be the last.

For Christmas Eve, we read stories from the Bible. We then fired up the generator and made it movie night. We had exactly four Christmas movies, but hadn't gotten the best ones for small children. We bought these before we had the twins. But we thought they would appreciate Elf. They would probably never get to see National Lampoon's Christmas Vacation. Not as long as we had a choice.

We watched the movie and went to bed without making our Christmas commitments. The distractions of the day took their toll on Madison and me. For tonight, we celebrated being alive.

CHRISTMAS II

Christmas Eve hadn't turned out as we wanted. I felt guilty that I hadn't been able to save the Dog Musher. I felt horrible about what I had seen. The images kept flashing through my mind.

I woke up earlier than usual after a fitful night. We didn't have a Christmas tree or any decorations. Christmas had snuck up on us.

I took the dogs out briefly. It was snowing again, lightly. The moon shone through the clouds, casting a pale light on our world. The trees sparkled with ice and new snow. It had warmed up. The dogs played a little more than I wanted, but they deserved to be happy. They were family members, too.

I ended up chasing them into the garage, where I wiped the snow off their bodies so when they jumped back into bed they wouldn't get any of the other sleepers wet.

I started the snow machine and slowly headed out. I needed to pick up where I left off yesterday. Back to the gas station to see what might be a treat for the twins. Maybe even something for Madison.

I took it easy on the trip. I wanted to revel in the morning, enjoy all that we had. Enjoy it without dwelling on material things. A dichotomy as I was in search of something material to give as a gift. What I really wanted was to see the happiness on their faces. All it would take was for me to be there when they woke up. It still wouldn't hurt if there was something to hand them, as well, would it?

With my trusty flashlight in hand, I went into the store as if it were a typical day. "Excuse me, ma'am. I need a little something for each of my children to give them on this fine Christmas morning. Would anything come to mind?" I asked the empty counter.

The aisles were clear. They hadn't been ransacked. Today was no different in my new norm of 'shopping.' Maybe I needed this sense of normalcy. Although I was a closet prepper, it was in the comfort of my own home, with plenty of power and a trip to the store only as far away as my Jeep in the garage. The only store left to me now was this gas station, which appeared to have made most of its money from alcohol and drink sales. The refrigerators were still filled with now frozen concoctions of all types – sodas, energy drinks, sugary teas, and beer. Mostly beer.

I wasn't interested in that stuff, even if it was thawed. And free.

I went into the candy aisle. I doubt there's anything as good as a frozen Snickers, so that was always an option. There was candy of various types, but I didn't want the twins to get a taste for things that were too sweet. I wasn't sure what the future held, but sugar wasn't going to be readily available. Honey maybe, so I looked at the Bit O' Honey candy bars. Those were good, but when they were frozen, they could be real tooth breakers. I put two of them and three Snickers in my pocket. Candy wasn't really what I was looking for, though. Something that's bad for you shouldn't be considered a treat.

On a spinning display in the corner were some travel games. I was surprised they had these kinds of things, but then again, Chena Hot Springs was almost an hour up the road if one were driving.

Travel Boggle. I put that in my pocket. A sliding tile math puzzle. A sliding tile word puzzle. The twins were two. These might be nice, but a little later in their lives. On the counter, there was a spinning display case with some cheap jewelry. I spun it and there they were. Two necklaces, each with one half of a heart. The heart would be whole when the two wearers were together. When they were apart, each would miss the other half. I took these. As the twins grew up, I hoped that they would look out for each other, take care of each other.

I arrived back home to everyone still snug in bed. The dogs had taken my spot so there was no hope of crawling back under the covers for me. So I made a cup of coffee. I had taken all the instant coffee from the gas station on an earlier trip. One has to have priorities.

I sat on a chair looking through the window to the yard and the woods. It was Christmas Day, a little over three weeks since we lost power.

If you haven't experienced it, you can't understand the beauty of Fairbanks in the winter. The colors are soft pastels. The white was bright and clean. Everything sparkled. The air was crisp. Fairbanks was considered high desert. It was dry and the snow was light, fine like powdered sugar.

The stars shine and the sky was full. The moon was so bright it cast shadows. Especially without any artificial lights, the sky was even clearer. I was still sitting there when everyone else began to stir. Madison was hugging the twins in close. The dogs were stretching and yawning.

"Merry Christmas!" I worked my way past the dogs and into the pile of humans. The twins were giggling and together they said, "Potty." We hurried up and put them each on their own mini throne, where they gave us the best gifts. On their own, they had learned what it meant to be potty-trained and that they'd decided to make it happen. We could not have been happier!

We made pancakes with the last of our shelf-stable almond milk. We took it easy with the maple syrup so we could continue to use that as a sweetener in oatmeal for the children.

After breakfast, I gave the twins their present. We put the necklaces on them, but saw that they were too young to have something like that around their necks. We promised to make them bracelets that they could put the charms on. They liked them and kept putting the two pieces of the heart together. They spoke to each other in their own language which only they understood. We could only watch.

I went to the garage and got one of the Snickers bars. I gave it to Madison on the sly. As adults, we had a different idea regarding treats. Madison took it and smiled at me. In no time at all, decadence had taken a back seat to necessity.

I'd lost ten pounds since the event. I expect Madison had shed a comparable percentage of her body weight. We didn't weigh ourselves that often. The scale worked, but the problem was in shedding enough clothing in our fifty-degree house to weigh ourselves properly.

We took sponge baths when necessary, but that was it. We still had not figured out how we were going to do laundry. We boiled water for dishes and, thanks to the gas station, we had an almost unlimited supply of propane and gasoline. We could continue to use our stove and generator. I needed to find a bigger generator. Then we could power the whole house. My small generator had a 220v outlet, but my dryer plug didn't fit it. I didn't have the proper plug. A good prepper would have thought of those things along with buying the right-sized generator in the first place.

The winter solstice was four days ago. That meant a little more light with each passing day.

It was crystal clear again, which meant that temperatures would drop further.

WHAT TO DO FOR
NEW YEAR'S

Every year for New Year, we had gone to Chena Hot Springs Resort to enjoy the springs. Even with everything else, why should this year be different? The resort provided its own geo-thermal power. It should be fully operational. Workers lived there as it would be too expensive and time-consuming to commute the hour-plus one way from Fairbanks. Many young people worked there to earn money for college. You couldn't spend money there so it made for a great way to save.

To make the trip, we needed another snow machine with a tow-behind sleigh. I knew there wasn't another set-up in our neighborhood. I took a trip toward Two Rivers. As I got further from Fairbanks, I figured it was more likely that every household had a snow machine.

I took it easy as I entered the first farm. I didn't want anyone to consider me a looter, although maybe I was. If I took a snow machine, it would be for our pleasure, but a backup could be critical if one broke down. Also with a second machine, we'd be able to both go 'shopping' and take the twins with us.

There were no vehicles that I could see and there weren't any tire tracks in three weeks' worth of snow. I still took no chances and yelled heartily from my snow machine. I waited. No answer. I gave it one more yell. Still no answer.

There were a number of buildings on the property. I figured the most likely to hold a snow machine was the garage. I looked in through the windows into the emptiness. No vehicles, although it looked like space was cleared for two. They had probably been caught in the city just like everyone else.

I got down on one knee and said a quick prayer for them. I had not been religious, until a month ago. Since then two, maybe three times, the world had tried to kill me. I had to believe that I was blessed. I couldn't let myself have survivor's guilt. There was no time for it. My family counted on me. I had to be there for them and be there with the right attitude. I got up. It was time to get back to work.

No need to defile their garage by breaking a lock when I knew it didn't have what I was looking for. Next up was the shed. It had a golf cart door so it could hold snow machines, or a riding mower. It had a key lock so I couldn't use my bolt cutters. Instead, I went with the sledgehammer. Using it like a ram, hitting the door right at the lock usually broke things open. This shed was no exception. The lock broke out, and I pushed the door in. Perfect. Thank God for people who were prepared to live in Fairbanks in the winter, and I thanked them profusely for sharing their wisdom with me.

Two top-end snow machines, both ready to go. They had towed sleighs that looked like undersized sleds as well. I choked one of the machines and hit the starter. It struggled briefly, then roared to life. Booyah! The sound of freedom.

I was trading up from a pull start to an electric start, and I liked it. I maneuvered the new snow machines and towed sleighs into the driveway. I put my old machine with the broken windshield and small sleigh into their shed and closed the door.

I tied a tow strap between the first and second snow machines. I hooked up the sleighs, one on top of the other, behind the towed snow machine. I reminded myself to dutifully document the exchange.

With the new snow machines and both towed sleighs set for travel, I was in a good mood. So I thought I'd look around before heading back. One never knew what could be found.

I put a five-gallon can of gas and a couple quarts of oil into the sleigh. They were undoubtedly for the snow machines, so might as well keep everything together. There wasn't anything else in the shed that I wanted to take. We didn't need anything else yet, so I wasn't going to break into the farmhouse. Maybe sometime I'd have to, but not today. No more 'shopping' than required. I didn't want to get greedy. We had what we needed for today and even for next month.

Although we could use more pellets. I figured I'd be critical low by the end of February or maybe even into March. It would still be deadly cold then. After the New Year I'd begin that search in earnest. If I had to change out the pellet stove for a wood burner, I would do it. But this was me and I knew it would be a painful installation that probably wouldn't work right at the beginning.

How long could we go without heat while I was taking one stove out and putting another one in? Could Madison and I manhandle a five-hundred-pound stove out and put another one in? It had taken four of us and a dolly to get the pellet stove into the house in the first place. The piped chimney wouldn't be too difficult, but without a Home Depot or Lowe's, I'd have to find the materials in other people's homes and dismantle them. That would be a sooty mess. That was enough thought on that topic. The right answer was to find someone who had a pellet stove. One extra ton of pellets, conveniently packaged in forty-pound bags, would take care of us through to the summer.

And putting those thoughts out of my mind for now, I pulled into our driveway with the two snow machines and two sleighs. All of us could go to the Hot Springs!

THE TRIP TO CHENA HOT SPRINGS

When I said all of us, I meant all of us. In the next few days, I had to train the dogs to ride in the sleigh. What a nightmare! They would ride for about three seconds and then jump out because they saw a mound of snow that needed to be sniffed and peed on.

I had to use the twins to help me train the dogs to ride in the towed sleds. We started with Phyllis. The twins held her and we took a slow spin around the neighborhood. She stayed between them for the whole ride. We did the same thing with Husky, although it took her some repetition to get it. The first time, we hadn't even reached the bottom of the driveway before she jumped out, dragging Charles behind her. Aeryn let go and laughed as her brother was pulled through the snow.

We put blankets in the sleigh and I built a rack with sides out of spare wood we kept in our shed. It wasn't pretty, but it did what we needed. The dogs would be behind a crate-like thing so they wouldn't be inclined to jump out. The blankets would give them a place to curl up once they relaxed. The trip to Chena Hot Springs could take two hours one way. The crate also partitioned the sleighs so we could bring a number of rudimentary supplies – tent, sleeping bags, food, water, gas, tools. All of that just in case. I didn't want to have to use any of it, but if we got stuck out there, we needed to be able to survive. It was like taking an umbrella when you think it's going to rain. Being prepared lessened the chance of needing what you were prepared for.

Like the twins remaining potty-trained – no accidents. It made our lives so much easier.

The day came. We left the pellet stove on. It would run until it ran out of pellets or the battery died. If all went well, then we'd be back before either of those things happened.

Dogs on the sleighs. One child on the snow machine with each of us. They would probably get bored, but we'd deal with that when the time came. Maybe we'd stop along the way.

I let Madison lead as she had not driven a snow machine before. We would stick to the road and maintain a steady pace of twenty-five mph or so until she was a little more comfortable. I had no doubt that she would pick up the pace on the straightaways. I would follow her far enough back to avoid the snow cloud her snow machine kicked up.

We set out. It was funny watching her navigate the first corner onto the highway. She almost came to a complete stop as she muscled the nose around. She gave me an unhappy look. I went wide around her and showed her how to let the skis take the machine around the corner. I gave it a little gas to help the skis dig in and corner smoothly. I slowed and looked back. She accelerated and slowed, accelerated and slowed. She was getting used to the gas feed. Once on the road, she passed me and continued toward Chena Hot Springs. We were on our way.

And an hour later, we were still on our way. But the pace was picking up. I raced ahead to give her the let's-take-a-break sign. We stopped in the middle of the road. First order of business was to let the twins relieve themselves. That was interesting. Snowsuits aren't made for field relief. Their little bodies shivered as they tried to go. We held them close while they finally did their business and then bundled them back up into their now cold clothes. The dogs frolicked in the snow. It was a bit deep for Phyllis, but Husky made a wide patch that Phyllis could follow. They ran back along the tracks we had made. Both were wearing coats as we didn't know how cold they'd get riding in the sleigh.

The coats were a good call. About five minutes into the ride, the novelty had worn off and they'd curled up as much as they could in the blanket, with their noses facing backwards, away from the wind. Next time, more blankets and maybe pillows to use as a wind-break up front and cushion in the back.

It was nice traveling with all of us together. We coaxed the dogs back into their traveling crates with Milk Bones, climbed aboard ourselves, and set out again.

The break helped. Madison was far more comfortable and almost immediately picked up the pace. We passed a few moose grazing on willow branches near the road. But we didn't pass any people or signs of people. Maybe everyone had left. Or hunkered down so much that they left no trace. Real preppers lived out here. People who understood what it was like to live off the grid. We were teaching ourselves quickly, but it wasn't natural for us. My first thought was to run a generator.

As we approached the Chena Hot Springs Resort, things looked normal. There were snow machine tracks in the immediate vicinity. There were dog sled tracks. The sled dogs were barking and yipping from the kennel near the road. There should have been about a hundred dogs there. It seemed like it from the noise they were making.

We pulled our sleds up to the main entrance where there was also the restaurant. We left the dogs in their cages, even though they were ready to get out. The door was unlocked so we went inside. As bizarre as it seemed, there was a young woman behind the counter.

THE HOT SPRINGS

"Can I help you?" she asked in a pleasant voice.

"I'm sorry. I didn't expect anyone to be here," I started.

"We've been out of touch for more than three weeks now. We have plenty of reservations on the books, but the state hasn't plowed the road. The phones are out, so no one is able to call and cancel and we aren't able to call them," she said. "We were getting worried."

I looked at Madison. Although the resort didn't get a great deal of traffic, I would have thought they'd be more curious. But then again, they were here to work for weeks at a time. From the looks of the parking lot, no guests had stayed. Our arrival drew a crowd, almost all of them college-aged.

We told them what we saw in the city, including what happened to our friends. We told them about the convoy of vehicles that left. I told them about the wolf pack and the Dog Musher.

The group gave a great deal of attention to our twins. The children enjoyed their new friends. Madison brought our dogs inside too.

"Would you have any fresh greens?" Madison asked. The resort maintained its own greenhouses. It had been a while since we had a fresh salad.

"You bet!" one young man offered. We were ushered into the dining room. They brought chairs for the twins. We put the dogs on leashes that they had in the gift shop. We didn't want them getting in the way or running into the kitchen.

Everything was fully functional. It was nice and warm in the lodge. It was light. It was normal.

But it wasn't normal. We were the only customers they had. They had been going about their business since the disaster that had befallen Fairbanks. Their lifeline had been cut and they hadn't even realized it.

A number of workers joined us to eat. Instead of eating in the employee lounge or somewhere else, the employees had taken to eating in the formal dining room, with the fireplace and the bar. We had nice big salads and the twins had mini hamburgers. There was fresh baked bread for everyone.

We weren't starving, but there is so much to be said for a good meal at a restaurant. Call this a little slice of heaven, at least for today. The crew took good care of us. When the meal finished, we offered to help clean up. No need, they said. It was nice to hear what had happened. They had a great deal to talk about among themselves.

"Is the pool open?" I asked.

"Of course. There's no one over there right now. Just help yourselves." I let them write down my credit card number to cover the meal whenever the power was restored. I gave them a $100 tip. I expected that I was still making more with my retirement pay than I was paying out in auto-payments. I couldn't be sure, but it's the thought that counts. I still had my wallet with me whenever I left the house. I didn't want to give that up. It was part of modern society. It was part of being normal.

We dutifully changed in the locker rooms, but left our clothes on the benches. I thought about locking up my rifle and pistol, but settled for taking those in the pool area with us. There were no other visitors.

We went swimming in the inside pool. The dogs ran around the pool and finally laid down on the rug by the door. We relaxed in the pool until our fingers were shriveled. Then we took nice showers to get the stinky mineral water off us. After nearly a month, a hot shower was incredible.

STAYING AT THE RESORT

We had taken our time and it was dark outside. I didn't want to drive back in the dark. I didn't think we had to. We dropped our towels in the bin and went outside for the short walk back to the main desk. Our greeter and the others were at the bar getting bombed. I guess the news of Fairbank's demise was harder on them than it first seemed. None of this group was from Fairbanks; they came from various places in the Lower 48.

They were occupied filling in the information blanks with various conspiracy theories. I put on my Intelligence Officer hat and boiled things down to the only facts we had. A nuclear device exploded somewhere on the west side of Fort Wainwright. It was big enough to level the city and make the enclosed area of Fairbanks radioactive. The detonation also would have created an EMP to destroy electronics on the circuit, such as the cell towers. Any communications would have to go through the city and there was no longer a city. The resort counted on the city so the resort was cut off. That was all we knew. Speculation didn't help anything.

I took the time to shake their hands. You can tell a great deal by looking into someone's eyes. I saw grief and frustration. These were connected youth of today and they were cut off from the world. I applauded their efforts to keep everything running. They maintained a level of normal despite the lack of guests.

"What do you intend to do tomorrow and then next week?" I asked. They didn't know. No one stepped up to lead them. They were a group of kids working their way through college. "Will you make it through the winter?" They looked surprised by the question.

"We have food and we have power. Do we have enough food for the dogs?" a young lady named Amber asked the group. They started offering bits and pieces of information from the areas they worked.

"I suggest you plan to spend the winter here. You probably won't be getting any guests. I expect that help will come at some point. We just need to be alive and healthy when that happens." Hope. I offered a lifeline for them. With hope, they would not only survive, but thrive.

"Since it's gotten late, can we stay the night?"

THE MAYOR OF CHENA HOT SPRINGS

Our after-dinner conversation became a team meeting. They looked to me to guide them. Maybe it was the Marine in me or, more likely, it was because I was older.

"You haven't had a guest in three weeks." It was a statement, but they nodded as if it were a question.

"I suggest that you all become the Community of Chena Hot Springs. What will it take to keep the geo-thermal plant running? What will it take to ensure you have enough food to sustain the community? What will each of you do to help the group survive?" They looked at me. No one talked.

"Let me offer an organizational structure to start with, but then it can be modified as you, the community see fit. Amber. You are the mayor." She shook her head. "Your job sucks the most. You need to know what everyone is doing and be everywhere at once. You will be the glue that holds the community together because you think logistics. Food. Water. Fuel. Power.

"Who understands the power plant here? Where do you get your fresh water from? Who manages the greenhouse? Who tends the kennel?" Because of where people were working, it was easy to align responsibilities with capabilities. Some people surprised us with their skills and backgrounds. Pleasantly surprised. We had an EMT in training. We had two farmers. We had one junior dog musher and one assistant to handle the dogs.

The key people, the previous management team, lived in Fairbanks. They'd left the evening of the first day after the detonation and never returned. We did not have a mechanic or a manager or a vet or a medic.

"My God, we don't have an accountant!" I blurted out. They looked at me and then started laughing. I wanted them to know that they had everything they needed. They had enough expertise to make this community work.

"You said that you only had one month of dog food left." The dog musher Abigail nodded. "Are there any hunters?"

"I got a deer once with my old man in North Dakota," a scruffy-looking young man offered.

"Shoot it?" He nodded. "Dress it in the field?" He nodded again. "Anybody else with experience hunting?" One of the housekeepers raised her hand. Becca. She was the youngest of the bunch.

"Here you go...?"

"Darren." He filled in his name for me.

"Here you go, Darren." I cycled the action on my rifle, emptying the chamber, and then gave it to him. "You and Becca need to get a moose. That will help feed the dogs and help you keep a fresh supply of meat here for everyone else."

"We have enough meat in our freezer for the few of us for another year if needs be. We are supplied to feed a hotel full of guests," the cook, Jo, added.

"Thank you and that's good. People are taken care of. Dogs will be taken care of. Everyone figure out the best way to conserve. How can you make the most of what you have here?"

"I'd like set times for meals. Everyone eats together and I only have to make one or two entrees for each meal. That would make things easier for me and then I could help out elsewhere. I'd like to learn more about the power plant..."

Our visit became a sharing of information, then a conversation, and finally a town planning session. Amber had shown Madison and the twins to the honeymoon suite. The dogs were enjoying the company of the humans. I expected Madison had taken another long shower and that the twins were sound asleep after a full day. Amber was back.

"Tomorrow morning, breakfast is at..."

"Eight a.m.?" Jo offered. I looked at her, then at Amber.

"Eight a.m.?" repeated Amber. No dissent. "Eight a.m. it is. Coffee starting at six thirty and I'll make that myself." She was off to a good start as the mayor.

I asked Darren to follow me out to our snow machine. I dug out the extra box of ammunition I had brought for the rifle. "Good luck." I shook his hand as I handed it to him. This group needed to believe it could be self-sufficient.

The dogs were outside with me, but I hadn't put on their coats or boots. Phyllis was running to stay warm. I had to keep yelling at her to keep her going in my direction. We finally made it to the building with our room, which was less than a hundred yards from the restaurant and main desk. Phyllis and Husky must have run a mile and marked every post on their way. I never thought that female dogs would mark like males, but they did. Phyllis even lifted a leg to do it.

I then joined my family in the honeymoon suite for a very relaxing evening in a warm bed with electric lights and running hot water. We easily accepted these creature comforts, but we no longer took them for granted.

RETURNING HOME

Morning came far too soon. I slept like a rock. Madison created a cocoon for herself and was a bump under the covers. The twins were wedged in between us, emulating their mother in near hibernation. The dogs were at the bottom of the bed. At least it was a king so I had some room. There's a lot to be said about waking up in a warm room and being able to use a flush toilet.

It was about five a.m., later than I usually awoke, but still earlier than the rest of humanity. I closed the bathroom door and took a long shower. It was so nice. Too bad I had to put dirty clothes back on. Then again, they didn't seem so bad when my body was clean.

I was surprised that no one had gotten up, but the humans were still out cold. The dogs lifted their heads. I shushed them and waved them out the door with me. They came readily. Their dog food was still in the sled. I'd get it on the way to the restaurant.

I put on Phyllis' coat and boots because it was cold out. Maybe minus ten. There were some external lights here. It was nice being outside in the morning and having light. We walked around the complex, staying in the lighted areas.

We walked into the pool building. The staff had stopped locking doors so everything was available at any time. The sulfur smell wasn't overwhelming and I got used to it quickly. The dogs didn't like it in there. Too steamy. No soft places to lie down. They worked me until I took them back outside. This was how it should feel when at a resort.

When we'd been outside long enough, we went to the restaurant. Everything was sitting out to make the coffee, so I started the first pot and set things out for whoever showed up first. After Husky snatched a muffin off the table, I moved everything to the top of the bar. Phyllis enjoyed part of the theft as the muffin broke apart when Husky tried to run under a table with it.

Amber showed up early. Others straggled in over the next half hour. Although they were not very talkative, probably due to the early hour, they had determined looks on their faces. I wanted them to believe and take hold of their circumstance. It wasn't of their making, and it wasn't of my making. It simply was.

Someone had set up a set of external speakers on the bar. I got my phone from the sled and hooked it up. I turned it on, touched my way to REM, and played, "It's The End Of The World As We Know It."

I danced by myself behind the bar. The younger group moved tables and danced in the dining area. I played it one more time. It became a singalong. Madison and the twins showed up halfway through the second playing. I took Aeryn by the hand and danced with her. Madison and Charles were much better dancers.

When the song ended, I let my REM playlist continue, but turned the volume down a little.

I turned to Madison. "What do you think? We go home as soon as it gets light?" She nodded. The resort was a slice of paradise in our bleak and cold world. But we hadn't packed for a long stay. "I think if the community of Chena Hot Springs lets us, we'll come here every week for an overnight." She nodded. The twins didn't want to leave. They wanted to go swimming again.

"Amber. Once it gets light, we'll take our leave and go back home." I reached out to shake her hand. "Thank you for stepping up. Things will be fine. You will make them that way." She nodded.

"I'll take care of your room. Just leave it as it is," Becca offered.

"No," I said emphatically. "You are no one's housekeeper now. You're the hunter. You need to help supply the dogs. They need you more than the sheets in that room. We'll clean it up ourselves. Just show me where the clean sheets are."

She ended up doing better than that. She moved the cleaning cart next to the door and left it there.

We cleaned the room quickly, even though we still had a few hours till daylight. We asked for tours of the various areas. We wanted to see the greenhouse. We needed ideas for when we built our own greenhouse. We had planned for years to build one, but I had not gotten around to it. Now seemed to be a great time.

The new Community of Chena Hot Springs happily showed us everything there was to see. We even went out to the kennel to meet the dogs, but we had to put Husky and Phyllis on leashes. They were hard to control when we saw all the dogs. There was much barking and pulling. It devolved into complete chaos so we cut our visit short and walked back to the lodge, dragging two very excited dogs.

HOME

We loaded up with a couple days' supply of lettuce and vegetables, started our snow machines, and waved goodbye as we pulled out. I smiled behind my face shield. We had a place to come to experience the old world until our modern conveniences were restored at our home. And maybe we had started something good.

A functional resort had value, even more so when the employees took full ownership of the operation. If management returned, I would like to think they'd be proud of their employees and how they'd maintained the facility.

It was amazing what a good night's rest can do. Madison was making great time. She handled the snow machine easily. We probably averaged fifty miles an hour on the straightaways and thirty-five or so on the corners. The snow was deep enough that the skis dug in nicely. We made it home in a little over an hour.

Maybe next week's trip to the resort, we could take our laundry...

Fully refreshed, we dug into our chores. It was below freezing in the house, but the generator started on the first pull, and with a fresh bag added, the pellet stove blasted to life. We took care of our lettuce, putting it in the laundry room which was between our great room and the bedrooms. When the stove brought us back to fifty degrees, the laundry room would hover somewhere between freezing and less than fifty. We made it our walk-in refrigerator. It was nice to have fresh vegetables after only eating canned for three weeks straight.

The greenhouse was moving up in priority.

Deep down inside, I felt that we would be cut off from society for a long time. We had seen nothing since that one airplane on the third day. We'd seen some smoke from fires. But until we visited the resort, we hadn't seen other people since the convoy. We knew they had to be there, but people in rural areas around Fairbanks are very private and able to take care of themselves. I thought we needed to make contact with more people, at least take a census of some sort.

Why us? By establishing the Community at Chena Hot Springs, maybe I had become the regional governor. Somebody had to if we were all to make it to that magical day when the world found us.

Whenever that day came, I wanted to be there. I wanted to know that I did what I could to help others, too. The death of the Dog Musher came back to me. He was one I didn't save, but wish I had. The world needed people like him, people who loved their dogs. I gave my rifle away in the hopes that all the dogs at the resort would survive.

And that brought me out of my reverie. I needed a new hunting rifle. I had some relics from the Cold War; AKs, SKS, and a Moisin-Nagant. Only the Moisin would bring down a moose, but it had a crazy safety. I only had twenty rounds for it, too. I needed something more modern. And we needed pellets. At least we no longer needed diapers. It's the little victories that make you smile.

"Who wants to go shopping?" Madison quickly overruled both twins. They had their lessons, already on the calendar, and they also had yoga. Madison had not practiced for two days and it was time. The twins could twist themselves into little pretzels. I swear it was if they didn't have bones. But this was a calming time for them and would be followed by a nap.

I left the dogs and headed out. After two days of excitement, the dogs would probably sleep for a full day before they were back in top form.

I needed to find a hunting rifle and pellets.

"SHOPPING" FOR A RIFLE

I expected the farmhouse where I found the two new sleds would have firepower on hand, so that's where I went. On this trip, I needed to get into the house. I checked around first to make sure that no one had appeared and stood ready to shoot an intruder.

There were no new tracks, except for those from one seemingly adventurous rabbit.

The door was standard for this area. Solid without a window. I had my bolt cutters and sledgehammer. When entering other people's homes, I tried to minimize the damage I did. These people didn't know it, but they were a lifeline for us. In a world where resources were scarce, we had to make the most out of what was available. I kept my list of what I had taken and from where. Maybe that was more for me than for those we borrowed from.

I walked around the house looking for the easiest way in. I checked the back door. It was unlocked. Once I cleared the snow from the porch, the door opened easily and I went in.

These people had not kept up on their housecleaning. Dirty dishes were piled in the sink, with more on the table. It was a mess. I stopped for a second and closed my eyes, thanking them silently for opening their home to me and praying that someone from this family was away from Fairbanks at the time. Maybe someone from this family survived.

There weren't any gun racks on the walls. I went upstairs. Nothing in the closets, from what I could see. I went back downstairs. There was a closet under the stairs. I opened it. This was where they stored their real gear. There were ammo cans. I pulled these out. There were a number of boxes of 300 Winchester magnum shells. I didn't think there was a better rifle for hunting moose or bear. But the rifle wasn't in the closet. There was a shotgun and ammunition for a variety of smaller calibers, to include full-metal jacketed rounds for my .45. I pocketed all the .45 ammo.

If the 300 Winchester was in the house, I had missed it. I looked in recesses behind doors and under beds. I looked for hidden compartments in the furniture, but nothing turned up.

What if they had taken it moose hunting, and it was still in their truck? Or maybe still in the gun case of their quad. They had to have a quad. It was a farm!

I left the house and went to the barn, where it seemed the barn was cleaner than the house. The hay was neatly stacked and things were in order. The quad was here and it had a rifle case. The case had a padlock, which my bolt cutters took care of in short order.

The rifle was there. A beautiful 300 Win mag. The owner must have dropped his entire PFD (Permanent Fund Dividend – Alaskans get a check every year based on revenue from the oil windfall years) on this rifle. Outside, I took off the scope caps and peered through. It looked like it had been focused at about three hundred yards. A nice shot well within the effective range of this rifle. I wondered if they had gotten their moose.

I slung the rifle over my shoulder and went back in the house. First thing I did was secure all the ammunition for it. There were only a hundred rounds, but it would do. I was back in business for when I needed to hunt. Or protect my family, although this rifle would not have been any good in the fight with the wolves. The 45-70 was much better for that. It had iron sights and an eighteen-inch barrel, almost like it was made for a firefight. Depending on how successful Darren and Becca were hunting, maybe I could trade them this rifle for my trusty cannon. I thought of it that way because the ammunition for it looked more like mini cannon shells than the sleek rounds of a high-powered rifle.

I checked the top freezer in their kitchen. There were some moose steaks and they didn't look like last year's packaging. They had to have a big freezer somewhere, probably outside where it cost nothing in the winter to run. Had there been one in the garage?

I took the ammunition, rifle, and a few moose steaks with me outside, closing the door behind me. I put everything on my sled, so my hands would be free for breaking into the garage. But that wasn't needed as the side door to the garage was unlocked. The freezer was inside. A big chest freezer filled with a variety of moose meat. The freezer had never warmed up after we lost power. This meat was in perfect condition. We could feed our dogs and ourselves for another year on what was in here.

Add this to the dog food stored at the Dog Musher's house and our dogs would live like kings. Madison and I had both lost weight since the detonation. There was always more work than could be done. We were constantly in motion and we burned calories heating our bodies since we kept our house at fifty. If we could find some pellets for our stove, then maybe we could turn the thermostat up a little. Fifty degrees was cold.

There seemed to be an unlimited amount of split firewood. Everyone had a wood burner. Most people were far more self-sufficient than we were. If it has to be purchased or manufactured elsewhere, it's not good for a prepper.

BENNETT ROAD

I needed to find pellets and further out was not the answer. Self-sufficient meant you made do with what was on hand, such as trees. They all had wood burning stoves out there. I decided that I had to risk getting closer to the city.

There was a road that paralleled ours, about a half-mile closer to the city, still on this side of the ridge. I reasoned that there would be no risk there. I cruised past the turn to our house and slowed to take the corner onto Bennett. I would look for homes with a chimney that did not have a supply of split firewood. This was like a military exercise. How could I get the most for the least effort?

I took it easy as I traveled up Bennett. It had recently been blacktopped and made for a smooth ride. Most houses were back a little from the road, so I slowed as I passed each, looking for what I considered to be the telltale signs of a pellet stove.

The last time I was on this road was before the detonation. There was a house that had a barn with horses. I wondered if they had survived. As it turned out, the horse ranch was the first house I came to that looked like it might use a pellet stove. I turned into their driveway and slowed as I approached the house.

Three shaggy horses were huddled outside the barn, eating from a rolled hay bale. They had survived and even looked healthy. But it had only been a month. They had to have emulated moose by eating snow when they were thirsty. The barn provided sufficient shelter from the weather. Maybe come spring we would need to do something with the horses if help had not arrived by then. Even if it was as simple as turning them loose when the hay ran out. I didn't want to see any more deaths of animals that had been locked up.

The front door was locked. I went around the back.

Footprints. Leading from the house to the barn.

ENDURE

I knocked on the door and yelled a greeting. I was instantly afraid. I had the new rifle slung over my shoulder and had a sledgehammer in my hand. I jumped down the steps into the yard, dropped the sledgehammer on the ground, and held up my hands. I stood there as a face appeared in the window.

She looked at me with wild eyes. Besides tending the horses, maybe she hadn't left the house in the past month. She might be running low on supplies.

"Are you okay?" I asked, my hands still in the air. "I live just over there." I pointed in the direction of our house.

She opened the door. She had a butcher knife in one hand.

"I'll stay here; I'm not coming any closer." I tried to put her at ease. "Is there any help that you need?"

She still looked at me, her mouth moving, but nothing came out.

"The horses look healthy. You've done a good job taking care of them over the past month."

"How do you know it's been a month?" she blurted out.

"I know because that's when a nuclear device detonated in Fairbanks. The city is gone. The blast did a lot of damage, and then the radiation did the rest."

Her mouth moved, but nothing came out.

"Did your husband work in the city?" It wasn't a question. She had been waiting for her husband for a month. She'd waited, not knowing.

He wasn't coming home.

Tears froze to her eyelashes. Her breath quickened, small clouds puffed in front of her. The knife fell from numb fingers. She turned and went back inside, closing the door behind her.

In a loud voice I said, "I'll come back tomorrow and check on you. I'll bring my family." I doubted she heard me.

I was done 'shopping' for today.

OUR FIRST LOCAL SURVIVOR

Madison thought we should be more active in finding survivors. Our trip to the Hot Springs had energized her. Madison realized that getting through this would be better if we didn't have to do it alone. Although she was an introvert, there was a certain solace in company. We had no intention of building a commune with everyone living under one roof, but we wanted to at least know where people were living. Maybe we could even map out the hot zone and help people stay clear of the radiation.

The next day, after sun up, we loaded up the twins and the dogs into their sleighs, fired up the snow machines and made the short trip to the woman's house around the corner. I hoped that her grief was no longer debilitating. Maybe the truth of the city's demise had helped her achieve some closure with the loss of her husband. I didn't know. I wasn't good with the emotional stuff.

We pulled down her driveway and unloaded everyone. The dogs raced for the fence so they could bark at the horses, who whinnied and were none too pleased with the arrival of our dogs. I thought I saw fresh footprints to the barn.

With Charles on my hip, I tentatively ventured up the back steps. The knife was gone.

I knocked on the door as her sad face appeared and looked at me. Seeing little Charles, she started to sob, putting her hand on the window.

I opened the door and she leaned out to hug me and my little man. Maybe her child had been in the city along with her husband.

She let me go, waving us all inside after her. The kitchen was immaculate, and even a little warm. Well, warmer than what we kept our house.

We put the twins down. Aeryn pointed to the woman and asked, "Why?" She wanted to know why she was crying.

"Why don't you ask her?" I suggested. Sometimes it helped to talk about your grief. Telling it to the innocence of small children could make the pain seem less.

Aeryn, still in her snowsuit, tottered over to the lady. "Why?" she asked in her small voice.

The woman sat down on the floor to be closer to her. Charles moved in close to his sister. We sat in chairs at the table.

"My husband took our son to the dentist on that morning and they never came home. They are never coming home, are they?"

For the children, the concept of never didn't have any meaning. They shrugged it off. They understood on the simplest of terms. Her family wasn't here so the woman was sad.

"What's your name? I'm Aeryn!" She brightened as she proclaimed proudly in her little girl voice.

With a tired smile, the lady looked at our little girl. "I'm Colleen. Nice to meet you." She held out her hand.

"I'm Charles!" Not to be outdone by his sister, he shouldered his way into the conversation. Colleen shook his hand, too.

"Hi, Charles. My son's name is Antonio and he's twelve." She started to cry again, quietly, with her head down. We had lost friends, but not family. We were blessed to be together through this. Colleen had to go through it all alone, only her horses for company. We pulled the twins onto our laps and sat silently for a while.

"What do you need?" I asked. "We happen to have some lettuce, if you'd like a salad…"

"I'd love a salad or anything that's not dehydrated." After finishing whatever groceries she had on hand, she'd started with their emergency rations. Most Alaskans kept thirty days' worth of food on hand in the form of a five-gallon plastic bucket filled with dehydrated meals. We had meals from our own stock, but as long as there was something else, we ate that first. No matter how well you prepare the dehydrated food, it is what it is, something to help you survive.

And it did its job, for Colleen anyway. It kept her alive.

I hoped we made a difference for her. She knew something was terribly wrong, yet she persevered. The human spirit is not so easily defeated. The Dog Musher saw his world taken from him and he couldn't move past that.

"Do you have a snow machine?" If she didn't, then she could ride with us. "We live just around the corner, but with the snow, it would be a tough walk."

"No, but we have a quad with tracks. I can follow you, but not too fast."

The horses had come up to the fence and the dogs were still barking. It was a little bit of chaos outside as both sides jockeyed for position as if they were going into battle. Or they were opposing sides in a rugby scrum.

We went outside, and there was much yelling and wrestling as we recovered the dogs and got them back into the crates on the sleighs. I went with Colleen as she opened the garage and got into the quad. Four tracks, in the shape of triangles, were where the tires should be. They looked like they'd have good traction and were wide enough to keep the quad on top of the snow.

It started after turning over for about twenty seconds. Ran roughly for another minute, then smoothed out. She slowly turned the steering wheel to exercise the connections. It hadn't run for over a month and she didn't want to damage any of the components. I think she realized that this was going to be her primary source of transportation until the spring. The truck in the garage would do her no good with the roads unplowed.

She pulled out and followed me to my sled. No sense in shutting the garage door. There was no heat to keep inside. I put Charles in front of me on my snow machine, and then our little caravan headed out.

RALLYING ONE SURVIVOR

It was approaching lunch time when we made it home, all of eight minutes after we left Colleen's horse ranch.

We parked our sleds and I stayed outside with the dogs while everyone else went inside. The dogs took care of business quickly as they knew there would be excitement indoors.

We prepared a big salad for Colleen and made moose burgers as the main course, using bread we had gotten fresh from Jo at the resort. We even had a tomato to cut up. Colleen ate like she was starving. She had probably lost weight in the past month, a great deal of weight. Her clothes hung loosely on her.

We finally introduced ourselves while we were eating. We talked about the community at Chena Hot Springs. It was nice to have fresh food. It was nice to know that we weren't alone.

We settled in after lunch, near the pellet stove. We turned on some music using my cell phone and our Bluetooth speaker. She closed her eyes and disappeared for a while. Not sleeping. She journeyed to another place where there was less pain. We put the twins down for their nap. They looked at us, but after a while, they drifted off into a restful slumber.

Colleen came back to us after a couple of Bob Dylan songs.

"Thank you for lunch," she started tentatively. "I didn't know what to do. There was no place to go. My phone was out. No power. We have a wood stove that we usually don't run, but I used it. We didn't have much wood, but our neighbors did. I borrowed some of theirs when ours ran out. They aren't home. No one's home." She looked down at her feet, at the dirty socks she was wearing.

"It's okay," I began.

"How is it okay?" she interrupted, getting angry.

"It's okay because it has to be. We have to all keep going until help arrives. I think that will happen after breakup." Breakup was the term used for the spring thaw. That was when the ice broke apart and the rivers started to flow free again. I assumed that the melting snow would take away most of the radiation. Then help could come and set up a relief station for us. Everything downstream might get contaminated, but not where we were, north of the city.

We hoped that Colleen was on the mend. She still suffered greatly from her loss, but maybe the worst was behind her. In one sense, it had been a month. In another, she'd known the truth for only a single day.

"We plan to go to Chena Hot Springs each week to check in on the community, but selfishly, to partake of the comforts of a normal world. They have power. And heat. And a chef! And we'll go swimming, but the dogs don't like the pool." We smiled. We would take a vacation each week, but we needed to bring things to the community to share. If we could find another snow machine, Colleen could go with us. She wouldn't stay at the Hot Springs because of her horses – they were her family, just like Phyllis and Husky were ours.

"Do any of your neighbors have a snow machine that you could borrow?" I asked while topping off the quad's gas tank.

She thought for a second and said, "I think all of them do."

"If you don't mind, I'll go back with you now and we'll see if we can find one that's ready to go." Then I added, "Do any of your neighbors use a pellet stove?"

LOOKING FOR MORE SURVIVORS

It didn't take us long to find a house with a newer snow machine in perfect condition. Colleen showed me to one of the neighbors who had both a sled and a pellet stove. I broke the lock on the shed and could see how uncomfortable Colleen was.

"I keep a list of what I take and from whom. If they return, I will pay them back. Right now? It's all for one and one for all. Anything everyone has is necessary to help us survive. After that, we can figure things out, but I don't think an insurance company expects anything to be intact. And I don't really care. The insurance companies and bureaucrats aren't here. No one has stepped up to even look for us, let alone help us.

"I feel bad for the people who used to live here. All of them have their stories. All of them meant something. I don't know if they were away or if they were in the city. In either case, none of them are here. If I wasn't here and somebody needed something I had to survive, they would be welcome to it." I looked at her. Despite my bold proclamation, I still felt badly digging around in other people's stuff.

"All right. I feel bad about it, but we're going to run out of pellets before we run out of cold. We haven't seen an airplane in a month. Besides you and the community of Chena Hot Springs, we haven't seen other people around here either. And I still feel bad, but we have little choice." I didn't tell her about the Dog Musher. His death might bother me forever. Unfortunately, I had to go back there within a month in order to get some dog food. I'm sure he would be okay with me taking it. I'd tried to save him.

I tried.

I pulled the shed door open. A high stack of pellets was on one side and a newer snow machine was on the other side, right in front of the double door. It was facing out and ready to go. I checked the gas – a full tank. I opened the doors to the shed, looking over the snow machine. They were all similar in how they started. Check the engine. Check the gas. Give the throttle a number of pushes. Choke it. And try to start it, whether a pull start or electric start. When it's cold, let it warm up plenty before revving it.

This was an electric start and it was ready to go. It seemed like it came to life with the second turn of the engine. It idled roughly at first, but it smoothed out. While letting it warm up, I started carrying bags of pellets to the sleigh. I figured I could drag maybe twenty bags, eight hundred pounds, behind my sled, my snow machine, without a problem. I was not going far and I wasn't going fast.

Once the bags were loaded and Colleen's neighbor's snow machine was idling smoothly, we were ready to leave. I shook her hand. "On Saturday morning, come by the house before sun up. We'll push off as soon as it gets light to make the travel easier. I think you'll enjoy it there. The young people have a lot of energy and the chef is magnificent!" She looked a bit down. "You can stop by our house anytime. I'm sure the twins will enjoy your company. But be prepared to teach them something. They get a few lessons every day." She brightened at that and nodded.

Colleen took the snow machine to her house and put it in the shed. She would hike back to pick up her tracked quad and bring that to her home, too. I pulled out, spinning a little until the sleigh started moving. It was nice to add the extra twenty bags to our stock. Our search for pellets had come to an end.

Today had not been a bad day. Colleen showed a spark of life, and we had gotten something we needed.

The chance to help someone else. It felt good.

EXTENDING OUR SEARCH

I spent the next day at the house. I had been gone too much lately. We were in a good place with our supplies. I had filled some of our neighbors' five-hundred-gallon fuel oil tanks with gasoline. The fuel oil was drained into two water carriers people had for their trucks. Most people in our neighborhood had those. You used to be able to pick up water from town and refill your own tank. We had water delivered. Since the detonation, we'd been siphoning water from our own tank as the pump needed direct-wired 220-volt power. Plus, we cut our water usage way back. It's surprising how little water you need when you don't have flush toilets, a shower, a washing machine, or a dishwasher. We had plenty of water and there was always snow that could be melted if need be.

We had food and we had heat. I ran the generator a couple times a day and stayed inside, reading with the twins, or building with Legos, or any number of other constructive things.

Colleen didn't show up that day, but just after sun up on the second day, she rode in on her neighbor's snow machine. She knocked gently on the door to the garage. We welcomed her in. She carried a book bag. We looked at each other.

She smiled warmly at the twins. "My son had these books. He outgrew them, but I think you might like them." She opened the bag and pulled out a number of Dr. Seuss books. We had a few of them, but many we didn't.

"Thank you!" the twins cried in unison.

"I like this one!" Aeryn was quite articulate for a two-year-old.

"If Miss Colleen would like, maybe she can read a story that you have not heard before." I smiled at them.

She proceeded to show each book, looking first to the twins and then to us. Madison nodded at One Fish Two Fish. Colleen put the other books down and started to read. The twins paid rapt attention as Colleen worked the rhymes and the rhythm of the prose. When she finished, they wanted her to read it again.

So she started over.

We wouldn't let the twins get a third reading. It was time for them to go outside and play. So we all bundled up and went outside. I asked Madison if she'd like to take Colleen on the snow machine to the gas station and look around. Madison had only been there once, so she liked the idea.

They headed out and I took care of the twins. It was too cold to make a snowman, but we followed our trail into the woods with the dogs. Everyone enjoyed being outside with the beauty of the snow frozen onto the trees. The sky was nothing but light pastels. The snow was pure white and sparkled.

When everyone was sufficiently cold, we went inside. Madison and Colleen returned with some little things. It appeared that Colleen had a sweet tooth by the bulge of candy bars in her pocket. We wished her well as she took her leave of us, thanking her profusely for her gift of the books and her time in reading to the twins.

And that's when we committed to seeing who else was out there.

GOLDSTREAM

On the day we last drove Goldstream we had seen an older lady in her yard. It was time to go back and see if she was still there, and who else may be around. I didn't want Madison and the twins to go. I wanted this to be as quick as possible. Maybe I was being overly protective, but I noticed that when Madison went to the gas station, she hadn't taken the pistol. She knew that since we had seen the wolves, we were supposed to be armed while outside. I thought we were supposed to. I thought we had agreed. Maybe I was too protective. That would probably change the longer this went on.

When would help come?

This could be a long trip if I ran into a number of people. I had the road map out of the phone book and dutifully put two numbers on the locations where the known survivors lived. 1 was for us. 2 was for Colleen.

I started a journal to keep track of the people. Maybe I'd consider myself the unofficial census taker. When help came, this resource would be helpful and save a great deal of time. In the interim, maybe we could save a few lives.

I took off right before sunrise. It was overcast, but still cold, so I didn't think it would snow. If it did, it wouldn't snow much. It usually warmed up above zero for the big snows.

I had the sleigh behind my sled with some things that people might need: a can of gas, some frozen moose meat, a small propane tank, a sleeping bag. Things like that. I had the high-powered rifle, just in case. I wore my shoulder holster with the .45 nestled under my arm. And I had my 'shopping' tools, too.

I had to go around ten miles before getting to the house where we had seen the old lady. The ride was uneventful, as I took Bennet to steer as far away from the city as I could get before reaching the Steese Highway.

There were numerous moose tracks crossing the Steese Highway heading toward Fox. The woods on either side of the road here were extensive. As I approached Goldstream, I noted a number of snow machine tracks. They ranged east, west, and north. It looked like many had used these roads. I was happy to see that we were not alone. Far from it, it seemed.

I picked up the pace as the sun peeked out over the southern horizon. I pulled into the driveway of the A-frame where we had seen the old lady. It didn't look like anyone was home. No tracks. No smoke. Windows frosted over. I got off the snow machine and went to the front door. I knocked. Nothing.

In the back, the door stood open. Something was under a foot of snow, partially blocking the bottom step. Probably a bag of trash. I stepped on it. It was solid. I continued into the house. No one had been home for quite some time. Logs were piled beside the wood burning stove, but it was cold. A pot was on the stove, a meal frozen within.

Whoever had lived here had left in a hurry, but after the power was out, unless they routinely used their wood stove for cooking. Many did that around here.

I checked the cupboards for food we could use. There was a small pile of vacuum-sealed meat that looked like moose jerky. I pocketed it.

When I went back outside, where I had stepped on the lump at the bottom of the steps, I could see what looked like a coat. I brushed off the snow. It was the old lady, long dead and frozen solid. I wondered if she had fallen down the steps or maybe even had a heart attack. It didn't matter. I said a prayer over her. One more victim of the calamity that had befallen Fairbanks.

I continued up the road on the sled, much slower this time as I looked for any signs that people were alive. The snow machine tracks looked like they came from one home up ahead. I pulled into the driveway. A slight curl of smoke came from a chimney at the back of the house. "Hello!" I yelled, with my hands up as I walked toward the house.

The front door opened and a man with a shotgun stepped out. I started to give my prepared speech on looking for survivors when he raised the gun and fired.

My face stung and I threw myself to the ground. It felt like I had been hit by a baseball bat. "Wait! Wait!" I yelled, as he calmly pumped another round into the chamber. I rolled away from that spot and jumped to my feet, turning back to my sled. He fired again.

I was thrown on my face as if a moose ran into me from behind. Pain!

I scrambled to my sled as he slowly came down the steps. I hit the starter and the warm snow machine burst to life. I gave it some gas while lying across the seat and did a partial donut as I sped away from the house. The snow machine bounced into the air as I clipped the ditch on the way toward the main road. The sleigh was still attached. I couldn't see if anything had fallen off. I wasn't going to stop and look. I raced back along Goldstream toward Steese. I slowed to take an inventory of myself. My face was bleeding where some pellets had hit me. The wounds were small. He must have used a light birdshot.

I looked back. Two snow machines were following me.

And they were gaining on me. With the sleigh attached, I couldn't outrun them. And even if I did, my tracks would lead these people back to my home. I couldn't have that.

This guy just shot me and now there were two of them chasing me. I could feel my anger rising. I could feel my fear that if I failed, I would be abandoning my family. Trying to be the big man, helping other people out, and I had put that which I held most dear in jeopardy.

Time to stop the madness.

I pulled into a driveway where a truck was parked and slid sideways to a stop, jumping from the snow machine and ripping off my glove at the same time. I pulled my pistol as I got behind the truck. One sled entered the driveway behind me, but slowly. The other stopped on the road. Their weapons were slung on their backs, their gloved hands on the handlebars of their sleds.

I leaned around the truck and took aim at the man on the road and fired once, re-aimed and fired again. A double tap. He rolled off his sled. The closer man accelerated directly at me. My breath froze in my chest. I tried to take a quick full breath so that I could aim, but no, my asthma was trying to take over.

I backed further behind the sled as he pulled a donut right in front of me. My head started to swim from lack of air. I fired at his back, and again, and a third time.

He leaned into his handlebars, starting to accelerate. I dropped to a knee and fired again, my aim still unsteady. As the snow machine jumped forward he rolled backward onto the ground.

I staggered up to him and put a round through his face. I kept going, aiming the pistol at the man in the road. He was trying to get his hand into his coat. I put my foot on his chest and shoved the pistol into his mouth. "Why?" I gasped.

He mumbled something. He couldn't speak with my pistol barrel in his mouth. He struggled weakly, trying to free his arm. I rolled him, then twisted his arm violently behind his back. Using my foot for leverage, I twisted his arm around at the elbow. Something snapped.

I rolled him back over. I grabbed his left hand and twisted it backwards. My movements were jerky from the lack of oxygen. I fell to my knees.

He contorted his body as he tried to get away from me. He was bleeding from somewhere, but with the snowsuit it was hard to see where.

"Why?" I yelled into his face.

"It's our world for the taking," he managed to say. I swung my pistol and hit him in the head, knocking him sideways. Fifty thousand people die and that was how he was determined to survive. His breathing grew shallow. I left him there as the pool of blood grew.

I felt bad about the Dog Musher. I did not feel bad about these two. Were there any more where they came from? Once my breathing calmed and I started to get enough air, I muscled my snow machine around to get it facing back toward the road. My head throbbed as it always did after an asthma attack. I thought for a second, then checked the two men. I put their weapons, ammunition, and snow machine keys into my sleigh. It was a small gesture, but hopefully it would send a message to anyone who saw the crisis as an opportunity.

CLEANING OUT THE RAT'S NEST

I drove back toward the men's home. I stopped some distance away and watched it closely, using the scope of my rifle. I took out a piece of my newly found moose jerky. It was good.

I knew that I should have felt something. I had just killed one man and left another for dead. But I didn't feel remorse over the killing. I was upset, but not about shooting the men. It was clear how far I would go for my family, if I was forced to defend myself.

If possible, I was even angrier now. How dare they put me in a position where I had to fight them! It was the survivors against the weather, against the animals. Not us against each other.

Was that a movement in the window? There was at least one more person in there. It looked like a younger woman, but it was hard to tell. The curtains were mostly closed. I took aim, thinking that I could shoot her through the window if she stopped to look out.

Which she did, but I couldn't pull the trigger. She looked afraid, not like a normal person who looked eagerly for their spouse to return. I'm not sure how stupid I had to be to continue to risk everything for others, but I started the snow machine and headed down the road.

I pulled in and turned sharply, facing mostly away from the house. I would be in a better position to leave quickly if needed. I kept the snow machine idling, while I got down behind it. "Hey!" I yelled. "Hey! Get out here!" My Marine voice echoed off the house. A young woman opened the door and stepped halfway out.

"Where are they?" she asked.

"They won't be coming back." I had my pistol out and pointed in her direction.

"Thank God," she whispered and turned to head back into the house.

I put a round into the door frame. "Stop, stop," she cried as she collapsed into a ball and covered her head. "I just want to get my coat and get the hell out of here."

"Hang on. I'm coming up. Keep your hands where I can see them, please." I moved toward her, keeping my pistol trained center mass, aimed at her body. She tentatively pulled herself upright. I waved at her with the pistol to go inside. I followed her into a filthy mess. "Tell me," I said as I kept my pistol pointed at her. "Are you with them?" I watched her face closely. She was afraid, but then she was angry.

"No! I'm not with them!" she barked. Her eyes said she was telling the truth. She looked away from me and then down at the ground. Her shoulders were slumped. Her posture submissive. I thought I knew what had happened, but wanted her to tell me.

"Is there anyone else here?" She shook her head. I put my pistol away. "Sit down," I told her. I cleaned off a place on an armchair for her, while I leaned against the couch. "Tell me what happened."

She began a convoluted story about her boyfriend, the younger of the two men and his brother. How they had spent the night before the event in the city stealing car parts. They were sleeping in after their spree, so they weren't in the city when they should have been at work. They survived the detonation because they were criminals. She was with them because she had dropped out of school and didn't have any other prospects. At least she didn't have to live with her parents, although as she told this part of her story, her eyes misted over.

No matter how strained your relationship, people missed their parents when they were gone.

She finally finished her story. She thanked me for freeing her from the hell the two men had put her through. Once the city was gone, they changed. They became domineering and drunk on power, as well as beer. They started their rampage by killing an old lady down the road who was outside getting firewood. After that, their goal was to leave no one alive. She showed me a closet that was piled with cash and jewelry.

I didn't want to know where they got that stuff, unless…"They didn't get any of this from the city, did they?"

She nodded. "They went down to the west side where there were stores. I think they cleaned them all out."

"Don't touch any of that. Did you go with them?"

"No. They wouldn't let me leave the house."

"You're better off. A nuclear explosion destroyed the city. Radiation killed those who weren't killed by the blast. This stuff is probably contaminated. Maybe everything they touched."

"That means me, too." She hung her head. "God is punishing me for what I've done with my life."

Maybe, I thought. *Maybe the consequences of your decisions are haunting you. Maybe you set yourself up for failure by being in the wrong place at the wrong time. When you know your boyfriend is a criminal and you stayed with him anyway? Well, maybe you're right.* I didn't say it out loud, but not saying anything confirmed in her mind that I agreed with her.

"Do you have a place to go?"

"Yes. There's a cabin up north that my family owns. I want to go there." She looked outside. "Where are the snow machines?" she asked.

"You can ride with me back to where the snow machines are."

She gathered up her things. She didn't have much. She wanted even less. She just wanted to be out of there.

Once packed and geared up for the cold, we went outside. I put her bag in the sleigh. I picked up my helmet where it had fallen off my sled when I departed so hastily earlier. I brushed it off with a glove and put it on. She climbed on behind me and off we went. It only took a few minutes to get to where the two snow machines were. The ravens had already been busy, and I didn't care if the older of the two was dead or not before the birds started to work on him. I hoped he suffered, just enough to make him feel guilty for what he'd done.

She looked at the young man in the driveway, even though it was a gruesome sight. Half his head was missing due to the close-up power of my .45. She spit on the gore and then turned without another look. She was obviously more familiar with the young man's sled. She started it up and slowly pulled out, making sure that she ran over the older man's body on the way.

She stopped, looked back at me with a smile, waved, and was gone. *She'll be fine*, I thought.

HOME

It was nice to get back home. The cuts on my face hadn't bled very much because of the cold. When Madison could get a good look at them, she found BBs that were still embedded. She pulled them out with tweezers while the twins looked on.

"They wanted to kill me," I started. I told her the story and, personally, I was glad that I had gone and not her. If she had run into them and something had happened to her, I would have probably ended up killing those two anyway, but the suffering attached with that would have been unbearable.

"I freed a young woman, their slave. I didn't save any others from them. I don't think I want to go back to Goldstream or anywhere around there. People are probably afraid and would shoot at us. We need to give it time. Let's stick with this side of Steese. This is our world." I thought for a minute, then added, "Maybe we can make sure that our world doesn't turn into anything like that. Just like those two decided to remake the world as they wanted it. What they wanted was for themselves. What I want is for our kids, for you to be happy."

I shook my head. "I'm not saying it right. I'm sorry. I'm so angry at people. How could they? We're better than that, we as a people, not just us."

Madison touched my face. She was so supportive. She married me because of who I was. This crisis brought the real me into sharp focus. I would do anything for my family and then I would do anything to build a world in which my family would be happy to live. Sometimes, these two priorities competed as they had today. I risked my life in trying to rally survivors, which put my family at risk. If I hadn't done that, then maybe, just maybe, those animals would have brought the fight to us. The fight would always be there, but if we picked where and when, wouldn't we be better off? But if we picked the fight, then wouldn't we be the bad guys? Did we know that we had to fight?

Madison, still holding my face, pulled my chin up until our eyes met. "I believe in you," she whispered.

THE WEEKEND

The rest of the week was thankfully uneventful. We took the twins to Colleen's house where she formally introduced them to the horses. The twins were mesmerized. Since they liked dogs, they saw the horses as really big dogs. Bigger was better, right?

Best of all was watching the twins sitting on the back of a horse with full winter hair as Colleen led it around. They changed positions a few times, each getting their fair share of time in the forward seat, holding the horse's mane.

We left the dogs at home for this visit. They seemed hell-bent on stirring things up as much as possible when anywhere near these super-sized brothers of theirs. If our dogs could have an arch enemy, the horses would be it.

On Friday evening, we were all getting excited to make a trip back to Chena Hot Springs. What did we need to take? What could we bring to the good people of the Community of Chena Hot Springs? How early could we leave to go there safely?

And then the snow started. When I got up on Saturday morning to make my coffee, a few inches had fallen and more seemed to be on its way. As long as it kept snowing, we wouldn't be able to go. I did not want to get caught in a snowstorm with the twins. We had our tent and sleeping bags, but I thought that was too much risk with no gain. We weren't tied to weekends anymore. When everyone else awoke, we'd break the news that if the weather didn't break, we would go tomorrow.

Colleen showed up ready to go and was equally disappointed. She went back home in short order.

We spent the day, everyone in a bad mood, blowing snow, shoveling snow, and generally feeling trapped. In our new world, we had little to look forward to. The days went by slowly, but in a blur. When we made our trip last weekend, we were so energized.

ENDURE

Everyone needs a weekend even if everything you do is simply for survival. Surviving takes work, but living is what we committed to.

As daylight faded away, the snow stopped and the last of the clouds marched past. We received about six inches of new snow, which we dutifully cleaned off. My tractor with snow thrower continued to work magnificently. If it broke down for some reason, then we would use the quad with the blade, still parked safely in Husky's shed. We hadn't taken it out yet, but it was available. As long as our generator ran, we'd be able to charge the battery. We had unlimited fuel due to access to the gas station. We were in a good position.

And we still needed our weekend. It looked like tomorrow would be the big day. A nearly full moon would allow us to leave before sun up. Colleen showed up early.

So away we went. The only ones not ecstatic to get on the road were the dogs. They had to stay in their crates on the towed sleighs. This time, they had blankets and pillows each, along with a rather rude amount of dirty laundry. They would be more comfortable and it was still warm from the recent snowfall. Temps were above zero.

The six inches of new snow didn't hamper our progress. Madison went first with Aeryn, Colleen and her snow machine were in the middle, and I pulled up the rear. I had Charles with me. Colleen was a long-time Alaskan and a very experienced rider. I expect that she could have made it in half the time if we weren't slowing her down.

We stopped mid-way to give the dogs a break and top off the sleds with gasoline. We hadn't burned very much fuel as we weren't pushing the speed. The dogs played a little in the snow, but it was too deep for even Husky to have fun. They were more willing to go back into their crates on the sleighs as there wasn't much fun without a place to play.

After the halfway point, there were very long stretches of straight road. We sped up. At one point, Colleen raced ahead. I think she was stretching the legs of her snow machine and feeling the freedom of flying over the snow. We maintained our pace and caught up to her finally. She was sitting by the side of the road, waiting. She put her helmet back on as we approached and gave us the thumbs up.

It was good to see her having a little bit of fun. The loss of her husband and son weighed on her heavily. She had gone through the deepest stage of depression by herself. She would always carry her loss with her, although I hoped that over time it wouldn't cause her so much grief.

We continued past Colleen and she raced to catch up. There was plenty of room, so she maintained a position parallel to Madison. They rode side by side as we approached the resort. We slowed and heard the sled dogs barking. We continued under the arch and across the bridge. Snow machine tracks crisscrossed the area. We rode up to the main office to check in and see what kind of progress had been made.

THE COMMUNITY OF CHENA
HOT SPRINGS –
A LITTLE DISCORD

Amber was at the desk and seemed relieved to see us walk in. The dogs nearly knocked us over racing past to say hi to their old/new friend. She ruffled their ears. "Let's go to the dining room," she offered, raising her eyebrows as a signal.

I didn't understand what she was trying to convey, but it became clear when we arrived in the dining room. Dirty dishes piled the tables and it was in a general state of disrepair. When everyone was in charge, no one was in charge. People probably rebelled right away from their individual roles. They hadn't worked out how to share responsibility for the jobs no one liked doing, but needed done nonetheless.

"No one wanted to clean up for Jo and Jo wasn't going to do it since she's not their servant?" I asked, although I already knew.

"How did you know?" Amber seemed surprised.

"Human nature. Simple as that." I started cleaning up one table of the dining room, then stopped. "Amber, let me introduce Colleen, a fellow survivor we met this week." They shook hands, then turned to look back at me. I continued cleaning the table and made a head gesture to another table. Madison dug in, then Colleen, and finally the twins. Amber watched us, mouth open.

"Why would you clean up after us?"

"Because we're all in this together. No one is better than anyone else. Everyone shares in the burden, everyone gives what they can. If I had a red carpet, I would roll it out for Jo to use. She is special. As are you. As is each person here. We represent a very small minority of people who survived the explosion in Fairbanks. We are all selfish and selfless, but humans demand some level of fairness, too. It doesn't matter that we should be happy that we are alive. That should be good enough, but it's not.

"It never is and never will be, because we're human. Once we've made it past one crisis, we race headlong to the next. It's okay, but it's something we need to address sooner, rather than later. We need to get through it and very quickly, too." We moved dirty dishes to the kitchen and started piling them with the dirty pots, pans, and everything used for cooking. It looked like about a week's worth of mess.

And it only took an hour to clean up as we all pitched in. When the end was in sight, I asked Amber if she could find Jo so we could pay homage and maybe get a nice fresh-cooked meal. We were willing to do whatever Jo needed from us, besides getting our undying gratitude.

We were putting the finishing touches on the kitchen when Jo came in. She looked a bit ragged, but brightened up when she saw her world returned to a level of order that made her comfortable. She directed us on where to put things away. We finished up strong and then I asked if we could make a fresh pot of coffee.

Of course Jo was upset when others treated her like their personal servant. Someone always had a problem with a menu item, many helping themselves by using Jo's kitchen to make themselves meals and then not cleaning up. People showed up at random times, despite the agreement on a set schedule. so someone always got a cold meal that was supposed to be warm. No one thanked Jo for her efforts and no one seemed willing to help her clean up.

Of course. Because no one had to before and change was hard. We would sit down and everyone would get to speak and then I'd tell them how it was going to be. We would build a work schedule and everyone would take their turn cleaning out the dog kennel, cleaning up after the meals. We would refine who was in charge of what and everyone would be in charge of something. Then everyone would also work as part of the team for everyone else. You better get along or there will be pain when you're working for the person you are giving a hard time to.

And always do whatever it took to keep the cook happy. This was a lesson I learned when embarked on the USS Belleau Wood as a Marine lieutenant. Our Executive Officer (XO) broke the ice cream machine on our second day at sea. We wore our flight suits with patches, so anyone from our squadron was considered complicit to the egregious crime of our XO. On ship, people liked their ice cream. No ice cream meant that the cook received a tongue lashing every day. He passed that on to us. We had to work overtime to get back into his good graces, including enlisting the aid of our Aviation repair team to fix the ice cream machine. They took time away from fixing airplanes, but for us, it was time well-invested. When the machine was returned to service after a week, peace returned to the ship.

Colleen worked her magic on Jo and they both went into the kitchen. There wasn't anything thawing that I could see. It didn't even seem like there was anything from the greenhouse on hand. We had hyped things for Colleen and she had her hopes up. I wanted her to share her story with Jo, how Colleen had lived for a month after the devastation. How Colleen had known, but didn't want to know. And now, she was really looking forward to a home-cooked meal with fresh food.

I dressed for the hike to the greenhouse. There would undoubtedly be work that needed to be done there, too.

THE GREENHOUSE

The greenhouse was a large facility dedicated to growing tomatoes, lettuce, green beans, peppers, cucumbers, and other greens and herbs. They said they could harvest a hundred heads of lettuce a week. I wonder how the master gardener had tempered that without the demand. I expected their compost pile was rather robust.

Or they could have stopped working the greenhouse altogether. Which is what it looked like. At forty-three hundred square feet, it made for an extensive workspace. There were hundreds of heads of lettuce in all stages of the life cycle. Many were beginning to rot.

Other plants overflowed with ripe vegetables. I didn't know how this place was supposed to work. Which vegetables were picked first? Which ones were composted? We took a couple buckets and picked some choice-looking heads of lettuce and some other vegetables for today's meals. I had no problem doing the work, but we'd have to find our gardener to show us what needed doing.

After Phyllis peed on one of the plants, I chased the dogs out of the greenhouse. They had a different perspective of what this building was for. Madison took them back to the restaurant. I kept the twins with me. They could pick some rotted vegetables and put them in what I suspected was the compost pile. If it wasn't, it was doing a great job of looking like it.

We only spent another thirty minutes pruning, picking, and straightening. The twins had lost their focus and were playing in the mud. It was time to get them cleaned up, and maybe Colleen and Jo would have something ready for lunch. I'd do the dishes even!

I wondered if Madison had found the laundry and gotten anything started. I could always do that in the morning.

I think I needed to talk with the group and try to remove whatever obstacles they had encountered. Adult leadership was all they lacked. Not being connected was taking its toll. None of them were professionals in the jobs they were doing for the Community. They were the best at what we had, but they hadn't committed to seeing it through. The more they thought about it, I expect the more they thought it was hopeless.

I needed to talk with them and bring everyone back into the fold.

RALLYING THE TROOPS

I brought the twins inside the restaurant and we cleaned them up before they were allowed to touch anything. It was nice being in a place that was warm enough not to wear multiple layers.

We took the vegetables to the kitchen. Colleen and Jo were chatting happily as they prepared something. I could smell bread baking. They grabbed the vegetables from me, and Colleen shooed me away.

Sometimes, all it takes is to get that first person to believe.

As I saw it, there was little difference between this group and a platoon of Marines deployed in the field. Everyone would be unhappy with something. What I had to do was convince them what was in their best interest. I couldn't order anyone here to do anything they didn't want to. Last week, I thought my efforts to allow them to buy into what they were doing had been the right approach. I may have been mistaken.

Maybe they were more like our twins than Marines.

Our snow machines outside let everyone know that we had arrived. We greeted everyone as they walked into the dining room. Many wouldn't look at me.

Shame was good. It meant that they had a conscience. I always had a hard time with passive aggression. I'm not sure how I would have responded to a stare-down either. I wanted this community to thrive, be the bedrock of a surviving world.

It wasn't enough to just exist. The Community of Chena Hot Springs was fully self-sustaining. It needed a little care and feeding, and then it could be whatever these people wanted it to be. We had no indication of when help would come, so we had to plan for the worst, hope for the best. Maybe the youth of today needed a timeline that was better defined.

Although it took most of an hour, we finally had everyone assembled. Everyone had eaten what was provided, without complaint. I urged everyone to take their own dishes back to the kitchen, rinse and load them into the dishwasher. Maybe coerce, or strong arm were better terms.

"Let me tell you a story," I began. People relate better through stories than other things we do to provide motivation. "Last week, when we came up here, we were so happy to meet all of you and see what you had accomplished here. We rested and enjoyed ourselves. We enjoyed your company.

"After we went back home, I was motivated to find more survivors, and tell them about a great place that still existed. A place where they could get back to how things were. How they could forget about the trials of living in Alaska without power, without help.

"The first person I found had been murdered. She was killed by people who preferred the new world, the world where they used violence to become kings. They gathered cash and jewels. They even grabbed a slave. I didn't know this when I stopped to talk with them. Their answer?" I pointed to the cuts on my face. "They shot me. Twice." People in the room looked shocked.

"I tried to run, but they chased me." I paused to let that sink in. "So I killed them. I killed both of them and left their bodies for the ravens to eat."

"Why would you do that? Why would you tell us?" Amber asked.

"I'm telling you because not everyone is like us." I gestured to include everyone in the room. "Some people are takers. They take from others. The only thing they give is pain.

"We've been here a few hours and we've done some dishes and picked vegetables. We don't need anyone to wait on us. We can take care of ourselves. But you know what? Isn't it better to do a little something for someone else? If you expect to get waited on, then you become a taker. If you appreciate it and help out, you're a giver.

"This world that's crashed down around us. There is no room for takers. We can't live with people like that." Some of them saw my words as a threat. They weren't, but perception becomes reality. I had to dispel that. "There's more to the story," I continued. "After those two men died, I went to their house. There was a young woman. She was their slave. She couldn't get out of that house fast enough. The only thing she wanted to do was get away from all humanity. She went to her family's cabin in the woods. I don't know if she got there or not or how she is.

"When help comes, what will they find? Not her. She's probably gone forever. But what will they find here?

"If you want, I suggest you take a snow machine and go to the city. See for yourselves what our world looks like. See what the total destruction of civilization looks like.

"What do I want? I want you to appreciate what you have. I want you to embrace your roles to help each other. If you're a taker, leave now, because we just can't have that."

Colleen stood up and walked over to me. She gave me a hug and then turned to face the group.

"This man saved me. He saved me, and he saved that young woman, and he didn't need to do any of that. He could have taken anything from me. There's nothing I could have done to stop him. But he didn't. He shared his family with me. He shared the fresh vegetables you gave him last week. And he asked me to come here. Take a hot shower. Relax in the pool. Enjoy more fresh vegetables.

"I lost my husband and my son in the city. They were there when it happened. They never came home. He couldn't do anything about that." She pointed at me. "But what he could do, he did. And he's done the same thing for you and what do you do?" She was starting to get red in the face. Her eyes narrowed.

"You act like a bunch of spoiled kids!" I hadn't expected that.

"I am embarrassed for him. What did he do? He cleaned up your tables and personally did your dishes. He didn't complain." Now I was getting embarrassed. The reason I cleaned up was very selfish. I wanted a good meal and there wouldn't be one if the chef was unhappy. I intended to clean up after lunch, too, because I had high hopes for dinner.

No one would meet Colleen's glare. Not even me.

"I'm sorry. I didn't mean to come up here and yell at everybody. I've lost almost everything that was important to me. If it weren't for my horses, I would not have made it. I still can't believe that my family is gone." She closed her eyes and stood there.

Jo got up and put an arm around her, guiding her back to the table so she could sit. Amber took the floor and looked right at me. "I'm sorry. I failed you and I failed the Community."

I laughed, which took her aback. "No, not at all. It's what we call growing pains. Everyone needs to figure out who they want to be. If help came today and somebody wrote a book about what you all did after the loss of Fairbanks, what would it say? I hope that it would say you learned and got better with each day. You helped. You built a sanctuary. You built a community." I could see them thinking about what they had done, what they would do.

But what could they commit to? I didn't see them coming together. Not yet, anyway.

Colleen stood back up. "If you'll have me, I'd like to stay a few extra days. I'm tired of being alone." Amber gave Colleen a hug and welcomed her. I watched the group. Two of the young men were put off. I wonder what they were thinking. Only one way to find out. I'd ask them.

"Can you guys give me a hand, please?" As the old guy of the group, these two didn't turn me down. They gathered up their dishes and walked with me to the kitchen. "What's up? I don't get the feeling you're fans of the arrangement?"

Anger. They looked at each other. They wanted to unload, but something was holding them back. "We can't fix it if we don't know what it is. Tell me," I coaxed them.

"You think we want to be here? A bunch of whiny girls. I came here to make some quick money, but this isn't my life. I'm not here to play Little House on the Prairie." And there it was. This young man wasn't able to accept his role in a new world, even if it was only temporary. The other was Darren, our hunter.

"I understand. Think what can be done about it. Darren, what about you?"

"I went out to hunt, but couldn't get a shot." Looking at the floor, he shuffled his feet uncomfortably. "I don't want to be here."

We had two very different problems. One was toxic. The other would be fine with a little attention. Both had egos that needed managed in a completely different way.

"What's your name?" I asked the first man.

"John," he said simply.

"Do you think you can make it to Canada? Do you think you can go for help?" I asked. The easiest answer for me was to get rid of the problem. Unless something significant happened, John would be a perpetual burden on the Community. "It's been well over a month and nobody has come? I can't believe they don't know, but how can we be sure?"

John brightened. The wheels were spinning. "I can take a snow machine. It's what, three hundred miles to the border from here? Over the hills to the Yukon River, then to Boundary, maybe Forty Mile?" He had looked at doing this. He had a way out if he wanted it.

I wasn't sure he would be able to bring help, but maybe it would give the others hope that we were doing something besides carving out a niche in this new world. None of them had signed up for homesteading.

"If you take Chena Hot Springs Road toward Fairbanks, you can turn off on Nordale Road that will take you to North Pole. It might be far enough from where the detonation happened to give you a free shot to the Alaska Highway to Tok and then Whitehorse. There are a number of small towns along the way. Each one could be an opportunity to find help." I wasn't sure if John could handle a couple hundred miles of snow machining Alaska's back country. I knew that I couldn't do it. Fairbanks to Whitehorse was seven hundred miles of open highway.

"Okay. I'll do it. For the good of the group," he sneered. I thought the sooner we could be rid of him, the better.

"You know, I should probably go with him…" Darren's statement trailed off. Darren had not found his niche. John was dominating him. Without John's negative influence, Darren would be a different person. I wanted the opportunity to help him realize more than being John's lackey.

"I think this is a one-man job. If John makes it, what, a week, two weeks? We should see help in less than a month. If no one comes after that, someone else may have to try it. We all need you. Both."

John stood tall and proud. He wanted the accolades. He wanted to be the hero. He didn't realize that being a hero was lonely. In the Marine Corps, the most heroic acts went unseen. Real heroes did the right things because they needed doing, not because they were going to get a medal out of it. John would get eaten alive in the Corps. He was probably getting eaten alive here by the "whiny girls."

John's departure was a necessity, whereas Darren's was not. Once Darren made his first kill and was able to provide something to the Community, he would probably be fine. He just needed some confidence and a sense of belonging. Over time, he could become a bedrock of the Community.

"Go get your stuff ready," I told John. "You might as well leave this afternoon if you can be ready. You'll be riding a great deal in the dark no matter what. Take the best rental sled and a sleigh. Take as much gas as you'll need." I offered my hand. John eagerly shook it. "Thanks, John. You're doing something for us that no one else can do." He smiled. Arrogantly.

It didn't cost me anything to stroke his ego. He truly was doing something for the Community simply by leaving. It was an easy way out for me, but harmony was fragile and I saw the chaos from the past week. Probably it was a lot of John's doing, but maybe not. We went back to the dining room.

"Hey everyone!" I said to get their attention. "John is going to take a snow machine to Canada to let someone know we're here and to send help." The looks on their faces was one of relief, but not because of the stated objective.

"Please help John with two weeks of food, a tent, sleeping bag, whatever so he can get on the road sooner. The sooner he gets there, the sooner help will arrive." I turned to Darren. "Let's do some hunting. No time like the present." John was out the door without another word. Darren remained next to me.

I turned to Madison and Colleen. "We're going hunting while there's a little light left anyway. Could you please clean up? I promise that I'll clean up after dinner." The twins wanted to go with me. They were trying to climb my leg. I leaned down on one knee and gave them both a big hug. "I think we need your help with the dogs. Someone has to look out for them while everyone else is working. Can you do that for me?" They didn't want to. They were of the impression that the dogs could take care of themselves.

Amber inserted herself into the conversation. "I need some help in the lodge. Can you help me?" She didn't even say what she needed, but the twins saw an adventure and off they went, including Phyllis and Husky. It didn't take look for the dining room to clear out. Everyone helped by taking their dishes to the kitchen. I sensed a new energy from the group.

I really wanted to go swimming. The hot water beckoned. A hot shower would have been nice, too, but sacrifices had to be made. Everything we needed to hunt was in my sleigh. Darren went to get the 45-70 rifle. I went to the kitchen to get knives that we'd need if we were successful in downing a moose. I grabbed table cloths as well to wrap the meat for the trip back.

HUNTING

This hunt was all about building Darren's confidence. I gave him the 300 Win mag and took my familiar 45-70 back. He liked the big hunting rifle better. For some reason, the scope drew him in. I preferred iron sights, but that was the Marine in me. I never used a scope when shooting the M16 and always felt comfortable. I'd qualified as an Expert multiple times, including a few high expert scores that I was proud of.

Darren showed me to an area some miles from the resort where he had last seen a moose. Although it would be best to take a bull, the dogs needed the meat so even a cow would do. I would only shoot a cow without a calf, though.

We stopped the snow machine on one side of a hill in a ravine. We unloaded our gear and trudged through the snow up the hill. This was slow going and I was huffing and puffing like a freight train. I wasn't having an asthma attack. This was age and old lungs speaking to me. Darren was kind enough not to say anything as he waited for me. We crawled the last bit to the top so no animals on the other side would see us. We were rewarded with a clear view of an open area. The only animal in sight was a raven. Natives would consider that a good luck omen. I considered it a lack of moose.

Going down the hill was far easier than going up. We continued around the hill to the next valley. This time we idled the snow machine on a shallow angle about halfway up the hill. Darren raised his eyebrows as he looked at me. "Sorry," I whispered. We walked the rest of the way to the top and this time we saw what we wanted: two cows and one calf grazing the willows.

I pointed and Darren looked at the moose through the scope. I saw him put his finger on the trigger. "Wait," I asked. "Which cow is the mother?" He looked hard trying to decide, then shrugged. He took his finger off the trigger.

We waited. The moose split up as darkness descended, casting long shadows into the valley. The calf and one cow were close together, while the second cow angled up the hillside. I pointed and nodded.

Darren aimed. I put my gloved hands over my ears. The rifle bucked as the round raced toward its target. The moose dropped straight to the ground. The other cow and calf bolted over the hill. The rifle's report echoed a few times and receded into the distance.

Silence and calm returned. The shadow of the evening crept over the downed moose.

I slapped Darren on the back. "I'll get the snow machine and meet you over there." The shot wasn't long, maybe a hundred yards. Darren got up and shook off the snow. He looked amazed, then a smile slowly split his face. I pointed to him. "You are the man."

I was feigning confidence. I had never field-dressed a moose, but we had to get it done before we headed back to the lodge. Not taking the meat now would be a waste, and we couldn't have that. The moose died for us and should be celebrated for its sacrifice. That's how Native Americans see it and they've lived off this land for ten thousand years. I would follow their lead, and hopefully, the land would take mercy on me.

FIGHTING A CARCASS

A real moose hunter once told me that you don't gut the moose. Skin it on one side, remove the meat, then flip it over and work on the other side. He said by doing it that way, you can get it done in just a couple hours and the meat isn't tainted. That's the approach I wanted to take.

We started skinning it and things progressed rapidly, until we started losing feeling in our fingers. It was cold and it wouldn't be long before the meat would get stiff.

"I want to share something with you," I started. Darren nodded, but kept skinning. "I've never done this before." He looked at me, then started to laugh.

"Well, we're doing it now, aren't we?" Just what the doctor ordered. Darren seemed like a new man. I felt sick to my stomach.

The lights of the snow machine shone on our work area. There was blood everywhere. My hands were stained with it. Hunks of flesh clung to the skin where I hadn't been too smooth with my knife. I butchered off one of the front legs. They are held on by muscle and tendons. There is no shoulder blade with a ball and socket.

I wrapped the leg in a table cloth and put it on the sled. We had to work the back leg together as it was a massive hunk of flesh. A great deal of meat clung to the over-sized bone. We muscled it onto the sleigh.

As we started cutting slabs of meat from the ribs, it became an exercise in production. I forgot that this had been a living animal only an hour earlier. We didn't bother cutting too closely to get every bit of meat possible. Speed was more important at this point.

We finished the one side. If anyone had been watching as we tried to flip the moose over, they would have been well-entertained. It would have brought to mind two monkeys with a football. The moose was not cooperating. We struggled mightily, as two whalers fighting Moby Dick!

Or two idiots who had no idea what they were doing. We eventually persevered, but I had to sit down and get my breath back.

"Well, that sucked," I panted. Darren looked at me, shrugged, and started skinning the other side. My head was swimming and I was starting to get really cold. We needed to make quick work of this and get back inside.

I dug in the best I could, trying to improve upon my efforts from the other side. I got the technique down of how to hold the knife, how to keep pressure on the skin to make the cuts more effective. The second side went much quicker than the first. We were putting the finishing touches on everything right at the three-hour point. And more importantly, it was dinner time.

With our towed sleigh loaded, we carefully re-traced our track down the hillside and onto one of the many trails around the resort. We took it easy, with two of us on the snow machine and maybe seven hundred and fifty pounds of moose on the sleigh, it was all the snow machine could handle.

It took almost no time to get back, as we had not gone too far. When we pulled up outside the main lodge, Madison's snow machine and sleigh were gone. I wondered where she had taken it. When we went inside, a bit bloody from our experience, she quickly came up to me. "John took my sled."

Yes. We were better off without him. I thought briefly that if I ever saw him again, I would shoot him, but that wasn't right. I wouldn't make it the easy answer to every dispute. And it really wasn't our sled anyway. We had 'borrowed' it, just like we were going to borrow one of the resort sleds to replace it. The real loss was the dog crate. The dogs would have to double up, but everything would work out.

Madison needed someone to tell her it was okay. I wouldn't let the cancer that was John continue to eat us after he was gone. With people like that, we got what we wanted, but he wouldn't let us get it in the way we wanted.

That's how narcissists control other people, I thought to myself. *Maybe I will shoot him if I see him again.*

A NEW DAY

We enjoyed a wonderful dinner. The mood was light and people seemed genuinely happy. I offered a toast to Darren for providing a moose to help feed the dogs. Abigail lifted her glass first, pleased with the toast. She hadn't realized the stress she carried worrying about being able to feed the dogs, her dogs.

We sliced out steaks for a future meal for us, while grinding up a small amount of fresh meat into burger for an easier meal to cook. Everything else was in the refrigerator, waiting to be ground up as dog meat. Tomorrow, they'd process it the rest of the way. Jo knew how to do that, and Darren and Becca volunteered to help.

The new Darren. He told Becca that the next moose would be hers and that the new hunting rifle with the scope made everything easy. They'd take it out and shoot a couple rounds each to get familiar. He suggested they wear ear plugs.

I especially enjoyed the salad that night. Having butchered the moose, I thought I had no interest in meat, although when they brought out the hamburgers, I had to dig in. Hamburgers with fresh tomato slices on fresh buns. I'm not sure I ever had a meal that tasted so good.

We even gave hamburgers to Phyllis and Husky, but without the fixings.

The twins enjoyed their child-sized portions, as they usually enjoyed their meals. They didn't seem to take this as anything special, except that they were surrounded by happy people.

I looked around the room at the variety of faces. Chris had been hired as a housekeeper. He didn't say much. In my mind, that made him more intelligent. When he did speak, you had to listen carefully, because what he said was important.

Felicia was hired to work in the greenhouse. She always watched what was going on. She smiled often, but it seemed forced and didn't smile when she thought no one was watching.

Emma was hired as a housekeeper. She was easy-going. Her joy at John's departure was apparent. It was like someone flipped a switch. I wondered what John had done, and it made me dislike him that much more.

Amber joined us at our table. "I think we should set up work schedules, to share the burden a bit. What do you think?"

I liked it. There are jobs that no one likes doing. Giving someone responsibility for doing the dishes in perpetuity was not going to work, but rotating it through a schedule would remove any individual anguish. People would be kings in their own area. Jo might never have to do another dish as long as there were people to help, and then Jo would take a turn in the greenhouse, at the kennel, elsewhere.

"Bring it up to everybody. This may be the missing piece that will bring everyone together. Everyone is a king and everyone is a pauper."

After dinner, Amber raised it as a proposal and said that she would set up a rotating work schedule. She sat down at the bar and started scribbling on a notepad. Jo stood up and apologized to everyone for not cooking for most of the past week. Lucas apologized to everyone for not taking the gardening seriously. He would remedy that first thing in the morning. The others followed suit. It felt like an AA meeting. Who was I to interrupt the reckoning?

I couldn't have been more pleased with the change in attitudes. Maybe instead of an AA meeting, it was an AJ meeting, life After John.

I was glad he was gone and hoped that we would never see him again. I didn't care if he was successful or not. As long as we kept a watch on the skies over Fairbanks, we could signal if a helicopter flew by. If John told people in a small city in Canada, there probably wouldn't be anything they could do. We were better off just waiting and watching. John was gone and that was all that mattered.

For the Community of Chena Hot Springs, it was a new day. And we had clean laundry. I was looking forward to a hot shower and warm bed. Until Jo showed up with ice cream and apple pie, then I was looking forward to dessert. After that, dishes, then we'd think about going to the room. It was nice to see the group's excitement about what their future held.

A FULL VACATION DAY

We took care of the dishes, got a hot shower, and settled in to watch a Disney movie they had in the recreation room. Everyone was satisfied and the twins were sound asleep halfway through the movie. We kept the movie playing while we retired to the bathroom for a hot shower together. We hadn't been intimate since the explosion. The twins were always with us, as well as the dogs, and it was cold in the house. We were always clothed in multiple layers.

It was nice getting naked with my wife.

The next day, I awoke early and took the dogs out. After playing for a bit, I brought them inside, and they were happy to get back into the big bed in my spot that was still warm. I went to the lodge to make coffee and listen to some music.

Glasses had been left out from the night before. I washed them and put them away behind the bar while I was waiting for the coffee. There was some fresh bread in the kitchen. I helped myself to some of that with jelly and a nice big cup of coffee. I made a fire in the fireplace, but only for effect. The dining room was well-heated. It made for a cozy morning.

There were numerous books lying around. I looked them over. One was a James Patterson mystery. I picked it up and started reading.

Time disappeared until people started drifting in for their morning coffee. Cereal had gone out of vogue with the fresh milk. There were cases of dehydrated milk, but that wasn't the same. Although I had to admit that I liked eating frosted mini wheats right out of the box. Toast made with fresh bread and plenty of jelly made a better meal than I deserved. There were no eggs, but there was bacon. Since Jo offered, I had to accept. Bacon goes with anything. It's the ultimate food accessory.

I helped clean up, although there seemed to be no limit of volunteers this morning. I thanked all of them personally with a handshake and gave Jo a bear hug with many superlatives. She was the only one who wasn't allowed to clean up. I expected lunch would be great and dinner spectacular.

I hurried back to the room to find Madison and the twins just getting out of bed. We quickly cleaned up and headed back to the restaurant for a more private breakfast. Everyone else was already out and about with their duties. Jo was guiding Darren and Becca in how to process the moose. That was going to be a sloppy mess, but there was only room for two people to work at one time. They would take care of it. Darren waved me away. Becca looked at him with a smile. Jo was pleased to guide the work, using a meat mallet as a gavel. I told them we'd return after a while to see if they needed help. I expected they wouldn't. Colleen had gone with Lucas to the greenhouse to help straighten things up.

I was happy watching my family eat.

"What was that? Which one of you gave bacon to the dog?" Two innocent smiles. I moved my chair closer to them. The dogs were drooling. It was disgusting. Worse than that, I was salivating, too. Ahh, nothing like bacon.

We then went swimming. The pool was a steamy ninety-six degrees and we had it all to ourselves. The world was back on track. After a long swim, we put the dogs in the room as we all dressed warmly. We would help out at the kennel before going back home.

There were almost ninety dogs here and they made quite a racket when we arrived. We went into the dog musher's office where more coffee was brewing. We asked what they needed. They had already fed the dogs, but it was time for waste clean-up. They had shovels and buckets. Madison took one, and I took one. We started at opposite ends and worked our way toward the middle. Ninety dogs can be very productive. I had to stop and empty the bucket into a dumpster three times before getting halfway. I think this meant that the dogs were eating well. They needed to run.

The mushers were both women and not too experienced, in their words. They loved the dogs though, and that made the difference. If they ran teams of twelve dogs, they could give all the dogs a run over the course of eight trips. That would almost be a full-time job. If they had half the number of dogs, it would be more manageable, but no one would approve killing dogs just because there might be too many. We didn't know when help would come, so we would make do.

It took us an hour and a half to finish the job of cleaning up. The good news was that it only had to be done like that every couple days. We were glad to save someone else from doing it. Although it was nice to go back into a warm building and drink hot chocolate.

The dog mushers had put the twins on a sled and taken it out. They were covered up with a blanket and happy as could be. Their faces were all red when they returned, but everyone was happy. Both of them wanted to become dog mushers. It was a laudable goal. We would see as they got older.

We went back to the lodge to clean up our room and get ready to go back home. Colleen had put a sleigh behind her snow machine. She found it in the snow machine garage. The sleigh was old, but looked to be in good condition. She told us to take her sled as she would stay for the week as long as we promised to check in on her horses every day. We committed to that easily. Colleen could provide the adult presence to help the college kids, although without John, I think they were already well on their way to being better than ever.

ANOTHER WEEK AT HOME, AND THEN ANOTHER...

The time seemed to fly by. We would spend a week at home, teaching the twins, making sure that the house was sound, 'shopping,' and other things necessary to survive. We'd race to the Hot Springs every weekend. Colleen would alternate one week there and one week at home.

And another week would go by and another. By March, we'd had some good warm spells. We were also up to almost twelve hours of light a day. We'd made it through the harshest part of winter.

And thanks to Colleen's missing neighbor, we had plenty of pellets, so we even turned up the heat in the house.

In the evening, the auroras kept us company. If the twins were sleeping, sometimes we'd wake them up. There's nothing like watching the northern lights dance overhead.

We spent a great deal of time outside with the warmer temperatures and increasing amount of daylight. We were always on the watch for any kind of aircraft. But there were no contrails. No sounds.

No airplanes and no other humans besides us.

I was surprised that none of the people in the caravan to Anchorage returned. If they had any problems, I was sure someone would have turned back. As a good Intelligence Officer, I maintained a certain level of paranoia, but I couldn't contemplate any scenario where this made sense. There were so few of us left north of the city. What about all the oil workers on the North Slope? What about all the people who lived further out?

In the winter, they had access by snow machine and dog sled. In the summer, there were dirt roads they could travel. They came to town once every six months to resupply or sell furs or do what they needed to do to survive in the remote areas. A significant part of Alaska's population lived subsistence lifestyles. Some might say it was living off the grid. Others would say that they never felt more alive.

Maybe it wasn't time yet for the subsistence people to restock.

There was one small island of civilization that we clung to. The Community of Chena Hot Springs had become a lifeline for us. Our days there were intoxicating. We enjoyed our trips and had made it often enough that we could get there in one hour. The snow machines were simple forms of transportation, not for joy riding. That's why we didn't own one before. I could not conceive of riding around in the snow and cold simply for the pleasure of the ride. I enjoyed the snow machine, but for me, it was a means of transportation.

And when the snow melted, we'd fire up the quad for the same reason. It was a means to an end.

The things we had taken for granted were clean laundry, flush toilets, running water – the little things. No longer. Everything we did to live took some kind of effort. We siphoned, we hauled, we melted, we recharged, and then we hauled some more.

The twins shared the work with us and we shared life with them. They were troopers. There were no terrible twos for the twins. They rose to the occasion and helped us to help them. Their classes were going strong. Their attention span was improving. They were well into a lifelong journey of learning. Would we have enough to teach them? Where would we be as they grew up? As they approached their third birthday that spring, they were stronger than ever and the whole world was before them.

We needed to think about their future in this new world. When would we have to decide about change?

SUMMER ALONE

We asked ourselves what would we do if help didn't come. There were only two choices: stay or go. Each decision would be significant.

If we decided to go, where would we go and how would we get there? What would be waiting for us along the way or even at the destination?

If we stayed, what would that mean? What would we have to do?

In my entire life, change was constant and I never liked it, until it was no longer a change. We moved eleven times in twenty years. Who likes moving? I thought we did as we looked toward the next great adventure. Maybe we just did it because we had to and we surrendered ourselves to our fate. We only owned three houses in our lives. One was purchased because rent was so high in Tampa, Florida. We purchased another in Pittsburgh to serve as our retirement home, but then Madison got the job in Fairbanks. So we sold our retirement home and bought our current home, which was by far the best place we've ever lived. We didn't want to give it up.

I didn't want someone who was 'shopping' to go through our home. Whenever I went into other people's homes, I never took anything personal. I took food, fuel, water, and things like that. I took some ammunition and some weapons. I took snow machines, sleighs, and a quad. I took things that insurance would replace. I closed doors behind me. If people returned, their homes would be intact, their personal items safe.

And I still maintained my list, although it had gone from very detailed, to general. I think I had the addresses right, mostly. If people didn't return, then there'd be no reason beyond my commitment to myself. That was enough. I would continue to keep track, even if it was vague. The list was getting fairly long. I perused it from start to finish. Had we really eaten that much?

If we stayed, what would we need for food, fuel? There weren't enough pellets for another winter if it came to that.

All of that aside, what did we really want?

I wanted a happy family. Despite the destruction around us, we had grown closer. We appreciated the little things. We appreciated each other. We could not have been more fully engaged in the growth and education of our children. From that perspective, it did not get any better. If we were to travel in search of civilization, would we have what we had now?

Once you ask the right question, the answer is easy. We would stay here, another year if needs be, and then we'd think about it the following year. After we came to that decision, the rest was planning.

We needed to garden and then can the food. We needed to find a water source. We needed to change out our pellet stove for a wood burner. We needed to bag a moose, then freeze it. We wanted a second generator, one powerful enough to run the whole house. There would always be needs and wants.

Our world was bigger than just our family. We had made it so. Colleen lived around the corner. We had started the Community and it was flourishing. We had gone no further than Bennett Road for the rest of the winter. I did not want to explore too far and wide in the area where the Goldstream brothers had spread fear. Maybe we'd rethink that come summer.

In the interim, we'd have to talk with the Community. I didn't think Colleen wanted to go anywhere as she had her horses to take care of. They were the last reminders of her family and she wouldn't let them go. We would let the others know what we decided and then see what they wanted to do.

Saturday came and we made our quick trip to Chena Hot Springs. With the warmer weather, the dogs enjoyed the travel more. There was still a great deal of snow and it was below freezing, but it wasn't mind-numbingly cold. We had a full day's worth of light every day, so our travel times weren't restricted. We had a big window to travel within.

Amber met us, as usual in the main lodge. She had covered the walls with butcher block paper where she kept track of work schedules, supplies, to-do items, repairs, and more. She had embraced her role as the mayor of the Community. Colleen had worked wonders with the group. She worked with everyone individually to help them appreciate what they had, improve on what they were doing. As a counselor, she was a natural.

When the group was together at lunch, I waited until they were done with their meal, then I spoke. "We have an announcement to make. Assuming help doesn't come, we've decided to stay at our home. I know we've talked about heading out to look for help, or just leave Alaska completely, but this is our home, and this is where we're going to stay. For now anyway."

They didn't look surprised. Darren and Becca sat closely together, holding hands. Jo was leaning closely into Emma. Emma was originally a housekeeper, but was now splitting her time between the kitchen and the kennel. The Community was becoming a real community, committing to each other, to a greater good.

It seemed that they also had talked about the big question – stay or go. Half of them were firmly committed to staying, while the other half were on the fence. At this time, no one had decided to go. I tried to fill the void and ended up spouting some Intelligence Officer nonsense sprinkled liberally with my fear of change.

"We don't know what's out there. Why no contrails, no airplanes? Why has no one come? What did the Two Rivers caravan find when they headed to Anchorage? What about John? Why have none of them come back?" I started with these questions to lay the groundwork of my argument. "It seems to me that there is something dangerous out there that's keeping people away from here. We need more information. Without that, it's a tough decision to leave. So, how do we find out what's out there?"

"We have a plane," Lucas offered. I had seen the airplane tied down off the small runway here at the Hot Springs. I hadn't thought about using it. The runway was still covered in snow.

"Does anyone know how to fly?" Nope. "Is anyone willing to learn using the Wright Brothers method?" As in, figure it out as you go... There were no takers.

THE COMMUNITY WORKS

Amber created work groups where three people would make a team for the day to work in areas not their own. She put herself out there a great deal, working somewhere every day. That's what leading from the front was all about. Two of the four main work areas, the kitchen and the kennel, were worked every single day, multiple times. The dogs required the greatest amount of care. Preparing food for thirteen people and cleaning up did not take a significant effort, but it couldn't be let go for a full day. The greenhouse required various amounts of work each day, depending on what needed doing. The power plant required someone to stop by periodically and check on valves and systems, but only required a full work detail once a week to keep sub-systems cleaned out and running efficiently.

They also took care of the pool as everyone used it. It was a good place to relax. In the time of guests, the rock pool outside was drained and refilled once a week. Since the loss of Fairbanks, they hadn't drained it once. Not many people used it this past winter, probably just to say that they swam outdoors on a day of thirty degrees below zero.

Even with the work schedules, everyone worked part of Sunday, but then everyone had the rest of the time off. With a two-hour commitment somewhere, that left the majority of the day free to do as you like.

Becca and Darren moved in together. As a couple, they took two connected rooms and turned one side into a living room and the other into the bedroom. They seemed happy. They made a dynamic pair of hunters. I gave them my 12-gauge shotgun to supplement their high-powered rifle, and they put it to good use. Four caribou and a flock of ptarmigan later, there was plenty of meat and variety for all.

The dogs benefitted as they were treated all the way around. Extra greens from the greenhouse went into their kibble, along with a fair bit of meat. By doing this, the hard dog food lasted much longer. The target of making it to spring would be easily met and they would now make it half way through summer.

A sickness like kennel cough passed among the dogs and many didn't survive. As it turned out, we lost thirteen dogs to the disease, many of them older. The remainder recovered and stayed strong through the rest of the winter. Everyone had their favorites. It seemed that no matter what work detail someone was on, they would find time during the day to visit the kennel. The dogs had their favorites, too.

Always trust a dog who likes a person.

Lucas was mechanically inclined and became the go-to guy to fix things. There was always something, from a busted water line to a bathroom fan to the water pump for the pool. Lucas was good enough in getting things back into operation. They weren't pretty when he finished, but they worked. So he was turned loose on the fleet of snow machines and quads to make sure that they ran when needed. He used a number of the vehicles for parts on the others. He kept running what needed to run. Darren and Becca had their hunting sleds always in top shape. There were a couple others that they used to break trails for dog sledding. No one used the snow machines for recreation.

With Jo and Emma paying more attention to each other, there was always two people in the kitchen, which kept kitchen duty to a minimum for whoever was assigned there for the day. They generally carried things from storage to where it would be thawed for preparation. Greenhouse duties overlapped with kitchen duties. It was more moving and cleaning than food preparation or cooking. Sometimes people would volunteer to make their favorite dish. This was encouraged as it kept people in touch with their lives from before and opened the others up to variety.

After things settled in and people got used to doing their share of work as well as leading a work detail, they got more efficient. Work that initially took six hours was down to four. Some things could be done in an hour. There were days where everyone checked in at all the work stations to see if anything needed doing. It had blossomed into a collaborative effort where everyone benefitted.

What did people do in their time off? There were numerous unheated cabins for camping and a yurt on top of the hill where you could go for the best views of the aurora. Some took advantage of this. If help came and they returned to their homes in the Lower 48, they might never get the opportunity again to see the northern lights, to experience the real Alaska.

They consolidated all the books in what used to be the gift shop. Amber had boxed everything from the gift shop and put it all in storage. It would be available if the resort ever opened back up for regular guests. Books filled a void, but also, many people had computers with digital books and movies. The resort itself had a small collection of DVDs for check out, but between the people there, they probably had many thousands of hours of digital movies and TV shows. By pooling what they had, they were able to load up a 1TB external hard drive with nothing but videos. Everyone could download what they wanted onto their individual notebook computers. Some movies were only available on people's personal iPads. To get one of these, you had to borrow the person's iPad. This usually meant watching the movie with the owner present. Who knows what else was stored on those iPads.

Surprisingly, the work-out room received a great deal of attention. Everyone was younger and still had things to prove, even if only to themselves. So they worked out. There were mini strength contests of all sorts. Everyone improved their health and fitness. The so-called lazy millennials of today were anything but.

They worked hard to achieve the common good. This system worked well for them, just like a Kibbutz we had visited in Israel a long time ago. It is amazing what happy people can accomplish. These college kids had been thrown off the deep end. They missed their families, and longed for a way to get word out that they were fine. Their families had to be worried.

But it wasn't time yet to take a chance. They all talked about who would be next to risk leaving and trying to make contact with the outside world, to get word back. They wanted to know what happened. We all wanted to know.

THE MASTER GARDENERS

My naïve prepping from the time before paid off in this case. I had purchased an emergency seed pack with thirty-two thousand seeds of a variety of vegetables and a book on how to grow your own food. It was March. We had to become experts immediately to start the seeds and then prepare a garden.

This was Alaska and, as the weather turned, we'd get more and more light until the mid-summer months, where we'd have light for nearly twenty-four hours a day. It was a prime growing season if we prepared everything properly.

The book became my new favorite. It stayed on the dining room table and no one touched it. I had a note pad as I laid out our plan of attack. Preparing seedlings, using a greenhouse, making sure the soil was ready, planting, watering, and more.

Moose. Where we established our garden, we had to keep the moose away. In no time they could destroy a year's worth of crops. There would be no recovery for us here. We couldn't simply run to the nursery and replace our plants. But we could always count on the Community as they were producing far more than they needed. We had a safety net. That gave us time to learn by trial and error.

We had a book and could leverage the wisdom of the authors. I wanted to be self-sufficient, while still appreciating the value of the safety net at Chena Hot Springs.

Gardening was a skill the twins could use no matter if we were rescued or not.

Rescue. An interesting word. What would we be rescued from? What were we really missing? The ability to flip a switch on the wall and have lights go on? To have constant heat without having to do any work? To watch television? We were certain that if help came, we would ask for things, but we wouldn't leave. The other world lost its allure. We had grown very close as a family. That isn't something to be rescued from.

What would happen now if we went back to the way it was? I was sure that we wanted more of this and less of that.

So gardening it was.

There was a creek at the bottom of the hill between us and the gas station. It was about a half-mile away, but once things thawed, we'd have running water. I had no idea how to check if the water was potable or not. As it was the only source in the area, we needed it to be good. I would have to follow the stream up the hill until it was well past any populated areas just to see. As long as there weren't any car batteries dumped in the stream or whatever, I thought we'd be fine. The wells in this area pumped water that smelled horrible. That would be an obvious bar to use. Pumped water. No one's well was pumping anything nowadays.

Soil was unlimited, but good soil was in short supply. I'd ask Colleen for some help. The horses produced a great deal of manure, and it needed to be moved out of the stables in any case. We could use the truck from the house on the corner of our neighborhood. We could do it, but it would take more work than what I had done in the winter. Siphoning and hauling wasn't that demanding. I was down to a lean hundred and seventy-five pounds. I lost a total of fifteen pounds over the winter. Not bad, and our trips to the resort probably kept me from losing more weight.

Three of our neighbors had small greenhouses, but without a way to heat them, they wouldn't do what we needed. I wanted to build a greenhouse on our parking pad and heat it using the generator. Once we started the seedlings, we couldn't take a day off. We could never let the greenhouse get below freezing. Water, heat, and light were critical for the plants at all stages. We had a plan. Time to get to work.

Time indeed

It seemed like we had all the time in the world. The only deadlines were of our own design. There was a certain freedom that we enjoyed. We received no bills. We traded in things and knowledge. We worked at the resort for the meals they provided. We weren't a burden on any other person. It was liberating.

We shared our time with those in the same situation, working hard day in, day out to survive.

There were two things I always had with me and that was my wallet and my .45. I hadn't needed my wallet since November, but I felt like I was missing something with an empty front pocket. My pistol was in my shoulder holster and seemed a part of me. I needed it at times when my life was in jeopardy. It was my safety blanket more than anything else.

And then there were the dogs. Phyllis and Husky were inseparable. They always stayed close to their humans. They understood their role as protectors of the twins, although the dogs probably caused more falls and scrapes than anything that threatened the two toddlers. I think our dogs would take on a pack of wolves to keep any of us safe. It was the same thing I'd do.

Our new world was so much smaller, yet more fulfilling. It was odd. How much life had we missed out on before? Everyone complained about the fast pace of modern society, but no one left their smart phone at home. We struggled for just one more thing, one more award, one more year toward retirement.

Now that we had time, we took the time to be thankful for what we had. Months after the world changed, we still reviewed everything we had done during the day to make ourselves just a little bit better. It wasn't about things. It was about what we did for each other, about what we did to improve ourselves.

My asthma bothered me a lot less nowadays, too. Maybe it was the weight, or maybe it was a diet that lacked junk food. Maybe it was the fitness. I was in the best shape I'd been in in a long time. Madison, too. She carried water and fuel and food. She drove the snow machine like a champ.

The best part of our day was reading to the twins in the evening. Where before, we would settle in to watch TV, now we would gather together and read. It didn't matter what we read. We had gone through numerous volumes of Dr. Seuss, but we also read them the gardening book, the Bible, *Master & Margarita* by Bulgakov. Anything and everything. When you read every day, you go through a lot of books.

GETTING READY FOR SPRING

We built our greenhouse using a big roll of Visqueen and two by fours. We built an inner shell and an outer shell to use the air gap as an insulator. We initially heated it with the kerosene stove burning fuel oil. We vented with a heat-driven fan and we used a two-foot-thick bed of wood chips and sawdust to help keep the heat steady. Once that was done and the wood chips heated, we removed the kerosene stove. There was no sense in poisoning our young plants with the toxic air.

I ran the generator so we could use an electric heater in the greenhouse. This meant that I had to run the generator every few hours. Madison would stay up later and I'd get up early. It wasn't optimal, but it was all we had until it got warmer outside.

We planted seeds for tomatoes, peppers, and green beans. When the time came we'd plant cabbage, kale, and other greens. In order to hedge our bet, we planted triple the number of seeds we wanted to get in plants. Just in case.

With the greenhouse, one of us had to stay home at all times. The twins would be really put out if they didn't get their weekly trip to the resort, so Colleen and Madison took them. They traveled light, pulling only one sleigh with the emergency gear (tent, sleeping bags, food, fuel). I kept the dogs with me at home.

This also gave me some freedom to 'shop' for things that we would need come summer. A truck with a trailer would be nice. Maybe even something like a backhoe, as digging an outhouse was one of the first things on my agenda when the ground thawed.

I saw twelve-hour workdays ahead. The twins needed to learn how to weed the garden. Well, maybe they were still too young for that. They would get their chance soon enough. We couldn't build the garden at our house. There simply wasn't enough water. The closest viable garden spot was a half-mile away.

It seemed like no matter what I needed to do, there were moving parts with missing pieces. I needed to get an inventory of what was available for us to use. I better pick up the pace of inventory management.

Not working was getting to be like a real job.

THE FIRST MEDICAL EMERGENCY

Madison, Colleen, and the twins headed out in the morning for Chena Hot Springs. They had to slow as the warmer weather was creating some icy conditions with the snow where we had hard-packed it on previous trips. They took a break halfway, but kept it short as they didn't have the dogs with them. A quick bathroom break, stretch the legs, helmets back on, and away they went.

They arrived at the Community a little after ten. When the engines turned off, there should have been the hum of a water pump, dogs barking in the distance, but there was more. A woman screamed hysterically. A man howled in pain. With the twins in their arms, Madison and Colleen raced past the lodge to see a small group gathered around someone lying on the ground.

It was Lucas. Madison couldn't see what the problem was, but she was sure she didn't want the twins to see it. Colleen calmly handed Aeryn to Madison and shouldered her way in to see what was causing the pain.

Blood flowed freely from Lucas's mangled arm. Amber was attempting to put a tourniquet on. Emma was jumping up and down, screaming uncontrollably.

In a voice that Madison had not heard before, Colleen pointed at Emma. "Get her out of here!" In a completely different tone, she talked to Amber. "I'll do it. I used to be a nurse. Put a half-turn as you tie it off, then it is easier to tighten." They had a thin flashlight that Colleen took and used to tighten the tourniquet. The blood flow slowed right away.

Madison was struggling with the twins and Emma. The twins were confused and afraid. Emma was still hysterical. Holding both twins, Madison kicked Emma in the leg.

"Get me some rags, we need to cover the wound." A t-shirt materialized and Colleen tied that around a vicious gash that started at Lucas's bicep and ended at his forearm. The muscle and tendons were cut to the bone. Lucas moaned in anguish, and his eyes rolled back into his head.

"What happened? Look at me," Colleen ordered as she cupped his face with her hands. "What happened?" she said louder.

The intelligence behind his eyes returned and he focused on Colleen. "Fixing the pump…exploded on me…still under pressure. I'm sorry." He started to sob and gag. Colleen turned him onto his good side as he threw up. He convulsed as the pain from moving his arm hit him. He screamed once more and passed out.

"Let's get him inside. Now, ladies!" Amber reached around his chest from behind and hauled him partially to his feet. Colleen picked up his legs. Jo had arrived, and she held his injured arm. They shuffled toward the back door to the kitchen.

They were putting him on the food preparation counter when he came to. He started thrashing about and Amber lost her hold on him. His arm was pulled from Jo's grasp. The tourniquet loosened and blood spurted.

"Stop it!" Colleen roared right into Lucas's ear. He settled down long enough for them to get him onto the table. Jo twisted the flashlight to tighten the tourniquet.

Colleen held his head firmly and looked him in the eye. "I need to sew this up and it's going to hurt, but I can't have you thrashing around." She looked at Amber. "Sewing kit?"

"We have a big first aid kit for the dogs and I know it includes sutures."

"Perfect. Take my sled and hurry." Amber bolted from the kitchen. Colleen took a closer look at the wound. If she could sew up the artery and maybe the tendon, she'd be able to save Lucas's arm. She wasn't sure how much use he would have of it, though. "Go get plenty of towels," she ordered Jo. Then added, "And soap and hot water. We need to clean this out."

THE TWINS UNDERSTOOD

Madison and the twins were in the dining room. She listened as Colleen gave orders. In the months that they had known her, she had never mentioned that she was a nurse. They usually got her talking about her husband and son. Even though they were gone, talking about them kept them real for her and seemed to give her a reason to move on. She was keeping them alive in the good memories she shared. She also spent time teaching the twins (and us) about horses. Horses weren't simple creatures. They required a great deal of attention.

The twins were concerned. They talked about Lucas's "ouchie" between themselves. Madison explained that it wasn't something you could kiss and make better. It needed real medical treatment, and Colleen was providing it. At this point, the best thing for them was to stay out of the way, although they wanted to provide moral support.

We could not have asked for better children. The fewer things we had, the less needy they became. Routine helped, especially a routine that involved all of us as a family. They were included in what we did, and the limits of what they could do were clear to them. They were open to doing more, of course, as they wanted to test their maturity. They had just turned three and it seemed to us that they were ready for kindergarten. We were blessed.

And there was work that needed done, so swimming was out for now.

Madison took the twins to the dog kennel and they all immediately dug in to the feeding and clean up. The twins weren't strong enough to pry the dog piles from the snow, so they kept the dogs occupied while an adult took care of the messes.

The twins were knocked down. A lot. Sled dogs like to run. They are active. The twins enjoyed it. They ran and giggled as the dogs easily ran faster.

They spent a good two hours helping Abigail, the apprentice dog musher. She was the most knowledgeable in the Community about the dogs and dog mushing, but this was her first year. She had a couple months' experience when Fairbanks was lost. She buried herself in her work with the kennel. She and Jo were the only two who did not serve on the roving work details, as their jobs were critical. Life was special, even that of the dogs. They required daily nurturing. Abigail gave them that in addition to what seemed like an endless amount of love.

As they finished the morning feeding, it was already lunchtime, but Madison was not in a hurry to head back to the lodge. She was afraid of what she would find out about Lucas. Delay wouldn't make anything better, though. If they needed any help, Madison couldn't provide it by hiding. So off they went, back to the lodge.

TRAGEDY AVERTED

Colleen looked exhausted, but exhilarated at the same time. It was hard to describe, maybe she looked like somebody who just won a marathon. Madison took this as a good sign.

"He's sleeping, surprisingly. He passed out as I was sewing things up, but he still had a strong pulse," Colleen offered before Madison asked. A half empty bottle of Scotch sat between Colleen and Amber. Madison's eyes narrowed at that.

Amber gave a tired smile. "That was for Lucas. It's all we have. And we used vodka as an antiseptic." The Community had been going through the spirits at a high rate, but the resort was well-stocked. Maybe some needed to be set aside in case of emergencies like this. They would have to think about that. Plus, there was the stock at the gas station. That had remained mostly untouched.

Having a nurse available was an amazing bit of luck. Lucas probably would have lost his arm otherwise, maybe even his life.

Having no medical care would make the new world a dangerous place. How long could we stay apart? How long would we have to?

Lucas's accident created a different sense of urgency. Madison knew that someone would have to head outside. Someone would have to find out if help was out there. And then do everything possible to get them to come.

Madison would not let it be me.

Jo and Emma were still cleaning up the kitchen. Emma had gotten hysterical since she thought it was her fault Lucas got hurt. She'd opened the wrong valve when Lucas had pointed at something by her. The pump he was working on exploded almost immediately since he had it half-taken apart.

She calmed finally as everyone told her it was just an accident. No one was an expert in what they were doing. They had to learn as they went. Emma returned to the world of reality. She rubbed her leg absentmindedly where Madison had kicked her. Madison left the kitchen for the dining room.

Lucas had lost a lot of blood. Without the ability to give him blood, he would need a great deal of rest and a lot of fluids. Someone would have to take care of him. Colleen said that she'd stay as long as necessary, but only if the twins promised to take care of her horses. This was their chance to contribute so they were all in. Both of them tried to squeeze onto Colleen's lap to give her a hug.

Madison went to each person, touching their shoulders and thanking them for their help. Lucas's accident could be a tragedy that tore the Community apart, or it could be a thing to unite them further.

Madison returned to the kitchen. It had been cleaned and some things were set out for lunch, but the only thing happening was Emma sobbing as Jo held her tightly, stroking her hair and cooing in a soft voice.

Madison began singing a chant that she'd learned as part of her yoga training. She closed her eyes and sang, her voice gaining strength. Peace. Love. Those things that ground a person. Emma needed the strength to get through today.

Emma stopped crying and listened. Madison's eyes were closed, and she was fully immersed in her chant. She repeated it a few times, then collected herself and opened her eyes.

"Thank you," Emma and Jo said together.

Healing.

The first thing Lucas did after he awoke was to tell Emma it wasn't her fault. He held her hand as she cried. But then that was it. Lucas told her that there would be no more crying. There was too much work in front of them to waste time looking back. Amber looked on as the two friends set things straight between them.

Lucas and Amber were starting to be more of a couple, but it was early in their relationship. They were still trying to figure things out.

Weeks passed before Lucas could get up and move about on his own. He was in a great deal of pain; the only drugs available were what they had on hand in the gift shop – aspirin, ibuprofen, over-the-counter stuff.

Lucas had matured since he first started working at Chena Hot Springs. He was there like everyone else to earn money, ostensibly for college, but that wasn't where his heart was. He wanted to be more hands on. He had expected to swap college for a good trade school. None of that mattered now, it seemed.

One of the books in the lodge's consolidated library was on the fundamentals of flight. Since Amber had prohibited him from working, he immersed himself in the book while also taking trips out to the airplane to get more comfortable with the physical side of it.

With each day he grew more confident that he could fly the plane. He studied the mechanical systems of the plane so he learned what each system was supposed to do and how it worked. He practiced with the controls. He had yet to power up the engine as his arm wasn't very functional. He was learning to do things left-handed. If he couldn't get his right hand up to speed, then maybe he couldn't fly the plane, but he could guide another person through the piloting process. Lucas could control the flaps, propeller pitch, and throttles left-handed.

A plan was forming itself in his mind that had the potential to give the Community a look at things hundreds of miles away. Lucas committed to make that happen. He continued his studies and became a new man. He worked with Colleen on what it would take to rehabilitate his arm. She gave him some exercises to start off with, but injury rehab wasn't her specialty. Once she got back home, she would check some books she had, but until then, he could start with some simple things.

He got to work and she left him to it, making sure that Amber didn't let him overdo it.

LONG DAYS

As March gave way to April, my work extended to almost sixteen hours a day, every day of the week. The seeds, the garden prep, the 'shopping.'

My scavenging had resulted in rolls of barbed wire, fence posts, clips, and all manner of hand tools. I couldn't sink the poles until the ground thawed, although I could bring in horse manure and good dirt that people had stored in their sheds, seeds and anything else I could find, especially commercial fertilizers.

I had to be careful with these as some weren't meant for gardens. Something like Sevin was a product to be used specifically to combat various bugs. I found both powder and liquid versions.

Since our garden was going to be a ways away from the house, I dragged someone's portable shed down there. That was a painful and time-consuming affair, but it gave me a way to store all the little things. Once breakup was under way, mud and standing water could wreak havoc on any kind of order. Since I was close to the stream, anything I had could wash away if I wasn't careful.

I looked at everything as irreplaceable. I was a slave to modern technology and needed all of it if there was any chance for us to have a successful garden. I didn't want to risk failure. We had to assume that we would need everything we grew to survive the next winter. Every day would be a battle to prepare. Sure, we had the crutch of the Community at Chena Hot Springs, but for ourselves, we needed to prove that we could survive on our own. Maybe that was my own ego, too.

My breaks consisted of reading to the twins, or helping them understand everything I was doing with the garden. Why was the fence important? What did I mean by prepare the soil? How could you tell the different seeds apart?

The only answer I had for the last question was because of the seed packets. They told me what the seeds were. Otherwise, I couldn't tell one seed from another. I was the world's worst prepper.

But we would learn together so we knew exactly what each seed needed in order to grow. Eating was not something to be taken lightly.

If it hadn't been for the greenhouse at Chena Hot Springs, the twins would have thought all vegetables came out of cans.

BREAKUP

Breakup in Alaska has been celebrated for generations, if not millennia. It is the way that the Arctic and sub-Arctic welcome springtime. It means standing water, running water, and mud. It is the transition from using a snow machine to using a quad. For us personally, it meant our travel ground to a halt until the roads cleared and the ground dried out.

This was the final bit of preparation time before the race to plant. The excitement was killing me. No it wasn't. More mucking about in the dirt. I was never born to be a farmer, but once again, I was doing what I had to for my family. Maybe I could convince Madison that there is nothing cooler than planting a garden. Then I could take over the twins' classes.

Actually, their classes needed to be about the garden and the outdoors, so we would all be at the garden regardless. Some would watch and learn and others would be mucking about in the mud.

As we waited for breakup to wring itself out, we made sure the battery on Colleen's truck was charged. I took the opportunity to charge the battery on my Jeep, too. It hadn't run all winter. I was happy when it started right up. I also fired up the quad, although I had driven that around a little bit at times. It would be a good ride. Although for trips back to the resort, we'd probably just take the Jeep.

I wish we would have found a Geiger counter so we could see if Madison's Jeep was contaminated. It would be the better ride. We hadn't looked for a Geiger counter. I wondered if there was one at the University.

After any spring rains and the final run off had gone down river, maybe we'd take a trip back. The route on Goldstream to Ballaine would still be clear. The original fire had not burned far, not even past the first hill. Everything was probably as we had last seen it.

With breakup comes warmer weather. There would be bodies; that could be a problem. I wasn't exactly queasy, but then again, I'd never seen anything like what we could encounter.

I wanted to know that Madison's Jeep was okay. I wanted to know if there was anyone on the other side of town. Once we got the garden planted, we'd have time to make a run. I could leave at four a.m. and it would already be light out. Maybe that was a better plan.

I had a gas mask in the garage that I'd bought surplus a long time ago. The filters were still sealed. I could wear the gas mask and a full set of coveralls. No exposed skin and breathing filtered air. I could take Madison's Jeep so if there was contamination still at the University, I wouldn't ruin my Jeep, too.

That would work. I'd talk Madison into letting me take another trip into the city. The Intelligence Officer in me begged for new information. Why had no help come? Where were the airplanes?

End of Book One

RUN

Book Two

BEARS WAKE UP IN
THE SPRING

The growl was loud and close. It was a rare occasion when I didn't have the dogs with me, but there I was, alone, calf deep in the mud, trying to dig my .45 out of my shoulder holster inside my coat.

I tried not to flail in order to attract less attention to myself, but this was a thin grizzly, freshly awoken from her winter slumber and not a T-Rex. She already knew I was there and was still trying to determine if I would be a good snack or not.

I wanted to be the kind that caused indigestion after tasting bad on the way down.

Or at least cause explosive diarrhea. I'm not sure the bear cared.

She continued sniffing the air as she approached. I knew I couldn't outrun the bear. Even if I tried, I expected that my feet would come right out of my boots. The mud was bad.

That's why I hadn't brought the dogs. I tried to take calming breaths, but my body was having none of that. My breathing was quick and shallow. Anxiety was an asthma trigger, and there's nothing that screams louder at your soul than imminent death.

"Come on!" I yelled. The bear hesitated, surprisingly. I hadn't been yelling at her, but at my recalcitrant pistol that was catching every fold in my jacket as I fought with it.

With one final tear, the pistol came free. I ripped away the piece of my jacket that hung from the hammer and took aim.

The bear seemed tentative, so I pointed the barrel in the air and fired.

The grizzly jumped up and started rumbling away.

I could hear my heart beating against my dulled sense of hearing as I watched her head toward the road, away from me and away from our house.

I came to the garden because I wanted to look it over, make sure everything was okay, and then go back home. I put my hands on my knees as I struggled to catch my breath.

As the bear disappeared over the road, I was happy that I didn't have to find out that my .45 might not stop a hungry grizzly.

A TRIP

Planting the garden was anticlimactic. We had prepared so well that nothing was left to chance. Planting our seedlings took a total of thirty minutes. The hardest part was getting them from the greenhouse to the garden site.

Green beans and tomatoes made up the majority of our garden. We had a number of peppers and a healthy amount of cabbage. After that, everything else was just nice-to-have vegetables. We even tried eggplants. We watered a fair bit after planting, but nothing to wash away any seeds. I had a manual sluice gate off the stream. It looked like a pair of two inch by twelve inch boards that were dropped into slots, providing a redundant stopper for the water, which flowed into channels around the garden where we could then manually divert water into the rows within the garden. If there was flooding, it wouldn't tear through the middle of the garden. Well, it shouldn't ruin the garden. I had no idea how much water my system would hold.

And that was that. A couple trips a day to check on the garden, making sure the fence was still in place, the plants were watered, and all weeds were pulled. And anyone could do that. It gave me time for a different trip.

Have you ever tried driving while wearing a gas mask?

That was a great challenge for me. I was completely bundled up, including where Madison duct taped my gloves to my sleeves and my hiking boots to my pants. These rubber boots didn't fit well, so they were expendable, just like everything I had on. Although, after losing all kinds of weight, my Swiss Tanker coverall fit well. I'd bought it surplus for a few dollars because it had an interesting camouflage pattern, but it had always been a little tight. It was tough material. Maybe a Geiger counter would tell me that I could keep it. We would see.

Even though I was breathing much better, probably due to getting in shape, my asthma still bothered me. I was taking my twice-a-day medications once every other day. It wasn't optimal, but it was stretching them out. I would run out soon though, and that caused me some anxiety. I was afraid of dying, gasping for breath.

The gas mask didn't help. I had to pull air harder to get it into my lungs, so I was breathing faster and getting less air. I had to relax. I rolled down the window. Madison was looking at me. "Get me a music CD! Something I like!" She went inside, reemerging quickly with a CD. I got out of the Jeep to get it from her. I didn't want her to get too close.

I held it up in front of the two eyepieces on my gas mask. Rush – *Signals*. That would work. I nodded my head and gave her the thumbs up. I put the CD in the player and turned it up. I had the windows rolled down as I drove off.

The first time I hit the brake pedal was a little bit of an adventure. The Jeep didn't stop. I down-shifted the automatic to second gear and then first. I worked the foot brake gently. It started to grip after getting exercised, and then the brakes worked normally. Maybe some rust. Maybe the hydraulics needed to lubricate the system. It didn't matter. Without any traffic on the road, I could have driven using just the hand brake.

The sun had cleared the road well, although some shaded sections still had snow. I easily avoided those. I drove fairly fast, even running the Jeep up to seventy mph on the wide-open stretches, just to feel it again.

This trip was about getting to the University, but it was also an opportunity to look for survivors. I slowed down and looked for signs. Without the snow, it was impossible to tell if anyone was traveling on the road. I could not believe that there weren't more survivors to the north. There were a number of communities there that were well suited for surviving the winter. Without the roads being cleared of snow, they would just now be venturing out for supplies. Maybe we needed to put out some kind of sign, either a warning or a note saying that there are other survivors. I would have to think about that.

We didn't want any empire builders showing up at our door.

I didn't see any signs of other people, but this was a snapshot in time. In the moment it took me to drive past a spot, if no one were outside or on the road, then it would seem that no one was there, when the truth could be the opposite.

If I could find a Geiger counter, then we would know for sure if we could expand our search area.

As I turned onto Goldstream from the Steese Highway, the bad memories of my last trip took over my mind. I started to breathe harder and harder until I was getting lightheaded. I slowed and pulled over to the side of the road. I guess I didn't need to pull over, but when you aren't thinking clearly, you do what is habitual.

I got out of the Jeep and took off my gas mask. I leaned against the fender until I was calm again. The idling Jeep was all I could hear, so I reached in through the open window and turned it off. I probably should have put my mask back on to do even that, but after an asthma attack, I never could think very clearly. I was always reduced to singular simple actions. And I was always exhausted afterwards. I think my muscles were crying out from being denied oxygen.

No rest for the weary, I thought to myself. I put my mask back on and opened the passenger door. I took out our clothes and boots that we had put there nearly six months earlier. I threw them into the ditch. I had all the windows down, but kept my mask on. I had to find a Geiger counter.

A TRIP TO NO-MAN'S LAND

The bodies of the two men were where I had last left them. One snow machine sat there, unmolested. I slowed down. A cloud of bugs hovered over the bodies. With my gas mask on, I couldn't smell anything, and I was happy for that.

Those men didn't belong in this world where we were all here together. What if we were rescued? Could I be arrested? Should I be? Those were philosophical questions for a different time. Without any signs that there would be a rescue, I had other priorities. But maybe those two bodies needed to go away. Then again, how many bodies were there, and who would look at them? Worrying solved nothing. Right now, I was looking for something to help us understand more of the world we had been thrust into. I refused to let those two scumbags steal any more of my time or energy.

I drove on, glancing briefly at the old lady's A-frame house as I drove past. She deserved better, but I couldn't take the time to bury her either. She would contribute to the circle of life in some odd way, whether through the ravens, the foxes, or something else.

Ballaine looked different than the last time we had driven on it. It seemed like the fire had reached farther up the hillside facing the city. The way was mostly clear, except as I got closer to Farmer's Loop where a number of vehicles were stranded on and about the roadway. I could see some had people inside. They were long dead. At least their windows were rolled up. I kept my eyes on the road. I didn't want to look at them.

Power poles had fallen, and their lines straggled across the road. I crawled over these to make sure that nothing wrapped itself around anything on the Jeep. It would be a really long walk back home if something happened to the Jeep now. I was wearing rubber boots that weren't comfortable. A long and miserable walk.

RUN

I drove halfway into a ditch in four-wheel drive low to avoid more wires. I had to take off my gas mask so I could see. I opened the door and hung out as I drove slowly. It was refreshing to be out of the mask. My head was covered with sweat where the mask had formed a seal against my skin.

Once onto Farmer's Loop, the road was more open, although there were a good number of dead vehicles, so I put my mask back on. Madison had told me that if anyplace had a Geiger counter, it would probably be the Department of Geology and Geophysics. This was the building next to where she used to work, so I knew right where it was. Getting there was effortless, after clearing the obstacles on Ballaine.

I parked on the road outside the facility and headed in. It was quiet, although I could hear songbirds. Anything living was a good sign.

I had my "shopping" tools with me as I figured I'd have to break locks to get into storage cabinets or past lab doors. I wasn't sure about metal doors and metal doorframes, but if I needed to get in, I'd find a way. I carried my pry bar, a sledge hammer, and a bolt cutter. There was an axe in the Jeep.

I looked for any place where there would be equipment. Offices might have what I was looking for, but a laboratory would probably be a better bet. As I walked into the department, there was a display case up front to lure potential students and keep current students excited about the world around them. As part of the display, I saw it sitting there, innocently. A Geiger counter. Could it really be that easy?

I used my sledge hammer to break the glass. It was a big pane, and it didn't go easily. My tanker coveralls protected me as larger shards fell toward me and shattered on the floor. I shook the glass off the Geiger counter. *What the hell*, I thought. I turned it on.

It came to life with minimal ticking. I waved it over some other things in the case. It picked up its pace a bit on some of the rocks, but otherwise it was steady and not in an alarming way.

I took it outside where the ticking was minimal. I waved it around the inside of the Jeep. It picked up a little bit on the floor where our clothes had sat all winter. I pulled out the floor mat and threw it away. The ticking slowed. I waved it over myself and was relieved to find that I wasn't radioactive. The Jeep was fine, too. I took the duct tape off my sleeves and pant legs. I was hot and sweaty. One normally wouldn't worry about such a thing except we only had limited water, as in no shower.

I started the Jeep and drove toward the city. I stopped often to test the air. Things weren't bad near the University. College Avenue was packed with vehicles and trash that had been blown into the road. It was impassable. I retreated to University and headed south. As I reached the intersection with Johansen, the Geiger counter picked up the pace quite a bit. From here, it was a clear shot east toward Fort Wainwright. The radiation must have swept straight down the road. I turned west, heading in the opposite direction.

Maybe I could check on the home of some other close friends. They lived on the opposite side of Chena Ridge. Then again, as I stopped where I was and looked around, this place was a wasteland. Dead vehicles were everywhere, probably from the electro-magnetic pulse. I wondered why our electronics still worked, but that was probably due to two large hills in between our home and the detonation. Not so anywhere in Fairbanks, which sat in a bowl between the hills. I drove up the back way toward the eastern side of the University. There was an overlook where one could see most of the entire city.

Once there, I took in the magnitude of it all. I used my phone to take a few pictures. I had it in an inside pocket and once I was clear of the radiation, I was able to take it out. I had my wallet with me, too. Maybe I didn't want to break those habits. They were my link to a world where I was more at home, to a world that didn't look like what was in front of me.

I looked for movement. Ravens flew about, not too far from me. I couldn't see any reindeer in the pastures off to my right. With no one to care for them, I wasn't surprised at not seeing any.

No people. The most disturbing view of all. I waited, watching and listening. Nothing.

I checked the time. I had only been gone for two hours, yet it felt like it was time to go home. I took off my coveralls, leaving me in my shorts and a T-shirt. It was too cold for just that, but I felt like I needed the freedom. I rolled the windows up on the Jeep and turned the heater on high.

I headed home.

MORE SURVIVORS

Madison wanted to go back into town and check on our friends to the west. I didn't see why we couldn't leave as soon as I topped off the tank on the Jeep. We could be back in town in less than an hour, and it still wouldn't be noon.

We loaded up the twins. They were excited for a drive. They enjoyed the snow-machine drive to Chena Hot Springs, but it was cold for them. They had goggles and little bike helmets we made them wear, but in the Jeep, they were in their car seats and had a good view out the window. We had to adjust the straps on their seats. We hadn't realized how much they had grown in the past six months.

We even packed a lunch for a picnic. And our usual tools, just in case, including our new Geiger counter.

The twins would see death in all forms. We would have to drive by the two men I had killed. We would pass cars with clearly dead people inside. They did not look like they were sleeping. They looked like the zombie apocalypse, although the twins would not get the reference. They would have to form their own opinions of what death like this meant. I didn't know if they were ready, but as long as we didn't let it bother us, they should be okay. They were going to see it sooner or later. I wasn't one for sheltering them, especially not in this new world where we found ourselves.

We drove off, taking the shortcut up Bennett to Steese on the way to Goldstream.

As we headed down the hill on Steese Highway, just after Bennett, we saw two trucks driving up the hill. This was a four-lane highway so we wouldn't pass that closely. I stopped close to the barrier dividing the lanes and got out, waving to them as they approached. I had my right hand on the .45 underneath my light jacket. As they got closer, I could see that it looked like a family or two. I relaxed.

They pulled close and stopped.

"Howdy!" a heavily bearded older man bellowed as he reached over the barrier to shake my hand. "You're the first people we've seen down this way."

"We're going to be the only people you see down here. Where are you coming from?"

"Circle," he replied with a nod. A small town about a hundred and fifty miles up the Steese Highway, it was named Circle because it was originally thought to be the first town inside the Arctic Circle. Unfortunately, the original settlers were off a bit, so Circle is south of the Arctic Circle. "What do you mean you're the only people?"

"A nuclear detonation destroyed the city. When you get on toward Farmer's Loop, you'll see. There's nothing left. Don't continue too far down that road. I think it's still radioactive on that side of the city. If you are headed south toward Denali or Anchorage, I recommend taking Goldstream around the city, and then jump onto Parks Highway west of the University.

"How many people are still up there in Circle?" I asked, looking about. The others had gotten out of the two trucks. They had two small children, a little older than the twins, so Madison started the introductions.

"Most people leave in the winter. I don't know, maybe seventy-five or a hundred people? We've come to resupply. We are about out of food and gas," the old man said.

"You won't find anything you need going this way. How about the gas station in Fox?" I offered.

"There wasn't anyone there. It looked like it was closed. We saw a lot of that on the drive."

"Let's head up there and see what we can find," I offered. Everyone repacked into their vehicles. They turned around and headed downhill. The fact that they were going the wrong way was old world thinking. There wasn't anyone here to go the other way. We met back up at the gas station.

It had been looted, but there was still fuel in their tanks. We got the unleaded open with little trouble. They had a hand crank fuel pump with them because they had brought a couple barrels to fill. We used some duct tape and a hose to give us the reach we needed to get into the tank.

We found some cans of Chef Boyardee in the store. There was a picnic table outside, and everyone gathered around it. We made introductions all the way around.

Bill was the grandfather. His daughter and grandson traveled with him. James was Bill's son. He drove the other truck with his wife, their two kids, and two dogs.

We broke out all the food we had and the canned goods from the convenience store to make a decent meal. It was energizing to help these people out, although the only thing we did was to get them some fuel. They still needed food. I wondered what kind of canned goods we would find at the Silver Gulch restaurant, which was right across the road. I suggested Bill and his son join me while we went to take a look.

Madison looked at me, not wanting to be left alone with strangers.

"Hell, what does it matter? Let's all go," I said to the whole group. We walked the hundred yards or so to the restaurant. The front door was open. The gift shop register had been broken into. I shook my head.

The bar area had been ravaged; broken bottles were everywhere. James corralled his dogs and put them back outside. We kept a tight grip on the twins so they wouldn't get into any of the glass. Then we chased them outside, too. All the children had a good time playing outside together. Bill's daughter and Madison watched them as we worked.

We looked for the restaurant's food-storage area. We went through the kitchen to a small room beyond. It wasn't as big as I'd assumed it would be. I'd always imagined vast warehouses supporting a restaurant, when it's usually little more than a large pantry. And that's what was here, although it was packed pretty tightly. Silver Gulch liked serving mostly fresh foods, so there wasn't much in the way of canned vegetables. There were various soup bases to which you could add fresh vegetables and voila! You'd have a custom soup. We handed all of this out.

There were bags of flour, sugar, salt, cooking oils, and everything to make meals from scratch. I'd never really thought about what they would have if they did their own baking. I'd always incorrectly assumed they had mostly premade dishes. Good for Silver Gulch! For what it was worth anyway.

Foods in the freezer were still frozen solid. That was a good sign. The family had brought coolers with them and filled them up with what they thought important from the freezer, as many vegetables as they could find.

They had to bring their trucks closer as they took most of what was there. We found a dolly and used that to carry out the supplies. After five trips each, we had taken everything that would fit in the back of their trucks.

Once the trucks were loaded, there was no reason to spend further time milling about. They wanted to get back home. I encouraged them to drive to town and take a look for themselves first. They needed to share what they saw.

WHAT NEXT

After we parted ways, Madison and I looked at each other. "We didn't really tell them anything about ourselves or how we survived." Was that the introvert in us? Or was it fear?

How much of our former lives was a façade? We were comfortable with each other and our own family, but we did not open up to anyone else. Before the explosion, we spent time with other people. Madison was a professor! She was constantly in front of others. She missed her life from before, or did she? I thought so, but I wasn't sure.

What did people in the Community of Chena Hot Springs know about us? How much had we shared with them?

I hate to say it, but we preferred this new world where we dealt with other people on our terms. This could be dangerous as the less we were with others, the less we would want to be around other people.

The twins seemed to enjoy the company. They played on the mining cars on display outside the restaurant. They even played some game with the other kids.

We still had time to go into town, but not enough time to explore. We headed out and took Goldstream. We followed it past Ballaine, where it turned into Sheep Creek. This took us around the back of the University where we could jump over to Geist and then Chena Ridge. We would avoid areas of damage from the explosion, the downed wires, and some of the fires. We would bypass areas that we knew were littered with dead cars and dead people.

As we approached the area on Goldstream where the two dead men were, Madison distracted the twins by making them look to their right. We raced by and kept going. The twins never saw a thing. I pointed to the old lady's house as we drove past and later to the two brothers' house. We continued past Ivory Jacks (always free parking, as their jingle used to state on the radio) to Sheep Creek Road.

Unlike our previous trips, we saw signs of people at home. We saw tracks trailing mud onto the road from more than one driveway that disappeared up the hillside. We saw smoke in the trees from a chimney.

We didn't stop. We were on a mission to see if our friends had made it. The far-west side of town looked more abandoned than damaged. The stores had seen damage, but from vandalism and theft, not the explosion. It didn't look like anyone had been there for quite a while.

We continued up Chena Ridge Road to the top of the hill, a right, then a quick left, and we were on the home stretch to our friends' house. They were a married couple, one a professor and the other retired at home. Sounded like Madison and I.

They had two trucks and a car, and all three of them were in the driveway of their log cabin. The initial impression was that their house was abandoned. But why wouldn't they take any of their vehicles? We stopped on the road and walked down to the house. The twins knew where we were and wanted to race to the door. I held them back while Madison knocked. No answer. She tested the door. It was unlocked.

She went in. I heard her gasp and she came back out, covering her mouth with her hand. She stumbled a few steps, then threw up over their porch rail. I immediately started herding the twins back toward our vehicle.

I went to Madison and held her. She slowly shook her head. I helped her back to the Jeep. She sighed. I didn't realize how much she had hoped they would come through it all. Our inner circle of friends had shrunk even further. "I don't know what to say," I told her.

"There's nothing to say. They're gone." She looked up at me and then at the serenity of their home. Only nature wafted on the breeze. Birds. Tree branches rustling. Something rooting around in the underbrush. The smell of spring. Puffy clouds in a blue sky. Madison calmed down quickly. We were resigned to tragedy in this world. We had our family, and that was always most important. It was our foundation.

"Do you think they'd mind if we borrowed their truck, assuming its electronics weren't burned out?" I asked. She looked at me oddly and then understood. Maybe a parting gift from our friends. If it had been the other way around, we would have readily given them everything we had. I expect that they felt the same way about us.

Madison got into the driver's seat of the Jeep and adjusted it for herself. I went back to the house. They kept their keys by the front door. They were still there. I had to look. They were coupled together on their couch, partially decomposed. I covered them up all the way. I took the keys and closed the door behind me.

Their generator sat on the porch, still connected to their external wall outlet. It was a powerful generator that ran their house when there was no electricity. It would do the same for most of our house. It was what I had been looking for. I unhooked it, rolling up the 220v cable. I moved the generator to the steps and then carefully bounced it down, one step at a time, stopping and balancing it on the third step up.

I tried to start the truck, but there were only the telltale clicks of a nearly dead battery. I asked Madison to pull our Jeep down so I could jump it.

Once started, I backed the truck up to the steps and muscled the generator into the back. I also took the two gas cans that they had. One was still half full.

I wondered if they had gone into town looking for supplies when it was still radioactive down there.

I turned back to the house. "Thank you both. You will always be our friends."

Madison backed onto the road. I followed her out.

WHAT TO DO ABOUT SURVIVORS

We drove back fairly quickly. I knew that Madison just wanted to be home. I wanted to be home, too. I would never forget what I saw. There was so much tragedy. So many people.

As I drove, I looked out and thought that maybe five or six homes were occupied. I couldn't see any of the houses from the road. Then again, maybe it was only one house with survivors and the same vehicle making tracks at the other houses. If they were anything like us, they needed to find supplies. Maybe they were better at the prepper thing than I was, but was anyone ready for six months when you lived this close to the city?

I might make a trip back here at some point, but not anytime soon. The survivors from Circle had gone back home. They would share and then those folks would probably dig in. They wouldn't have to be ready for an influx of the summer people. I couldn't believe that anyone was coming back. Not this year.

It was springtime. The weather had turned and the city wouldn't kill you. Not the western side anyway. I expected anything towards the army post was still too hot to survive. Maybe even down towards North Pole. There was a back way to North Pole on Nordale Road, off Chena Hot Springs Road. That was how John would have gone.

I didn't expect him back, but was curious as to what he had found. Did he get the sickness, radiation poisoning? Who knew what his plan was once he left the Community. His absence was one of the best things that ever happened out there. One person. A cancer to all. Look where they were now!

And then there was Colleen. She was making do. Her engagement with the Community had brought her back to life. Although, when she thought no one was watching, you could see her sadness. She would never be the same, could never be the same. We didn't know her before, but I knew she had to be different, happier then.

I would always want to return home at the end of the day. Home. Where we lived now, austerely, but it was our home, and we were comfortable there. I think we were the happiest we'd ever been.

THE PLANTS ARE GROWING

As our garden came in, I was like a little kid at Christmas. Shoots appeared from the seeds, and the seedlings started expanding like mad. We even heated the garden with a small fire when it was too cold.

We watched the temperatures closely, and as it got back toward freezing, we covered everything up. On our little weather station in the house, we were able to set an alarm to go off when temperatures hit thirty-five degrees. It was annoying, but it would only take one freeze to ruin everything. We planted much earlier than the norm of Memorial Day, but we needed the extended growing season. I wanted everything to come in fully before the fall cold set in. I also wanted a chance to replant if we did something wrong.

We still had a number of seedlings in the greenhouse. We even planted new seeds, just in case. The greenhouse was nice and warm as the spring sun hit it. We didn't need to use the generator to heat it any more.

Plus, we had the greenhouse at Chena Hot Springs if anything went terribly wrong. As it was, we got our fresh vegetable fix every week. We could have grown lazy and counted on that, but we needed to make do on our own. What if the Community decided that they would all leave? Then, we'd support them, but it would mean the demise, over time, of the facilities at the resort. With nine people, they were able to keep up, mostly. But it took a great deal of work.

If they left, it wouldn't take long, I supposed, and it would be no more.

If they left, would we move there? Could the four of us keep it up? Interesting thought, but my preference was that they stayed. It was selfish, but I hadn't pushed my opinion on them. They gave us a vote in their affairs, but we had not exercised it. We would not exercise it. Their destiny was theirs to control.

And in the interim, we had a garden to tend. The thing with maintaining a garden was that you had plenty of time for philosophical thought. That's probably why people like J. R. R. Tolkien had masterful gardens.

After it warmed up, we moved back into the rest of the house, opened the windows, and let the good air flow. We even had our friends' generator hooked up through our dryer vent and plugged into the dryer's 220v plug. With standard power (alternating current vs direct current), it doesn't matter where the power originates as long as there is only one source. With the power, our water pump ran and, amazingly, our sewer line to the septic tank had not burst. We had running water again, which was a bit dangerous as we were limited to how much water we had in our tank.

Some things you just don't need to worry about until you need to do something. Then you do what needs to be done and move on. We worried a great deal less nowadays. We knew what we were capable of, and we knew we were going to survive. We had a plan that probably mirrored the plan of people from hundreds of years ago. Heat, water, food, shelter. And enjoy the heck out of life.

TAKING FLIGHT

It had been two months since Lucas's accident. His arm was back to about fifty percent. He could feel his fingers and manipulate his hand. He had little strength, but he was able to manage. He learned that he could do a great deal with his left hand, but writing and eating remained wholly right-handed endeavors.

He had also found avgas and was able to get the plane started. He taxied it around the runway and on the parking apron. He was getting comfortable working it. He felt ready to take flight, but wasn't ready to go alone. Amber tried to talk him out of it.

The two had become a couple since his injury. I'm not sure it was love as much as convenience. They respected each other and were friends, which is probably more than many modern couples have. It was working for them.

But she saw all risk without any reward. If Lucas found someone out there, then what? Would he be able to land and talk with them? And then what? Paradise wasn't just up the road. Not everyone would fit in the plane. It would take numerous trips to get everyone out.

Or, as Lucas phrased it, it would *only* take four trips to rescue everyone.

As far as navigation went, Lucas had planned to fly along known roads; however, when he turned on the GPS, it was fully functional. The satellites were in orbit and effectively broadcasting.

This was interesting for me as it suggested our issues were more local. No world at war. No aliens. I know, aliens? I had no explanation for what had happened to so many people or why no one returned after they'd left. I still couldn't figure it out, but having GPS was a huge bonus. It meant we could take direct flights where we wanted to go and greatly increase how far we could fly and still get back.

I said we because I wanted to go with Lucas. I trusted him to do the hard part of the flying, but I really wanted to see what else was out there. I didn't believe that the risk was too great. We would do some local flying first in order to learn the aircraft and, most importantly, learn how to take off and land in a safer environment. Amber felt better that I was going, but Madison? Not so much.

The day of the first test flight came, and we were stoked. It was probably the excitement of the flight. Or it could have been the adrenaline rush of imminent death. Regardless, we tried to stay positive.

We practiced while sitting on the apron. Flaps, throttle, air speed, pull back on the stick, ease it forward, back off the throttle a little, retract the flaps, and so on. We finally taxied down to the end of the runway and made a tight turn to face into the wind. I knew we could do it. We had the basics of flight down, but if there was an emergency, we were screwed.

Standing on the brakes, we throttled forward until the engine raced. Lucas let up on the brakes. We started moving forward slowly and then more quickly. The aircraft pulled a little to one side, and Lucas turned the yoke, a little too much. We zigged, and he pulled us back.

We hit our speed, ninety miles per hour, and Lucas pulled back on the yoke. We lifted gently into the air. We stayed in a shallow climb as our air speed picked up. We retracted the flaps and picked up more speed. We then throttled back once we were at five hundred feet and flying southwest toward Fairbanks. We started a gentle turn so we could circle around and try our hand at landing.

We started losing altitude. More rudder. More throttle. We picked up speed and climbed. Our little Cessna made a tight turn, even though we weren't trying. As we transitioned through the wind, the movements were exaggerated. Lucas needed to compensate by being more deliberate. We flew to a point a mile off the end of the runway and then turned back to line things up. We descended. Too fast. Then we steadied the airplane. We descended a little, then back up, then back down.

Flying wasn't as easy as it should have been. Push down, you go down. But the airplane wanted to do all kinds of other things.

We lined up with the runway. Everything looked good. We lowered the flaps half-way. We stopped descending. Lucas tried to ease the yoke down, but we stayed level. We pulled back on the throttle a little, and we started to slow down, too much.

Stalling was the worst thing we could do. We gunned it and retracted the flaps. We zipped straight down the runway, about a hundred feet high. We climbed back to five hundred feet.

"Whadda you think? That could have gone better, huh?" I asked, starting to laugh. If we landed, Madison would drag me from the plane and I would never get back into it. Lucas laughed, too. There's nothing like two idiots teaching themselves to fly a stolen airplane.

The second pass was anticlimactic. We descended on a steady path and dropped our airspeed safely at the end of the runway. We touched down, cut the throttle all the way back, and stopped with a huge safety margin. We gave a thumbs up to our better halves and turned around for another run. Had we stopped, my wife probably would have gotten the finger-across-the-throat signal indicating that if we didn't die, they'd kill us.

The second take-off and landing were smooth, as were the third and fourth, and, by the fifth time, we no longer had any spectators. That was what we were waiting for. It was now safe to pack it in for the day.

Lucas wanted to thoroughly inspect the airplane. He remembered how everything fit together. He wanted to make sure that nothing had loosened up and that there was plenty of oil and then get an estimate of how much fuel we had used.

I just wanted to go for a swim.

After taxiing up to the avgas pump, Lucas shut it down. We shook hands, and after we got out of the airplane, I gave him a big bear hug. Hope was something that kept men alive far longer than they should have lived. Lucas had given all of us hope with his dream of flying.

THE BIG TRIP

With our touch and gos, everyone had calmed down. Once again, I had underestimated the power of worry. They honestly thought we were doomed. Our first attempt at landing confirmed that belief. Madison was still mad at me after an hour in the pool.

I had truly enjoyed flying around. The next day, we would try to fly to Delta Junction to see what was down that way. If we could land at a small airstrip and refuel, our range would be almost limitless.

We took off in the late morning under a cloudless sky. It was June, and we would have daylight for almost twenty-four hours. The weather was perfect for flying. We stayed at a thousand feet and headed south. Our GPS showed us a straight route over small hills. We could see any obstructions well before we reached them. The GPS gave us an estimated flying time of forty-two minutes. That was about perfect. No matter what happened down there, we had plenty of fuel to fly back. A trip all the way to Tok would require a refueling. We hoped we could find avgas in Delta Junction.

We didn't know what to expect. I brought along all my "shopping" tools, including the Geiger counter. I also had my trusty .45 and the 45-70 rifle. We had sleeping bags and a tent in case something happened to the plane and we had to hike back. That would be miserable. I patted the dash on the plane, wishing it great health.

We flew over a herd of caribou. The wide-open space was like a nature park, unspoiled by man. No cars were driving. It was warm, so it was doubtful we'd see smoke from a chimney, especially since it was forest fire season. We could see areas of smoke at the extreme range of our vision.

If there was a forest fire close to the resort, our only recourse would be hope. We couldn't put it out. We could only run from it.

We followed our GPS directly to Delta Junction. The flight was uneventful, which was probably the best thing that could have happened.

We didn't need excitement. The plane was simply a very convenient form of transportation, although it carried a certain amount of risk. As long as everything worked like it was supposed to, we were safe.

We flew toward the Tanana River, north of Delta Junction and then headed south. The airport was on the north side of the small town. As we approached, there weren't any immediate signs of life, but south of the town, the destruction was obvious. Fort Greely had also been the recipient of a catastrophic explosion.

"I'm not sure we want to land." I unbuckled and contorted myself to lean into the back and get the Geiger counter. We circled once while I got things ready. "Let's try a low pass over the civilian airport."

We lined up on the runway and dropped to a hundred feet as we cruised past. I held the Geiger counter's probe out the window and didn't get anything.

"Let's do a lazy 's' as we head south. If things get hot toward the base, we can come back. I think it's okay to land."

Lucas gave me the thumbs up, and he climbed a little before executing the first turn. I checked the Geiger counter.

Nothing. We approached closer, and then it started to register. It picked up rapidly as we approached a point that could have been ground zero, right at the front gate. "Get us out of here!"

Lucas firewalled the throttle and climbed, turning back toward the north. "Land?" he asked.

I nodded and pointed to the north side of town. He made one turn and then brought us in for a flawless landing.

Before we got out, I checked the Geiger counter again.

The battery was dead.

ATTACKED

"We were attacked. Attacked by someone who could make nukes," I said as I thought out loud.

"Wouldn't we have seen the missiles?" Lucas asked.

I thought about it. They didn't use missiles. "Low tech, man. They used trucks with a bomb that they detonated at the gate. In Fairbanks, it looked like ground zero was at the main gate off Airport. Here, same thing. What other way would you attack a missile defense base? It's kind of ironic."

"But who would do something like this?" Lucas wore an expression of disbelief. Maybe he hadn't contemplated it. Once past the initial shock of their situation, he had accepted things as they were. Although the world was a turbulent place, I had never thought a direct attack like this was possible. 9/11 was terrible, and it showed what a small, dedicated group was capable of doing. However, this was the use of nuclear bombs in multiple locations. I expected we'd find something similar southwest of Fairbanks, too. That's why no one returned once they'd left.

I didn't like our President's foreign policy. He showed too much weakness, too much vulnerability. America's job was not to be liked by everyone throughout the world. Other governments would always envy us, and that was dangerous. The danger magnified if they weren't afraid of us.

"Somebody who hates us enough to destroy what we have. We haven't seen any signs of soldiers. Maybe there is a front, but it's a long ways away. Maybe there is no fighting. Who knows how many bombs were delivered right to our front door?" Rhetorical questions never invited a conversation.

"No one's coming to help us, are they?"

That was the real question wasn't it? Isn't that why we took the risk of flying? I thought.

"I don't know, Lucas. If we were at war, I would have thought there'd be more signs of, well, war! No missile trails heading over the poles to bomb the Russians. Nothing heading west to go after the Chinese. No combat air patrols over Alaska. No military convoys on the roads. Well, not as far as we saw."

"What do we do now?" Lucas asked.

I was reminded of Bob Dylan. "We keep on keeping on."

DELTA JUNCTION

We sat and looked at each other. We had already taken a reading, and things looked perfectly safe here. If there was residual radiation, it would be most harmful if we ingested anything. So we tied scarves over our faces and wore gloves, which we would leave behind.

"Don't kick up any dust. Wouldn't that be precious if we flew back in just our underwear? What would the ladies think?"

Lucas nodded. We looked around to see where we needed to taxi. It looked like people used the roads to taxi to different parking areas. We went to a small hangar on the north side of the airport.

"Let's see about the avgas," he suggested. We parked next to a tanker truck. I tried knocking on the side of tank, but I couldn't tell if it had gas or not. I climbed on top and opened the cap. It smelled like gas. I waved Lucas over with his hand pump.

We pumped the first bit out on the ground to make sure. It looked fine. And the truck had a good load. We would be able to restock some of our avgas at the resort. We filled our gas jugs, and used them to fill the tanks on the airplane. Lucas had a thought.

"Why don't we start the truck and use its pump?"

I looked at him, finished pouring my can into the airplane, and then went to the truck.

No keys.

There were a few airplanes in various state of repair and only one building. The hangar side door was unlocked. I went in and looked around. There was an airplane with its engine disassembled. It looked to be the same model as ours, but I couldn't be sure. I yelled out, "Hey Lucas! Are there any parts you need for the airplane? Any spares you think you might need?"

He came in and looked the plane over. I went to the desk and looked for keys. Nothing. This truck was probably stopping by to top off the tank outside the hangar. Whoever had driven it probably still had the keys on him, wherever he might be.

Lucas settled on a spare battery, which he loaded into the back of our plane.

I didn't want to stay here any longer than we had to since it could be contaminated. Without the Geiger counter, we couldn't be sure. We went back to fueling the plane and then got back in, tossing our scarves and gloves on the ground before we closed the doors.

The plane fired right up, and we taxied back to the runway. We looked at each other. I held up my hands in a gesture of "I don't know."

"Continue south along the road?" he asked.

"I think we need to be careful. Let's follow the road, not so high that we won't see people and not too low in case there's radiation."

WE FOUND THE MILITARY

Lucas was getting good at flying the plane. I didn't need to do anything. Even with his bad hand, he could manipulate the controls. He was a natural.

We stayed low and flew relatively slowly. We looked for signs of life. We didn't know what else we were looking for. Maybe signs of combat? It was Alaska's interior, how would foreign troops get here? That wasn't reasonable. But where had all of our people gone?

We followed the Alaska Highway for twenty miles, then fifty miles. There was a great number of abandoned vehicles along the road, which in my mind was typical of a hurried evacuation. We were all eyes as we looked for any sign. About twenty-five miles out from Tok, we spotted an airport. The GPS said it was Tanacross. I thought if we were to find anything, it would be in the larger city of Tok.

As we approached, we finally saw what I thought had to be there. It looked like a military checkpoint – a number of HMMWV military vehicles, a five-ton truck, a GP (general purpose) tent, and a couple armored vehicles. They looked like U.S. military. Getting closer, we could see people in uniform running to and fro. All of a sudden, a red flare shot skyward in front of us.

Lucas panicked and turned the yoke hard, banking north, away from the checkpoint. As we leveled off, I looked back out my window and could see a machine gun on one of the vehicles firing. "Dive! Go north! Faster!" I yelled.

Lucas took us down as close to the ground as he dared. Once out of the immediate view of the checkpoint, Lucas throttled back. Our engine was running close to the red line.

I came up with a quick plan based on my impression that these were the enemy. We couldn't have them following us.

"Let's climb to where they can see us, make the fuel mixture as rich as possible so we start making some smoke and noise, and then we bank hard and dive toward the northwest. We stop the smoke and get on the other side of those hills. Then we follow the valley back up toward Delta Junction. We can refuel there and then get the hell home."

Lucas embraced the plan and firewalled the throttle to gain some altitude quickly. He richened the fuel mixture, and the engine immediately started sputtering, but it didn't smoke anywhere as much as we'd hoped. He heeled over using the rudder and then backed off the throttle. We glided downward. We hoped that it looked like we had lost control and had gone in for a rough landing. Lucas adjusted the fuel mixture and gave it enough throttle to keep us airborne. We were running as silently as we could.

It still sounded loud to me.

Into the valley and between the hills we flew. We couldn't see behind us. We couldn't see to the sides of us. We could see ahead and a little above us, but that was it. Our priorities had changed from finding people and information to simply surviving the day.

"Do we have enough gas to make it all the way to the Hot Springs?" I thought it better if we didn't stop. If they had military vehicles, then they probably had airplanes and helicopters. Military helicopters were faster than we were. If we had to stop, then we'd have to hide and wait for things to blow over.

"We have plenty and a good reserve to boot," Lucas nodded, determined to get us home.

He was energized by the low-level flying. I hung on for the ride, much of the time spent looking out the windows for any signs that we were being followed. We were really low. I figured we'd find tree sap on the undercarriage, if we made it home alive.

Lucas wasn't worried. He followed the GPS straight back to the Community. He picked up altitude as we approached so we could improve our descent angle. He brought us in for another smooth landing. He wasn't even sweating. I was a wreck.

Lucas was energized like he'd just won the Super Bowl. I suspected he had some Honey Badger in him.

HERE FOR THE DURATION

As we all discussed what we'd seen, things didn't make sense to me. Why was our military firing at us? If they weren't ours, how did a foreign military get our equipment? Why didn't they chase us?

It was troubling having more questions than answers. At least we knew that we were cut off. There would be no help until the military issues were resolved.

"What if we're in a demilitarized zone of some sort?" I thought out loud. "Maybe they weren't trying to shoot us down, just scare us back inside. We were really close to them. They shouldn't have missed us. Plus, what about the flare? Why fire that if you're just going to shoot us down?"

"Why in the hell would they make us stay here? We can't leave?" Amber was upset. Both she and Madison were happy to see us return, but when they found out we'd been shot at, their demeanor immediately changed. No, we weren't going anywhere anytime soon. I agreed. I had no desire to get shot at again.

I expected Lucas would be back in the air today if he could. It would probably be a while before he could talk Amber into another flight, as it should have been. Once the soldiers checked, they'd figure out that we never crashed. The good news was that Alaska was a big place, and there were an endless number of small airstrips. Many people had carved them out of the woods by their cabins. It wouldn't take much to hide the airplane and ourselves. The geothermal power generated no smoke. One thing we couldn't hide was the kennel. The dogs had a big footprint, but from afar, someone might not see the dogs. I didn't know what to do about that. As long as we kept to the shadows and stayed inside, maybe no one would know we were here.

Fear. What would it take to live a life without fear?

Our fear was the life or death sort. It took its toll on us. We would give the situation a few days and then go back to our normal routine. If we buried our heads, then what kind of life would that be?

We needed to talk with everyone about what it would look like to stay here for another year or more. We didn't know how long we'd have to survive on our own. We didn't even know who the good guys were, let alone if they would come.

I needed asthma medicine, which meant that we needed to find a D-cell battery because we were going back into town. I wanted the Geiger counter to work.

AIRPLANES

We didn't even have to wait one day before we had our answer. Two fighter aircraft made an appearance to the southwest, between us and Fairbanks. We yelled at everyone to get under cover. Madison ran to the kennel to let them know we were hiding.

The F16s flew as a pair. The lead aircraft was high, while the trail followed lower and to the right. We watched as they made a long, slow loop, disappearing into the distance. Madison returned with Abigail. We all stood outside the lodge, watching and listening. All of a sudden, the lead aircraft appeared above a hill. We hadn't heard it as it skimmed the deck on its approach toward us.

"Inside!" We scrambled through the door as the jet went by. He was going fast. We ran to the windows to look out. We couldn't see anything. Then the second jet roared by, bombs and missiles loaded under its wings; a drop tank filled the centerline position.

We waited. Fifteen minutes later, we went outside. The air was clear and warm. What had the aircraft been looking for, and what had they seen?

"Let's have lunch," I offered. Everyone looked at me like I was crazy. "We need to talk about what we're going to do next. We might as well eat. Who knows how many good meals we have left."

Since this was a military issue, they deferred to me. My wife had served four years, so that made us the only veterans. No one else had even studied military history. Their only frame of reference was what they saw on television.

For my part, I had no idea what we were up against. I didn't know why they would be after us. Our survival drew unwanted attention to us. If helicopters with a big red cross on the side appeared, I would have been relieved.

That's not what we got. We were on the receiving end of warplanes flying in a combat formation.

Jo was a little rattled, but she rose to the occasion. She took what she had thawed out for dinner and made it lunch. Moose steak, potatoes, plenty of green beans, lettuce, and tomatoes. We were having everything that we made available here. The moose was from a young bull that Becca had shot before the snow melted.

"Maybe we should have somebody out on watch?" Lucas offered.

"Then what would we do?" I asked a bit sarcastically. I was angry at the situation. I couldn't imagine our military turning against other Americans. "If we saw helicopters or armored personnel carriers inbound, then what?" No one had an answer. "We need to decide what we are going to do based on what we think they want. They saw us. Then they came to find us. They shot at us when we approached their checkpoint, but they didn't bomb us when they found our home. What are their boundaries?" I finished that thought with the question to which I had no definitive answer.

"Now is when we make a choice. We make the best decisions we can with what we know and then live with the consequences. Sometimes, the world delivers what it will, even when we've made good choices."

THE UNKNOWN FEAR

"What are we afraid of?" They looked away from me as I tried to make eye contact. "We're afraid of the unknown. All of us. It's been half a year since someone bombed Fairbanks. And the military finally shows up, but they're not here to help us. They shoot at us and then chase us with fighter aircraft! What the hell is that all about? Why are they after us?" More rhetorical questions. These people did not deserve to get beaten down.

"Look at you," I calmed my tone, speaking more softly. "You're good people. You worked here because you wanted to make money to go to school, to improve yourselves, move up in the world. That choice should not have led to a life of hardship. But it did. Then again, your decisions mean that you are alive today. If you were in Fairbanks, you'd be dead. If you were at Delta Junction, dead.

"Six months. You've not only survived, but you've made a good life here. The longer we can hold out, the more likely things will get resolved. This is the United States we're talking about! It will eventually get fixed. And we'll still be alive. Every day we survive is one day closer to getting back some of what we've lost. We will be here when that time comes."

"What do you think our chances are?" Jo asked me.

"I think our chances are good. I've been thinking about why this is happening, why no one has come back after they've left. Maybe they think we're contaminated from the radiation. Maybe they think we'll be the leaders of the zombie apocalypse!" No one smiled. There was no place for humor in this conversation, but that's how I coped. That's how I kept control of myself.

"I think there's still a war, and we're in the middle of it. But it's being fought somewhere else. Our military has agreed somehow to maintain a demilitarized zone, and we are right in the middle of it. If they evacuate us, then what happens? For Madison and I, our whole world is our family and our home, and we don't want to leave. For you guys, maybe evacuation is the best choice. I don't know. I don't know what they think we are or what they intend to do with us. What if we're considered prisoners of war? Refugees? The same government that couldn't get us help in the past six months is going to take care of us someplace else? That's not my idea of my future." No one talked. Everyone's eyes were still on me.

"What's next, you ask? Here's what I see, what I think they'll do.

"It starts with the reconnaissance of the resort, which I assume the F16s did. Next, if someone thinks they saw something, there will be a more dedicated reconnaissance or even a reconnaissance in force. There's no way we looked like a threat, so I don't expect they'll come rolling up here in tanks or that they'd resort to simply bombing the place. That didn't seem to be the goal, otherwise, the F16s could have easily done that.

"If their goal isn't to destroy the place, then maybe they are just rounding up people. I don't know if that is good or bad. If they wanted us to land the airplane when they saw us, they could have simply waved when we flew past, maybe fired up a green flare. Green is good, right?" Most people nodded. I still had the floor.

The military was a foreign concept to them. They didn't have a frame of reference from which to form an opinion. They needed more information. I needed to choose my words carefully. If I recommended a course of action, they would probably accept it. I would not surrender to an unknown authority, and I didn't think it was best for the group either. I was thinking of protecting them through a disinformation campaign.

"I, for one, have no intention of dealing with a military that shot at civilians. If anyone comes, I suspect it will be in the next day or so. I don't think they'll come by ground – too many hot spots between that checkpoint in Tok and here. So I think they'll come by helicopter. I think that if we want to meet with them, we want to do it on our terms. Until we know what this is all about, I suggest we not be here when they arrive.

"Let's leave a note saying that we are trying to make it to Canada. And we disappear."

"I will stay and take care of the dogs," Abigail immediately jumped in.

"If they come and take you away, what do you think they'll do with the dogs?" She hung her head. They would leave them in the kennel, where they'd die.

"What happens if we turn them loose?" I asked.

"They run away," she answered, still looking down.

"Can we try it? Maybe turn a number of the dogs loose and see what happens while we're getting other things ready? In the end, it's your choice, but I'd like you to have options that give both you and the dogs the best chance for survival."

"I'll do it." It didn't sound like her heart was in it. "I'll take care of it now. I have what I need over there. I can stay or leave from there." I'd heard that she had taken to bringing some dogs inside the dog musher office where she'd moved a mattress. She slept in a pile of dogs. I'm sure she was never cold or lonely.

"Thanks, Abigail. We don't want to see anything bad happen. We didn't ask for any of this, but we have to deal with it." We needed to hurry and I was starting to lament our situation. These people needed their orders, and they needed a timeline to execute.

"Our choices are simple. Stay or leave. If we stay, then we go about things as we always have. Madison and I will take the twins to our home. Colleen?" I looked over at her.

"Going home," she replied. Others nodded. No one wanted to stay at the resort. At least with the Community, they knew what they had. No one was willing to brave a hostile unknown.

"There are houses in our neighborhood where people can hole up. We'll leave a note on the door here. It will say that we've headed east, toward Canada. That we were afraid and didn't want to die. We can draw a line on a map, too. They'll like that. We need someone to hide in the hills and watch, for maybe a week or two. I really want the military to come, confirm that no one is here, and then move on and leave us alone."

"I'll stay," Darren offered. He and Becca had been sitting silently, holding hands.

"And I'll stay with him. We can hide in the hills and watch from there. No one will see us," Becca said firmly.

"Take a quad. After they've come and are long gone or if they haven't come after two weeks, come and get us." I told him the directions to our house. I didn't want anything in writing, just in case they were captured. There was one turn after fifty miles – the directions were simple.

"Everybody else, pack the minimum, and let's get on the road in thirty minutes." It was not an arbitrary amount of time. It had taken almost a full day for jets to come looking for us. If they reported back that they thought they saw something, it would take time to put a response team on a helicopter and then fly two hundred miles to get to the resort. We should be able to make it to our home outside Fairbanks well before a helicopter could see us.

What they showed up with would give us an idea of their intent. If they arrived in transport helicopters and few troops, which I suspected, then they intended to evacuate us. If they showed up in gunships and with a large number of troops, then our decision to hide was best. In both cases, we needed to not be here if or when they arrived.

"Darren. If the only thing that shows up is a white helicopter with a red cross and no armed troops, maybe you'll want to go introduce yourself. Don't tell them where we are, but leave a note in the yurt if there's no threat. I would love nothing more than to be wrong about all this."

He and Becca both nodded, jaws set firmly. They didn't believe the Red Cross would show up any more than I did.

Everyone packed quickly and paired up on the quads. The good thing about our sleight of hand was that we didn't have to make it look like no one was here. Quite the opposite. We could leave the greenhouse and even leave things in the refrigerator. If we lost power, then we'd lose some food, but we'd deal with that if it happened.

We stopped by the kennel on our way out. Abigail was in the process of letting all the dogs loose. They were running around, but not running away. We all pitched in to help. She still didn't want to leave. Someone had to feed them. I told her our plans and that Darren and Becca had already departed to hide on a hill to the northwest.

She liked that and offered to hide in the hills to the southwest. She could return daily as needed, always staying under cover of the trees, and still take care of the dogs. She didn't need a quad.

She also had her pack of dogs that wouldn't leave her side.

Everyone took turns giving her a quick hug, and then we headed off, careful not to hit any of the dogs that were now running everywhere. We got to the road and some of the dogs followed us, running alongside the vehicles. We sped up until they fell behind, and then we hit the gas. We had agreed on keeping good spacing between the vehicles. That would limit our visual footprint should any helicopters sneak up on us. In our Jeep, we would arrive earlier than everyone else. We'd wait at the turn-off to our house. I didn't know what the top speed was for the quads, but I didn't want anyone to push it and wreck on the drive.

We made it to the turn-off to our home in record time, forty-seven minutes. The others cruised in over the next hour. The skies remained clear, without a sound from any aircraft.

TEMPORARY HOUSING

We rallied at our house as people arrived. We hid the quads under trees or in sheds. As usual, we brought a bunch of vegetables back from the Community. They would go to waste otherwise. We even still had some halibut in the freezer from last year's fishing trip. That could be a treat. We would fire up the grill and do our best. We might as well make the most of our exile.

Maybe we would take everyone to see the city.

We settled people into where they would be staying. There were two couples and two singles who needed beds. There were a number of houses in the neighborhood that were in good shape, ready for guests. We had an extra bed in our home and Colleen had extra bedrooms. No one would be left out.

Who wanted a house to themselves? Jo and Emma volunteered. Amber and Lucas thanked Colleen for her hospitality, along with Felicia, the woman who took over in the greenhouse when Lucas moved into full-time maintenance. I'd ask her to take a look at our garden to see if she had any suggestions.

Chris stayed with us. He had hired on as a housekeeper, but after the guests stopped coming, he became a general helper. He was always in a work group as he did not have an area where he was in charge. He was very quiet. As a matter of fact, I'm not sure I'd heard him speak more than five words at once. I didn't care that he was black. He was just like everyone else – doing everything he could to help us all survive.

And that made him a good man, something we all aspired to be.

We asked everyone to come back around five, after dropping their things off and getting the lay of the land. It was new, so people were a little adventurous, the reasons for being here, quickly forgotten.

As long as we didn't have a visual footprint, something that someone in an airplane (or helicopter) could see on a fly by, we should be safe.

RUN

We were fifty miles from where they might have seen us last. I hoped that Abigail, Darren, and Becca would all be safe.

As it turned out, we didn't have to wait long.

THEY CAME, THEY SAW, THEY LEFT

The next morning, bright and early, I was outside with Phyllis and Husky. I heard the quad from a long way off. Someone was coming. I suspected it was Darren and Becca. They didn't seem to be in a hurry. I strolled out into the road to wait for them. I waved as they rolled up.

They stopped and got off. Both were smiling.

"It worked, man!" Darren said, shaking my hand. "A helicopter came about three hours after you left. They stayed only ten minutes, and then they all jumped back into the helicopter and flew out, directly east along the route you drew on the map."

"They never came back," Becca added.

"That is great news. Did they find the airplane? I assume they didn't see Abigail."

"No and no, I don't think so. Abigail is still there? We saw the dogs running free. They ran up to the soldiers when they landed, but the soldiers chased them away."

"Abigail hid in the woods as a compromise. She wasn't going to leave her dogs. Tell me, how many soldiers came, what kind of helicopter was it, and what kind of uniforms were they wearing?"

"The helicopter was big, a big bulbous nose for the pilots. The helicopter looked filled with soldiers who wore camouflage, with helmets. I don't know, soldiers."

I would have thought any Army actions here would be in the Blackhawk, or maybe the Chinook. It didn't sound like a U.S. helicopter.

"Two big rotors, front and back, or one main and a small tail rotor mounted perpendicular to the ground on a skinny boom going back from the fuselage?" I asked.

"A small tail rotor. And yeah, a long skinny boom. "

"What did the engine intakes look like? They were over the cockpit, right, not on the side of the engines?"

"Two round ones, like a jet engine would have, side by side, and yes, right over the cockpit. What's it mean?"

I pressed forward with one final question. "What kind of guns were they carrying?"

"We were a ways off, but they looked like AKs."

"I think you saw an Mi-8 filled with soldiers. No room on it for passengers. That means the Russians," I said, gritting my teeth. "It means they weren't going to evacuate us." I swallowed hard.

"It means we're at war, and we're losing."

A WORLD AT WAR

A world at war? Or maybe it was just Alaska at war. I still thought that we were in a demilitarized zone. What if the weak politicians had negotiated a stalemate where the territory between the militaries was declared no-man's land. It had been irradiated from the nuclear explosions, and almost all other survivors had tried getting out. They may have been corralled and not allowed to return. Maybe that's why no one came back.

Where did that leave us? If our own people shot at us to make us turn around, and our own people flew out to find us, but the Russians were the ones to put troops on the ground, then there had to be some kind of agreement.

Our own people had shot at us when they shouldn't have missed. Not a single round had penetrated the plane. The red flare, a warning. The F16s flying low and fast to make a great deal of noise. And almost six hours for us to run and hide.

That sounded more like malicious compliance from people whose orders had to be carried out, but whose orders went against the very fiber of a soldier or airman's being. I could see it. "In order to keep the war from spreading beyond Alaska, we've agreed to allow Russia access to all areas northwest of this line. We will help them find any survivors, who will be resettled to locations outside the zone. Thank you for playing."

We needed to lay low until the immediate threat passed. Then we needed to keep laying low.

When we got everyone together, the initial joy at seeing Darren and Becca was muted when everyone realized that our changed lives also meant a changed existence. So we had another what-do-we-do-now meeting.

I was fresh out of ideas. Maybe we could approach it by looking at what we *didn't* want.

"I'm not surrendering to the Russians. Ever." I'd rather live in the woods like a caveman. I wouldn't let the twins or even our dogs get taken by the Russian military. I'd fight. And I'd garden, can vegetables, and do everything we had been doing. What could change?

But for my family, we sure as hell couldn't run to the hills and make do. Life in Alaska required one to be far more deliberate.

Since they flew in, maybe that meant ground troops would not be permanently stationed in the zone. If they saw something, they'd come. So we needed to make sure that they didn't see anything.

No more flights in the airplane. No smoky fires during the daytime. No big heat signatures. Nothing to make us stand out. Or we could leave for Canada. We could get there going overland, although it would be far easier and quicker in the winter on snow machines. As always, this was a mutual decision between Madison and me.

She had already reached her conclusion. Her words made the decision make sense.

"We'll be fine right here. We have what we need, and they don't know about us. We'll keep doing what we've been doing. We'll just stay out of sight while doing it."

"I don't know why, but I like our new life. I like what we have. If we give up, will we be allowed to go home? Unless I know that answer is yes, I don't want to take the chance. I want to stay," Amber said firmly.

"Me, too," Lucas committed, standing and giving Amber a hug. Everyone else gave their approval for the plan to lay low. To keep on keeping on.

Awareness and readiness did not equal fear. If any of us were going to live in fear, then we wouldn't be living.

A NEW NORMAL

A nd yet another new normal for us all. After two days, the eight people from the Community returned home to Chena Hot Springs. We continued our gardening and were pleased with how everything was going.

We constantly looked over our shoulders. We would stop and listen. We were always armed.

We told ourselves that it wasn't fear, but we were afraid. How could we not be? Maybe the real word is that we were courageous. There was something out there to be afraid of, but we were standing up to it, even if only in a small way.

I had to build a small shed to house our generator. I double insulated it and put four heater vents on it in the hopes of dispersing the heat enough that it wouldn't light up an enemy's infrared goggles.

We also needed a wood-burning stove. We hadn't found enough pellets to keep the pellet stove alive for another winter. One thing we hadn't counted on was the extra manual labor provided by the Community. I had real doubts that Madison and I could move a five-hundred-pound pellet stove out of our house. With the help of our friends, we made quick work of the change out.

The pellet stove was moved to our shed. We disconnected the wood burner from the house on the corner and moved that, with the help of our friend's truck and a dolly. Our vent pipe was four inches, leading to an eight-inch roof vent. We needed the wider pipe all the way. I'd take care of that during the rest of the summer.

We needed to find and stock up on glass jars for canning. We had our book on gardening and it had a section on canning. With the generator, we'd also be able to freeze things. When the winter cold came, the freezer would already be sitting outside. At that point, it would be a big cooler, not needing electricity.

We needed to stock split firewood. In the immediate neighborhood, there were probably hundreds of cords. With the truck we had "borrowed" from our friends, we could easily move as much as we needed in a very short time. I thought we could put half in our shed and half in the garage. We didn't want anything out in the open.

Marines took the war to their enemy. Marines sought to impose their will. In this case, we wouldn't be doing that. Our only chance to survive against a vastly superior enemy was to not exist, at least as far as they knew. I hoped our note ploy would keep them guessing. They didn't fly regular reconnaissance flights over our area. We would have seen something. I assumed they were only in a position to react. Without seeing anyone, they would go back to waiting. At least that's what I hoped.

As part of my note, I put "the two of us are going to hike to Canada since we crashed our airplane...." Since they could only confirm that they saw the two of us, we didn't need to give them a bigger target.

HOW DOES ONE PUMP A SEPTIC TANK?

After weeks of nothing unusual, we fell back to our old routine. We were stocked with firewood to last the entire winter. Our neighbors' fuel oil tanks had been filled with gasoline. We were able to pump some fuel oil from the tank at the gas station, so we filled our tank. With the bigger generator, we could run our home heating system. We had hot water. We had enough electricity. It was almost like we'd returned to how we'd lived before the attack on Fairbanks.

To get to this point, I was working almost eighteen hours a day. I was exhausted. I was on my feet all day and working, always lifting or moving something. If anything needed to be tended to, hauled, fixed, or built, then I took care of it. The one thing that remained for us to ensure a comfortable winter was to pump the septic tank.

I thought we could do it if we had the truck that the septic pumping companies used. Without that, I wouldn't know where to start.

I needed to find a truck that could do the pumping. Maybe there was something in Two Rivers. I took our truck in search of a different truck.

When Chena Hot Springs Road was used by thousands of people daily, it was constantly in need of repairs. It was amazing how well it held up without any traffic. I usually drove down the centerline, but still adhered to the speed limits. The law didn't matter anymore, but I didn't want to risk getting into an accident. I wore my seatbelt too, just in case.

Two Rivers is not a big town. I knew it wouldn't take long to search it. I drove up and down the roads, checking driveways leading into the trees. I drove slowly on the dirt so I wouldn't kick up a big dust cloud. I lived in constant fear of being seen. I wanted to think that I was being prudent, but my caution was driven by fear.

I never found anything that looked like a pump truck. I continued up the road to the next small community. Same thing. Long driveways into the woods and no trucks. When I was turning around after driving down one long driveway, a door to the house popped open, and an older gentleman stepped out, waving.

Wasn't that a pleasant surprise! First, that he didn't shoot at me and, second, that he had survived. We had driven past his turn-off dozens of times and never knew he was here.

Then an elderly lady joined him on their porch.

Leaving my rifle in the truck, I got out with my hands up.

"Fellow survivors! It is great to see other people." They smiled broadly at me, and we shook hands, but the older lady wasn't into that, she grabbed me in a big grandmotherly hug. There's no doubt she felt my shoulder holster under my jacket, but that couldn't be helped, and she didn't seem to care.

"We've been by a number of times, and I never saw that you were here," I told them.

"We usually keep to ourselves. I tried going into town a couple months back, but the city was gone. So I came back home. There wasn't anything that we really needed, although I would kill for a cup of coffee." He must have driven by when we were visiting the Community. "Come on in and sit down. Martha makes a great cup of tea." She beamed at the compliment and went back inside. He leaned close to me and added in a conspiratorial whisper, "You haven't got any coffee, have you? I don't have the heart to tell her that I don't like tea."

I laughed long and hard. Of all the things going on in this world...

SAM AND MARTHA

Sam and Martha had lived in Alaska their whole lives, nearly seventy years. They'd bought this house exactly thirty-five years ago to set themselves up for retirement, which they had enjoyed for the past six years. Their cabin was without electricity and running water. There was a stream out back where they pulled their water. They had a huge old-growth forest behind them where they managed to cut enough wood for heating and cooking through all the cold months.

They were the epitome of preppers; they were completely self-sufficient. I was awed in their presence.

The inside of their cabin was lined with shelves, completely packed with books of all sorts. They had oil lamps for light. A big garden was out back, and there was a door leading to what may have been a fruit cellar. If it was below the permafrost, then it would act as a walk-in, year-round freezer. They didn't need much from the rest of humanity.

"This is a good cup of tea, ma'am," I said, not looking at Sam as I didn't want to laugh at his expression.

"Let me guess. You're a coffee drinker, too." It wasn't a guess. I think Sam underestimated her. I smiled uncomfortably, but Martha was so grandmotherly, she made it all seem okay.

I told them everything we knew, right up to the helicopter full of Russians searching for us.

"We were here when this was only a territory. Even then, the Russians thought it was theirs. When we found oil, the Russians made noises about getting their cut. Maybe they finally thought they were strong enough to take it back."

"Or that we were too weak to fight for it." My negativity lingered. I had spent a great deal of my life as part of an American military. Peace through superior firepower and all that. It pained me to see us negotiate away a part of our country, giving up on our own citizens.

"Would you like to take a trip to Chena Hot Springs? All the modern conveniences, including fresh vegetables!" Their garden was in the process of growing. They wouldn't be able to pick anything for at least another month. Their eyes lit up thinking of fresh food.

"And you can take a swim in the pool," I added.

"Not that into swimming, but a fresh salad would be nice. We're almost out of gas though. I don't think we can make it there and back." There was an old truck parked beside the cabin. It probably didn't get very good gas mileage.

"I have ten gallons with me. Take it all. We have plenty more to share." They looked at each other.

"How can we say no to that?" Sam leaned over to shake my hand.

"There were a number of young people working there when we lost Fairbanks. They run the place now. I call them the Community of Chena Hot Springs. When you get there, go to the lodge and find Amber. Tell her that Chuck sent you. They will all enjoy hearing your story." I thought about it for a minute and then added, "As for payment, since they work for themselves now, we always join the work groups and pick vegetables, or clean the dog kennels, or work in the kitchen. I see that you two aren't strangers to work. I suspect everything you have here you built yourselves."

"Mostly him," Martha pointed and smiled again. If only all people were as happy as these two, then the world would be a pretty good place.

We went outside, and I was getting ready to leave when I remembered what I had come for. "You wouldn't know how we could pump our septic, would you?" Sam shrugged his shoulders and shook his head.

Damn.

ABIGAIL

When Amber and the group returned to the resort, they couldn't find Abigail. They went to the kennel, yelling for her and continued in the direction she had gone. They gave up the search after a couple hours. They grilled Darren and Becca to ensure that the soldiers hadn't done something to their dog musher. Darren was certain they hadn't. Soldiers barely made it to the kennel before they were called back and flew off.

Someone would have to wait in the tree line where Abigail said she would feed the dogs. They would wait for a day before scouring the woods and hillsides.

Darren volunteered to wait, but Becca waited while Darren headed into the woods. Since he was the designated hunter, he took it as his responsibility to be able to track. He didn't know what he was doing, but that didn't mean he wasn't going to try.

With his trusty 300 Win mag hunting rifle, he gave Becca a kiss and headed into the woods. There were a number of trails, so he walked alongside each, looking for footprints in the dirt. He found only dog tracks, and they were everywhere, going in every direction. It didn't seem like Abigail had come this way, until Darren walked on the trail itself.

He saw the weeds, but it didn't immediately register. Something didn't look right. A brighter green against darker green all around. He leaned in for a closer look. Someone had stepped through the weeds, upsetting one single plant. A small human footprint was underneath, leading up the hill.

Of course she hadn't walked on the trail for the same reason Darren hadn't walked on it. It was demeaning that he thought she had no woodcraft. He stood up and looked around. "Why would I think she's stupid or even naive?" Darren asked himself. Male arrogance? He needed to get over that. There were three men and five women here.

Five and seven if he counted us, the frequent visitors. Everyone had a role to play, and everyone was good at filling his or her role. Otherwise, how could they have come this far?

Had they learned that much from each other? Maybe Abigail had learned things from Darren and Becca when they didn't realize she was paying attention. What had they learned from her? Darren needed to listen better. He started to laugh. Isn't that what wives complain about most, that their husbands don't listen? How had Darren fallen into that trap? He would have to ponder that lesson later.

Leaning his face into the weeds, he looked in the direction the footprint pointed. There! More disturbed under growth. Then beyond. Once he had his head on straight, her trail looked as obvious as if there were neon arrows pointing the way.

He picked up his pace, staying on the dirt, which was starting to get overgrown. No one had tended to any of the trails. There were no visitors to use them. He stepped from weed to weed, leaving few footprints, should the soldiers return, but he didn't think they had any woodcraft. He had watched them as they took no care in how they searched. *Bulls in a china shop*, he thought.

Abigail's prints departed from the network of trails and headed over the hill. He hadn't expected that. He thought she would put herself in a position where she could see the resort. She hadn't. Her job wasn't to watch, though. It was to return twice a day to feed the dogs. And to not get caught. They couldn't find her because she was hiding.

Once over the hill, Darren started yelling for Abigail. It wasn't long before the dogs started making noise, and he heard her trying to shush them. Which only made them more excited. Darren kept yelling as he walked straight toward the commotion.

Abigail had set herself up in a small hollowed-out spot under an overhang. Six or eight dogs were running around.

"They're gone, and we are back to business as usual, sort of," he said with a smile. As Darren and Abigail walked back, Darren showed her the trail she had left. She nodded and looked closely. He could see the wheels turning. If there was a next time, she would be much harder to follow. He was impressed. He also took a good lesson away from it all. Never underestimate people by assuming they don't know what you know.

THE COMMUNITY
REFRESHED

Once Abigail was safely back in the fold, they debated whether to return the dogs to the kennel. In the end, they dismissed it. With some natural selection, the number of dogs would be reduced. The stronger and more loyal ones would remain. They would pull out the females and keep them within a fenced area for the time they were in heat. They weren't ready for full on dog fights over breeding rights or a mass of puppies.

Unfortunately, the dogs were leaving a healthy mess throughout the compound. Maybe come winter, they would rethink where they would put the dogs. The smaller the space, the more prolific they would appear and the more often the area would need to be cleaned.

With everyone back and all in one piece, work had piled up. The plants in the greenhouse needed to be picked and weeded, and the next round of vegetables needed to be planted.

The geothermal power plant needed a little more than routine maintenance, like ensuring that the R134a coolant was filled and that the water pumps were cleaned out. The plant moved vast amounts of water, up to fifteen hundred gallons per minute. Those pumps and their filters were critical. If they weren't well maintained, there could be a catastrophic failure. The turbine spun at 13,500 rpm. If anything failed, the entire system could go off like a bomb.

The Community also had to determine their food needs to get everyone through the next winter. They needed to start freezing or canning. As a matter of fact, the ice museum was still operational, making it the biggest walk-in freezer in Alaska. They would take advantage of that, but just in case, they would go with a full supply of canned goods and a full supply of frozen food. This would give them triple the quantity to survive on as they would have fresh food from the greenhouse as well. All in all, not a bad goal.

They went to work with a new determination, while still keeping a wary eye on the sky.

THE NEW ALPHA

It had been almost three weeks before we ventured back to the Hot Springs. I had forgotten that we'd let the dogs loose. I figured that once the troops left, Abigail would round them up and get them back to their posts and doghouses.

That wasn't the case. As we approached, it was a yapping free-for-all. Dogs were everywhere. Phyllis and Husky got pretty excited, as in, completely incensed. We weren't sure what we were going to do. We hadn't bothered with leashes since Christmas.

"We can't just let them go. Husky will be fine, but Phyllis will be overwhelmed." I was dismayed. I didn't want anything to happen to Phyllis, she had helped us through it all. "Do we have a rope, anything to use as a leash?"

"In the back. I'll get it," Madison offered. She opened her door and got out. Phyllis, like a shot, came over the center console and was out the front door, almost knocking Madison down in her headlong rush. Madison started yelling and chasing after her. I jumped out. Husky, following Phyllis' lead, came out the door after me.

Immediately, Phyllis was surrounded by dogs in a typical greeting. She started growling, and one of the sled dog females growled back. Before we could work our way through the mob, Phyllis and the other female were fur over paws fighting. Phyllis outweighed the sled dog by some thirty pounds, but the Alaskan husky was quicker.

That didn't last long. Phyllis bowled over the other female in a bull rush and clamped down on the other dog's ear. She shook her head, just to maintain the other dog's attention. It was yelping in pain, and then it stopped fighting. Phyllis wouldn't let go. Her jaws were locked in place.

We finally made it through the other dogs to her. It took a while and much yelling to get her to let go. The other dog's ear was mangled and bleeding. Once the other female was free, there was a complete change in the rest of the dogs. With her victory over the Alpha female, Phyllis was now queen of the pack. Although I held a tight grip on her collar, I knew that we couldn't keep her leashed forever. In this world, you wanted the Alpha on your side.

I let her go.

"What are you doing?" Madison yelled at me, as she tried to get past me to Phyllis. I held her back.

"See? Phyllis didn't kill the other dog." Wasn't that our worry? We didn't want anything to happen to her, and now nothing would. I put my arm around Madison, as we watched Phyllis tear into the middle of the pack, tail wagging and play biting. Even the defeated Alpha joined in, tail up and running alongside the others.

"We better do something about that ear. Abigail!"

THE INTRODUCTION

The past couple weeks had been stressful, so we took the twins swimming. It was always relaxing to float around in the ninety-six-degree water of the pool. We even took the opportunity to go to the rock pool outside. At a hundred and five degrees, more or less, it made for a deep-muscle-cleansing experience. We only went down as far as the bottom of the ramp, so we could stay close to the twins. They were sitting in the shallows at the top of the ramp.

We wrapped things up lazily and headed inside for some nice long showers. As we walked out of the pool house, we saw a massive pile of sleeping dogs under the trees. We had to look around to find Phyllis. She was off to one side, but still a part of the pile. Husky was nowhere to be seen.

"Phyllis!" Her head rolled around, and her eyes cracked, barely. "C'mon Phyllis! Let's get some lunch." I had never seen her this exhausted. And sore. She was probably older than most of the sled dogs, but she had tried to keep up with them. Some straggly-looking dogs started getting pushed around like stuffed animals as Husky raised her head from the bottom of the pile. "You, too," I told her.

They walked slowly over to us. I scratched behind their ears and held the door for them.

Madison went into the kitchen to see if she could help while I got the twins ready for their lunch. Their highchairs were a permanent fixture in the dining room. As people did, everyone had their own table with their own chairs. Everyone sat in the same place every day, even if only one person was there. People can only tolerate a certain amount of change. They liked certain things to remain constant, predictable.

Amber and Lucas were the first ones to join us. They were both especially attentive to the twins, giving me a cursory greeting on their way in. Then again, the twins were fun most of the time, and they loved the attention. I was certain that trouble would start soon if one perceived that too much attention was being paid to the other. I'd let it run its course.

People filtered in over the next ten minutes, the last ones being Sam and Martha. I rose to greet them and everyone looked on in silence. Martha had a tray of cupcakes held out in front of her. She smiled sweetly at everyone and introduced herself and her husband, Sam. She put the tray down and then gestured for everyone to please help themselves. As a guest, one always brought something for the host.

For people who lived alone, Sam and Martha worked the crowd like professionals. They listened carefully as everyone said their names, repeating them back to help them remember. And just like that, Martha was off to the kitchen.

"Sam, can I offer you a cup of coffee?" I said with a huge grin. He looked at me like a sailor who's been lost at sea finally getting a drink of fresh water. I got a cup from the pot that was always on. It was a little stale, maybe even burnt. "It's been cooking for a bit, so it could be strong. I'll make a new pot."

He took the cup from me and looked into the blackness of the liquid as if trying to divine the future. He carefully took a small sip, closing his eyes as he held it in his mouth. He finally swallowed and then took another drink, bigger this time.

"That's really good!" he exclaimed to everyone's laughter. Martha's face appeared behind the door to the kitchen. She shook her head and smiled at her husband.

THE GROWING COMMUNITY

With the two new additions to the Community, we now numbered fifteen. This could have created a minor controversy as everyone already had their seats. There were no spare chairs at the tables.

But this was easily remedied. A small table was brought from the back room and butted up against one of the other tables. Two chairs were added and Sam and Martha had been officially welcomed aboard. I let them in on the inside joke of "assigned seating."

Lunch started with a salad, as usual, and the main course was a beef stroganoff that Jo and Madison had put together. Martha offered to clean up after lunch, and Chris said he would help her since it was his turn.

Sam wanted to see the geothermal power plant. He had been an engineer and thought it sounded interesting. Lucas said he'd be honored to show Sam around.

It was a good day. As Sam had shown us, it was important to appreciate the little things. To Sam, bad coffee was better than good tea. Seeing people laugh made everything okay. It said that at least in this moment in time, life was good.

The meal was exceptional, as always, and we complimented the chef. Jo stood and took a bow, and Sam and Martha started clapping. We all joined in.

As the clapping died down, Amber and Lucas stood up. "We have an announcement," Amber started. My mind immediately leapt to the conclusion that they were getting married. I wondered how we could accomplish that.

"I'm pregnant," Amber stated tentatively. Madison was the first one up to give Amber a hug. The others were stunned into a brief silence, but then the congratulations started. Colleen took a more clinical approach in that she wanted to "look things over."

My only thought was, *They could still get married.*

Martha beamed the look of a grandmother. I wondered if they had children. I assumed they did as they had pictures in their cabin that gave the impression of a big family. I would have to ask.

With a maybe November due date, we had plenty of time to get ready, whatever that meant. Even though we had twins, I had no idea what needed to be done. I'd leave that to the experts.

"Amber! Let me offer a toast in congratulations to you and Lucas," I said. We lifted our glasses of Coke and spring water. "I want to say that you have been stalwart from day one, the first day we came to Chena Hot Springs. You helped everyone to keep things running. You carried us all on your shoulders and have become a good friend." There were a few hearty agreements, while others nodded. Amber was well liked. "You know we'll do whatever you need us to. So what do you need?"

She and Lucas smiled as they held hands. I hadn't been sure how they would turn out as a couple, but it wasn't my place to judge or even guess. It was my place to support my wife and children and do right by the others. That was all. Sometimes I could be such a wiener. And here, while they were making their big announcement, I was thinking about me. I clamped down on myself and focused on them, hearing Amber mid-sentence,

"...incredible journey, in the company of friends. You guys have always been so supportive and helpful to me. We appreciate the offer of help, but I don't know what we need. Any suggestions from our mothers out there?" She looked at Madison, then Colleen, and finally Martha.

Despite our attempts to break down gender barriers, there we were. Three mothers and one mother-to-be heading into the kitchen to talk and clean up. The rest of us carried in all the dishes and cleaned off the tables in the dining room. Madison came back out and grabbed the twins, giving me a quick kiss before herding them into the kitchen.

"Well, it's just us," I said to Phyllis and Husky. The others went their own way, many going with Lucas and Sam to the power plant. Felicia was headed to the greenhouse.

"Could you use a hand?" I asked

She nodded. Once outside, Phyllis and Husky disappeared into a newly energized dog pack, while Abigail started chasing the former

Alpha female. We had forgotten to tell her about the dog fight. She didn't seem phased by the dog's injury as she got ahold of the dog's collar and pulled her toward the new infirmary, a small cabin just outside the lodge.

Well, it didn't matter which dog did the biting, did it, so I didn't share what I knew. I didn't want to get in trouble with Abigail.

SPENDING SUMMER PREPARING FOR WINTER

The summer passed quickly. We tended our garden. We gathered jars and Ziplocs from other people's long-empty homes. We even found a vacuum-seal machine with a number of bags.

As we were waiting for our first crops to come in, we tried our hand at fishing the Chena River. We hoped that any contamination had washed away, allowing the salmon a free shot upstream. It wasn't to be. The only fish we caught were grayling. So we filleted our catches and ate them fresh. We didn't have enough to make it worth our while to freeze.

The first crop to come in was the green beans. We nurtured them from the start. Madison's parents always had home-canned green beans available. We had developed a taste for them long ago.

We froze half the green beans and canned the other half. We did something wrong in the canning process as only half the cans sealed. We ate the ones that didn't seal and then went back to the book to try and figure out what we'd done wrong. Then we brought in the experts.

Sam and Martha came by for a visit. We stocked them up on gasoline, filling a fifty-five-gallon barrel that we strapped into the back of their truck, so they were far more mobile. We tried to talk them into "borrowing" a better truck, but they wouldn't have any of that. We respected them for their convictions and hoped that their truck wouldn't break down at an inopportune time.

We had our gardening books, but we still had some trial and error. With their guidance on round two of canning, everything went perfectly. Just a little more salt here. Hold the pressure for one more minute there. There's nothing like wisdom gained from experience.

We didn't have to go very far to find wild berries where there wasn't any competition except for birds. We picked gallons upon gallons. The twins' fingers were blue and red, I thought maybe permanently. We made jellies out of some and froze the rest. I could probably go months without seeing another berry, although we exhausted all the sugar we'd found while "shopping." Martha was comforting during the whole process.

We had our twenty cord of wood in place. We did test runs with the wood stove, and it worked great. I needed a lot of kindling. I was so bad at starting a fire that even the twins were embarrassed.

We never found a source for more kerosene. Burning fuel oil in the kerosene heater just didn't work. It mucked up the wick and belched toxic smoke.

With the big generator, we could run our boiler and all the water circulation pumps. We filled two aboveground five-hundred-gallon tanks with gasoline from the gas station to keep the generator going, also making sure we had enough water to get us through the winter. We increased our storage capacity to about four thousand gallons, but that meant we had to put a number of five-hundred-gallon tanks into the garage. If it wasn't firewood, it was water tanks. We had no room for our vehicles. Those would have to stay outside in the weather, although we had enough power to plug in their block heaters. We needed more heated garage space. Maybe next summer we'd add on. There was enough building materials around that I could use.

We had fully embraced our new world, no longer expecting to be rescued or that we'd even leave. We spent all summer getting ready for winter. When the cold and snow came, we would be ready. We wouldn't have as many tomatoes as we had hoped. Some of them just weren't growing like they should. I had a recipe for green tomato salsa. We would make that.

Aside from being successful getting ready for the winter, my biggest personal win was in finding more asthma medication. I took care with the ones I had, finally running out in June. By August, I couldn't take it anymore. I ran out of breath easily while doing things that I had to do. I woke up in the middle of the night, gasping for breath. I needed the medications or I would go downhill even faster. The thought of leaving Madison alone with the twins in this environment was too much.

I took our trusty Geiger counter and drove to the west side of the city, then to the Walgreens there. Fred Meyer was next door, but was half caved-in from the original detonation. I intended to search both. I brought my "shopping" tools, along with a full coverall, the gas mask, gloves, and the remainder of a roll of duct tape. The world will truly end when one runs out of duct tape. It will be the last thing used to repair the old technology.

Walgreens was a little radioactive on the outside, but not too bad. My ad hoc radiation suit, gas mask, and gloves protected me. The store had been looted, but they hadn't gone after what I needed. Inside the store, I realized that there was almost no contamination. I kept on my suit as I would have to go back outside, but I took off my gas mask and put it on the front counter. I was having a very hard time breathing while wearing it.

The cash register had been broken open. I snorted. How's that money serving you now? I expected that the two I shot were the ones who had been here. It made me angry all over again to think about them. They killed survivors while searching for a valueless treasure.

I let the thoughts go. I climbed through debris in the aisles. Many of the shelves had fallen over. Animals had been in here.

I went back to the pharmacy where the decomposing body of the pharmacist was slumped over his long-dead computer. I didn't touch him. I knew what my medications looked like. From television commercials before, I thought that Advair might be a reasonable replacement. It was better than nothing. I thought of that as I came across some boxes of the inhaler on the floor. I took them all. I kept searching. I found one of my two medications. They only had twelve, thirty-day packs of these, but that meant two years of medication, four with rationing. I was so happy. I opened one immediately and took a puff. I waited a few breaths and took another, breathing the medication in as deeply as I could. If only I could find the same thing in my one other inhaled capsule.

On the way out, I checked through the aisles. I found some honey and took that. I also took a number of candy bars as a gift for the young folks of the Community. They had burned through the stock of candy quickly last winter. I also found plenty of beef jerky. I took that, too. There was a good deal of canned goods, although most of it was processed food that wasn't good for us. We didn't need that stuff anymore. Or want it.

I wanted to find my second medication, so that meant I had to brave the falling-down structure of Fred's. The pharmacy was toward the front of the store, where the caved-in roof was the worst. I had to break down the half door from a kneeling position since there was so much debris on top, held up by the shelving and remaining walls. I crawled into the back. It took me two hours to search an area the size of our great room. It was dark and dusty. I found more Advair, but none of the capsules to complete my original prescription. It would have to do. At least I had more than when I started.

I left with my treasures and went home. We could return. Because of the caved-in roof, Fred's canned foods were protected. This would be a source of goods for years to come. I wondered why survivors from this side of town had not cleaned out the store. Maybe they were afraid of the radiation, as they should have been and if they knew about it. We had the benefit of a Geiger counter. The inside of Fred's grocery store was not toxic. Maybe it was the falling-down roof. Knowing didn't matter. The important thing was that we had a mostly stocked grocery store to ourselves.

Were the other survivors still here? Or did they try to get out and were caught on the road by the Russians? We'd probably never know. It didn't matter if we found out or not. I had what I came for, and we were ready for winter.

RIDING HORSES

Colleen was a godsend. She was a nurse and had nursed Lucas to health. She would do everything she could to help us with Amber's baby. We would have been at a loss otherwise.

Colleen took a liking to our twins. She spent a great deal of time with them, teaching them about her horses. At first, they only rode with her. She told them they didn't get to ride on their own until they could properly care for the animals. They learned to brush them and feed them carrots. Their little hands were at risk, but Colleen watched them closely and taught them well.

With only a blanket as a saddle, she would lead the horses by rope while the twins rode. It was nice to see. I think the twins saw the horses as really big dogs. And they loved dogs. With the free-for-all dog frenzy at the resort, the twins were always at risk of getting mowed down, but they took it all in stride. Over the past year, they had slept with Phyllis and Husky. I don't think they could sleep without having a dog by them. They treated horses with the same degree of companionship.

Colleen knew that she would have to spend more and more time at the Hot Springs just to make sure that the new mother and baby would be fine. She decided that moving there would be best. They were able to fence in an area she could use as a pasture. So she loaded her horses into her trailer and made the drive. She took very little in the way of personal things. I think it was more than a move to help out the Community. It was her way of closure, of reconciling herself with the past and moving on with her life.

Almost all of us carried the burden of the time before. Madison and I didn't know about the rest of our family members. We were the only ones who lived in Alaska. We believed the rest were fine, but they didn't know about us and had to suspect the worst. We couldn't help that. Maybe John had gotten through and delivered our messages, although that was doubtful. John was a scumbag.

The twins were devastated when Colleen told them she was moving to the resort. They wanted us to move, too. This created some strife on the home front. They didn't get over it as we had hoped. They brought it up daily and seemed genuinely angry with us. This went on for weeks, until it snowed, then we had other things to think about.

THE FIRST SNOW

The first snow came on September 15th. We were scrambling! There were still tomatoes in the garden along with a number of peppers and other things.

When I got up in the morning and saw that it was snowing, I let Madison know that I was on my way to the garden. I took the quad and bolted off, the dogs racing after me.

I haphazardly picked everything remaining. The snow had not yet settled on the plants so I hoped that they hadn't frozen the vegetables and ruined them.

I filled bags with everything left. Some of the peppers were too green, little more than fiber with no taste. We could still mix it all together and create some kind of sauce. We could not abide wasting any of our work. We had enough to eat, but we'd worked long and hard on our garden. As I liked to tell people, I fought a bear to maintain the sanctity of our young plants.

Sam and Martha showed us how to build our seed stock for the next year off what we had grown this year. Those were already safely stored in a cool area of the house.

We didn't quite have all of our winter gear ready either, like the snow machines and our tractor with the snow thrower. That wouldn't take long. Either it worked or it didn't. Charging the batteries would be easy. We had power almost constantly, only shutting the generator down for a little while here or there. Although that probably needed to change. We needed to learn to live without electricity. And probably propane and gasoline, too.

That would be the hardest part. We liked having mobility. Well, I liked being able to drive, whether it was the quad, a Jeep, the truck, or a snow machine. Even the airplane was a bash, but that nearly resulted in our total demise, so we could do without flying.

With the snow, it might melt or it might stay. We were entering the in-between time. Too much snow to drive the Jeeps, but not enough snow to drive the snow machines.

The dogs enjoyed new snow, especially when it was still relatively warm. With temperatures around thirty, it was prime outside play time. After getting the vegetables indoors, everyone was up. We put snowsuits on and, as a family, made snowmen. We made one big one that would be the dad, then a slightly smaller one that would be the mom. We made two small ones for the twins. Then they wanted to make a snow horse. That was a challenge that required a little more planning.

We had been out all morning, and now it was time for lunch. We chopped up some of the freshly picked vegetables (none of them ripe) and doused them with olive oil and spices. It was all we had left; the dressing ran out long ago. We had some moose burgers, without buns, with rice on the side. We were blessed in being able to provide a meal like this in these days. We had never even come close to getting hungry, although we usually never gorged. We ate what we needed and no more.

Together, we plotted how to build a snow horse. When we went back outside, the work went quickly. It had warmed above freezing, and the snow was really sticky. It stuck together well. Our snow horse came together, but it looked more like a four-legged Frosty the Snowman or maybe the Stay Puft marshmallow man. This helped the twins a little. They now had their own horse in the front yard.

If the snow melted, we would head up to the resort and check in on Colleen. Hopefully, they had been successful in moving a load of hay there. Sam had said that he would help her with that.

I expected Sam and Martha to winter in their cabin, but they were invigorated by the Community. They provided knowledge and guidance; they were helpful; they were good people and, most of all, they were needed. Everyone needs to have a purpose beyond simply surviving.

They decided to move to the Hot Springs full time. Sam was a dynamo in the power plant. He understood how it worked and what needed to happen to keep it working. Martha was great at maintaining good order and discipline. She would be there whenever anyone needed something. Need, as in someone to listen, a cup of tea to hold something warm, a helping hand to wash the sheets. She was everyone's grandmother, and she broached no disrespect. If Jo said lunch would be ready at one o'clock, Martha had everyone there on time, cleaned up, and ready to eat.

Martha had a way about her. Sam assumed the role of grandfather and took over Amber's duties as Mayor as she got farther along in her pregnancy.

The Community was getting excited about the prospect of growing. The destruction of Fairbanks and then the helicopter incident had changed their attitude toward their future. We were on our own, and we had to assume that it was for the duration. We didn't know if we would ever return to a normal life, definitely not here, but maybe not somewhere else either.

With the snow, we found ourselves isolated from the Community and the others we had brought into the fold. That meant there was more time for us to spend on ourselves. We got the assembly line ready and went to work preparing the vegetables to make a pseudo-salsa.

When the weather allowed it, we would head to the resort so the twins could see the horses. No, that didn't mean this afternoon and probably not tomorrow either. More disappointment from the young ones.

CLEAR ROADS AND CLEAR SKIES

It only took three days for temperatures to climb back into the fifties and most of the snow to melt. As promised, we headed to the resort.

We took the truck so we could deliver a load of fuel to them. An extra fifty-five gallons would come in handy for the snow machines and some other pieces of equipment.

With the sun getting lower on the horizon with each day, many areas of the road were shaded. We slowed as we drove through the remaining snow. We had our special winter tires on, our Blizzaks. These did great in the snow and cold, but were spongy in the summer. I had no way of putting our summer tires on because we didn't have them on rims. I had always taken them to a shop to get changed over.

More confirmation – I was the world's worst prepper. I should have had them on their own rims.

We had almost come full circle from the winter before as the new winter approached. We had improved our lives considerably over the past year. I can't imagine what it would have been like if the twins had refused their potty training. The fact that Fairbanks was no more and so few people were left alive was reduced to my own personal view that misery consisted of changing diapers.

I was so shallow.

Since we had brought the truck, it was a tight squeeze with the dogs and two car seats. We managed, but the drive took longer than usual because of the snow. When we finally arrived, we were all happy to get out. The dogs darted off into the pack. We unbuckled the twins and went inside.

Jo was sitting in the dining room, watching a movie on a TV that was set up on the bar. She had her feet up and seemed to be enjoying a mixed drink. It wasn't even noon yet.

"Is everything okay?"

She looked at us. She was very relaxed, her eyes dilated. She slowly smiled.

"Are you stoned?" I blurted out before thinking.

"Hey! That hurts!" Then she started giggling. "How can you tell?"

We went from surprised to shocked. In the uncomfortable silence, one little voice spoke out, "What's stoned?"

"Apparently Jo is, so let's go check on the horses." The twins were instantly distracted, and away they went with Madison running after them. I was sure they would follow up later until they were satisfied with a definition that made sense to them.

"We were cleaning out a better set of rooms for Amber and Lucas when we found someone's stash. It was only a couple of joints that Emma and I shared. Emma! What do you think of the weed? Emma?" I looked around and found her on the floor under the table with the coffee pot. She was sleeping, crumbs from something she'd eaten scattered on the floor around her.

"Uh huh." I wasn't sure there was anything to do. "I'm going to see if anyone needs any help. Don't hurt yourself." Jo seemed to be moving in slow motion. I doubted she was capable of anything more than falling off her chair.

Martha was in the kitchen, busily getting lunch ready. The smell of fresh bread made my mouth water.

"Martha! You could possibly be the absolute bestest ever. By the way, I have to ask, where did you get the eggs?"

She shooed me away from the oven as I was about to open it.

"I'm afraid the stock of frozen Egg Beaters is getting low, so enjoy bread now while you can," she suggested good-naturedly.

I guaranteed her that I would. I expected the stock of most things was getting limited. Vegetables, moose, and caribou would become the staples. But that would keep everyone alive until they could work on something next year that they could turn into flour. Is there any way chickens would survive in the wild up here? Probably not. But there were ptarmigan. Maybe we could capture some and see if they might produce eggs. Probably not there either.

WHAT'S THE WAY AHEAD?

I'd ask Sam. He'd have ideas about eggs and flour. I was certain they would be good ideas, too. The man was a survival genius.

Although it was a beautiful fall day, I thought that planning would be beneficial. Becoming self-sufficient was going to be critical come the new year. We would run out of plenty from before, leaving us with our wits and what we could grow or create ourselves.

It was a big challenge. It also changed the dynamic. It begged the question of what were we living for. Where did we want to be in five years? What about twenty years? Was it possible to think that far ahead?

What happened when we ran out of ammunition? And gas? The ammunition could last our lifetime if we used it only when hunting big game. The gasoline would run out within a year or so, even if we were able to stabilize it. In either case, we'd have to figure out how to survive without it.

What kind of world would the twins grow up in?

It was making me sick to my stomach thinking about all these things. I was having serious doubts. I had never shared with Madison or the twins how afraid I was for our future. I was afraid every time my breath caught and my asthma acted up. I couldn't guarantee how much longer I would be around. I wasn't that old at fifty-three, but my lungs were compromised, and I would not receive any more health care. I was on my own.

But I was the positive guy! Look at the remains of the snow men in our yard. Miserable people don't make snow families.

The twins were happy. They had us, and they had their friends in the Community. They had Colleen and her horses. They had Abigail and the dogs. They were learning. Their little purple fingers knew how to pick berries. They understood that animals are our friends, yet every now and then a moose will sacrifice itself for us. We say a prayer and thank the animal for living well.

I'm sure everyone undergoes a crisis of faith at some point. I couldn't let anyone see me like this. I needed for them to believe, because there had to be better out there. The war would have to end at some point, and relief agencies would stream in, proclaiming their own greatness as they provided materials and people. Look at me, helping survivors!

I didn't like that world either. It would take generations to build a new world, a better world. I gave myself ten years to influence the future. The twins would be thirteen years old. They would have to be ready to carry humanity forward, regardless of anything else. In the other world, they would have been learning things that meant something, but not how to survive. What did they need to learn to build that better world?

I sat on a bench outside the lodge. A number of dogs came by to give me a sniff. Once they learned that I didn't have any treats for them, they ran off. I leaned down with my head between my knees. I was going to be sick. I jumped up and made it to the bushes just in time to lose my breakfast and too much coffee. As I hit bile, it was tinged with blood.

I'm sure it was from all the stress I put on myself to get us ready for winter. We were ready. It was time to relax. My personal crisis probably generated enough extra acid to put me over the edge. I hadn't felt badly lately, a little upset stomach here and there.

I needed to de-stress. So of course I would not tell Madison. She'd freak out about it. And we needed to talk about what we wanted for the twins in ten years' time. I needed that. They would get an accelerated education. They would have to grow up more quickly than either of us liked.

After all my contemplation and puking blood, I was no closer to an answer. It weighed on me.

Once again, I found myself seeking Sam's counsel. What drove him and Martha to remove themselves from society, then reenter it as they had?

SAM'S WISDOM

I found Sam in the geothermal power plant building. He was tinkering with something while the pumps hummed. Everything was running smoothly. I expected no less.

He was alone.

"Sam!" I shouted as this was not a quiet place. He motioned me toward the door. We went outside.

"How do you do it, Sam?" I left it open-ended.

"Do what?" He didn't like to waste time. He needed more information to give a better answer.

"Keep going like you do. Your cabin. Not interacting with people. What's it all for?" I continued. "Aren't we supposed to make sure things are better for our kids? Is that what we're doing here?"

"You are giving them a chance to make their own way. If it's better for them, it's not because you gave it to them better. It's because you helped them to make it better for themselves. Did you like what you saw from young people before the explosion?" Sam asked. I shook my head.

"Little kids with cell phones. Video games. Kids in college protesting everything, affecting others who just want an education. Think my way or you're wrong!" I kicked a dirt clod into the bushes. "Outrage. People were offended all the time, outraged at nothing. Then when something important came along, there was no energy left."

"I see." Sam put his weathered hand on my shoulder. I looked at him. "Where are your twins right now?"

"They are at the stables, with the horses. Why do you ask?"

"Is that a waste of their time?" he asked as we shuffled back toward the lodge.

"I don't think so. Colleen's been teaching them how to care for the animals."

"Life lessons, Chuck. And Abigail has been teaching them about the dogs. And Jo about cooking. And you about gardening."

"Little things here and there. I don't expect them to start their own garden next year or build a kennel and breed dogs." I was probably a little more sarcastic than I had intended. My stomach was churning.

"Sure. Not this year, or next year, but what will they be capable of in ten years?" I squinted back at him.

"In ten years? I would be surprised if they weren't fully capable of taking care of themselves and probably take care of us, too.

"They'll be thirteen at that point, right? Instead of playing video games or dicking around with their phones, they'll have life skills." We reached a bench. He sat. I took the spot next to him and leaned forward, my head dipped down toward my knees.

"Once they've learned their own way, then all you need to do is be there for them when they ask for help.

"We didn't know what happened when Fairbanks stopped being. We lost contact with our kids. Maybe we'll hear from them again. Maybe not. But we know what they are capable of." Sam hesitated, picking at something under his fingernail. His eyes misted over. "So we waited. Then you came along. And now we have another family. A new chance to help make tomorrow just a little bit better than today. The best thing we can do in life is prepare for tomorrow, while living today."

"Living today," I repeated. "Surviving today, maybe." I was feeling down. I was afraid. Afraid that my health had gone the wrong way and that I was putting my family at risk. I had helped them survive today just to expose them to greater risk tomorrow. My stomach rebelled, I started to gag, and then I threw up more bile. Sam sat with his hand on my back, just being there for me. He saw the blood.

"I see," he said simply. "Let's get you to Colleen and see what she thinks." He helped me up, and we walked toward the stables.

JUST A LITTLE THING

"Alcohol consumption?" Colleen asked. I shook my head and held up my hand with the zero sign. "Any cases of stomach or esophageal cancer in your family?" I shook my head again. "Stress?" I forced a laugh. She knew what my to-do list looked like.

"I can't tell you what you have for sure, but we'll treat it as if it is acute gastritis. We'll change your diet a bit and then give you a heavy dose of antacids. And stop worrying about everything for Christ's sake."

"What if it isn't gastritis?" Even with Colleen and her set of skills, we were in a bad place if we needed more in-depth medical treatment.

"See? More unnecessary worry. If it is something where you need surgery, I'm afraid there's nothing I can do. So we'll treat it as if it isn't serious, because it can't be. We're going to treat it as if it's acute gastritis because that is what it must be." Colleen was firm on this point. She punched me in the chest.

I'm sure she had been a great mom. I should have felt more relieved. We had experienced the loss of our friends, but not our family. Look at what Colleen had gone through. Sam and Martha were bedrock. Amber ran the community.

Together we were making our lives mean something. Still, I expected that the others battled their own demons as I was battling mine.

"Listen. You saved us all. But you don't have to do it every day. We can help you to help us. Tell Madison what you've got. I'll announce it to the others and put you on light duty. Isn't that what you military types call it?" I nodded.

"Big tough men, all of you. Get over yourselves." With that, she punched me in the arm and whisked herself away, leaving me sitting in the ad hoc horse stable. It made me proud to think she thought that about me. I didn't like seeing people suffer. I liked laughter and people having a purpose. Maybe helping our small community survive was more important than anything I had done in my previous life. By surviving each day, we earned another day to try for something a little bit better. We all carried the weight of the world on our shoulders, but it looked like what would fit in our own two hands. Maybe that wasn't such a big weight after all.

Sam had joined Madison and the twins in feeding carrots to the horses. I expected that the horses would eat our entire crop if we let them. As I watched them from the doorway of the stable, Madison looked at me. She knew something was up. I couldn't believe my initial plan was to not tell her. I waved her over. Sam waved, too, and then pointed to the twins and nodded. He would look after them.

"My stomach's pretty upset. Colleen said I have gastritis. Too much stress, so I'll be hanging out on the recliner, watching TV." I took a fake step away. That earned me a punch in the back. "Hey!"

"I'm talking with Colleen to find out what's really going on." She wasn't amused by my attempt to paper it over with humor.

"I threw up blood. I feel like garbage."

"I told you that you were driving yourself too hard. We are fine. We were fine hundreds of gallons of gas ago. We were fine ten cords of wood earlier. We were fine with one winter's worth of canned vegetables. But no, twenty cords, a freezer full of beans, no place to put any more moose. What else do you think you need to do?"

"Sit back and watch TV?" My voice came out weaker than I had intended. "We will spend the next six months having fun and relaxing!" I proclaimed boldly. She smiled.

"I'll be lucky to get you to relax for six days."

THE BIG RESTOCK

Martha served up a fabulous lunch, but Colleen and Madison wouldn't let me have any of the tomato sauce – too much acid. I had bread and some peanut butter. I had a big salad. I drank water. And I chowed a handful of Tums.

Colleen made her announcement regarding my light duty. Everyone agreed. They said nice things about me. I felt much better. My stomach felt better, too.

I slid my chair over to Sam and Martha's table and waved Jo over. "What do our supplies look like?" I knew the answer to the question, but I wanted to hear it out loud.

"Almost out of everything that we didn't grow or kill ourselves," Jo responded.

"When I was on the west side of town last week, the Fred Meyer grocery store lost half its roof, but it was mostly intact. The caved-in part was alongside the grocery shelves." I let that sink in. "It's been almost a year. If we wait too long, dry goods will go to waste. The summer wasn't too hot, so maybe we didn't get too much spoilage." I was being selfish as I really liked a good meal. I liked fresh-baked bread. I liked coffee. I liked a lot of things from the before time. And they were there for the taking.

"You thinking a grocery run?" Jo was getting excited. She had been hired as a cook, but was a chef at heart. She could see the supplies in her mind. She was thinking about enlarging her culinary repertoire.

"I think we can do that. If it's okay, Chuck, I'll manage the food run. You can stay here and watch things. I haven't been into the city yet. I think it's my turn. We'll be there and back in less than a day." Sam was excited about a store run, too.

"Sam, the coffee aisle is outside the collapsed section of the roof." I waited as his ears perked up. "It looked untouched."

"Now you know why I have to go," Sam said with a laugh. "I think we're running low." Jo heard us and shook her head, holding her hand out, showing that we were stocked with cans of coffee above her head.

Sam put together three teams driving all the vehicles, with the horse trailer and one flatbed trailer. They cleaned the trailers and truck beds and then gassed everything up. They would head out first thing in the morning. I asked that they keep spacing of maybe half a mile between the vehicles. I didn't know if any bad guys were watching. A convoy might trigger an unwanted response from a Russian helicopter.

Madison watched me closely to make sure that I wasn't going along. She wasn't going either. She would stay to work with the twins and keep me out of trouble. Amber was staying. Felicia was staying. Chris wanted to go, but he usually didn't speak up. So I asked him directly, and he confirmed that he would go if they needed him.

When we were on the run from the Russians, we took almost everyone from the Community for a short stay in our neighborhood. Outside of that, these people had been here for almost an entire year. Yes. Anyone who could go, should go. Everyone deserved a shopping trip.

I briefed everyone on the radiation threat, that they shouldn't spend any more time outside than they absolutely had to. They should wear scarves or something over their faces while outside to reduce the risk from contaminated dust.

They could stop by our house on the way and get the Geiger counter so they could be more certain of the threat. I also asked that they put more gas in the generator and reserve tank, then fire it back up. Then we could stay a few more days without the freezer thawing. Lucas told me that he'd take care of it.

I spent the rest of the day doing very little. Floating in the indoor pool. Floating in the rock pool. Watching television. Reading to the twins. Talking with Sam.

And thinking. I was always thinking about the details of an operation. Before Sam left, I had suggested that he bring along some materials that they could use for bracing fallen beams and such and levers to move material out of the way. That might give them a little better access. Who knows, that last bag of flour might then be within reach. Or more likely, that bottom row of canned coffee was right there!

Before they'd left, Sam had quipped, "If I see decaf, I think I'll leave it. I don't ever want to think that I'll be so desperate for a cup of coffee that I'd be willing to drink decaf. I'd rather have a cup of Martha's tea." He looked around quickly to make sure she hadn't heard him. "Don't tell her that…"

WE STAYED THE DAY

We stayed the day together at Chena Hot Springs. My list of things to do was minimal and supposedly light, but nothing was easy.

We fed the dogs, which was an exercise in complete chaos. Although we would put out enough moose meat and dry dog food (we had taken the Dog Musher's complete stock earlier in the summer – I'm sure he would approve) for all the dogs, they all went after the first scoopful. I poured and jogged while Madison threw the strips of meat into the makeshift trough. They eventually spread out, but it was quite the ruckus.

Abigail told us we were down to less than fifty dogs. Natural selection, adventurism, whatever the reason. The remaining dogs were both loyal and hearty. She kept them in shape, using the wheeled sled to keep them familiar with the harness and their role in pulling the sled. Some of the dogs no longer liked to pull, so they weren't hooked up. There were plenty who did though. The twins wanted to learn dog mushing, but they needed to get bigger. Abigail suggested that if we found children-sized dog sleds, she could rig a team of two or three dogs for the twins to learn to drive.

That was an interesting concept. Dog mushing at three years old. What would have been unfathomable a year ago made sense now, and practical sense.

The twins tried to help feed the dogs, but were mobbed, knocked down, and beat up as the hungry animals ripped the moose meat out of their small hands. At least no one was bitten. That happened the last time that they'd helped deliver the meat, but that taught them to be a little more respectful of what the dogs could do.

Then we went to the greenhouse and worked there for a bit. Felicia had everything under control. She gave us easy things to do. We didn't have to plant anything, just water and pick the ripe vegetables. The Community had trimmed back on what they planted. Now, they had only three or four heads of lettuce ripen each day as opposed to a hundred a week when guests were still coming. Same for all the other vegetables, although with the horses, maybe they would need to ramp up production. The horses could eat a hundred heads of lettuce a week, along with the peppers, green beans, and anything else that would grow. But I'm sure Colleen had already thought about what the horses needed and put in her order.

Nothing to worry about. Maybe another soak in the pool. This time, we took the twins with us.

It was very nice to relax. Felicia, Amber, and Martha were the only ones left behind besides us. Martha promised to make us lunch.

Amber was doing laundry. Everyone changed their own sheets, but they didn't have to launder them. They piled things up and, as part of the work groups, people rotated through doing the laundry. They could do it all in a couple of loads, so people looked forward to getting this duty. It only took a few minutes' worth of work over the course of two or three hours.

We spun up the DVD player and watched the old animated Disney *Pinocchio*. The twins loved it. That made it a timeless classic. Next up would be *Snow White*, the original color animation. I was glad that the resort had these on hand. It always made for a nice visit.

It also gave us time to think about how we were raising them. Movies represented a time to relax, maybe even learn to dream. The rest of the time, they were learning and doing. They were listening as we read and even trying to read for themselves. They were learning to build, even if it was only with their Legos. Light duty for me meant light duty for them, too.

Look at how far we had come as a family. I couldn't imagine anything different or better. Maybe we had done what we could, but we needed the twins to grow up, be responsible. We never knew when they'd have to fill in for one of their parents.

Life was dangerous, though probably less dangerous than before, when they could have been run over in a parking lot. The dangers now were fewer by orders of magnitude. We weren't exposed to disease, although I wasn't sure about the mosquitoes in the summer. Who knew what they had gotten into?

RUN

I couldn't control that any more than I could control a wolf pack. Address it, and move on. We hadn't seen the wolves since they had attacked the Dog Musher. I think my 45-70 had made an impression on them!

The movie credits rolled, and the twins cheered. Everyone loves a good story. I scooped them both into a big hug. If they were to tell their story, it would be a good one, wouldn't it?

"Let's see what's for lunch."

THE HAUL

It was a huge relief to hear the convoy pull back into the parking lot of the resort. They were honking their horns to get our attention. They hung out the open windows, yelling and cheering. We went outside, clapping and hollering.

From my initial impression, I couldn't see what they hadn't taken. It seemed like they had emptied the store. From fifty-pound bags of rice to small jars of pickle relish. They even had packs of tortillas.

I have to say that I was very happy to see case upon case of various salad dressings. I liked the fresh vegetables, but they needed a little extra something. I guess I was old school that way.

Lucas made a beeline for Amber, while Sam went to Martha. Everyone hugged. There is nothing like the pure joy of a successful hunt. They had gone on an adventure, to help themselves, to help us all. They had taken a risk going to town, but they'd won a victory for the Community.

Darren and Becca held hands, looking through the horse trailer. People had their personal favorites. I wondered what they had their eye on.

"Jerky," Darren said as I looked questioningly at him. He pulled a pack out of his pocket and offered me a piece. I looked over my shoulder for Colleen. I didn't see her. I took a piece. Jerky was timeless. I chewed it, savoring its salty goodness.

"What are you eating?" Colleen had materialized in front of me. I hadn't realized that I had closed my eyes. I could only stammer. I kept chewing, so I could put the last piece in my mouth. Too late. She ripped it out of my hand. Madison appeared right behind her and glared at me.

"I, I, I…" I was at a complete loss for words. Darren shrugged. Some dog came running by and took the jerky right out of Colleen's hand. He took off, chased closely by two other hungry dogs.

Jo took over and saved me from further embarrassment.

"All right, people! Let's get this unloaded. We have a feast to prepare!" We lined up to pass boxes and bags into the storeroom. "Not you!" Jo shouted, pointing at me.

"I'm just getting the twins. That's all. Everyone stop yelling at me." I leaned down on one knee to scoop up the twins, but instead, got a face full of Husky. Then Phyllis jumped in, too. I herded our two dogs and the twins into the dining room. We needed some music. This was a celebration.

I put on Led Zeppelin, their first album. I had all their albums on my phone, which I always had with me, although it was only on when I used it to play music.

My wallet was in my pocket, too. I wrapped my hand around it. It had a comforting feel. When this one wore out, what would I do? Probably sew it up and keep it going until it could go no further. The same thing I expected from myself.

WINTER

Winter came a full month after the great raid on the grocery store of Fred Meyer. We had gone back to our house and weren't doing too much. We spent a lot of time playing outside with the twins. Since we had power, we used our blower to clean the leaves off of our driveway and out of our yard. I put my chainsaw to good use, knocking down a couple trees that we might have problems with in the winter. I didn't care if any trees fell into power lines. That was a concern for a different era. The here and now depended on the integrity of our home and, secondarily, access to the road.

And at some point in the distant future, I would have to cut and split firewood.

Unless we moved to Chena Hot Springs. I knew we didn't want to make the trek to Canada while the twins were still small. We also liked our home as it was, but were we so resistant to change that we maintained our home when the Community could use our help? We would have to talk about it. Our equipment would start breaking down. We'd run out of gas. We wouldn't be able to maintain our home. Why wait until we had no choice? What kind of message did that send to our fellow survivors, our friends?

Colleen, Sam, and Martha had all moved to the Community. With each person, the Community became stronger. With the first child born, the Community would become a real place where children could grow up.

Which brought out something I was afraid of, that the twins would be denied the opportunity to find someone to share their lives with. I wanted more children to be born, and then they would have choices, assuming nothing else changed between now and when they hit that age. That was a long ways off. For it to come to fruition, we'd have to do as Sam suggested. Plan for tomorrow; live for today.

RUN

I checked the snow machines, oiled them, charged the batteries, and took each for a test drive. Everything was in good working order. The belts were in good shape. Although we'd ridden them one hundred miles every weekend last winter, they weren't hard miles. We didn't drive them over rocks or into gullies. We kept to the roads, and that kept our snow machines in good shape.

During the down time between summer and winter, I fabricated better sleighs to tow behind the sleds. These were bigger, without being wider. There was a better place for the dogs to sit, while still having enough room for cargo. These were the things I had wanted last winter when we made do with what we had. This winter, we were in a better place.

The wood burner worked well to heat the house, although it took quite a bit to get used to cooking on it. We had many an undercooked or overcooked meal before we learned.

We still had propane, thanks to the gas station, but that might not last the winter. We still kept it as a backup.

We ran the generator for a few hours in the morning and then again in the evening. We didn't run it overnight. We used rechargeable flashlights for light the rest of the time. We didn't need to charge a battery to run the pellet stove. The wood burner didn't use electricity. In other words, we didn't need to run the generator at all, although it was nice having running water.

The outhouse would never make for a comfortable reading room. When it was warm enough to relax, the bugs were out. When there were no bugs, it was cold. It took all the fun out of taking care of business.

I never was able to figure out how to pump the septic, but we probably only had six or seven months of use on it, so we could probably get through this winter without any problem. I didn't want to risk a backup or a break in the line. We'd do without indoor plumbing except as a last resort.

STAY OR GO?

That still did not help me understand why we were so determined to stay in our house. A year after the detonation, we knew what we needed to survive. It wasn't much from the past. Arms and ammunition, seeds, food, water, fuel. Maslow comes to mind. Artwork, trinkets, souvenirs, Marine Corps memorabilia. None of it mattered in this new world.

We may find ourselves spending more and more time at the resort, until one day, we simply don't come back to the house. Our house wasn't built for living long term without electricity.

It was soon to be a relic of a more technological time. As were we. The twins could be the foundation of a new generation that needed no electricity.

The most important thing was that they were happy. This is the lesson that I constantly relearned. When we beat back one threat to us, I looked for the next. I looked to build one good thing on another, never satisfied with reaching a goal. There would always be a new goal, and it would be just out of reach. That was my personal problem, and I wrestled with it daily. Madison knew it was there, tormenting me.

We couldn't make our house anything like what the Community had. We could live alone, but if we were able to shape our interactions with others, then we could be true to ourselves. True to our introverted selves, that is, while still contributing. It offered us the opportunity to balance our privacy with our commitment to the group. It offered us the chance to raise our twins in a way where they could choose friends, family, and strangers.

Our dogs were pack animals though. They seemed to thrive in the chaos of the sled-dog pack.

Last year, when we made the decision to stay, we didn't have as much information as we did now.

If we left today to winter over in the Community, the only thing I would feel bad about was all the work that we'd done to get ready to spend winter in our home. That wasn't time ill spent. It gave us options and, in this world, options are good. If you had no options, then you would be forced onto a path you may not like. So our preparations were sound. We could transport a great deal of the food to the Community, so it wouldn't go to waste.

I had learned what it took to garden and grow, can and freeze. We had all learned, and that made the time spent even better. We'd given ourselves options and the ability to give ourselves more options in the future. I'd talk to Madison and see what she thought.

THE BABY

As October approached November, the Community buzzed with anticipation. According to Colleen, Amber was progressing nicely. And she now had company because Becca was now pregnant, too, and due in May.

Everyone pitched in to set up one of the guest rooms as a birthing room. It had a cooktop to heat water, plenty of extra towels, an oversized Jacuzzi tub, and all the medical supplies that Colleen thought she needed. She had never delivered a baby before, but she had brought her books and studied up.

The first false labor came at three in the morning. Everyone jumped to it, groggily at first, but after spending the next three hours in the birthing room, the contractions went away, and most people staggered back to their beds to get more sleep. It was still dark, of course. This was Alaska in the winter. Sunrise was probably closer to ten a.m. Did we remember to do the daylight-savings thing? Maybe we had no idea what time it really was.

Amber's water broke two days later, again at three a.m. The baby was coming.

Amber was howling in pain. Lucas was a wreck. Colleen's nerves were frayed, and she was tired because she hadn't caught up on sleep from their trial run. Jo helped with filling the tub, but it wasn't going fast enough, so she started yelling at Lucas, who was by this time completely incapacitated. Abigail had practiced as Amber's Lamaze coach, but she was nowhere to be found.

We were at home when this all happened, so we heard it secondhand.

In the end, Colleen lost her patience and chased everyone out of the birthing room except for Lucas. She had to grab him by both arms and shake him like a rag doll.

"Your job is to hold her hand. That's it. Now do it!" Colleen screamed in his face.

"I think I'm gonna puke," Lucas mumbled weakly.

"If you puke, aim it that way." She pointed away from where she was working. "And then I will punch you in the face as hard as I can!"

"I'm here for you," Amber gasped between contractions. Then squeezed Lucas's hand to the breaking point as another contraction wracked her body. The pain took away his nausea. He locked eyes with Amber and attempted to soothe her. Colleen was happy that he had pulled his head out of his butt and started to help. He had the easiest job. She would still probably kick him later.

"That's it, that's it. I see the baby's head!" Colleen exclaimed. "One big push. Now!" After the head, Colleen helped work the shoulder out, and then the rest of the baby's body followed. The little girl started crying as Colleen wrapped her in a soft towel. She supported the baby's head and carefully handed her to Amber. "Say good morning to your daughter."

And that's when Lucas passed out cold. Colleen kicked his leg out of the way as she helped adjust Amber into a sitting position. Amber looked alarmed.

"Don't worry about him. He'll be fine." Colleen waved dismissively. "Men…"

CHRISTMAS

We decided that we would move to Chena Hot Springs, but after Christmas. We were very comfortable as the generator supplied the power that helped heat and pump the water that allowed us to use the inside toilets and the shower. We were warm and clean.

I didn't think we needed to top last year's heart pendants that we gave the twins. Christmas wasn't about giving bigger and better. We'd had that conversation last year. How well I remembered how Charles had turned me in for feeding him McDonald's French fries.

The twins were a mature three, going on four. They would now have to act as older cousins for Amber and Lucas's daughter, Diane. They had responsibilities. We thought that was good for them.

Maybe our one present was something we could do for the new parents. The resort had cribs for guests with babies, but didn't have a changing table. I knew where nice changing tables were located. We could get one and refinish it, personalize it for Lucas and Amber. It would take work, but it was something that we could do as a family.

When we talked, we wholeheartedly agreed that our present would be a changing table. Madison also suggested a rocking chair. We would give presents to others this year, not to ourselves. We had everything we needed, and even everything we wanted, although I would always want just a little more for my family, something just a little bit better, although they didn't care about that.

We missed Thanksgiving. We hadn't thought about it. So we decided to make Christmas a celebration of thanks. We were thankful for everything we had. We were healthy. We had not needed to fight off any wild animals so far that year. The twins were growing and contributing. Sam and Martha had become like the parents we left behind in the other world. We had grown very close to them. The twins had even started calling them Grandma and Grandpa. When at the resort, we were surrounded by good people. We were thankful for that.

We'd prepare one final feast at our home. We had some potatoes from the Community, along with carrots and onions. We had a moose roast that we could cook in the oven. In the time before, we had a magnificent kitchen. We had a number of different crock pots and roasters. We had a pan for every occasion and almost any kitchen utensil you could dream of. In the end, we went with a few cast iron pieces that worked well on the wood stove. It would be a treat to dig into our repertoire of goodies for one last hurrah.

We'd clean up, put everything away, and leave the house to freeze. We wouldn't lose what was important. We'd make trips back to pick up stuff and transport it to the Hot Springs, eventually moving everything we could use.

And with that, we had a plan and a new direction. Was it really a new direction? Most likely it was more of what we liked, with less of what we didn't. Maybe we were surrendering to my need for civilization. Manual labor was hard enough without the assistance of power tools. I couldn't imagine having to cut firewood without a chainsaw or electric log splitter. I dreaded the thought.

We wouldn't have to worry about that at the Hot Springs. We knew the routine, and it was time consuming, but not anywhere near as physically demanding as what we needed to do to maintain our own home.

Our Christmas would be about bringing joy to others. We would go through our stuff and see what would make good presents for them. And then we'd have to get on that changing table so it would be ready in time to bring some joy to the new parents, although I expect a good night's sleep would bring more joy than a changing table. With our gift, we would empathize, and the twins could take their rightful place as the over-protective cousins.

THE BIG MOVE

We had enough food and fuel to last us through the winter, but we were leaving almost all of it behind. This was therapy for me regarding working for better. Work hard, and when better appears, seize it, even if that isn't what you were working hard at initially. My stomach started churning again. I needed to get my priorities straight, reconcile what was most important, and not worry about work done that seemed wasted.

Look at how excited the twins were. They didn't care where they slept each night. They wanted to see the surprise on Amber's and Lucas's faces when we presented the changing table. They wanted to work in the stables every day, taking care of the horses and maybe even learn to ride on their own. They wanted to build their own dog-mushing teams. Madison was happy that they were happy. She was also happy that I wouldn't be alone when working. There would always be someone nearby to check on me. My stomach issue scared her, but she didn't admit it. I didn't tell anyone that it was acting up again. At the Hot Springs, it would be easier to stick with a non-offensive diet.

So we loaded everything into the sleighs, and we were traveling heavy. The dogs were squeezed into one crate because the other sleigh was loaded with a changing table and a rocking chair, both wrapped together in a blue tarp and tied down tightly. We had gifts of all shapes and sizes piled in the back. We had some clothes. We each had a child perched on the seat in front of us. We didn't want to stress out our snow machines, so we traveled at about half speed. The snow wasn't very deep. We didn't want any accidents.

It was our longest trip yet, and I was more than ready to get off the snow machine when we finally pulled in. Madison was too. Phyllis and Husky were beside themselves as we got mobbed by the sled dogs when we arrived. We turned Phyllis and Husky loose into the middle of kicked-up snow, yipping, and flying fur.

We wanted to warm up before we unloaded anything, so we went into the dining room. It was just after lunch on Christmas Day. We had left home when it became light outside, but with the solstice recently behind us, we were limited to about four hours of quasi-daylight. We'd used up the majority of that time getting here.

"We expected to see you here yesterday," a tired Amber said as we arrived. She had her sleeping baby cradled in her arms.

"We thought we'd wait until Christmas to arrive," I answered as we continued taking off coats and other layers.

"Christmas was yesterday."

Without missing a beat, Madison chimed in. "Orthodox Christmas isn't for another two weeks, so we could be way early." She smiled and held out her arms for the baby, whom Amber readily surrendered. The baby remained asleep. This was the danger zone. I was torn about taking a turn. I could only lose. If the baby woke up, I would be a buffoon. I couldn't risk it. I paid closer attention to getting the twins ready to grab some lunch. They each wanted to get in close to the baby. Their mother accommodated them by leaning down.

"Not sure how we could have gotten that wrong. Our smart phones are still pretty smart. They wouldn't have led us astray." I powered mine up. I'll be damned – December 26. I showed it to Madison. "See! I told you Christmas was yesterday." She looked at me, sighed, and then shook her head and went back to showing the baby to the twins.

I went outside. I wanted to get the gifts for the others out of the weather. I took the blue tarp off and manhandled the changing table inside. It should have been lighter. Same thing for the rocking chair. I put them in the alcove of the gift shop and covered them back up with the tarp. I brought in a fairly large bag that contained our gifts for everyone else.

I put the bag behind the desk at the lodge entrance.

We talked to Amber about joining the Community permanently. She reassured us that we were more than welcome, with only one condition. She made me promise that I wouldn't let Lucas go up in the airplane again. There was nothing to worry about on that point.

We moved into our room, which the group had kept for us throughout everything. We still had the honeymoon suite, although we had tried to give it up on a number of occasions over the past year. The group gave us credit for getting rid of John and helping to bring harmony to the Community. We appreciated it and felt most at home in this one room. Plus, it had the oversized shower for couples. It was hard to turn that down. Really hard.

When everyone rolled in for dinner, we greeted them with a hearty Merry Christmas, followed by my explanation of the time warp that cost us a day somewhere. Jo rolled out yet another wondrous meal, owing to the extra supplies from the great raid on Fred Meyer. We insisted that we would clean up, but first, we had some things to give out.

I had raided my military memorabilia for unique and small souvenirs that we could tell a story about as part of the gift. I started with Darren, as the hunter. I gave him a Ka-Bar fighting knife from my time in the Marine Corps. Its leather sheath was worn shiny. I had tied paracord to the tip of the sheath so I could keep the knife secured against my leg while crawling through the brush. I had sharpened it to a razor's edge. It was the knife of a warrior. That wasn't whom I was anymore, but Darren would go to the ends of the earth to find game to feed us all. I also gave him extra boxes of rounds for his rifle. It was all the 300 Win mag shells I could find.

For Becca, we brought one of Madison's old camouflaged uniforms, including a field jacket with liner, along with UnderArmor to wear as a base layer. As a hunter, she needed the best to keep her warm while she stalked her prey. Becca appreciated the extra clothes. She'd been making do with clothes not tailored for hunting. We thought she deserved better than that.

For Jo, we brought our Pampered Chef utensil collection. There was even a pickle grabber. It was an eclectic mix of niche kitchen items. She beamed as she thought of uses for each.

We had something for each member of the group, even Sam and Martha, although they said that their joining the Community was the best Christmas gift they could have gotten. I suspected it was second best – word that their kids were okay was probably at the top of the list. I gave Sam a special Marine Corps Ball coin, commemorating the values of the Corps. It was small, but it meant a great deal to me. Sam hadn't served, but he understood. We gave Martha two tea infusers, along with the rest of our loose leaf tea. She insisted that she would share with Madison every day until the tea was gone.

We saved the changing table and rocking chair for last. Amber and Lucas had undergone a monumental change in their lives over the past year. From two people working at a resort, to new parents helping to lead the Community. I'm not sure if they could have been happier with the furniture. We even had the height right to minimize the stress on their backs when changing little Diane. Unfortunately, we couldn't provide any disposable diapers. They were stuck with cloth, but at least they had access to a washer and dryer.

With that, we toasted to our friendship and the great things that our combined futures held. We depended on one another, and that meant I could sleep soundly at night. These were good people who would look out for us all.

IT WENT BY FAST

Our first winter as full-time members of the Community went by in a blur. Amber tried to make a motion that I be made Mayor. I politely declined. I would become a tyrant, something I feared. I also had my gastritis under control, and I wanted to keep it under control.

I dabbled in a little bit of everything, including writing our memoirs. I interviewed everyone to document their backgrounds as a part of the Community's history. We even did a presentation on the big screen television where everyone cheered and added more anecdotes.

Madison was occupied building a full curriculum of classes. The twins would need formal schooling soon because they turned four toward the end of that winter. Madison refused to compromise on this point. As the children grew up, they needed to get a base education, most importantly in how we learn. Then they would learn critical thinking. With her plan, they would complete their college-level educations by the time they were in their mid-teens. I didn't try to dissuade her. This was her forte. If anyone could pull that off, it would be her.

I remained constantly alert for aircraft. I couldn't believe that we had only been targeted one time and that the Russians were so easily lured away. There was something going on that I could not figure out. Maybe there was some clause regarding the joint U.S./Russian security of the demilitarized zone. Maybe they had handed it over to the lawyers to work out, so it would probably be a quagmire forever.

Maybe they would forget about us as people lost interest in the wilds of Alaska. They were probably rebuilding. If Washington had been hit, then that would take priority. Had to take care of the politicians first. I suspected that I would speculate for years and never come to the right conclusion. As long as they didn't bother us, we were free to make up any stories that fit the few facts we had.

Martha left us that winter. She passed away in her sleep, Sam beside her. It was tough seeing an old man cry, so we cried with him. We put her body in the ice museum until we could dig a proper grave. Sam visited her often, while spending a great deal of time whittling a grave marker for her. It turned out to be a magnificent sculpture and was a proper tribute to her and to his love for her.

Besides Martha, we had no other surprises that winter. We had plenty of food, and everything worked like it was supposed to work. Sam's loss probably encouraged him to increase what he felt he needed to pass on regarding engineering in general and the systems at Chena Hot Springs in particular. He knew about small engines. We temporarily lost one of our snow machines that I was attempting to overhaul under Sam's watchful eye. I learned a great deal, but we had to completely tear it apart after I had it all together because of something I had done wrong. Who could have known that if you didn't get the keyhole retainer right, the engine wouldn't run....

Diane was five months old when Becca and Darren's baby was born. He was a strapping lad with lungs on him that could have given bagpipes a run for their money. Everyone got to share in the experience whenever little Bill woke up hungry. I called him Master William as he had the voice that could call moose from two hills away. When he grew up, we wouldn't let him forget what he did to the Community's calm. Abigail said that she could hear him from the kennel, so she took to sleeping with the windows closed.

The twins turned four right around Bill's birthday. We had a big celebration, that included presenting the twins with their own mini dog sleds that Sam and I had constructed from birch boughs.

We made a few runs back to our home to pick up other things and supplement the already abundant food supply at the Hot Springs. More than a year later, I still had a number of specialty mustards at home. I eventually brought all of these, too, as they made our moose burgers unique.

In the background, we almost always started or ended an evening with REM's "It's the End of the World as We Know It." And I felt fine.

I made sure that I touched my wife whenever I was near her. We would hold hands while eating, so I learned to eat left-handed. I committed to this physical link of what it meant to live for today, while planning for tomorrow. Why eat if there wasn't going to be a tomorrow? We worked with the twins on one thing or another. They were learning to hold their own when they went outside.

The sled dogs created a certain amount of chaos at all times. The twins learned karate moves to deflect a dog's energy past them and then kept walking as if nothing had happened.

Despite our best efforts at controlling breeding, we had three litters of puppies that spring, not the least of which was from Husky. She hadn't been spayed by the time we rescued her, so she was an open target. Not sure which of the males was the father, I gave them all a good tongue lashing when we realized Husky was pregnant with a litter.

Eventually, Abigail corralled the dogs and tied them back to their posts. The number of adult dogs had dropped to about forty, and we had twenty-four puppies. Those little fellows were cute as can be. Phyllis adopted all the litters, although she deferred to the mothers. She still took it upon herself to provide some training to the little ones. Once they were mobile, they would mob the Alpha. I don't know if that was a motherly instinct or what, but Phyllis took it all in stride and played her role well. We did have to bandage her tail more than once. A pit bull's tail isn't furry like an Alaskan husky's. It seemed like the puppies made it a game of trying to bite Phyllis' tail. More than one puppy got nipped when it got caught.

Returning the dogs to the kennel created a new calm at the resort. You didn't have to watch your step or be on the lookout for getting bowled over whenever you went outside.

BECOMING MORE ISOLATED

We lost one of the snow machines on a run back to our home. I think we blew the engine. It made for a short trip as we piled on one sled and its towed sleigh for a return trip back to the Hot Springs. We figured this was the start of many vehicle failures. None of them had been serviced for at least a year and a half. They would fail, and we couldn't replace them. As the gas started to get bad, they would fail more quickly. Our time with gas-powered machines was drawing to a close.

With an eye toward a final trip, we took all the wheeled vehicles we had and, once the snow cleared sufficiently, we made one last run to Fred Meyer to clean out the store. We tried other places as well, taking everything that wasn't nailed down. It took two trips, and when we called it a day, there wasn't much left of value in the small slice of the city that remained. We cleaned out the pharmacy at Walgreens. Maybe Colleen could set up something like a formal clinic for us. With our growing population, who knew what would crop up.

As we transitioned toward summer, we needed to look at the myriad of things that we needed to do to get ready for winter. It wasn't as daunting here since we had power. There were fireplaces, but they were more for show. We didn't need to put up much split firewood. All the wood we needed could be done in a single day.

The big event was fixing the roof of our main lodge. We only had three ladders and no shingles. None of the places in Fairbanks that would have had shingles survived. We had to go "shopping," in my use of the term, elsewhere. There was a small subdivision that had been under construction in Two Rivers, only about thirty-five miles away. We took the convoy to see what was available. Sam looked like a kid in a candy store. He had clearly gotten over his aversion to taking other people's stuff. I wondered how the insurance companies were handling the complete write off of a state? "Sorry, war clause, no money for you…"

When we talked about the new homes being built, we envisioned something a little different. We were thinking that we'd whip in, take building supplies that were neatly piled, and then return home. But Fairbanks had been attacked at the end of November, which meant new construction had already been underway for a while. The roofs were finished, and the houses were already enclosed. We'd have to take the shingles down, one by one. If we wanted anything else, we'd have to dismantle the house. Emma volunteered to take word back to the Hot Springs, while the rest of us determined to stay as long as it took to get what we needed.

Three days, four stitched-up cuts, and two mashed fingers later, we had our vehicles loaded. I gave the finger to the construction site and was glad that I'd never have to look at it again. We were hungry, thirsty, and tired. Most importantly, we hadn't repaired our own roof yet.

When we did get things set up, it went quickly. Everyone helped. Jo even set up a barbecue outside. Not having dogs running everywhere had its benefits. Although we all loved the dogs and most visited the kennels daily, there was a serenity in not having their hungry eyes watching every bite you took.

We built a scaffolding first, and then a couple of us worked the old tiles off. Sam led the process of putting the new tiles on. No one was overworked, and, at the end, I took the time to enjoy an ice cold beer. I usually didn't drink. One beer made me feel bad, so I didn't have a second.

These things kept us close. How much did companies pay to create artificial team-building events? Here, we were getting the ultimate experience. We still found some petty things to create conflict, but they went away quickly.

Becca heard someone call Bill "that little hell spawn," and she was miffed for a few days. But Bill made everything right by finally sleeping through the night. After everyone got more sleep, things calmed down quickly.

People settled in to doing the things that needed done, helping one another with chores, and just being friendly. It reminded me of episodes of *Gunsmoke* or *Little House on the Prairie*. Everyone knew everyone else, and most people liked and looked out for one another.

We had plenty of food. We committed to learning what it would take to make flour since fresh bread was always a highlight. Sam and I spent a lot of time wandering the hillsides, talking about it and other things. We also figured that we would need animal transport at some point. Sled dogs were fine in the winter, but in the summers, we'd need horses.

Unfortunately, Colleen's horses were all mares. We had to take a lesson from the natives, which meant capturing caribou and domesticating them. That would be tough. We'd have to do it if we wanted milk, unless wild cows were running around somewhere. Doubtful as they couldn't survive the harsh cold. Maybe we could try domesticating moose. Alaskan natives had done it at one point. I'd seen pictures at the University.

ANOTHER YEAR

The second summer turned into the third winter, which transitioned to the third summer. We ran out of flour, salad dressing, mustard, barbecue sauce, and those things that add flare to the meal. We learned that everything tasted great without the extras, although that didn't keep us from trying to make our own condiments.

It took a few tries to make our own vinegar. After that, we set up a mini-vinegar factory to make the one thing we could use for everything, from cleaning to making our own salad dressing. We had to be careful with the dressing. Our vinegar had a hearty kick.

The Community adopted the babies, so no one had to raise their children alone. Diane was a cute little girl, shy and really smart. Bill was Bill. He was precocious and always in motion. We had to take turns watching him because he wore everyone out. He loved the hills, taking after his parents even at an age where he hadn't been walking for long. I swear he went from crawling to running in the course of a week.

Emma and Jo wanted to have a baby of their own, so they contracted with Chris. It was the twenty-first century, and although there was no anonymity, they were all very adult about it. It didn't take long, and Emma became pregnant. At the same time, Colleen became pregnant. Although Chris had been spending more and more time at the stables, it was interesting that no one realized that they had become a couple. Colleen was about fifteen years older than Chris, but in the Community, character trumped all. Chris was probably the best of us. He didn't complain. Unless you looked closely, you didn't see that he worked harder than anyone. He was quiet, and often we let him sit outside a conversation. That reflected on us, not him. He was better than that. He was better than us.

In the third year, Amber and Sam asked him to be Mayor. He didn't want to accept, but we supported the motion so strongly that we left him with little choice. He was a natural leader, and his motives were always what was best for the Community. That was also what made Amber so effective. We had foisted the role of Mayor on her, too. I liked our version of elections. One should always be suspect of a person who wants to be elected into a public-service position. I don't believe anyone is that selfless. If they were, they would already be contributing to the greater good without having to stand up before God and the world to extoll their own virtues.

Amber was happy to step back and, with Madison's help, become one of our teachers. We didn't call any of it daycare. We were raising the children to be productive members of our small society. I could not have been more proud of my family and the role that they played.

The twins were growing up in a world that we had never envisioned for them. There were sixteen of us and that was every human being that they knew. They knew all the dogs by name. Husky's puppies weren't good as sled dogs since they were a little too beefy, so the twins each adopted one as their own. Having four dogs in our rooms was a bit much, so we acquired two small rooms in the lodge and gave the twins their own rooms. That was an interesting development, which led to room inspections, which led to some wailing and gnashing of teeth, which led to fewer room inspections. It was surprising that we had raised slobs. I take no credit for that.

We left the resort only a couple times that third summer. It was becoming too risky. The Jeeps were dead. The trucks were mostly dead. No one wanted to break down fifty miles from the resort. We always took bicycles with us when we left, just in case our last two vehicles went belly up. We weren't opposed to walking, but why, if you didn't have to?

We were more successful at fishing that third summer. We drove a dog team down the road, using the wheeled sleds. That was a wild ride, but it got us where we wanted to go. The stream was cold and clear. Since it hadn't been fished for a few years, the grayling had grown numerous. We even found deeper holes where rainbows were hanging out. It was nice taking a big haul of fish back to the Community. We even had enough to share with the dogs. They deserved a treat after dragging us down there and back.

After Martha passed away, Sam seemed to age quickly. Although he had fewer and fewer chores, he tried to work even harder. At the end of the third summer, his heart finally gave out. We dug his grave next to Martha's. We set some wood aside for a monument that we'd work on over the winter. He deserved it. He deserved a nice monument next to the one he had carved for Martha.

The twins were more torn up than I would have thought. Sam and Martha had only been in their lives for the last couple years, but in their view they had just lost the last of the only grandparents they had known. They were too young when they met our parents to remember them.

To get them out of their funk, we constantly bombarded them with questions about what Sam taught them about this or that. Sure. We put him on a pedestal for them, but he was on one for us, too. He'd had a gentle way of sharing his in-depth knowledge of any topic. He was the encyclopedia to which we no longer had access.

With Sam's passing, I became the grand old man of the Community. I had been before Sam and Martha joined us, but after that, Sam showed the power of a true patriarch. I would always pale in his shadow, and I was good with that. Everyone has their unique gifts. I wouldn't let us down, but I wasn't Sam.

So we moved forward with more canning, more creative condiment development, broader growing, and still no flour. We'd have to figure that out.

We captured two caribou. Females keep their antlers throughout the winter so they can protect their food supply from the lazy males. Ours were female. We were so happy when we finally got them in the enclosed pasture with the horses. One problem though. Whenever we tried to interact with them, well, they had antlers and weren't afraid to use them. I got my head racked pretty hard once. I woke up back at the lodge with Madison looking at me, wearing a worried expression. I had twelve stitches to remind me that domesticating a wild animal could be dangerous. I pitied the person who tried to milk one.

We had plenty of meat and plenty of vegetables. The geothermal power plant continued to work well. Sam had trained all of us on the system, so we knew what to look out for. As long as we had power, we had it all.

JUST BECAUSE YOU'RE PARANOID DOESN'T MEAN THEY AREN'T WATCHING YOU

I was always wary. Charles and Aeryn probably thought I was a bit of a nut, looking at the horizon. Stopping and listening. "Dad!"

They were learning to hunt. They were skilled in the woods. They were five going on six years old, but they were seasoned in what hunting was all about. They said prayers over the downed animal. They respected the sacrifice. Their little hands were more adept at intricate skinning than I was. They could field dress a moose, with help, as a moose was simply too big for them to lift even a single leg.

Our fourth winter arrived as winter always did in Alaska. A little here, a little there, a brief respite, and then snow and lots of cold.

Unfortunately, unwanted company arrived as we approached the winter solstice.

We saw the jets before we heard them. A flight of two, they looked Russian to me, maybe MiG-27s. They made one pass relatively slowly. We hadn't practiced our emergency evacuation in a long time. I hoped that everyone remembered what we used to do. I was outside and immediately raised the alarm. Others heard me and picked it up. People poured outside and raced for the nearest woods. I saw the twins running ahead of Madison with the dogs close on their heels. Emma was very pregnant and making the best time she could. I ran back to help Jo with her and we all waddled and frog marched as fast as we could. Colleen and Chris were at the stable on the other end of the runway. I hoped they were able to take cover.

The second pass was coming in much faster. We pushed Emma to the ground and shielded her with our bodies. We never saw the bombs drop, only felt the concussion and the debris as our world was blown apart. We shook ourselves off and continued to the woods. Emma was in a bad way. I thought she might be going into labor.

The jets made one more pass, dropping one bomb each which leveled most of the remaining compound. We waited in the woods, huddled together for warmth. Not all of us had jackets on. I was proud that people remembered what I'd tried to teach after our first encounter with the military. Time was more critical than any one thing. Get out first, we'll figure out the rest later.

We had put together a cache of goods at the yurt on the hill. The couples all ended up there for a night away on occasion, so it didn't hurt having extra stuff that anyone could use.

Last time, the helicopters arrived about five hours after the jets. I didn't know if the helicopters were coming or not, but didn't feel like they would. If the helicopters were coming, they would have no need to level the compound. I figured that they simply wanted us to not exist. Maybe the negotiations for the territory had finally concluded. I could see our government caving, believing that no one was alive. It seemed that the Russians were trying to make our nonexistence a reality.

In any case, we couldn't stay here. We made a stretcher out of two poles and two coats and carried Emma to the stables. Terrified horses had bolted, knocking the door down. They were still running mad in the pasture. Our two caribou were gone. I expected the fence was down somewhere.

Colleen took over with Emma, trying to calm her down. Jo was helping. There was no room for the rest of us. We went back to the compound. Chris continued to the kennels to check on Abigail.

There wasn't much left. We found things we could use as rags, some frozen food that we could salvage. None of our canned goods survived. Canning was a misnomer as we used only glass jars. They couldn't withstand the concussion from the bombs.

We had to decide on a course of action, just like last time. Stay or go?

WE CAN'T STAY

We lost one of our own in the bombing, a minor miracle and a tragedy at the same time. Felicia had been in the greenhouse. When we found her, there wasn't much left. The greenhouse had provided no protection from the bomb blast.

We broke up into two groups. One was at the stable helping Colleen with Emma. The other was at the kennel where the building was still mostly intact. One side of the structure leaned, but had gone as far as we thought it would. A number of dogs had succumbed to falling debris. Abigail was in tears.

I looked to Chris. "What do you think, wild man?" He looked out over the kennel. Even now, he didn't look rattled.

"Are they coming back?" Then he added, "What do we have left?" He had gone straight to the kennel, not looking closely at the destruction in the main compound.

"I don't think they'll be coming back. Why? No power. No food. No water. No shelter." I was not trying to be dramatic, but it came across that way. He narrowed his eyes as he looked at me. "It's all gone."

Chris moved over to Abigail, who had survived it all without a scratch.

"Abigail," he said softly, putting a hand on her shoulder to get her attention. She looked at him, trying to blink the tears away. "How many dog sleds can we run if we hook them all up?" We had all trained somewhat with dog mushing, but we had very few lead dogs.

"Let's get the sleds out and start hooking up the dogs. I think it's time to leave, and we have a long ways to go," Chris said calmly, but with determination. The decision was made.

We all pitched in getting things ready. We were able to save a couple of the less injured dogs. The others had to be put down. I took care of that myself, remembering a long time before when I had put down a dog in a house not far from our own using the same pistol.

I had a good deal of ammunition left because I stored all of it in our long-dead Jeep at the side of the compound. The Jeep had come through the explosions with scratches and dents only. The buildings on the other hand succumbed instantly to the high explosives.

I had all of our traveling kit in the Jeep, a tent, sleeping bags, some bottled water, "shopping" tools, our little BioLite camp stove, and other such items. We had carried this kit for years, not ever needing it. We didn't want to ever have to use it, but unfortunately, now it would get its chance to help save our lives. I pulled out the two duffels containing our gear and put them on the hood of the Jeep.

I turned back to look at the compound and watched the glow from our smoldering home for just a minute. There was nothing to do there. It was time to get to work to ensure our survival.

TODAY'S MY BIRTHDAY

Emma was in a great deal of pain. She wasn't communicating, so all Colleen could do was make her press forward with the birth. She put a blanket down and tried to make Emma as comfortable as possible. The baby was coming, no matter what.

Jo held a flashlight, but she was shaking badly. Madison was doing all she could to try to calm Emma down. Colleen knew something was wrong when blood came out the birth canal. They needed the baby out now. Because of the light, she couldn't see the top of the head. She felt Emma's abdomen and it seemed like the baby was in the right position.

"Push!" she yelled. "Push!" The head started to appear and Colleen helped guide the baby out. The placenta had broken apart during the events of the day and that was the blood and gore that preceded the baby. Emma calmed immensely after the delivery of her little boy. He had a blend between her pale skin and Chris' dark skin. He had a full head of curly black hair. Covered in afterbirth, he was a mess, but a beautiful mess that Jo and Emma were proud to call theirs.

Colleen was worn out. She was about eight months pregnant herself and this had been a trying day. She staggered away, bundled herself up, and fell asleep in the corner of the stable.

Little Tony was a trooper from the word go. It seemed that he had had plenty of the birthing business and fell fast to sleep after he was cleaned and fed. Emma fell asleep with him. Jo wasn't much better off, but we needed her help. We needed to get ready to go.

MUSHING THE BACK COUNTRY

We were able to hook up five sleds, although Abigail wasn't certain about their effectiveness. She had two strong teams. The twins each had their own six-dog teams pulling small sleds, Husky's puppies being half of their teams. They were fun to watch, but this was going to be real. The worst that could happen was that we had to abandon their sleds and some of the dogs. No one wanted that, but we couldn't stay. With the twins driving their own teams, we gave twelve more dogs a chance to live.

The third big team was mostly untrained, but without the extra sled, we couldn't carry everyone and our supplies.

I would lead the way in my stalwart snow machine, the one that Sam had me tear apart over and over. I knew the machine, and I knew it would run. I filled the sleigh with five-gallon cans of gasoline. If we were able to stick with the shortest route, we only needed to cover a few hundred miles to reach Canada. The towns of Boundary, Forty Mile, or even Dawson awaited us.

We hoped.

Jo helped us gather what food items we could find. We did not have very much. We needed the stores at the yurt on the hill. I took the snow machine on a quick trip. I filled the sleigh with blankets, food, and drinks. It still wasn't very much. We needed water. We had smoked moose at the kennel for the dogs. It would feed us, too, because it had to.

We needed to head east, northeast. If we hit the Yukon River, we could follow that into Canada. It would be longer that way, but manageable. I needed to be able to navigate the route, in the dark of winter. My stomach twisted into a knot.

RUN

I wasn't confident that I could do it. I met with Darren and Becca. They had traveled into the hills around the Hot Springs on quite a few hunts. They weren't familiar beyond about fifty miles, but that was much more than what I knew.

I changed places with Darren. He'd take the snow machine, and I'd ride with Madison in the number-three dog sled. We'd keep the twins by us. Abigail would drive the number-one team, carrying Emma, Jo, and the baby. They hooked up a sleigh, but didn't put much in it. We didn't have much. They used the blankets to pack under and over the riders.

Becca would drive the number-two team with Chris, Colleen, little Diane, and baby Bill on board. She wouldn't tow a sleigh behind her as she was already traveling with a full load.

The twins loaded their small sleds with food, water, Phyllis, and Husky. We had no other choice. We were fleeing for our lives. It wouldn't be pretty, and it wouldn't be fast.

But it needed to be fast. We couldn't survive in the wilds of Alaska as we were. I didn't know how many of us would survive the trip. We knew we couldn't stay. We had two bad options to choose from. Or did we.

As we were doing our final checks and getting people settled, Darren, Abigail, and I came to Becca's sled. "What if we go to our house back toward Fairbanks? Then we can take the southern route. It's longer, but if we keep abreast of the roadway, we'll be able to avoid the bigger mountains as well as find shelter. We might be more exposed, but if we try to go east through Alaskan wilderness for three hundred miles, I don't think we'll make it. We have a new baby and almost no supplies. Let's go toward Fairbanks and set up to do this right. We aren't ready for this, and I'm not ready to see anyone else die." I hung my head as I finished my speech. I was exhausted, and we hadn't taken the first step away from the resort.

"Thank you." That's all Chris said. I could see the relief on his face, on all their faces. I felt it energize me. I wanted to believe that the Community would be okay. This gave us a better chance. We were too close to plunging into the abyss. I was so afraid that I wasn't even sure that I could mush the dogs away from the compound.

Note to self: If a decision is so bad that you are panicking, change the decision.

Colleen was especially relieved. Going through the back country, we knew we couldn't take her horses. By taking the roads and staying out of the mountains, we gave her precious friends a chance at life. Colleen raced back to the stables and saddled up two of the three horses. They had calmed down over the past few hours and returned to the stable, only to find that they had to stay outside. Colleen rode her horse and Chris rode the other. This helped to reduce the weight on the sleds and gave us a fighting chance.

Darren and I switched places once again, Madison joined me on the snow machine. We turned our convoy around and headed down a real road with a destination less than a day away.

IT SEEMED SO CLOSE

Fifty miles is a ridiculously long mush for a five-year-old with a six-dog team. We stopped multiple times to let them rest. We even switched out, letting the twins ride while Chris and Jo took turns mushing the sleds. That was taxing as the humans had to half run to keep the sleds going. Colleen followed along with the other two horses in tow when Chris wasn't riding. The riders shuffled around the sleds until I lost track. I told Darren to make sure we didn't accidentally leave anyone behind.

About halfway there, only twenty-five miles in and twelve hours later, we daisy-chained the twins' teams, leaving a ten-dog team to pull Chris (with Phyllis and Husky on board), while we threw the other small sled atop the sleigh behind my snow machine. I put both Charles and Aeryn in front of me as I drove the sled, while Madison moved to Becca's sled to help with the babies. This made all the difference. It only took four more hours to cover the last twenty-five miles. When we were only a couple miles from the house, I raced ahead to get the wood burner fired up.

I even tried the generator, which came to life, albeit roughly after I thought my arm was going to fall off from pulling. The gasoline was starting to go bad, but it had a little juice left.

I shut off the pumps. The house had been frozen for too long. I didn't want to risk a burst pipe, not because of damage to the house, but because we needed all the space we had so people could recover. It would be a tight squeeze, but it was a means to an end.

The twins had curled up and gone to sleep on the couch. They were still wearing all their gear, but it was cold in the house. I was tired, but they were exhausted. We would need to train with the dog teams a great deal in order to make the trip. We were going to run our own Iditarod, but without any support and with five small children, maybe even six.

I'd been awake for nearly thirty hours and, as the adrenaline wore off, I felt bone tired, but there was still too much to do to stop.

I plugged in our electric heaters in the various bedrooms. It would take the edge off so people could sleep. I opened up the garage so we had a place for some of the dogs, although it was still filled with wood and water tanks. They would be exhausted, too. There were enough trees around that we could tie off other dogs to those. It was cold, but not to the extreme. Or we could use the fenced yards in the neighborhood. That would probably be better. At this point, we needed every dog we had to give us the best chance. Those we weren't able to hook up with teams had run with us. I hoped that many of them had made it all the way.

We needed a break.

At least we had some water here. We needed more bowls. I was tired and simply moving around was painful. Maybe we could sleep for a while first.

Our good people all mushed in together. First and foremost, all the babies needed to get inside where it was warm, get changed, and maybe even eat something. The mushers tied off their teams and brought out anything that would hold water. I used the hand pump to get water from our tank. Everyone got their buckets and bowls to their teams for a big drink. They passed out some smoked moose, now frozen solid, for the dogs to munch on before sleeping.

The humans were too tired to chew frozen meat. We squeezed into our house, and most people grabbed a spot on the floor to lay down. Madison and I took our own bed. The electric heater helped, but it was still cold. We slept in our clothes. I awoke when Bill let out one of his earthshaking cries. He calmed quickly when Emma gave him some now thawed smoked moose to gnaw on.

THE FIRST NEW DAY

I got up, but moved pretty slowly. I ached all over. I had no asthma medication left and was struggling to get a deep breath. There was no time for any of that. We had all of our canned supplies that we had left behind when we moved to the Community. The frozen goods had thawed and refrozen. They were no good.

I put a number of jars of green beans in the kitchen. It was now warm enough in the house that they would thaw. What we lacked in variety, we would make up for with quantity. There were leftover seasonings we could use on the beans. We could fry up some moose.

Then we could take stock of our situation. We were running for our lives, so we would make do with less. Just how much less was the question.

The twins slept like they were dead. So much so that I checked to make sure they were still breathing. I was proud of them. We had asked them to be adult too early in their young lives. And they gave us everything they had.

I went to our outhouse. It was cold. I had gotten spoiled with a heated suite and flush toilet. I wanted to be spoiled again. I was getting too old for this. But there was a world of pain and trial in front of us. If a better world was out there, we would have to earn the right to be in it. We would have to beat the odds one more time.

TRAINING

We spent the morning recovering, eating, drinking water, and resting. We were all thankful that we had not tried to head east yesterday, or was it the day before?

The sled dogs seemed like they were ready to go again, which was good since they had a great deal of work ahead of them.

In the afternoon, we hooked up the twins' sleds and one other team. We had to practice. We also needed to scout our route south. Nordale Road, the route I had recommended to John years ago in order to bypass Fairbanks, was where we'd practice. We would take that to a point where we could see North Pole and then return home.

The twins didn't want to do it. They were still tired from yesterday's run. Abigail mushed our third dog team to provide some training for them, with Madison riding. The twins each took their own sled. Charles had Phyllis as a rider. Aeryn carried Husky. I watched my family mush away. Although I considered all the Community as my family, there was no substitute for flesh and blood. I felt helpless, but Madison was with them. She carried my .45. It would have to be good enough. I had the snow machine, and if they weren't back in four hours, I would go find them. And I'd bring my 45-70 rifle.

The time went quickly as we worked through what we had. Colleen took Chris and the horses to her old house. She said that she might have some things that we could use. I think she wanted to let Chris into more of her old life. She was a far different person from the woman I'd found.

She stabled the horses and fired up her old wood burner. They would stay there to free up some room in our house. There was even some hay left for the horses. It might be bad as it was old, but it was all they had. They came back for dinner after preparing the old stable for the horses to bed down for the evening.

RUN

I was fixing what looked like our breakfast when I realized that four hours had come and gone. I asked Jo to take over as I couldn't eat while they were still out there. I bundled up, put on my helmet, and fired up the snow machine. I took it slowly out of the neighborhood and opened it up a little when I turned onto Chena Hot Springs Road. I kept the speed down as I didn't want to accidentally run into them. They had no lights. The headlights of the snow machine were all we had. I followed their tracks onto Nordale Road, but needed to go no farther. I could see them up ahead. The dogs were running well. The small teams and two sleds were side by side as they climbed the hill toward me. I turned the snow machine around so the lights weren't shining in their faces.

The twins looked tired but confident when they came up to me. I waved them onward. Phyllis tried to jump out, but Charles got her to sit back down. Husky was off before Aeryn could say anything.

The twins both mushed like champions. Abigail and Madison passed me, giving the thumbs up on their way by. I gave Husky plenty of love, and then she was off, chasing the dog teams. I followed them well back, which gave them light to finish their run. Their first real training run was complete.

For the first time, I became curious as to what they had found.

TIMING

Once they got back to the house, it took them a while to get settled. Abigail insisted that the twins take care of the dog teams themselves. If we got separated, they needed to know what to do since the dogs were their only means of transportation.

They fed the dogs and used blankets scavenged from other houses to bed them down. They provided water and watched as the dogs curled up, keeping their paws and noses inside their fluffy tails.

We welcomed the dog mushers back into the house with cheers and much clapping. The twins ran the gauntlet like NBA players heading back into the locker room after a big win.

And we ate moose and green beans like it was the best meal we'd ever had.

They had gone farther than they had intended because the road was open and the going smooth. They made it almost all the way into North Pole when they turned around. There was a little more uphill on the way back, otherwise they would have made it home sooner. All in all, it was a good training run. They learned that the road was open and North Pole was still there.

After cleaning up, we had a big meeting because we needed to make some decisions.

Chris stood as we sat around, some on chairs, some on the floor. Then he started in his soft, but authoritative way. "We decided to leave because we couldn't stay at the Hot Springs. We couldn't save Felicia. We couldn't save our home. But we saved the children. We saved the horses. We saved most of the dogs." Chris paused to take a drink of water. No one else spoke.

"If we don't have one another, we don't have anything." He paused to look around. "I believe we need to leave for Canada. If we stay, we die. If we go, we could die on the way, but we will at least have tried. I vote for the chance at life. I for one want to live." He looked purposefully at Colleen.

It didn't sound like Chris was asking people to vote. We couldn't stay. That was all there was to it.

"Chris is right. We need to leave," I chimed in. "We need to leave within the week. I think we have enough food to take with us so that we can survive a week to ten days. If we average fifty miles a day, we could get to Canada before we run out of food. If we go slower, then we'll need to find food on the way."

"Colleen and I talked. If we leave within the week, she shouldn't deliver while we are on the trail. One week helps Tony gain a little strength so he can manage, although it will be hard. If we wait until Colleen delivers, then Tony will be better off, but we'll have no food to make the trip. We have a couple rifles, so we could get a moose, but we have nothing else. We aren't carnivores, we're omnivores. The horses won't have anything to eat soon either. I know it all looks bad. Emma? Jo? The greatest risk is yours. What do you want to do?" Chris closed his speech. There would only be two votes. Whatever Emma and Jo decided, we would support. It's what we did as the Community.

Emma hugged Tony tightly and sobbed softly. Jo wrapped her arms around the two of them. Aeryn kneeled down in front of them, putting her little hands on their shoulders until they looked at her. "We can make it," was all she said. She had no idea what Canada was or where it was. She only knew what she knew. She trusted us all. She loved the dogs. She had endless faith that we were destined to live.

They pulled her into their family hug. Bill let loose with a window-rattling howl. He had never gotten over sharing his super power with the rest of us. Becca pulled him in, looking to see what was wrong. He had touched the wood burner and had a small burn on his hand. She and Darren soothed him, while Diane ran over to give him a hug.

The Community of huggers. We figured that Canada would welcome us with open arms.

"We'll be ready when we need to go. Just tell us the day," Emma stated softly.

And that was that. We needed to gather our wits, whatever supplies we needed, balance our loads, and get to getting.

But first, a good night's sleep. We needed fresh minds to take on the wilds of Alaska. And possibly the Russians. And then whatever else the world held in store for us.

THE ROAD TO SOMEWHERE

It took us five days to complete our rest and preparations. Then we left our entire world behind for the whole world that was in front of us.

I'm sure that plenty of people have been on a road to nowhere. Maybe that was the road to Chena Hot Springs. It ended at the resort, and the bombing ended the resort. That made it a road to nowhere. That's why we turned south on Nordale Road. We were now on a road to somewhere; at the very least, it was a place that I called hope.

It would have to carry us hundreds of miles. Without it, who knew what would become of our little caravan.

It consisted of five dog sleds and their teams, one snow machine, and three horses. It looked just like the group that had traveled fifty miles less than a week prior, but that was an unplanned trip made in fear. We claimed that this was different and that we were ready.

The snow machine was in the lead, and broke the trail. It pulled a heavy sled that helped compact the snow, making it easier for the dogs to run. The first team was the best dog team. They helped make the trail for the others. The next two were our twins with their small sleds and six-dog teams. Following them were the last two dog teams, not traveling as heavily as the first team. Bringing up the rear were two people with three horses. The horses carried a fair amount of weight, and the snow did not provide the best footing. We estimated that they could travel thirty to forty miles per day.

Even though that could make our trip last two weeks, we refused to split up. It was all or nothing.

The first day went smoothly as we traveled on established roads. We made it to Salcha, where we were able to find a barn. We arranged concrete blocks inside and built a small fire. We were careful to keep it contained. It was enough to warm things up above freezing, but not too much beyond that. The horses sheltered in a lean-to outside, while all the dogs slept inside with their mushers and families. Everyone benefited from the shared warmth.

Emma's baby was restless all night. He had slept during most of the trip. Being under a bundle of blankets and inside Emma's coat was probably like being in the womb. Emma stayed up, walking around and rocking him, doing her best not to step on any tails. She kept the fire going as well. Shaking out and drying diapers near the fire wasn't optimal, but she made do without complaint. Jo took a turn walking around with the baby, too.

Colleen couldn't get comfortable, and Chris did all he could to help her. No one slept well. It was cold, maybe minus ten or twenty degrees Fahrenheit. We were tired but not exhausted. We had traveled thirty miles. The horses had kept up. None of the dogs had any problems. Phyllis and Husky were bored and would run alongside the sled dogs at times. They knew when they needed to ride, so we let them do as they wanted.

Tomorrow night we'd probably sleep better. At some point, we might have to take a break for a day and let everyone rest up. Lucas and Becca could go hunting and hopefully come back with a fresh kill. We would plan that for Delta Junction, less than seventy miles away. In the morning, we'd push early and go as far as we possibly could. On our third day, I planned that we'd hole up in the hangar that Lucas and I had found at the Delta Junction Airport.

DAY TWO OF THE GREAT ESCAPE

When the time came, people simply got up. It wasn't like waking from a refreshing sleep. Emma and Tony had finally fallen asleep, and we felt bad waking her to get her into the dog sled. We ate what we could. The dogs had a little smoked moose, but we could see that they were still hungry. Iditarod and Yukon Quest dog mushers slept on the ground with their dogs and mushed up to two hundred miles in a day.

We had covered thirty, and it was already wearing us down.

I had it easiest on the snow machine. It was still running well. I'd give it a snort or two of avgas when we got to Salcha. That should help add some kick to my remaining supply of gasoline. My ride was smooth. We were on a roadway with at least a foot of snow. By riding the roads, we were able to avoid drifts and other places where the dogs and sleds could have trouble.

We figured that we would be safe on the highway until well past Delta Junction. With the detonations at Fort Wainwright in Fairbanks and Fort Greeley in Delta Junction, no one had probably traveled these roads in many years. It was dark during most of our travel, so the dog sleds and horses were safe. I had the headlights on the snow machine, but I didn't use them as often as I probably should have. I traveled slowly at times, but I'd also race ahead and return to pound down the snow of deeper areas. I didn't want to get too far in front of the dog sleds. I feared the snow. If snow came, it could quickly hide my trail that the others were following.

It remained cold out. As such, I figured I could stay a mile or two in front of the lead team. If it did start snowing, then it would warm up.

We made good time in the morning of the second day; the dogs were still fairly fresh. With only four hours of daylight, one could easily think it was much later, or earlier, than it really was. So three of us wore watches.

We called a stop at about nine thirty a.m. in what used to be a rest area. There were outhouses, which were welcomed. Since we'd been close for a long time, we had gotten past our inhibitions. If you had to go, you had to go. The men showed no shame, while the women were more civilized, and, in the end, people respected one another's dignity.

We gave the dogs a little more meat than we intended, but they were doing the hard work. We trimmed our own rations back as we were along for the ride.

I pulled Darren aside. "We need to kill something," I said.

"I know. I'm seeing tracks on the road, but I can't see any moose without more light." He licked his lips. "Even a caribou would go down pretty well right now." We watched as Colleen and Chris kicked some snow away from a grassy patch where the horses could find something to eat.

"When it gets light, I'll look for fresh tracks. I don't think we can wait until Delta Junction to feed the dogs what they need. I'll talk to Chris."

I joined Chris and Colleen to help clear some grass for the horses. It was frozen and snowy, but they would make do. They'd survived more winters in Fairbanks than just the last three.

Chris agreed that we needed to get some fresh meat for the dogs. It wouldn't hurt if we could get them something green, or even dry dog food.

"I guess I could race ahead to the next community and do some 'shopping.'" I had lost my cell phone in the bombing, but I still had my wallet and my "shopping" tools, my trusty sledge hammer, pry bar, bolt cutters, and even the Geiger counter. I thought of myself as the post-prepper, prepper reborn. It was a mouthful, but while riding the snow machine, I'd had a lot of time to myself to think.

Little Diane was getting into it. She was mobile, but we didn't have good snow boots in her size. She wore three pairs of socks to shore things up, but she still struggled through the snow. Becca was cleaning Bill up from something that he'd gotten into when he let out one of his bellows. She had to be deaf by now. I was amazed that she didn't jump like the rest of us. Darren put a calming hand on Bill's little shoulder and spoke to him soothingly. I think he might have been teething. A little snow on his gums helped.

We wrapped up after a longer break than I had intended.

The twins took care of their dog teams like adults. They even politicked to get some more meat for their teams, using those big eyes of theirs. Madison and I gave them our ration of moose meat. It wasn't much. My sled didn't need food to run. I could lose some more weight as I was far from skinny. I was still heavier than the day that I'd graduated boot camp. Madison was lighter than when we'd met. I didn't think she had anything left to lose. But if we were successful this day, then we'd eat well tonight.

I talked with Abigail to move Darren into the lead position of the dog sleds, putting him behind me. If we saw a moose, he could take his team to flush it toward me. I had my 45-70 rifle and my .45 pistol. I needed a shot within a hundred yards with the rifle to make it count. If I used the pistol, I needed to be right on top of the moose, and then it wouldn't be pretty. If I tried to use the snow machine to run down a moose, we could travel too far away from the roadway. I could wreck the sled. I thought of all kinds of bad things that could happen. Flushing a moose would be best.

It was too bad that we'd lost the 300 Win mag in the bombing. We had to count on my trusty shoulder cannon, but it had limitations.

We saddled up our caravan with the plan to stop whenever a moose was sighted. The horses brought up the rear. If we got a moose away from the road, we might need the horses to drag it to a place where we could butcher it. The horses shied at the smell of blood, but we had little choice. We might need them. Colleen and Chris hoped it didn't come to that. She was in no condition to fight a horse, and she was our best rider, of course.

We didn't need any of it. I saw no fresh moose tracks, even though I covered maybe a hundred miles by ranging far and wide away from our direction of travel. Our caravan continued down the main road as we discussed, and I met up with them at different times. I didn't need to say anything. I simply shook my head. They could all see my lack of success.

DOG FOOD

We found a home with an RV-sized garage not far off the road. There was also a big fenced-in area that looked like a former kennel. I broke into the house and the garage without the least concern. I had long ago lost my list of what I had taken. It didn't matter anymore. This was survival, and I would do what I had to for my extended family. I'd do it without remorse.

We found bags of dog food. Eighty pounds would go a long way. Although we had about fifty dogs with us, they were mostly lean Alaskan huskies, marathon runners all. They weighed between thirty and forty pounds each. Phyllis and Husky were bigger, but they were the exception.

We still needed something to eat. In my mind, I kept planning for two more weeks. Always two more weeks. That would give us a reserve because professionals talk logistics. Without food, our journey would end very quickly.

Chris and I went outside to take care of our personal business. I looked around to make sure no one was near. "Chris. How would Colleen be if we have to kill one of the horses to feed the dogs?"

Chris hung his head low. I wasn't the first to think about that option. "She would hate you forever."

"Yeah. That's what I thought. We'll know it's time when the dogs can no longer pull the sleds. Even then, I'm not sure I could do it. Colleen doesn't need to know we talked about this."

"She already knows. Not you, I mean, but that dogs have eaten horsemeat for millennia. It would be more natural than we admit." Chris finished his business and turned toward me. "Take that rifle of yours and go get a moose. You're the one who showed us more options lead to better decisions." He held his hand out to me. I took it, and we shook. "Give us more options," he encouraged.

RUN

It was another clear evening, which meant it was cold. I couldn't sleep. I was worried. I felt it was my responsibility to feed us, so I got up. I refilled the snow machine and took off down the road. I had the lights on and did a lazy "s" pattern to show the road and what was on either side.

JOHN

While trying to run ahead in our limited daylight and hoping to see a moose, I almost drove through a sharp corner. I slid the snow machine sideways, stopping in time to avoid a gully beyond. There was a barrier beside the road, but it had been broken through some time ago. The edges were rusted.

The snow covered what looked like a snow machine pulling a sleigh. I climbed down to see what was in the sleigh and was rewarded by finding jerky and candy and other things necessary for survival on the open road.

Hey! That was our blanket.

I dug through the snow to find the snow machine that Madison used to drive.

I looked for a pile that might be a person.

I found a mound of snow on the other side of the gully. I dug into it and found a body, mostly decomposed, but the helmet was familiar.

So this was all the farther that John had made it. With the snow machine, this was a little over one hundred miles from the resort. John probably died the night he left as he raced ahead in the darkness, counting on the snow machine's headlights to show the way.

What an arrogant ass.

The way the sleigh was packed tightly, much of the supplies had survived the past three years. I started to dig out the sleigh, hoping to drag that back to the top of the embankment. Once I got to the gas cans, I put those aside. I didn't need that fuel. It was probably bad.

After that, the sleigh was much easier to move. I worked it free of the snow and ice. I tied one end of a rope to my sled and the other to the sleigh in the ditch.

It pulled up the embankment and onto the roadway. After moving the food supplies to my sleigh, I pulled John's sleigh into the middle of the road where the others wouldn't miss it. The sleeping bag would come in handy, as would the tent.

I drove on, looking for the ever-elusive next meal.

CHASING CARIBOU

After about twenty miles farther south, I saw what looked to be a herd trail that crossed the road. It had to be caribou. Moose didn't travel like this. I stopped and searched through the torn-up snow. Plenty of droppings – caribou. They were faster than moose and smaller targets. I turned off the road and followed their trail. I tried to judge how many were in the herd, but that was beyond my capability. The snow was tracked heavily in a swath fifty feet wide.

It seemed as if they were walking. The tracks were close together. They couldn't be far. As I continued on for a couple miles, the track length increased, and the ground churned up more deeply. They had started to run. I assumed that they'd heard the snow machine. They'd headed for a wooded area. As I swept my headlights, I still didn't see the herd, but there was an open valley to the right. Maybe I could get past them before they were through the woods.

I accelerated away from the trail and tried to flank the herd. The valley paralleled the trees for some distance. I raced ahead and then turned down a trail into the woods. I slowed and shut off the snow machine. I could hear them.

Were they coming this way? I jogged ahead, staying close to the trees where there was less snow. My breath came in ragged gasps. I had to stop. I was getting lightheaded. I tried to listen, but asthma attacks always made my eardrums pound. I couldn't hear much, but I started to feel the vibrations in the tree I was hiding behind as the herd approached. They were coming right at me. The woods weren't thick, but there weren't long lines of sight. I leaned my rifle against the tree and took out my pistol.

I tried to calm my breathing as I waited. The first doe shot past me before I knew it. I stepped out from behind the tree, surprising a buck. I snapped off two rounds, hitting him only once. He reared, then turned sharply to run away from me. I put a round right behind his shoulder, and he dropped with his first jump. I aimed again as another caribou started to veer away from me. One shot took a female in the back leg and she went down, struggling to drag herself with her front legs churning. Another frightened doe almost ran into me. She got one round in the chest between her front legs. She slammed against me as she tried to get past, going down on her side. She huffed once and stayed down. I dropped behind a tree, only able to concentrate on my breathing.

After a few minutes, my head cleared enough to go after the injured caribou. I followed her blood trail about fifty yards where she continued to struggle wildly. I put a round into her to end her misery. I kneeled next to her and offered a prayer for her sacrifice. She would help us make it that much farther. She gave us a better chance to live.

I dragged her back along her blood trail to where the other two caribou were. Her legs kept getting caught up in the snow. It took all I had to get her back. I was exhausted and having a hard time breathing. My hands were shaking, which always happened after an extended bout without being able to take a full breath. I expected I was turning blue.

It was dark in the trees. The blood trail stood out as a path, but nothing else was obvious. I couldn't find my tracks leading to where I had ambushed the herd. How far did I run, fifty yards maybe? This was me. It wouldn't have been too far. Where was my rifle? I couldn't think clearly.

I sat down for just a second. Leaning against the tree, I fell sound asleep.

WHERE IS HE?

Madison knew that I had left. She knew why and was not happy. But she also knew there was nothing to be done about it. "From each according to his ability, to each according to his need." Although she wasn't a Marx fan, she was an academic, and in order to understand, one must study all sides of an issue. In this case, Marx applied perfectly. It needed to be me. If the snow machine broke, I had the best chance to fix it. I could shoot, and we needed the food.

She wished me well and curled up with the twins and their dogs. Phyllis and Husky worked their way into the pile. Phyllis, being a short hair, wore her coat, but she still appreciated the warmth from the other dogs, which they willingly shared with their Alpha. It was good to be the queen.

Chris cuddled with Colleen and prayed hard that I was successful. He didn't want to see her have to decide which horse would die to feed the dogs.

Darren wished that I had asked him to come along, but knew why I hadn't. I wanted someone there who could protect the Community. Chris wasn't even armed. Darren had my AK-47. I'd left it in the house when we moved to the resort full time. We had no need of it. The AK wasn't a good hunting rifle, but it was available. Darren carried a number of loaded magazines. There wasn't any other ammunition for it.

Darren had the unspoken role of protecting the group. He or Becca swore to stay on watch at all times. Becca was every bit as committed as Darren. Their baby, Bill…when Bill woke up, everyone woke up. We loved them all.

Amber remained stalwart. She helped us all see the positive side of things. Despite our trials, she continued to teach Diane things like patty-cake. Amber didn't complain. She kept her family close, making sure that they slept well. Little Diane was bundled up in an odd assortment of clothes, but it wasn't like we had much choice. The twins were in the same boat. They had clothes that were pinned and hand sewn.

Jo was probably the most put out of all. As the master chef, the Community revolved around the meals she provided. They acquired the things she needed to cook the things that people liked. She made magic happen with meals when we ran out of variety. We didn't have any of that anymore. She was in charge of the food distribution, but we were on reduced rations. The dogs were fed well enough. The horses got only what they could scavenge.

Emma was doing the best she could. Her entire experience with motherhood was a life on the run. She kept her baby warm, but the diaper rash was inevitable. At least we'd found some talcum powder in the house here. It looked like the residents left in a hurry, so almost everything was left behind, like the dog food. There was very little canned food. It looked like that was the one thing they did take, or maybe they never had much of it in the first place.

Little Tony was not gaining weight as he should. He seemed okay, but our life on the road was not the best for a newborn.

Jo and Emma talked about staying behind, if we could find a place that would support them until the baby grew stronger. We didn't want to split up, but losing someone because we didn't split up didn't pass the logic test. Chris, Amber, and Colleen talked to them to see what needed to be done. If we found a cabin with a good supply of wood, water, and maybe a few cans of food, and if we were able to provide them some moose meat, and if, and if....

We had hope that this trial could be managed. That we could get to Canada, a free Canada. We needed help.

When everyone woke up, Madison looked for me. Becca had been on watch and knew that I hadn't returned. She shook her head when Madison made eye contact. Becca looked quickly away.

"We have to go look for him!" Madison blurted out to no one in particular. Aeryn gave her mother a big hug.

"Don't worry, Mom. It's Dad. He'll be fine." Charles seemed unconcerned. The undying faith of children in the superhuman abilities of their parents is a universal constant. The twins had more faith than most as we had seen them through all kinds of challenges. We sold them on a positive attitude. They seemed confused that their mother was concerned. So they went about their business to get ready to mush on.

Chris let Madison know that the snow machine track was clear as it continued down the middle of the road in the direction we were going. It would make sense to follow.

The Community shared a brief and meager breakfast before getting on the road. Darren took his team in the lead and set a pace faster than any of the previous days. Chris and Colleen with the horses soon fell far behind. The twins lost pace as well, starting to fall behind, too. Abigail had to slow her sled so she didn't run over the twins.

"I'll get in front of the twins and we'll keep them between us and you," Abigail shouted to Becca and Madison. She pulled the sled over and let Becca catch up, then told her what she intended. Becca gave the thumbs up without taking her hands off the sled.

Abigail gave a hearty, "HA!" and they leapt forward. As she got even with the twins, she told them what she was doing. They gave her a quick nod. They were all business while mushing. They loved it. They were one with the dogs as they maintained their momentum.

Abigail smoothly moved in front and slowed her pace. They chewed through ten miles, then fifteen. It was past the time where they should have taken a break, but Darren was nowhere to be seen up ahead. They needed to keep pressing forward just in case someone up there needed help.

They stopped when they rounded the corner where John had gone through the guardrail. They cleaned out the sleigh that I'd parked in the road and pushed it to the side. Without a second look at what had been John, they mushed the dogs forward.

When the caravan hit twenty miles, the dogs were starting to slow down. They had about reached their limit and needed food and water. It was getting light, and the group needed to stop.

That's when they saw the tracks up ahead. Darren had stomped out a big arrow turning left at the churned up snow where the herd had passed the night before. The snow machine track was very clear on top of the hoofprints. They knew immediately that I had gone after the caribou. In the daylight, they could see the track disappear into the woods some distance away. They finally caught sight of Darren. He was fading out to the right of the tree line.

The group members looked at one another. It would be hard for the dogs to run through all the hoofprints. Abigail suggested everyone take a break here, and she would follow the tracks with her sled. She had the best dog team, so she could follow the quickest with the least wear on her team. She was also better suited to get into the open area away from the hoofprints.

They helped her unpack to make her load as light as possible and then watched as she mushed the team alongside the herd tracks.

Lunch!

I slept for a long time. I woke up lying in the snow, drool frozen into my newly growing beard. I needed to clean the caribou before the meat was lost. In the dark, I gutted the animals, one after another. Then went back to cleaning them up more. I was famished.

As the world's worst prepper, I had never mastered the art of starting a fire without a match. I had one of those magnesium rod and striker things, but I was rarely successful in making fire. And that was the case here. I wanted to cook some of the caribou to help keep up my strength. In the end, I ate some of the backstrap raw. It wasn't as bad as I thought it would be, but then again, I hadn't eaten for more than two days. Hunger is the best condiment, or so they say.

I was removing the head from the third caribou to help make transport easier when I heard Darren yelling. I cupped my hands and shouted back. I could hear him call his team to a halt, and then he ran up to me. He had been worried. It was never my intent to make anyone worry. I only wanted to find food.

He broke into a huge grin when he saw the three caribou. He gave a hearty whoop of joy. Now it was quite clear where Bill had gotten his lung strength.

And then he asked what help I needed. We went through a short list. I was still tired and hungry.

"Now that I've done all the hard work, maybe you can help me get these loaded?" I asked Darren with a wink. "By the way, you wouldn't have seen a snow machine around here anywhere, would you?"

It was embarrassing that Darren found it before I did.

Abigail was happy to take two of the caribou on her stripped-down sled, while I put the third on mine. The dogs looked on hungrily, so we cut off some healthy mini-steaks for each of them. They wolfed down the meat. We brought out their bowls and used the heat from the snow machine engine to melt snow for them to drink. They needed water and that's all we could manage.

Once we were going back toward the road, I went ahead to meet up with everyone else and, most importantly, to let Madison know that I was okay.

I could see them cheering as I approached. I stood on the snow machine, pumping my fist in the air and pointing back to the sleigh with the caribou. I took it easy as I approached, not wanting to drive the dogs into a frenzy.

Madison wouldn't hug me. I guess that I was a little messy from cleaning the caribou in the dark. In lieu of a hug, she gave me a big smile and a punch in the chest.

From the twins? "Hi, Dad." They weren't even looking at me. "Can we get some meat for our dogs?" they asked in unison. They had never been worried.

With the arrival of the first caribou, Jo took it upon herself to make things happen. She whipped out a knife from somewhere and prepared to butcher the caribou. She looked around.

"Can we find a house or somewhere we can do this properly?"

I looked down the road. There might be something up ahead. I started the snow machine and raced ahead. A mile away I found a cabin that looked like it would work. I left the snow machine at the end of the driveway. The cabin was small, but there was a big lean-to for firewood. The lean-to was mostly empty. It would have to do. I looked inside. There was a central table, a bed off to one side, a counter, and a wood-burning stove. I went back outside to get some firewood. They had matches and proper kindling, so I was able to start a fire in the wood burner.

I heard an odd noise and went back outside. A black bear had found the caribou and was tearing into it. My rifle was still in its case on the side of the sled, so I pulled out my pistol and started shooting.

This made the bear mad. Thank God he wasn't that big, maybe only two hundred and fifty pounds. He jumped down and made to charge at me. This pause allowed me to shoot him three more times. He went down in a heap. Keeping my eye on him, I jogged out to my rifle. I put one round from the 45-70 through his skull.

I caught him before he ate too much. And this gave us another hundred and fifty pounds of meat. I'd heard that black bear tasted pretty good. I guess we'd find out.

As Darren and Abigail mushed their teams back toward the road, they saw everyone waving as they traveled south. Even cleaned like they were, the two caribou made for a heavy load. Abigail manhandled the sled up the incline and turned south, following the others. Darren dropped his snow hook and stomped out his previous arrow. He made a new one pointing down the road. Chris and Colleen had not yet made it, so they needed the sign to show them where everyone had gone. There were still hours of daylight remaining, but clouds were beginning to settle in.

As everyone mushed their teams to the cabin, the smell of the bear sent the dogs into an uproar. Phyllis jumped off the sled and stood near the dead bear, barking and showing plenty of teeth. Husky joined her, but she just didn't have it in her to be that angry. She gave up after a short time and settled on sniffing around the area. Phyllis had to be physically dragged away from the carcass, only to escape and go muzzle deep into the bear's neck.

THE SMOKE HOUSE

The snow started to fall, and Chris and Colleen were still nowhere to be seen. Darren told me that I was to stay, and he would take the snow machine out to look for them. We heard it start and then slowly move out. With the snow, he didn't want to run headlong into three horses.

Jo managed the processing of the caribou and the bear. In the end, we had hundreds of pounds of meat. She wanted to smoke some of it so we could eat it as we traveled without having to make a fire. All the rest could be left to freeze. The dogs were perfectly happy eating it that way. After the last few days, we figured they'd be happy with anything to eat, even if it was raw and frozen.

Although meat was the only thing on the menu, we welcomed it. As soon as the first bits were a little crisped, we passed them around. We ate a little at a time, for a long time. It seemed we couldn't get enough. Finally we had eaten our fill. Jo set up a little containment using some sheeting from under the bed. We wired it all together, roughed in a couple shelves and Jo turned the wood burner into a smoker. The whole cabin filled with smoke as much of it escaped our crude construct. I waved Madison outside where we intended to set up our tent. Unfortunately, it was on the sleigh behind the sled that Darren was driving. We went back inside, staying close to the partially opened door. The smoke was really bothering me.

I had to go back outside where I leaned up against the cabin and wrapped myself in blankets. The next thing I knew, the snow machine was back. Three horses slowly made their way in. One was limping badly. I forced myself up to see what was wrong.

Colleen had moved onto the pack horse as Winnifred, her riding horse, had gotten hurt. There was a nasty scrape on the mare's foreleg. We got the horse into the lean to, and dug out the first-aid kit, which was fairly substantial thanks to our Walgreen's run and consolidation of everything from the resort. It had been at the stables during the bombing, so it was fully intact, albeit a little dusty, as we'd used it only a few times in the past three years.

Colleen used the antibiotic ointment on the horse's leg scrape, placing a gauze pad over top and taping it on with athletic tape.

While Colleen was working on her horse, Darren had gone inside to bring out a heaping plate of fresh-cooked caribou. Chris and Colleen ate heartily. Too bad we didn't have anything for the horses. We'd have to dig around the gullies for any tufts of grass. No mowing had been done in years, so there had to be heavy growth somewhere beneath the snow.

"You think we can take an extra day to rest?"

Chris nodded. I shook my head. "We're about twenty miles from Delta Junction, maybe even less since we're only going to the airport. We can almost walk it. Can Winnifred make it? Then we can maybe find something a little more substantial for the horses to eat. And us, too. Then we can rest. We have plenty of food now, thanks to a generous herd of caribou and one overzealous black bear."

I thought about it for a little bit more. "I can shuttle someone into town so we can travel a little bit lighter, and maybe that person can start looking for things that we need. Are you up for it?" I didn't think Chris would be. He wanted to stay with Colleen. Not waiting for Chris to answer, I pressed on. "I'll ask Darren."

The smoke had gotten so thick in the cabin, I could hardly see. It burned my windpipe. I went back outside with a racking cough. Madison came outside when she heard me. The twins followed her. They held their scarves over their faces. I looked at Charles. "Can you get Darren for me, please?"

A DAY OF REST

The snow tapered off quickly, leaving little more than a dusting behind. As the front moved south, Darren and I saw it as an opportunity for a quick trip to Delta Junction. I wanted someone to go with him as my last foray alone could have ended tragically. In the end, since Darren was going, Madison suggested that I go, too.

At this point, everyone was standing outside, and we feared that the cabin would burn down. Smoke poured out of the now open windows and door. Jo was trying to figure out how to rescue the caribou currently in our failed smoker.

The last thing we wanted was to kill everyone we were trying to save.

Darren and I hopped aboard my sled and were gone before anyone could change his or her mind.

The road from here to the airport was almost straight. The trip took no time at all. As we pulled in, I powered up the Geiger counter. Nothing more than the usual background radiation.

We went into the hangar that we had visited before. Everything was as we had left it. Darren said that he would stay and scout the immediate area. I wanted to go back and maybe start shuttling people here. It was early enough and, with the dogs fed, we could probably get most of the people moved. Chris and Colleen would stay behind and rest their horses.

It made the most sense. At the smoke house, we had to sleep outside. Here, everyone could be inside where it was a little more comfortable. We'd send "shopping" parties into town to find supplies, like any canned goods, and any other things that might come in handy.

I went back, rallied the troops, and, although they'd already mushed twenty some miles today, without complaint, they started to hook up their teams. I held little Tony inside my coat as Jo and Emma rescued the smoking meat. It started by throwing handfuls of snow on the fire. I didn't think it possible for the smoke to get worse, but it did. That lasted only briefly, and then they were able to get back inside and throw everything into garbage bags.

We mushed on.

Phyllis and Husky rode with the twins. The dogs that weren't hooked up ran alongside the teams. The people held their positions. It was dark, but the snow was fresh, and the moon was coming up. Dog mushers learn the trick of looking about fifteen degrees offset from the normal line of vision. This maximizes the amount of light that can be interpreted by one's mind. It makes it possible to see details when light is very low.

As usual, I ran out in front. I had already made two trips on this highway, one down and one back. This was my third, so the snow was getting well packed. The dogs found good footing, and the teams made good time.

Abigail was behind me, further smoothing the trail for those following. And we continued, without a break, until five very tired dog teams showed up at the hangar. It had been almost four hours since I'd left Darren there. He was nowhere to be found, but surprisingly, there was a propane-fueled heater blasting refreshing warmth into the hangar. There were three extra propane bottles sitting to the side as well.

It felt like heaven. This was the perfect place to rest for a day.

We unloaded everything into the heated building. The dogs tried to pile in front of the heater, so we had to put up makeshift screens, which they quickly knocked down. We wanted to keep the dogs from getting too close to the heater so they wouldn't catch on fire.

We ended up moving the heater outside, with its nozzle poking through the door. We blocked the opening with sheet metal and insulation. We put fire extinguishers close by, even though we weren't sure they would work. As usual, we went with the best we had.

Everyone picked various spots around the hangar to lay their blankets and their stuff. We consolidated all the food into one of the planes parked outside. We didn't want to lose anything to predators. The smell of the meat could draw them from miles away. At least locked outside, the meat could freeze while it was still protected. It was above freezing in the hangar, and until the caribou was fully smoked, it would spoil in the heat.

We'd figure out everything we needed to do for the rest of our trip tomorrow. Or maybe even the next day. We had already traveled about a hundred miles, and we now had more food than when we'd left. I'd never doubted that we would make it to Canada, but I hadn't been confident at the outset that all of us would be there together when we stood on Canadian snow.

I looked around at the group – a baby, a toddler, children acting like adults, and people from a variety of backgrounds. Our family. Everyone needed to make it out. That's what the Community stood for.

A LONG REST

Chris and Colleen showed up the next day, looking none the worse for wear. Winnifred was barely limping. They seemed happy to arrive.

Little Tony had gained some color and was looking healthier after a day in the warmth where his mother had plenty to eat.

So our one day of rest became two weeks. We scavenged this section of town, finding sufficient canned goods for a great number of meals. We found a barn with old hay. The horses ate at it like it had been served up on a golden platter. Winnifred's wound closed up without any sign of infection or swelling. It left an ugly scar, but that didn't matter.

Tony gained weight quickly. We moved Emma, Jo, and the baby into a house with a wood burner where they could stay warm all the time. They had plenty of water and food. They even slept in a bed.

Each day, we spent the daylight searching. At dusk, we gathered together for a meal. We all held hands in silence. Some might call it prayer. We called it our renewal of faith in one another and in God and in thanks for another day. We took nothing for granted.

I wasn't religious, but there were so many things out of our control that could have conspired to kill us all. They didn't. Whether blind luck or simply beating the odds, it didn't hurt to be thankful. It didn't hurt to keep karma on your side.

We even managed to surprise a moose casually walking through the city. This led to a chase with the snow machine, some patience, and a lucky shot. He was a big bull, the kind that many looked to mount on their walls. We didn't need his rack, although it was almost as wide as I was tall. We were in the sixty-inch club, which was completely meaningless now. We were more than pleased to remain members of the "survive to live another day" club.

We had been fairly thorough in our "shopping." One place we hadn't gone was the post office. I thought I'd give it a try. Who knew what kind of packages were in there, waiting on people who would never claim them. Maybe someone had ordered a satellite telephone.

The outer lobby was open, but we expected the counter and access to the packages to be secured with heavy barriers. I didn't know if we could get past them, but thought we might find something useful. We had time, and we were committed.

As we went through the lobby, I noticed a sign on their bulletin board. It had "Alert" in faded red letters. It also had the Russian and U.S. flags. I took it down and held it in the dim daylight.

"All personnel must leave the disputed territory within two weeks and report to the resettlement officer. Anyone remaining after that date will be considered a terrorist and will be eliminated.

The disputed territory is anywhere in Alaska north of Ketchikan.

There will be no further warnings."

The message was repeated in Russian. It was signed by the Russian-U.S. Armistice Committee.

It was dated three years earlier, right around the time Lucas and I had made our flight. I expect that the U.S. pilots who saw us weren't quite sold on the "kill all the Americans" approach that the letter seemingly mandated. That's why they had given us the time we needed to escape.

I wondered how the natives in villages throughout Alaska responded to this mandate. Probably not well.

I abandoned my plan of breaking into the post office. I wanted to think about this some more.

ON THE ROAD AGAIN

We didn't even realize that we had been living on borrowed time. Three years after the fact, and the Russians were cleaning out the remaining pockets of people. I had always wondered why everyone disappeared so quickly. The bombings didn't kill everyone, but no one seemed to be around. People tried to drive out and were immediately detained and resettled, whatever that word meant. Were they sent to Siberia or allowed to stay in America?

Had we lost territory in the war? After so many years of jumping at the boogeyman, our government wasn't ready when real bad guys came. I knew that they caved. They sold us out. They no longer needed our oil. They prevented the mines from expanding their search for precious metals and coal. They restricted fishing and then approved farm-bred, genetically modified salmon for sale. The politicians didn't need Alaska. They didn't even want Alaska. Too much wild west for their taste. Washington D.C. was four time zones away, and it seemed that for Alaska, that was one time zone too many.

I didn't know if the checkpoints were still there. I didn't know what we would find if we made it to the Canadian border. Had they signed a non-aggression pact? Would they turn us over to the Russians or simply turn us away?

We couldn't stay here as the Russians seemed more than ready to enforce the edict of the alert. Three years later, they had to eliminate any survivors just to save face. The U.S. government probably didn't want to know about any of it. Bury your heads, and you won't see evil.

Was Tony strong enough for the last couple hundred miles?

Was Winnifred healed enough to at least carry herself?

As we progressed into February, we had at least eight hours of daylight, along with hours of visible twilight. This would give us more time to navigate the back country. If there were any observers still at Tok, we would need to head off the road fairly soon to stay far away from them. I figured it was only a hundred and fifty miles if we headed straight east, crossing Highway 5 south of Chicken, and continued due east into Canada. There were a couple valleys we could use to follow to the Yukon River and then stay on that north to Dawson. We could have a total of two hundred and fifty miles remaining. Ten days at a slow pace. Five days if we hurried.

That meant ten days of food for us and all the animals. We'd found some bags of dog food, but those were used up in the two weeks that we'd sheltered in the hangar. We ramped up our production of smoked moose, keeping the smoker running twenty-four hours a day until we had hundreds of pounds of it. The rest was frozen in small strips that the dogs could readily eat. Who would've thought that after the apocalypse, Ziploc bags would be at a premium?

With the sun came limited warmth. It wasn't as cold as it had been in January, but it was far from warm. Temperatures would remain well below freezing for the rest of our trip. Everyone now had sleeping bags, along with some of our original blankets. We didn't have time to tan the hides, but we did what we could with the stinky moose hide, leaving the hair on it for extra protection. Same with two of the three caribou hides and the bear hide. Riding in the dog sled could be as trying as it was boring and cold. Having a hide to sit on made things a little more comfortable. Phyllis and Husky were the only riders who would not get the luxury of riding on a hide, although we padded their sleds with extra blankets.

We also found another dog sled with an old harness. We could hook up a sixth team, which would improve what we could carry and all the dogs would contribute to pulling. Everyone would have a place without having to double up. Our planned pace was twenty-five miles a day, but with the lighter loads, I thought we could easily manage fifty miles. The horses would have to set the pace. If the way was clear and the footing sound, they could manage the longer distance, but there wasn't anything to feed them besides the frozen grasses we would find along the way. Could they walk two hundred and fifty miles with limited food?

We would find out.

THE FIRST CASUALTY

We received our answer on the horses rather quickly.

On the first day's travel from Delta Junction, we set a strong pace. The way was wide open across grasslands with little change in elevation. I thought we might make it all the way to Highway 5. Getting a hundred miles behind us on the first day would cut our trip to just a few days. That was wishful thinking.

We made the first twenty-five miles without a problem. The dog teams stopped twice to let Chris, Colleen, and the three horses catch up. Colleen said that they were maintaining a pace where the horses wouldn't need to rest, so when they arrived, we set out again. We drove another ten miles in record time, maybe less than hour. The snow was firm and the route level. The dogs were at their best.

The twins' dogs were probably the most tired. Their sleds weighed maybe a hundred and fifty pounds, but they only had six dogs pulling. The twins always had to run with the sled to help get things started, but once they were going, it was better.

We waited and waited for Chris and Colleen to catch up. It was light out, and there were no obstacles. We should have been able to see them. I took the sled and raced back.

Colleen, at eight-and-a-half months pregnant, was lying in the snow with her arms around Winnifred's neck. I pulled up on the side away from the other two horses. Chris shook his head. Winnifred's leg wasn't healed at all. It readily broke when she stepped into a hole. I could see where she'd tried to run a few steps, leaving a bloody stump print. And she had fallen. The animal's eyes were wide open because she was terrified. Both the other horses were stamping anxiously. Chris grabbed my arm and pointed to my pistol. He motioned for me to give it to him.

Pointing the barrel toward the sky, I handed it butt first to Chris. I pointed to the safety – it was on. He nodded and went to Colleen's side. He whispered into her ear and she started sobbing. He held her close and then helped her up. He helped put her on the pack horse and smacked the animal's rump. It jumped a few steps before settling into a slow cant.

I didn't realize he was waiting for me to leave, too. I looked at him. Tears filled his eyes. I couldn't let him be someone he wasn't. I took the pistol back from him and told him to catch up with Colleen. I would be along shortly

He thanked me with a look and then kicked his horse into a gallop.

I pulled the blanket off Winnifred's back and folded it. I wanted to muffle the sound of the pistol. I waited until they had covered some distance, just in case the pistol shot was too loud. Winnifred was suffering. I couldn't wait any longer.

"You've been a great friend," I stumbled through the words "and a beloved member of our family. Please forgive me." I pulled the trigger. She thrashed once and was still.

What had I become?

Nothing new. It's what I'd always been.

CONTINUING ON

I caught up to Chris and Colleen within a minute. I couldn't look at them as I drove past. A couple more miles and I caught up with the rest of the group.

We had passed Healy Lake and were now well into the back country. Hills that wanted to be mountains loomed in front of us. We had a valley picked out that we could use to get through. I could see the entrance not too far away. I pointed to it.

"Let's bed down there for the night." But everyone wanted to know about Chris and Colleen. I put my helmet back on before answering. "They're coming," is all I said. Madison knew something was wrong, but I didn't want to talk to anyone. She put her hand on my arm, but I shook it off. That hurt her. I reached back and took her hand.

"I'm sorry. Winnifred didn't make it." And again, "I'm sorry." I put my visor down and slowly pulled out of our temporary camp.

I took it easy on the drive to the valley. I didn't want to put any stress on the snow machine. It had turned out to be the workhorse, our link to keeping the Community whole. It was the reason we had food.

I picked a spot where trees blocked the wind, creating a snow break. It gave us sheltered ground to camp. We'd take that anytime we could get it. I looked back at our caravan. The horses were dots on the horizon. The dog teams were about half that distance away. I had time.

I scouted the valley ahead, but I didn't want to go too far. I couldn't sit still while everyone else was still out there.

I forged ahead. The valley made a direct line to the northeast. It seemed fairly open. I cruised along the valley floor, not seeing any obstacles. There was a greater base of snow than I liked, but it was cold enough that the dogs would most likely not sink in. These were optimal conditions. I figured we had covered forty miles that day. That cut almost a full day off of our trip.

We couldn't put Colleen and her baby at risk by pushing too hard. The unborn baby was every bit a member of the Community. He or she would be born as a result of it. I thought of their baby as a miracle baby.

When I drove back after covering an uneventful ten miles or so, I paralleled my first track. This gave the dog mushers some options. I tried to keep my tracks as straight as possible since not all the wheel dogs had embraced their roles. If a turn was too sharp, they would take it straight and get tangled up in the rigging. No matter the age or training of the dogs, they could all pull straight without any problems.

I refueled the snow machine, checked the oil, and tightened things that had gotten loose. It was ready to go for the next day. I set out the things I had and even managed to pull together a few fallen branches to make a fire. We had found matches in Delta Junction, otherwise I probably wouldn't have had any success.

The fire was burning well in a small opening between sturdy spruce trees when Abigail drove her team in. She put them off to the side and fed them. I provided some water from snow that I'd melted over the fire. The dogs drank this up and wanted more. I started round two of melting, and Abigail joined me with her own pan. Nothing like a metal dog dish to use as a multi-purpose tool.

"How many dogs have problems?" I asked.

"Two or three is all. We may have to cut one loose from Becca's team. He's limping pretty badly. It's hurting the rest of the dogs on the team. He'll take down the whole team if we keep trying to run him." Abigail was analytical when it came to the dogs. They had jobs to do, and she expected a certain level of performance. I think she also understood that when she said we'd have to cut one loose that meant we'd have to leave him behind to fend for himself. It was probably a death sentence.

"What about the twins?" I asked, looking for something positive. I was already proud of them, but I wanted someone else to tell me that they were doing well.

She laughed. She knew I was fishing for a compliment. "There is no way on this earth that there is anyone their age who is as good as they are." She smiled. I didn't expect the ultimate superlative, but it was very nice to hear.

"Thank you. That means a lot to me."

Her smile faded. "What happened back there?"

"Winnifred didn't make it." I got up and headed into the trees to find some more deadfall. I didn't know when I would be willing to talk about it.

My fear was that this would only be the first loss we suffered. We were far away from our goal, but we were so close, too. Across a big plain on the other side of these hills was Highway 5. Through another range and we would find the Yukon River, well inside of Canada.

About two hundred miles to go. Only eight days if we covered twenty-five miles a day, but we were managing more than that. I wanted to be there now, but less than a week would work, especially if we didn't lose anyone else.

The rest of the Community made it to the campsite over the course of the next hour. The twins arrived after Abigail. They were tired and thirsty, but they made sure that their dogs were fed and watered first. I encouraged them to take a drink, which they did out of the dog bowls before putting them down for their teams. I pulled each of them aside for a big hug. They didn't ask why. They probably knew. Only two horses were following them.

The other three teams were bunched up and arrived at almost the same time. Becca had a gap on her team where she had already removed the injured dog. Once they arrived, the dog jumped out of the sled where he had gotten a ride. He couldn't put any weight on one leg and hopped over to get to the water dish with the other dogs. Becca didn't leave him behind. No one wanted to see anyone left behind.

It took Colleen and Chris another two hours before they finally made it to our campsite. Colleen got off her horse very gingerly, even with Chris helping her. I faded into the trees. We could use some more wood.

When I got back, I stayed as far away from Colleen and Chris as I could. But that didn't help. Chris hunted me down.

TOMORROW

"What's tomorrow bring?" Chris asked as he squatted next to me. I looked up at him, not understanding the question. "Today is over, my friend. It is as it had to be. Tomorrow, Colleen and I will ride in the sleds. We decided that the horses have a better chance to live if we let them go free. Our baby will have a better chance at life if we can get to a hospital. It wouldn't be good if the baby was born out here."

"No. No it wouldn't," is all I managed to say. Chris slapped me on the shoulder as he stood up. I looked up. He held my eyes for a second and then walked away.

Chris stood at the campfire and warmed his hands. Everyone else was sitting, still chewing their dried, half-frozen moose. Nutrition did not have to taste good or be easy to eat. Cans of baked beans had been dumped into a pot and were heating on the fire. These hit the spot, but there wasn't enough to let everyone eat their fill.

Chris stood up straight and called quietly for everyone's attention. "Today was a tough day. We left a warm shelter to cross the unknown in the hope that something better waits for us across the border. We know that nothing good waits for us here. If we tried to stay, it would take us, one by one." He shuffled his feet. He'd had a long time to think of this speech, but when he actually had to make it, the words weren't coming easily.

"Colleen and I are going to set our horses free. We've chosen our baby's life over the lives of our horses. It has to be that way. We don't want to see another put down. And we don't want to hold up the rest of you. You deserve better. We're sorry, and we want to make it right." Everyone talked at once, protesting his apology. He didn't know what else to say to them. The twins hugged each other and cried.

I stood up. "We didn't choose this!" I said, much more forcefully than I intended. Everyone stopped and looked at me. I stepped closer to the fire. "We didn't choose any of this. We did the best we could with what we had." I hesitated, the fight gone from my voice. "I've killed people. I've killed animals. I didn't do any of it because I wanted to. I hated it, but it had to be done.

"Survive. One word. One little word that drives everything we do. Whatever gives us the best chance to survive is what we'll do. It's what I'll do. It'll be easier once we're there to lament the past. But until then, we can't waste the energy. We need every bit we have to take the next step, and then the next, and the next. Until someone else provides us with shelter and food. Until there is a someone else, we have to do it ourselves, just like we've done since the war started. A war we didn't know anything about, but were right in the middle of.

"We had no choice. Just like now. No choice but to go on." I let the silence continue until people started looking somewhere other than at me. Then I continued.

"I've already scouted ahead, and the valley should make for a quick run. We can make good time. By the end of tomorrow, Highway 5 should be in sight. From right now, we may be less than three days away from the border. Since we are picking up the pace and should arrive sooner, what do you say the dogs get an extra ration of moose?"

The twins were the first to cheer and immediately got up to take care of their teams. I went back into the shadows of the trees. My noble steed was already fueled and ready to go. I saw Madison comforting Colleen. They had sat together since Chris and Colleen had arrived. Chris disappeared, probably to take the reins and saddles off the horses, untying them for the last time.

Madison stopped Lucas and talked to him briefly and then came to find me.

"I'll ride with you. Colleen will ride with Abigail. We're shifting around a little. Chris, Lucas, and Darren will mush as they're the best ones we have. It's better if they can help push the sleds along. Jo and Emma, Becca and Bill, Amber and Diane will ride in the sleds." She snuggled up next to me. "We're all going to make it."

I looked at her. It was impossible not to smile. I had been given the greatest gift when she agreed to marry me. And then there were the twins. What more could anyone ask for?

"McDonald's."

"What?" she asked.
"Dawson better have a damn McDonald's."
"Yeah. I could go for that too…"

HIDING IN THE OPEN

As we left the hills behind, the open plain through which Highway 5 traveled was open. Really open.

We made quick runs north and south of our trail, but there was nowhere to hide. In the summer, the brush probably would have helped, but in the winter, we were visible to anyone who looked.

We'd arrived in the middle of the day. I didn't want to find out if the Russian-U.S. Armistice Committee had checkpoints or personnel in this area. I figured that if we saw them, they would have already seen us. It was best to be completely unnoticed. Infrared to detect heat sources had much less range than the human eyeball.

We couldn't travel in the daylight, and we couldn't use lights at night. We had to slow down.

My stomach started churning. I felt like the whole world was watching me fail.

We were close, so close to escaping from Alaska that I could taste Canada in the air. Hope gave me energy. Hope made Canada the best place in the world.

And reality said that it was probably more snow and remote terrain that we'd have to slug through. What if Canada refused our entry? That was too much to contemplate.

Madison knew what I was thinking. She watched my body language as I slumped over the handlebars of our snow machine.

"It'll be all right. We're going to make it. We are so close now that we could sprint across the border if we had to."

I understood her words to mean that we put the twins on the snow machine with us and leave everyone else behind. I turned around with a scowl on my face.

"What?" Madison asked, not understanding my expression.

"We'd leave the others behind?" I asked incredulously.

"What?" she asked a second time, before it dawned on her what I was thinking. "Of course not. We'd run, all of us, through the night, until the dogs were ready to drop. If you think I'm going to abandon our family or give up now, you don't know me very well," she shot back.

I laughed softly. "You know I wouldn't leave anyone behind. It bothers me that we had to leave the horses, both of them." I looked for something positive to say. "You know what doesn't bother me?" She shook her head. "That John crashed your sled." I nodded for emphasis.

A BLUR

We stopped around midday and waited until the sun began to set. Then we made an all-out sprint to see how far we could go before it got too dark.

We stopped around midnight.

The teams were exhausted. My thighs hurt from the crouch I maintained to absorb unseen bumps. My back hurt from when I didn't crouch and we jammed against something. The shocks on the snow machine weren't in their prime. This was probably the last run for my stalwart iron dog.

I remember that we were always tired. We were sleeping in three- to four-hour blocks before running again.

The dogs kept up the pace and seemed happy to do it. We fed them well as we had almost double the provisions we needed. We were eating less, but we mattered less than the dogs. They would carry us across the finish line.

We saw Highway 5 only when we physically crossed it. No vehicles had traveled it in so long that it blended into the landscape. The road signs were covered with snow. The only reason I saw one was when I almost ran into it. The highway was important as a waypoint on our journey. It was meaningless as a road. The enemy didn't use it that way.

They had helicopters and could find us from the air.

We needed to get into the back country again. I wanted to conduct a reconnaissance using the snow machine, but if I were seen, they could backtrack my trail and find everyone else.

The best course of action was to not be seen, so I decided that there'd be no reconnaissance north or south. We needed to head straight east. The Community needed to finish the run across to Canada.

If anyone looked, they'd see one trail making a beeline for the border. Abigail followed the snow machine's path, and everyone else followed her.

The second day went by quickly as we realized we were close. We had covered more than two hundred miles since we left our home, two hundred and fifty if you include our wild ride from Chena Hot Springs. We weren't Iditarod racers. We were just a bunch of people and their dogs on a journey to a better place.

We hoped it was better anyway. We had no way of knowing for sure. Hope was what drove us forward.

When we reached the last mountain range between Alaska and Canada, we stopped and spent the night. We all needed the rest. It was too late in our flight to make the mistakes that tired people make. We needed the daylight for us to continue safely. We were close now, and it would be reckless to get hurt.

We camped among the trees on a hillside the day before we were to cross the border into Canada. We'd had good weather for the past few days, which necessitated us running much of the time in the dark, but it was getting overcast. We figured it would soon snow. What would Canada be without snow?

Not Canada! We had a good laugh at our own joke. The Community was in good spirits. The snow would mask our final passage out of Alaska. I thought that we were supposed to feel relief, maybe even joy at our accomplishment.

I was sad. Alaska was our home, but that was a different Alaska.

We awoke as Phyllis growled and then started barking. Husky joined in, wagging her tail as if the pizza man had just arrived. I pulled my .45 out, having no idea what the commotion was about.

A cow moose bolted through the middle of our camp, knocking over a dog sled, throwing its contents in a wide arc away from us as it disappeared into the dark. It was followed closely by a yearling moose that plowed through a pile of sleeping sled dogs. A second cow ran through the camp a moment later. We only saw flashes of brown and the whites of its eyes. The moose hadn't expected to come across the Community, otherwise they would have avoided us altogether.

We must have slept too close to willow trees.

We rallied to recover what we could from the overturned sled and the sleigh it towed. The sled could be repaired but the sleigh was a complete loss. I surprisingly wasn't worried about the sleigh. Our dogs and teams had already shown what they were capable of. We'd continue, and we'd be dragging one less item out of Alaska. We snuggled back into sleeping bags, blankets, and dogs.

We woke to a heavy snowfall. A good six inches of snow was already on the ground, and the near white-out continued. The question was, did we push forward? With the lights of the snow machine, I could see a hundred yards. I didn't want to lose anyone in a mad rush over a cliff, but I felt like I'd be able to keep us on a clear path. We debated, but everyone wanted to go. We were exposed to the weather, but they wanted to be done with the journey, have the hardship behind us.

I couldn't guarantee that when we crossed the border there wouldn't be more hardship. Once we crossed, we still had a ways to go.

So we pressed on. Madison sat with her back to me on the snow machine so she could watch Abigail. We stayed barely in front of her team, and that helped Madison keep an eye on Aeryn just beyond. She tapped me on my right leg to go faster, left leg to slow down. We continued this herky-jerky drive for quite some time before we came to a rather large river that was frozen over.

I looked left and right. The snow was letting up, but we still couldn't see very far. I was positive it was a river and not a glacier. We'd been descending for half the day. Then it dawned on me.

We had reached the Yukon River.

We stopped Abigail and asked her to wait. Madison turned around, and we drove up the river a little ways and then back down. It couldn't be anything but the Yukon.

That meant we were in Canada.

DAWSON, YUKON TERRITORY

We set up camp on the bank of the river although everyone was excited to go on. It was getting late. We thought it best if we arrived in the middle of the day. We would need help as we had almost no money. Colleen, Madison, and I had our passports, although mine was expired. Many had no identification at all. We didn't have anything for the new babies: Diane, Bill, or Tony.

We would find out tomorrow. We didn't know what day of the week it was, but we needed to end our run. I hoped beyond hope that Dawson City had not been affected by the war, that we would find food and shelter there.

And information.

We camped for what we hoped was the last time. We stayed close to one another as the sky cleared for a beautiful sunset. Ravens flew by, letting us know that they'd seen us.

Ravens were good luck in Alaska. We waved at them and thanked them for being there.

We stayed wrapped up for a long time that night, but few slept well.

Everyone got up before sunrise. We took our time packing and eating because we wanted to travel in the daylight. So close to the end of our journey, we didn't want to take senseless risks.

We lost two more dogs overnight – maybe the weather finally got them or they crawled away because of an injury, we'd never know. Becca's (Darren's) team was down two dogs, so I told them to hook Husky up. She was a powerful dog, I thought. That made for quite the comedy. She'd ridden hundreds of miles on a dog sled, yet when she was hooked up, she seemed to have no idea what to do. She'd have to figure it out. We were going to run straight, so all we needed was her power.

Everyone else was ready. I had to avoid the temptation to race ahead and see. I was impatient. Not knowing was difficult for me. Almost too difficult, but finally the time came for us to head up river.

Madison hugged me tightly when we pulled out. I maintained a pace just ahead of the dog teams. It didn't take long before we came across snow machine tracks. A great number of snow machine tracks. And dogsled trails, too.

I sped up, and soon Abigail was far behind us. Madison started hitting me on the shoulder and pointing past my helmet.

I saw them, too. Lights up ahead. Coming toward us.

I turned around and raced to Abigail to let her know, and then I headed back up river. As the other snow machine approached, it slowed down. The driver was wearing a regular snowsuit, a big knit cap, and goggles. I breathed a sigh of relief that he did not look to be military. We waved him down.

The moment of truth.

"Can I help you?" he asked. Normal. Nothing unusual about meeting another snow machine traveling along the river.

"I hope you can. There are a bunch of sled-dog teams behind me." He stood up and craned his neck to see Abigail in the lead. "We finally made it out of Alaska. Is there someone in Dawson City we can talk to? Maybe get a place to stay, something to eat?"

"Alaska! We haven't seen any refugees for what, three years now? We used to have a refugee center, but that's not open anymore. They came for a little while, but then nobody," the man said as he rubbed his face in thought. His eyes smiled, and I felt the stress of the journey leave me.

"I'm sorry. Let me introduce myself. I'm Mike, I run one of the grocery stores in town, but since we're closed on Mondays, I thought I'd do a little snowmobiling. I'm glad I did. It's not every day you get to meet people who escaped the damn Russkies. You give us all hope, buddy!"

"Thanks, my friend. We can follow you, but take it easy, our dogs are tired." His smile told me that he understood my whole meaning.

We waited until everyone caught up with us. Husky didn't want to stop running when the team was called to a halt. She wanted to run up to the humans, as Phyllis had done.

Phyllis wasn't sure about Mike, but warmed to him quickly when he produced a small piece of salmon jerky for her.

Once we had everyone together, I asked Chris to follow Mike first, with Emma. After all, Chris was the Mayor and Emma was our former Mayor. Who better to arrange things on our behalf? Madison and I waved to everyone as they went past. The twins waved, giving us big smiles, but quickly put their hands back on the sleds. We followed the group to make sure we didn't lose anyone at this point. After a mile or two, I pulled to the side of the river. There were some rocks where I hid my rifle and pistol. This was Canada. I didn't want to make it all this way just to get arrested. If we needed to be armed, then we'd lost.

There was no fight left in me. I went from relief, to joy, to exhaustion in the space of minutes.

We caught up to the teams and, in less than an hour, Mike took us to what looked like a boat launch. The Community mushed up the bank and into town. Mike called two people who must have then called everyone else. Soon, there was a big party greeting us kindly, giving the dogs love and affection and making cooing sounds at little Tony. They shied away from Bill after he let everyone know that he was mildly perturbed at something.

Mike helped us bring the dogs to an area where they would get water and food. It looked like a stable or a semi-open warehouse. What mattered was that the dogs were sheltered. Those with babies went inside while the rest made sure that our dog teams were taken care of, fed and watered, and safe for the rest they deserved.

As a group, we went inside.

Officials showed up, a policeman and a representative from the territorial government. We were being treated as heroes. Word spread quickly that we had escaped. Anything that gave the finger to the Russians was being applauded.

Any anxiety that we may have had evaporated. We were going to be well taken care of. They secured rooms for us, even bringing clothes (we looked like bush people). We walked together to a gym in a nearby school where we were happy to enjoy the showers. We stripped out of our old clothes and piled them separately. I expected that they'd be burned, but Becca and Darren wanted to keep their hunting clothes. They'd grown fond of them.

Once we were clean and in our new, borrowed clothing, we didn't know what to think or what to do. We'd been the Community for years, but now, there were so many new people, and we didn't have our daily chores, our routine to fall back on.

I called a meeting for the Community. We sat on the bleachers while the good people from Dawson who were helping us sat nearby.

I took the floor with Chris beside me. "If you're like me, you're wondering what's next. Well, I don't know. What have I said? Live for today, plan for tomorrow?" The group nodded their heads. They all looked too thin in their new clothes which fit better than anything we'd worn in years. The Community looked tired, although it was barely after noon.

"With the incredible people from Dawson's approval, I think our plan for tomorrow is to do what we do. We'll take care of our dogs. We'll make sure we have enough to eat. Tomorrow, we'll plan for the next day. But today, the only thing I want to do is enjoy life." The twins both stood and cheered. Their little voices echoed within the gym. The people from Dawson stood and started clapping. The Community stood as one, cheering and clapping.

I shook Chris' hand and sat down in the front row, next to Madison where I could hold her hand. The twins were in the next row up and they both leaned over my back and pulled on my ears. They were the only ones who had any energy left.

Chris started speaking, softly as he did, which quieted the crowd as they craned their necks to hear him.

"I usually don't say much, and I don't see a need for a lot of words here. I think there's only a few words that matter. We made it. All of us." Then the real cheering began. The Community left the bleachers to group tightly around Chris. Charles and Aeryn gave Colleen a hand up and stayed at her side as she waddled to the center of the pack to hug her partner.

The Mayor had entered the gym during my speech. I was happy that she'd stayed to the side. Many politicians want the spotlight on themselves, regardless of what is going on. That wasn't her thing, and she deserved our respect for it. When we finished, she finally took the floor and talked to us. She started by shaking everyone's hand and congratulating us all on our incredible journey. She looked forward to hearing more at a banquet that was being put together in our honor.

We didn't know what to say.

We left the gym and walked the short distance to a restaurant with a CLOSED sign in the window. It was warm inside, and we started to shed layers. The food was good. The welcome was friendly.

To me, it looked like we were all introverts. Maybe you are born with it, and maybe some people learn it. I could see that no one was opening up. They answered the questions, but they weren't going out of their way to start conversations with the new strangers.

I asked to see our benefactors separately, waving at Chris to join me. It was always important to set expectations so people weren't disappointed for the wrong reason or weren't working at cross purposes.

When we were alone, I took a deep breath and then spoke quietly. "We've lived apart from other humans for the past four years. Please forgive us if we seem aloof or less than appreciative for everything you've done for us. It's not you. We need to get used to humanity once again, used to civilization." I took a drink from the bottle of water they'd given me. It tasted different than what I was used to, but it was still good.

The Mayor started to protest, but I raised my hand to stop her. "Give us some time, and you'll see that there are no better friends than us. And now, some administrative garbage. We have three babies without birth certificates. Out of all of us, I think we have two passports, three if you count my expired one. I can vouch that these people are the kindest and best people on the planet. I can tell you that I believe they are all Americans in good standing, but I expect that when you check, probably all of us have been declared dead. I don't know how we'll deal with any of it, but the only way we'll survive it all is with your help. You've been incredible for us so far, and here we are, asking for more."

The Mayor stood tall and put her hand on my chest. "We will contact your embassy, and we will get it all sorted out before you do anything else. Don't you worry yourselves about any of that. You have a home here for as long as you need it, for as long as you want it. If you want to go to the States and have to leave your dogs, we will find them good homes. We may not have a lot in Dawson City, but the one thing we have plenty of is hospitality." The others nodded vigorously in support of the Mayor.

Chris stepped up. "Please, have patience with us as we assimilate and get our affairs in order. Thank you for not rushing us and our decisions. For the past two months, we've been running through the back country of an Alaska without power, without any support whatsoever. We spent that time thinking about how to survive, not about what to do next. It will be nice to be able to take our time and be comfortable while we talk about what we want for our future. For me and my partner, I think our baby will be born right here in Dawson City. I expect that to happen any day now," Chris ended with a smile and sparkling eyes. He tripped over the word *partner*. I thought he was going to say wife. Maybe they talked about it, but it didn't matter before. In our world at Chena Hot Springs being married was unimportant. Maybe it wasn't here either. Yet one more thing we needed to figure out.

"And we don't have any money, as far as we know. Sorry about that," I said so only the Mayor could hear. She pushed me away and laughed.

We returned to the group. Madison looked at me oddly, wondering why we had to have a private conversation with the Mayor and the others from the town.

The Mayor saved me from having to answer.

"Good people from the Community of Chena Hot Springs. It is our distinct pleasure to take care of you until such time as you decide what you want. We don't care that you don't have any money," she smiled and looked at me. I couldn't meet her gaze. "We know that you've lived apart from the rest of humanity for a long time, and that it will take you some time to get used to us. I hope that someday soon, you'll be able to call us friends. You've thanked us profusely for the meager help we've provided, but we need to thank you for standing up to the Russians, for surviving when everything seemed to be against you. We offer our hospitality for as long as you need it. As Mayor, I will do everything I possibly can to get your papers, documents, whatever you need to go or stay, in good order. We'll make some phone calls this afternoon to get the ball rolling."

One of the other Canadians produced a notepad and started getting everyone's full name and birth dates that the Mayor could share with the U.S. government. I was happy that they were handling that paperwork. I couldn't stomach dealing with the administration that abandoned an entire state and all its people.

When she mentioned the phone, I waved to get her attention. She joined us, and Madison asked if she could use the phone. The Mayor slapped her own head and pulled her people together. Everyone who had a cell phone plan to call the U.S. at no additional cost volunteered to let the survivors from the Community use their phones.

You never forget the phone number that you grew up with. Madison punched in the numbers, as if she had just made the same call yesterday. A tired, older-sounding, but very familiar voice answered. "Hello?"

"Hi, Mom. We're coming home."

EPILOGUE

It only took a week to get all of our paperwork in order so we could go back to the States. In that same week, news of our escape from the Alaskan DMZ went viral. Reporters and news crews started showing up. The city's available rooms filled up with visitors of all types, and our privacy ended. We took to staying in our rooms or working with the dogs. The twins liked the attention, just until they hated it. They were the media darlings. Diane was a favorite as a toddler, and Bill chased away even the heartiest reporter. Little Tony found his way into the arms of every female reporter, but he was never more than one step away from Jo or Emma.

During the week, we made arrangements for our weapons, even the pistol, so I took my snow machine, which was very happy to get filled with fresh gasoline, and picked up my firearms that I'd stashed under a rock along the frozen river. The local police put our weapons and ammunition into their storage locker. They were there should we need them again.

Volunteers took care of our every need. We never lacked for something to eat. I think we all gained at least five pounds that first week, maybe ten, but we were okay with that. I think we'd been on the verge of starvation.

Abigail spent nearly all of her time with the dogs. There were a couple kennels left in Dawson, owing to its place on the Yukon Quest route from before the war. A young man ran one, having taken over from his father who had retired and moved to Arizona. This young man and Abigail hit it off as there was nothing either of them liked better than the dogs. So Abigail took all the dogs and moved in with the young man at his kennel.

That was accomplished in less than a week. The twins were put out as they considered the six dogs from each of their teams as their dogs. Abigail assured them that their teams would be ready whenever they needed a mushing fix. Abigail also suggested that they think about moving up to twelve-dog teams as they were ready and could easily handle that size team. That made the movement of the dogs to the kennel much easier for the children. They wanted to get back into the weather and practice mushing the bigger team. But that would have to wait for a different time.

Two crates were supplied so we could take both Phyllis and Husky to the United States. But then we didn't need them as someone was so taken with our story that they sent their private jet to take us wherever we wanted to go. We wanted to go back to Pittsburgh, but on the way, we'd drop off Darren, Becca, and little Bill in Portland, Oregon, which we discovered was her home. Darren lived in northern California, so they'd drive to his parents' home.

We'd also drop off Amber, Lucas, and Diane in Boise, Idaho, Amber's home town. Lucas wouldn't tell anyone where he was from, which didn't matter to any of us. The reporters seemed to take it as a challenge, which made Lucas quite uncomfortable. We didn't know if Lucas was his real name, and we didn't care. The embassy ginned up papers for him so he could enter the United States. Even they weren't going to break up a family at this point.

Even Phyllis and Husky got papers. They were less than amused with the shots from the vet, but everyone took their medicine as we prepared to head south.

The big day came, and we said goodbye to Chris and Colleen and Emma and Jo, who'd decided to stay until Tony got bigger. Abigail stayed because of Phillip, the kennel guy, and all the dogs. We couldn't have been more pleased because we knew our dogs would be well taken care of. Chris and I had pulled Phillip aside and made certain that he understood if we received a call from Abigail and she was crying, we'd be back, and there would be hell to pay. Phillip promised to treat her well. Chris and I probably looked far meaner than we really were, but we had to make the point.

With the twins and our dogs, the small jet was packed to the gills, but we had almost no luggage, so we were well within weight limits. When we took off, I looked at Lucas, remembering the last time we had flown.

He looked back knowingly and started to laugh. We fist bumped as the jet raced into the sky. Our better halves shook their heads.

Next stop, our hometowns. After that, we had an invitation to the White House and a special offer from the President himself. Now that the next phase of the treaty was in effect, he needed people to resettle Alaska before the Russians did. We had yet to decide whether we'd go to the White House and visit the man who'd abandoned us. We also had to look at the Americans who voted him back into office during our time out of contact.

That was all water under the bridge. We had to live for today.

But we knew we'd return to Alaska. There was no doubt about that.

End of Book Two

RETURN

Book Three

HOMECOMING

There's nothing like returning home to a ticker-tape parade, but that's not what we wanted. A limousine met us at the airport, which was a nice touch, but completely unnecessary. All our family members wanted to give us a ride, but sometimes, you have no choice. That was the life we left behind when we went to Alaska in the first place. I took one step from the plane, saw the crowd, and was already homesick for the Community and the resort. My heart pounded.

There were too many dignitaries to mention. They didn't matter. Madison's mother was propped up in front of the group as we walked off the plane. We waved, thinking that's what the people expected. Photographers surrounded us as Madison and her mother hugged, both crying profusely. I tried to put the circus out of my mind. Our families thought we died, and years later, we were reunited. That's what mattered.

They wanted to whisk us away as soon as we landed, but we politely refused while the twins took Husky and Phyllis for a well-deserved break in the closest grass. I'd had a week of glad-handing to improve how I answered the now commonplace questions.

"How did you survive in Alaska for four years? Right in the middle of a war zone, too. I can't imagine..." It began the same way every time, and they didn't want to hear the real answer. I learned to cut out the four years of boring survival stuff and give them the tidbits of action.

I left out how I killed the two criminals. That would have to be my secret. I hadn't thought about it in years, but had to be careful what kind of stories I told. I didn't want to diminish the world's view of their new hero, did I? We only wanted to be left alone, and that wasn't going to happen.

I needed Madison to help me keep my ego in check. It was hard to be humble and be the center of attention. She didn't want any of it. She only wanted to go home and try to catch up with her mother. Four years is a lifetime when you're supposed to be dead. The good news was that her only brother and his wife had a baby. Madison could be the cool aunt and her mom had three grandchildren to spoil.

The dogs finished their business. Although they were on leashes for the first time in years, neither dog seemed to care. They were happy to be with us. We piled into the limousine for our ride to Mom's house on the other side of Pittsburgh. It was a tight squeeze as the dogs took the area in the middle to sniff and assess everyone they didn't know. We had to pull them back. I wasn't surprised that Phyllis didn't like the mayor.

We'd lost control of our lives, I hoped for only a brief period of time. We were headed downtown to a reception and media event. Madison was livid, but only I and her mother could tell. She clenched her jaw so tightly that her lips were white.

"Mr. Mayor, until a week ago, my mother-in-law thought her daughter and grandchildren were dead. I'll come to the reception, but the rest of my family would appreciate their privacy," I asked soothingly.

"Don't be ridiculous! You are heroes of this nation, and you deserve to be celebrated. We'll make it quick, if that's okay?" He didn't ask like it was a question.

How about you stuff your celebration up your ass you freaking jag-off! I thought in my harshest internal voice. I loved the Pittsburgh term for an asshole. Jag-off. It was a great slur. My expression must have given me away as his aide tried to come to the rescue.

"I'm sure we can reach some accommodation, as everything is already set up. We'll make it quick; the car will be close; and we'll keep the engine running. How does that sound?"

"I appreciate your consideration, but we weren't consulted on any of this. We are private people. Remember where we lived? Alaska is not Pittsburgh. We don't like crowds, and my dislike of politicians is growing exponentially," I said coldly. I hadn't intended to add the bit about despising politicians, but the "don't be ridiculous" statement grated on my soul.

"Well, we can, well…" the mayor sputtered.

I had made my point. Now was the best time to negotiate a compromise. "Madison and her mother will stay in the car with the dogs. Charles, Aeryn, and I will join you for the reception. I will make some remarks if you wish, extolling the virtues of Pittsburgh, and how it set us up to survive." The mayor hesitated before answering as he looked me over. "I'm not your enemy, Mr. Mayor. We've been gone a long time and this is all overwhelming. A week ago, we were sleeping on the side of a mountain with our dogs when a moose ran through our camp. We hadn't eaten a decent meal because we were running from an enemy with MiG fighters who had just dropped bombs on our head. We aren't quite yet in the party mood."

The mayor brightened up. "How could we be so callous. Of course that will work for us. Give us thirty minutes of your time and we'll get you home without further issue. We'll also assign police to your home so that your privacy is respected. You will have gawkers and well-wishers of all sort, as I know. Trust me!" he said with his most charming smile.

We smiled back, mechanically. I nodded as well and shook his hand.

I looked at the twins. They were each holding one of our dogs. I took a knee in the middle of the limousine where I could get close to them. "We'll leave Phyllis and Husky in the car. We don't want them to get anxious because of all the people. When we get out, stay close to me. People will ask questions, but don't answer them until I say it's okay. Think about what it was like mushing your own dog teams! Six-year-olds everywhere will be envious," I said as I ruffled their hair. They calmed down, although I couldn't guarantee they'd stay that way once we were mobbed by strangers.

"Mr. Mayor, can we keep people from pressing in on us? We would appreciate a little bit of space. I don't want to find out that these two are claustrophobic," I asked, trying to improve our chances that the twins wouldn't be in a position to answer questions unsupervised. No one needed to get too deeply into what we had to do to survive. The twins would be perfectly honest, but I suspected the reporters wanted dirt, wanted something to catch the readers' eyes. No one wanted to read about my trials in figuring out we couldn't pump our septic tank.

I laughed to myself. And then there was the great gardening adventure. Sitting there, willing plants to grow. Much of it wasn't very exciting.

The mayor watched me closely. "We'll do everything we can to protect your privacy and to hold the wolves at bay," he said in a well-practiced calm and reassuring voice.

Too late for that, jag-off, maybe you should have asked us before we arrived? I thought again in my sarcastic inside voice. This time I smiled and nodded. "We lost a man and his dog team to a wolf pack. We battled the wolves and it wasn't pretty. I can't express how important it is to me that I don't have to fight off any more wolves," I said, letting the double meaning hang there in front of us all. Madison gripped my arm tightly and pulled me back into my seat.

After that, everyone focused on the dogs and gave them an excess amount of attention. It held further conversation at bay.

A RECEPTION

The reception was a blur. There was a gauntlet that we had to walk through, but as soon as we got out of the car, the driver closed the doors and drove away, giving Madison and her mom time alone.

Charles was on my left and Aeryn on my right. They held tightly to my shirt as I waved at the crowd with both hands. I pointed to everyone wearing a Pittsburgh Steelers jersey. They'd won another Super Bowl in our time away, and that gave me all the fodder I needed for small talk. We wanted to watch replays of some of the games, at least the playoff run. In some ways, it was nice to be back. It was nice to believe that things could be normal.

We had yet to decide if we liked this normal. We'd had no time to ourselves since we flew out of Dawson City, and we needed time. Once we figured out how much money we had, we'd rent a cabin in the hills and disappear until we could get our heads wrapped around our new old world.

All the people. Everything looked the same. I assumed our country would be at war, but no one acted any differently. It seemed too normal.

When was the last time we were in Pittsburgh? Almost five years ago? I couldn't remember.

I continued to wave to the crowd as we were shown to a small platform with a lectern on it, topped with a bush of microphones bearing the labels of radio and television stations.

There weren't any chairs for the group. I took that as a sign that the comments would have to be quick. We arranged ourselves around the mayor who stepped boldly to the front and center.

Show time.

"Ladies and gentlemen, fellow Pittsburghers!" He held up his hands as the crowd cheered. At vantage points beyond the crowd, large cameras from the major news networks had been set up. We were live nationwide. My mouth went dry. I licked my lips, but it didn't help.

"A son and daughter of Pittsburgh have come home to us after surviving in the Alaskan Demilitarized Zone for four years! And they raised their children in that environment. These children here were two when Fairbanks was destroyed. Now look at them!" He stepped aside so the cameras could zoom in on the twins. I hugged them to my body and smiled. "And now a few words from the man himself, the Pittsburgher who saved twelve other lives, Charles Nagy!" The cheering was humbling. I never wanted this, but here I was. And there were more than twelve of us, counting the babies, but who was I to correct a moron?

I raised my hands for quiet, and the crowd calmed down. There was one final shout of "Go Steelers," to which I gave a thumbs up.

"I can't thank the people of Pittsburgh enough, for what this city means, and for the warm welcome we've received. I thank the mayor personally for taking time out of his day to orchestrate this. And let me tell you, we don't deserve this," I said while looking at the faces of the people closest to me. People shouted back that we were heroes.

Not in my definition of the word. I leaned closer to the microphones so I didn't have to feel like I was yelling. "We did what any of you would have done. We took care of our family, and when we added other survivors to that family, we took care of them, too. Just like anyone does in this great city!" I stepped back to let them know I was finished. I turned toward the mayor to shake his hand. He beamed and nodded to me.

Politicians were exceptional at reading people. He knew that I didn't like him, but I'd kept my side of our deal. He owed me, and he knew it. I gripped his hand tightly while holding my smile. He tried to reciprocate, but I had four years of hard labor behind me. He couldn't hold up. I let go and he didn't rub the circulation back into his hand. I appreciated his self-discipline, if nothing else.

We left the stage and tried to hold off other questions as we made a beeline for the limo which was now behind us. There was another gauntlet that ended with a wall of people. We stopped half way as the mayor made to shake my hand, then thought better of it. He leaned close and made his apologies that he wouldn't join us for the rest of our drive. He'd respect our privacy by giving us the car to ourselves. I thanked him profusely as I gave his shoulder a light squeeze. I wasn't sorry if I hurt his hand, but I'd made my point, and he gave me what I wanted.

This also meant that we found ourselves without our government handlers. The bastard turned us over to the media, lock, stock, and barrel. At least there were police present. I leaned toward the nearest officer and asked for help in getting to our car. He nodded and said, "Semper Fi." Once a Marine, always a Marine. I clapped my fellow veteran on the back and we fell in behind as he plowed through to the limo. Once there, we turned to face the reporters who were a bit put out at not getting individual time with us.

"We'll set up a separate media day, if that works. Get with the mayor's office tomorrow as we should have a time and date. The kids would love to talk about what's it like to mush your own dog team across three hundred miles of Alaskan wilderness, counting on only yourself and your family. Thank you!" I ended with a shout. We crawled in quickly and shut the door.

Hijacking us on our way home? I hoped his office was flooded with calls from the media.

HOME

We made it home where more family waited. This time there was a meal prepared, and although people asked questions, they were from family. They mostly wanted to see that the twins were okay. No one could believe how big they'd gotten. Last time we were home, they were only a year old. Now at six, they were like little adults. They both had scars on their arms. Charles had one on his face that would be there forever. He'd fallen through a sticker bush while picking berries. It would have been fine, but he kept picking at it, saying that it itched.

There was nothing that compared to my mother-in-law's cooking. We ate far too much, until I was almost sick. The twins controlled themselves, surprisingly. Their diet had been so limited that they liked more bland cooking. Moose and canned green beans, four-year-old rice cooked in a pot on the wood-burning stove.

Every meal was a feast back then. It was just us. No distractions. I wondered about getting another cell phone. I brought my old one out of Alaska, but it would no longer hold a charge. Now I'd be able to download all the pictures I'd taken. Thousands of them, of us, the city, our home, and of the Community at Chena Hot Springs.

We met our new nephew. He was two and what a blast he was. He was completely unafraid of our dogs. The twins liked him right away. He was their only cousin.

They'd named him after my wife and me. Maddie Charles wasn't a usual name, but after meeting him, we had no doubt he'd make it work.

We were happy when everyone left. I knew we needed help to manage our lives, so I called an old friend from the Marine Corps who'd moved into public relations after he retired. We hired him as our agent. He said he'd drop everything and meet us the next day.

We strolled outside. The weather was nice enough that a flock of turkeys made the mistake of venturing into my mother-in-law's yard. Phyllis and Husky went after them with a vengeance. They'd learned to hunt ptarmigan to help put food on the table. The two dogs treated the turkeys like a future meal. We didn't stop them as they each caught and killed a wild turkey. The dogs happily brought them to the house. I asked Madison's mother for knives so we could clean the birds. They'd make for a great meal. It was nice to have spices again.

My mother-in-law was shocked, but when Madison shrugged then nodded, she understood that we didn't want the turkeys to go to waste. Wishing she hadn't seen it wouldn't make them any less dead. We rewarded the dogs with Milk Bones. It had been a while since they'd gotten such treats. They might never get moose again, so Milk Bones it was.

My friend, and now our agent, made sure we didn't get any more surprises like the mayor had given us. We could live our lives on our terms, while fulfilling our duties to a grateful nation.

As it turned out, everyone was overjoyed that a group of survivors made it out three years after the DMZ had been supposedly vacated. Although the Lower 48 wasn't at war, in their minds, anything that showed the Russians to be liars was embraced fully. Especially since we were proof they tried to bomb us instead of evacuate us. That violated terms of some agreement somewhere that people trotted out when it suited them. It meant nothing to me.

We had an agent. I shook my head after getting off the phone with the President of the United States. Another politician, but this was the same guy who'd abandoned us, then declared victory by keeping the war away from the continental United States. I thought it looked like lipstick on a pig. The President, however, said something that caught my ear and made me think. He mentioned that in the next phase of the treaty, Alaska needed settlers to establish a new foundation from which America could regain ownership of the contested land. I wanted to know more, but he offered that we talk in the private setting of the Oval Office.

Our agent arranged everything. All we had to do was show up at the gate. My friend also took care of things to ensure we made enough money in our fifteen minutes of fame that we'd never have to work again. The money people were throwing at us for this or that was obscene. I was offered millions for my memoir, as an example.

We also had the power of the White House to clarify that issue where my retirement pay had been stopped when we were declared dead just after Fairbanks was nuked. They owed me a great deal of back pay. Our life insurance policies had both paid my mother-in-law. She was happy to give us all the money, but the insurance companies were making noise about getting their money back.

Our agent took care of that, too. We kept the money, and all we had to do was a thirty-second commercial.

There was plenty of time for us to be alone and enjoy the company of my wife's family. My parents had both passed away in the last four years. I called my siblings, but didn't make any plans for a visit. I didn't feel like traveling. My friend was a godsend. We did plenty of interviews, but from a local studio that was video-conferenced with places like the Today Show out of New York City. They pushed hard for us to travel, but our agent shut them down.

We also called our fellows from the Community. Everyone was getting more attention than they wanted. We were of a like mind that our privacy was paramount. Those faring the best were still in Dawson City. They had joined a new Community, bigger than ours, but it felt about the same size. People kept to themselves.

I was surprised to hear that Chris and Colleen's baby had not yet been born. We wished them well as we always did, and gave Colleen our best. Madison and I could both see her smile as she thanked us for our sentiments. The twins missed the Community. They were the only family the two had known, and they were comforted by what the others would do for them. Maybe they got that from me. It took a long time before I gave anyone my full trust. I was open with everyone, ready to shake a hand, but my pistol was always within reach.

Although we wouldn't take it to Washington D.C. They frowned on armed patriots showing up on their doorstep, bizarrely enough.

THE WHITE HOUSE

My friend and agent accompanied us on our visit to the President. We spent some time talking over ways I could avoid showing my disdain for the man. Whatever we wanted to get from the exchange would have to be done with tact and grace.

That caused me some anxiety. I had to treat it like a stage production where I played a role. I spent half the five-hour drive trying to get into character. A nice guy, appreciative of everything the government had done for us.

I felt sick to my stomach. I must have turned pale, because Madison put a hand on my back and told me put my head between my knees. I was pleased that I didn't have to drive, as we were riding in another limousine. I'd quickly gotten used to getting chauffeured, probably too quickly.

I was better driving my snow machine or even a dog team. I was more me because I had time to think. The so-called "normal" world moved too fast for us. I wondered how long it would be before it came crashing down around our heads.

All we had to do was survive our fifteen minutes of fame, and then maybe people would leave us alone.

We met the Press Secretary at the back gate to the White House and he escorted us in. We passed through a metal detector and everything we carried was X-rayed. It made sense to me that we could have been a threat to the President, but he invited us, which made it worse to get checked as if we were vagrants off the street.

We had to wait in an outer office until we were appropriately summoned. We should have been flattered, but we weren't. I could feel my blood starting to boil. I felt like a bad kid waiting outside the principal's office while he talked with my parents. And then I looked at our two six-year-olds. They stood there in their new clothes, looking proper. They had more patience than any first grader I'd ever met. They were far more mature than they should have been. The trial of our lives made them grow up. Too fast? No. They grew as fast as they needed to, as fast as they wanted to.

The door opened and the President walked out, which seemed to take the Press Secretary by surprise.

He greeted us warmly and apologized for the delay. He was much taller than me and cut an imposing figure. The President used to be the most powerful man in the world, but that was before this one lost American territory to an enemy. I shoved that thought to the back of my mind as we took our seats on the couches in front of the President's desk.

"First, Chuck and Madison, Charles and Aeryn, I want to welcome you to the White House. And second, I want to apologize on behalf of the United States for your hardships in Alaska. The attack came as a surprise, the destruction so complete that few survived and most of those suffered from radiation sickness. We will get Alaska back. Our flag has fifty stars because there are fifty states." The President ended his short speech with a nod as he looked at each of us. The twins sat patiently, but none of it meant anything to them.

To us, it meant a great deal. "Thank you, Mr. President. We needed to hear that, and it was best hearing it from you," Madison said. I looked at her in surprise. She was an academic and could readily speak to any audience. She had prepared herself better than I had. I let emotion cloud my words, and I didn't bother trying to hide my feelings.

You can always learn something. I gave her hand a squeeze. I couldn't have been more proud.

"Thank you, Mr. President. I know we have some things we need to talk about that you mentioned on the phone, but first, would you be so kind as to let Aeryn and Charles tell you what it's like to mush a six-dog team across Alaska?" The President snickered. He'd had small children once and appreciated their candor. He asked the twins to teach him how they did it.

The two stood up, which we weren't prepared for, and adjusted the coffee table as if it were the sled. Then they put people in each of the positions, lead dogs, swing dogs, and wheel dogs. They explained that the six-dog team didn't have any team dogs, but Abigail had promised them twelve-dog teams upon their return, and then they'd have two or four team dogs. The President and I were the lead dogs, which was odd since all of the lead dogs on the twins' teams were females. They must have understood innately how politics worked.

The President's photographer snapped a number of pictures and the most popular in the next day's papers was one where the President and I were laughing as we crouched forward to lead the "team" deeper into the snow of the Great White North. The Chairman of the Joint Chiefs and the Secretary of Defense were the swing dogs and Madison and the Press Secretary were the wheel dogs. It was a good picture and one that we'd keep with us forever.

After the twins ran through the demo, they went on a private tour of the White House with the Press Secretary. I asked if a Marine could accompany them as that was the level of protection they were used to. The President appreciated my position and asked a Marine in Dress Blues to make it happen. He saluted smartly and followed the group out, returning shortly after making the arrangements. He nodded to me with a tight-lipped smile.

I hoped that I'd get a chance to talk with him and other guards before leaving.

"I'll get right to it. If we leave those two kids of yours alone for too long, they'll take over the world," the President said with a smile. "One clause we worked into the treaty with Russia is the reestablishment of American settlers in Alaska. We figure that the Russians want the oil-rich north slope, but it is barely habitable.

"If you didn't know, they dropped a nuke in Prudhoe, so the pumping station and much of the pipe is gone. It would be an extensive effort to bring it back on line for even a fraction of the oil it used to pump. We think they have something in mind, but we're sure they won't be successful. That leaves the rest of the state. If we can colonize it with more people faster, when the final count comes we'll get to retain possession. And I agree, we shouldn't have to work the angles to keep something that is ours. But resettling puts the UN behind us. Although this is a UNSC issue, we've both agreed to waive our veto authority in this regard. We have the votes, as long as we have the people settled.

"And that's what we want from you, your Community, and anyone else we can get who wants to live a subsistence lifestyle. There is the one catch. The settlers cannot receive any governmental assistance. They have to make it on their own. This is why we know the Russians won't be able to recover oil on the Slope. They can't do that with what they can carry on their backs while trying to survive inside the Arctic Circle. We'll catch them cheating and we'll present that evidence to the UN.

"Are you in?"

I looked at my wife. She smiled and nodded. "It's hard to say no to that." I stood and offered my hand.

As he took it, he said, "There's one more thing. We've made some progress in stem cell research. If you stop by Johns Hopkins this afternoon, they'll be waiting for you. How'd you like to breathe again?"

I was shocked. I stepped back and looked up at the man. What had he just said?

"The doctors pulled your records from the VA and they think they can get you back to seventy-five or eighty percent lung capacity. Does that sound like something you'd be interested in?" the President asked.

"I, I don't know what to say," was the best I could come up with. I hoped that meant I wouldn't need to take medications anymore or at least fewer of them. It sounded like we had to go with what we could carry. "Of course we'll stop by Johns Hopkins.

"I have something," the Chairman of the Joint Chiefs said.

I interrupted him, "What could be more than that?"

"We're recalling you to active duty and promoting you to colonel." The Chairman smiled broadly as he delivered the news. He held out his hand.

I looked at him stupidly. "Say what?"

EXPERIMENTAL PROCEDURE

The Chairman explained that I didn't need to do anything while we were still in the Lower 48, but that being active duty was a way for me to draw full pay and be the head of any military operations in Alaska. He didn't elaborate, saying that I'd get briefed at the Pentagon over the next couple days while I was undergoing the stem cell procedure.

Madison was not good with my return to active duty. I promised her that I wouldn't put on the uniform. To maintain our neutrality as settlers, I didn't think I could be active duty, but that was for the bureaucrats to figure out. The way I saw it, I was going to get paid for doing what I was going to do anyway.

And if they could repair my lungs, I'd get on my hands and knees and kiss their feet if they asked for it.

The five of us arrived together at Johns Hopkins and, as promised, they were waiting for me. My friend and agent, Frank, said he'd take the twins sightseeing while Madison and I stayed at the hospital. Today's part of the procedure would only take a couple hours. Tomorrow would be an hour, with an hour every two days after that, but the follow-up procedures would be done at the VA hospital in Pittsburgh.

I cleaned up as if I was going into surgery. I had to scrub my body down with antiseptic and put on the funky blue gown that was open in the back. As usual, I had to ask myself, what's up with that?

They explained that the procedure involved taking stem cells from my bone marrow, which meant inserting a needle through into the larger bones in my arms and legs, the femur and humerus. I understood there would be some pain, but nothing prepared me for it.

Getting a needle as big a soda straw jammed into your leg and through the bone about made me bite through my lip. I sweated profusely and hyperventilated, solely because of the pain. It was only one needle, yet the pain extended through my whole body. Finally, one down and three to go.

They gave me oxygen and an IV with saline solution. I'd get antibiotics and pain medicine once the procedure was complete. I urged them to hurry.

They had to pound on my other leg as I had tensed up to the point of cramping in anticipation. The needle went in and sweat or tears ran down my face. I didn't care which. I had my eyes closed, and I could hear Madison's voice, seemingly coming from far away. When they pulled the needle from my leg, I howled in agony. My back hurt from arching against the pain.

When they inserted the needle into my arm, that's the last I remember of the procedure. They complimented me afterwards, telling me that most people passed out before then. They'd never had anyone remain conscious through the whole bone marrow extraction.

The doctor announced that he had enough stem cells. I would not have to get violated by any more pencil-sized needles.

Once it was over, I was in a much better mood, but I needed a shower. I was soaked in sweat. We called Frank on my new iPhone that AT&T provided as part of a short commercial we did for them, along with a significant sum of money as we showed some of the pictures I'd taken using the old phone. The screen wasn't even cracked. AT&T's byline was that their phone survived a nuclear attack. Buy AT&T. I reminded them that we hadn't had service the past four years, but their marketers said that didn't matter. It worked for us.

Frank didn't care where or how we got our phone. He said that he'd be right back with the children, and then he'd take us where we were staying. After he became our agent, we were taken care of without having to worry about any of the details. We didn't know where we were staying, but we expected something nice. We didn't think we deserved it, but that's beside the point.

Frank directed our driver back to the White House where we were set up in the Lincoln Bedroom.

That was a treat. Too bad I had to leave early the next morning for briefings at the Pentagon. Madison and the twins enjoyed breakfast with the First Lady while Frank gave me a muffin after he picked me up. I had to admit that the coffee in the White House would spoil anyone. We had coffee the entire time in Alaska, except for a few days while mushing for our lives. Even then, whenever we entered a house or business, they almost always had coffee. You know what's better than nothing? Four-year-old stale coffee.

MILITARY BRIEFINGS

The military wanted to take my old cell phone to download all the pictures. I told them to get bent. Then a general showed up and ordered me to give up my phone. I wanted to tell him the same thing, but took a different approach.

"Listen, General, you and I both know I'm back on active duty because the President feels guilty about losing Alaska. Maybe my recall made him feel better. I don't know, and I don't care. This is my private phone, and I'm not giving it to you. I am more than happy to share the pictures, but this phone is not leaving my sight. I haven't downloaded the pictures since we escaped. I'd like to keep them. And for a few million dollars' worth for my memoirs, these pictures will save me a lot of writing time." I stood unmoving as the general tried to glare at me.

"When we were there, in the DMZ, soldiers, our soldiers, shot at me while we were only trying to survive. I don't who issued those orders, but don't let them get anywhere near me." I leaned close to him, and although he was physically bigger than me, he withered. The United States military firing on its own within the United States had to make him sick to his stomach.

He gave up quickly. Maybe he wasn't a fan of how the war was managed. We had that in common. I wasn't a fan either. Maybe he realized that I wasn't asking for much. They could have the pictures, just not the phone.

He waved an Army master sergeant over and directed him to have IT come to the conference room with whatever they needed to download the pictures. He also told him to bring an extra thumb drive to give me a copy. I appreciated the gesture. It saved me from doing the same thing later.

That reminded me. I needed to download all my music to the new phone. I wanted to use it when I no longer had service upon our return to the Great State. I wanted to download more music, too. I expected

Madison would do the same. Money was no longer an issue. Only our time seemed to be at a premium.

The Pentagon's IT guru showed up. The Air Force sergeant looked like a little kid to me, but they said he was the best when he showed up. There was nothing extraordinary that needed done. I even typed in my password so they could access the phone, which then made it look like the same iPhone connected to the same laptop in tens of millions of homes around the world.

There were thousands of pictures, so it took almost thirty minutes to download everything and another minute to copy the pictures to a thumb drive.

I put the phone back in my pocket next to my new one when they were done.

I thought they'd go away and pore over the pictures, but they didn't. They projected them onto the screen in the conference room, thumbing through quickly, but stopping at all the ones of a destroyed Fairbanks. The mood in the room sobered immensely. The destruction looked horrific on the big screen. The pictures I took from the overlook at the University of Alaska Fairbanks showed the worst of it.

A colonel requested a map of the city and asked me to show everyone what happened, including follow-up. I asked for a map of Delta Junction and then a road map of all Alaska.

I pointed to the gates at both Fort Wainwright in Fairbanks and Fort Greely in Delta Junction where I was certain the nukes had been detonated. I showed where the checkpoint in Tok was three years ago. They knew about that, though. It was a U.S. military operation. They also knew about the overflight of Chena Hot Springs resort by the U.S. F-16s shortly after our unfortunate encounter at the checkpoint.

Both pilots had been court-martialed for not dropping their bombs. I stood up and pounded my fist on the table. "What the hell?"

"Sit down, Colonel. We didn't have to tell you that, but thought you deserved to know. They insisted on the court martial to shine the light on failures of our government, and you know, none of this leaves this room. Do you understand me?" I nodded and sat down, freshly disgusted.

"But it never went public. They were tried in private, convicted, and given Administrative Discharges under Other Than Honorable circumstances. This was the lightest punishment they could be given because they pled guilty. They should have said not guilty because of an illegal order to fire on American citizens. You have my word that both men are doing just fine in the private sector. An OTH discharge isn't a bar to employment."

I closed my eyes and took deep breaths, a calming technique that Madison had taught me to help with my gastritis. When I opened my eyes, they were all looking at me.

"I'm good. Shall we continue?" It was also unnerving to be called Colonel. I'd been a civilian for a long time and had grown accustomed to the freedom that entailed.

The briefing picked up where we'd left off. I could tell they wanted pictures of the MiG-27 attack, hoping to confirm the treaty violation. The question of, "There's nothing else?" tipped their hand.

"I'm sorry. It was late morning when they attacked. We lost one of our people in the bombing and then everything else was about getting the hell out of there. I didn't have any time to take pictures. From then on, we were running for our lives. For what it's worth, we never saw another Russian or trace of a Russian for the rest of the trip." I detailed our travel route on the overall map. They copied it down on a printed copy. We hadn't seen anyone or even any signs of human beings when we traveled through those areas, and there was some value in that.

We finally finished the debriefing. I was amazed at how well they squeezed fifteen minutes of information into two hours, but despite the fact that everything had changed in my world, nothing had changed anywhere else.

They escorted me to the administrative section so I could fill out paperwork. With my recall to active duty, I thought they'd take care of these things.

They didn't do any of it. I was handed a stack of blank forms an inch high. I filled out the first one with my mother-in-law's address and stopped. I returned to the counter. "Here you go. I'm done filling these out."

"But sir, you've only filled out the top page. We need all these forms filled out in entirety. If you don't have addresses of your references, you can bring those back to us tomorrow."

"No. I'm done filling out forms. The only thing that's changed is the address. I'm not providing references and I'm not putting the same information into thirty different forms."

"But sir, you can't get paid if you don't fill out the forms," the young enlisted man insisted.

"I have all the money I need. If you want my pay, you fill 'em out." I made to leave but the young man called over his supervisor, the Staff Noncommissioned Officer In Charge, who then attempted to threaten me. When I cocked my eyebrows at her, she retreated and called in the Administrative Officer. The major was used to dealing with intransigent senior officers and said that I should fill them out to set a good example for the junior personnel.

I leaned close so only she could hear me. "I was involuntarily recalled after being retired for more than ten years. In all that time I never filled out any forms like that, and I'm not going to return to that life. There is nothing in here that you don't already have. If you can figure a way to streamline the system, you'll be doing all the services a favor, and that's how you set a good example. Refuse to blindly follow what everyone knows is ridiculous. I won't be stopping by tomorrow. The only thing I expect is that you'll take care of it. You're wasting my time. You're wasting their time, and I expect you're in violation of the Paperwork Reduction Act with the vast piles of paper printed in this office. With that, I'll wish you a good day."

I left without waiting for my escort and was lost within five minutes. I milled about until I ran into someone who looked like they knew where they were going. After that, I was happy to be free of the Pentagon. I had no idea who my supervisor was and if he or she called and tried to chew on me for anything, I would give them the finger and hang up.

It didn't take long. I was in the car with Frank, headed toward a hotel when my phone rang. It was some general who was yelling into the phone. I put it down until he stopped. "Are you done?" I asked, which sent him into a complete frenzy. He finally ran out of steam and asked if I'd heard what he said.

"Listen, General. I didn't ask for any of this. I refuse to tolerate the stupid bureaucracy too many people seem to embrace. If you don't know, I'm being sent back to Alaska, a place without power, communication, a grocery store, anything that suggests a modern society for probably the rest of my life. I really don't care about your damn forms. I don't care if you want to court martial me. I don't care if I draw my pay. And frankly, I don't care that you've pulled rank on me. That's not how you're going to make any of what DoD wants important to me. Is that clear?" And I hung up.

He was kind enough to not call back. I appreciated that and was glad not to talk with others about such inane issues as some damn form.

SCHOOL

It took three visits over three days to the hospital to get my treatment started. It was a simple IV adding the separated stem cells that were juiced with something unpronounceable. Once in my blood stream, the stem cells were transported to my lungs where they stopped and collectively repaired the damage. They told me it would take a week to start noticing a difference and two months before I would realize the full effect of the treatment.

That's how long we had to wait. It was late March, so we thought we'd get the twins into a real school so they could learn to socialize, maybe play a sport. Upon our return, my mother-in-law was waiting on the steps to the house. We'd been dead for four years. She quickly got used to the idea that we were alive, because she hadn't given up, but then we went away again. We hadn't yet told her that we were going back.

That could wait for another day. The twins tested into second grade although they were only old enough for kindergarten. We sent them to the public school. We drove them the first few days, but after that, the school requested that they ride the bus like all the other students. They weren't that much smaller than their classmates, but when we observed them, they seemed far more mature. They liked playing with the other children, but they didn't know the games. They were both fast and strong for their size. This didn't help them when playing soccer with the older children. Their foot skills weren't great because they'd never played before, and they were consistently getting roughed up.

They didn't care about the bumps and bruises. They were used to getting bounced around. They cared that everyone wanted to be their friend, but no one was. The jealousy from the other children was obvious in how they looked for ways to find out things about the twins, and then take those inside notes to others. They made fun of our children from the darkness of the shadows.

One day we received a call from the principal. He had the twins in his office and required our presence. We bolted out of the house, concerned at what had happened.

When we arrived, we were quickly shown in. The twins sat patiently in chairs across from the principal's desk. They ran to us and we picked them up, putting them in our laps as we sat down. The principal wasn't pleased. Maybe he expected us to ice the children while we received his verdict.

From our point of view, we were happy that they looked okay.

"There was an altercation, and your children have injured a boy from their class," the principal said without preamble.

"Why don't you tell us what happened, Aeryn?" I asked as she was usually the one to come clean quicker.

"A boy was pushing me around, and Charles beat him stupid," she said matter-of-factly.

"You should have gone to an adult!" the principal interrupted.

"I didn't see why. We took care of it," she responded. I bit my lip to keep from laughing. I looked at Charles, and he just rolled his eyes. The principal did not take my smile well.

He didn't take it well at all. He asked that the children wait outside. We sent them. Once the door was closed, I watched the principal as he leaned forward in his chair, taking a deep breath from which to express his concern at our parenting.

I jumped to my feet and slammed into his desk. He lurched backwards, almost tipping his chair over. I took charge of the conversation.

"When I grew up, we got into scuffles. We fixed things ourselves. And then we became friends. I'm happy to see those two think the same way. They are six years old and in second grade. Where were the adults when this was going on? You don't have the foggiest of what those two have been through. The adult wasn't needed to protect them, but to protect the other children. The twins are survivors. You do understand that they can defend themselves from any and all predators. Why? Because up until two weeks ago they had to in the only life they've known. You call us down here, and you have the audacity to come at me because they protected themselves. Maybe I should beat you stupid, too. What do you think of that, jag-off? Well here's our answer – they won't be back. They'll continue through homeschooling where they will finish high school while you still have these kids stuck in middle school."

The principal's lips were working, but nothing was coming out. His head was turning purple as his blood pressure soared out of control. Being grossly overweight had a tendency to do bad things to one's body.

I pushed the desk a few inches closer to the man, then offered Madison a hand up. We casually walked out of the office, leaving the door open. The twins followed us into the hallway. I took Charles' hand and Madison took Aeryn's.

"Maybe you shouldn't have done that, Charles," I said, not accusing him of anything. I knew what his answer would be.

"I couldn't let him pick on my sister. Those other kids are kind of mean." He hesitated before continuing. I waited. "We really don't like it here."

"Me neither. Don't worry, you won't have to come back." They brightened appreciably. Madison gave me her angry look. She was the academic and I hadn't given her the chance to speak.

"I'm sorry," I pleaded. "He made me mad. It was all I could not to punch him in his fat face!"

Her eyes shot wide, and she nodded toward the children. "Here in this world, we don't settle our differences with violence," she said calmly. "We settle them with words, as your father did with the principal. It's important that we continue your education at home so we can focus on those things you need."

We hadn't told the twins that we were returning to Alaska. We could delay that for a while. As soon as they knew, they'd stop trying to learn about civilized society.

Civilized. What a word. If that's what the principal was, then I wanted no part of it. The Pentagon's admin section? I walked away from that, too. Maybe I was no longer suited to live among civilized people as I had no tolerance for pandering, being indirect, talking behind people's backs, or outright lying. There were so few people who could be trusted. Besides Frank and my wife's family, there was no one else. There was only the Community.

I counted the days until we could go home. Alaska waited for us.

TWO MONTHS LATER

I finished my memoirs in six weeks and turned them over to the publisher. That was the single best payday of my life. I'd never seen a real check for seven figures before, but there it was, in my hand.

Our bank was more than happy to reestablish our accounts that they'd closed when we were declared dead. They even gave us our previous account numbers. I deposited the check. They considered us to be their best customers.

More pandering. I could do without that, although we shook hands and smiled as if there was a relationship based on more than money. There wasn't.

We had more money than we could use, even after paying the taxes. So we added Madison's mother to the account so she could take what she needed. She wanted to quit her job to be at home full time with her daughter and the twins.

That's when we had to tell her that she shouldn't quit. She needed to have something to keep her busy after we'd gone. And then she broke down completely, and there was no consoling her. We suggested she come along, but that wasn't going to happen. She finally had her children and grandchildren in one place but they lived worlds apart.

She didn't want to pick one child over the other. We told her about the problem in school with Charles and Aeryn. The twins would never get along with the children here. For them to fit in, they'd have to trade who they were. Madison and I didn't want that.

We started making phone calls to the other members of the Community. The stories were the same. None of them were able to re-assimilate into modern society. I told them we were going back to establish a settlement and this time, no one would be trying to kill us. It was us against nature to decide which country earned the right to resettle the great state of Alaska.

RETURN

We'd be cut off, but everything we built would be ours. I didn't know if we were up to the challenge, but the government said there would be plenty of volunteers with special skills who could go with us: engineers, farmers, woodsmen, and more.

Abigail confirmed that she'd go and Phillip would come, too, giving us a second strong dog musher and handler. She talked with the twins and told them that their teams were mostly ready, but they'd have to decide which twelve dogs out of sixteen potentials they'd like.

The twins wanted to leave right then, but we had our affairs to settle before heading out. Our fifteen minutes of fame petered out quickly, resurging for a brief period with the publication of the book. We were happy to be out of the limelight.

I received a call from Mr. Bezos, our benefactor, the one who'd sent his jet to Dawson City for us. The fact that we were going back was a secret, but somehow he knew. He had something he wanted us to do.

A SPECIAL PERSON

The man's private jet landed at Latrobe Airport east of Pittsburgh. We met him there and went into town for lunch. He didn't beat around the bush.

"My daughter was one of a few who stayed over at Denali after the summer tourist season. She was coming home at Christmas that year," he said, his eyes started to glisten with tears as he relived a painful memory. "After it happened, I personally went to the resettlement camps in Washington and in southeast Alaska, talking to anyone and everyone. No one had come from Denali, but some people had attempted to pass through. The Russians had a military checkpoint there. In the official reporting, there was a 'safety' stop north of Anchorage, but nothing as far north as Denali. The officials documented the checkpoint in Tok even, which corroborates your story.

"I've used up all my resources trying to find her but no one's been allowed back, until now that is. I will pay you all you want, do anything you ask of me, if you'll only go to Denali and try to find her. I'll give you a satellite phone so you can call," he said quietly. "So she can call."

He stared at his hands. He was probably younger than he looked. The worry regarding his daughter had aged him, as it had done to Madison's mother.

No one should lose a child. And no one should have to continue without knowing. I looked at Madison and she shrugged but then nodded.

"I'll do it. I'll run down there, and we'll look for her. Where did she work and were there any other places she mentioned, a favorite camping spot or something like that?" I continued with the questions until I was sure he had nothing else for me. The situation piqued my interest. The President had implied that there may be others who survived. I was certain that there were people secreted away in dark corners of the interior mountains who lived the subsistence lifestyle. They might never be found.

If there was any hope for survivors in Healy, the town at the entrance to Denali National Park, then we had to look. I didn't want to walk that whole way.

"Do you know how to refresh old gasoline?" I asked the man.

"No, but I have engineers who can help you…"

BACK TO DAWSON CITY

We returned to Dawson City on the summer solstice. When we exited the private jet, Husky and Phyllis ran down the airplane's stairs and across the parking apron to jump on Abigail. Phillip was with her, as was Chris, Colleen, and their baby girl Hermione. They were both huge Harry Potter fans, it turns out.

Jo and Emma had never left Dawson as they wanted Tony to get stronger, which he did, more than doubling in size since we last saw him. When we were able to fight our way past our dogs, we were pleasantly surprised at how everyone had more meat on their bones. Civilization had been kind in some ways.

Lucas and Amber followed us off the plane, holding Diane's hand as she was big enough to negotiate the stairs on her own.

Becca and Darren were already in Dawson City. They'd gone on an extended camping trip in the woods of northern California because they found the world of their former lives so stifling that they couldn't live in it. They'd run away and were happy when we finally got in touch. They couldn't think of anything better than returning to Alaska as settlers, so they took a commercial flight to Canada as soon as possible.

Most of us cringed when we heard Bill bellow something at his parents. At a little over two years old, it appeared he had two speeds: high gear and overdrive. We were happy to see him, too, despite that fact that we weren't happy to hear his lungs were stronger than ever.

As were mine. The stem cell treatment made me feel like a new man. I had more energy than I thought possible. I had one medication that I took once a day, but I could carry ten years' worth with us, without taking up much space. If we didn't have some type of commerce reestablished by then, we probably would have failed.

Looking at the group of close friends who'd become family, I didn't see any of us considering failure as an option.

RETURN

With a new determination we gathered at Abigail and Phillip's kennel outside of town. We finally had the privacy we all sought, along with the camaraderie we'd missed. They say you can't choose your family.

I think they're wrong.

THE RETURN

The sun shone twenty-four hours a day this far north. We weren't constrained by the light although it was hot out, relatively speaking. We had wheel carts for our dog sleds. These rickety contraptions would get us where we wanted to go, but the ride would be nowhere near as smooth as what we'd experienced on the way out.

The added bonus was that we could use the roads this time. I purchased a four-door quad with a trailer where I put my trusty snow machine. It had been completely rebuilt. I brought along extra gasoline, but most importantly, I had the knowledge to recover and reinvigorate old gasoline. I'd have to filter it and juice it up, but then we'd be able to have a running vehicle again. The best way to use old gas was in an old engine. Vehicles from the 1960s or 1970s could burn any type of gas, especially once it was spiced up with a little avgas. We knew where there was plenty of all types. I was certain that we'd be riding in vehicles sooner rather than later.

I had a small toolkit with the quad in order to work on old engines. The usual tools were easy to scavenge. As long as they were out of the weather, they wouldn't rust in the dry interior of Alaska. The tools I carried were to set points within the carburetor, fuses, and the more unique items that might not be readily available.

I forced myself to stop thinking about everything I had in front of me. I looked over the group, the new people selected in secret by the United States Government. Under the Treaty, there could be no government sponsorship of settlers, but they did it anyway. They told me that I could turn down any of the selections, but I was given no options. Being the military governor of the territory carried no weight.

Besides all of the member of the original Community of Chena Hot Springs, we added only four people. I figured that austerity had lost its attraction or the government's efforts to market the new homesteading had fallen flat. I looked at the newcomers and wondered.

Ben was an older native Alaskan, an Athabascan. He knew fishing, and he knew the area around Fairbanks. With the resort destroyed, we intended to establish a settlement on the southwest side of Fairbanks or even Nenana, about fifty miles to the south. We needed access to the river as we needed access to the water for fishing and power.

Ben's wife Clarisse was a joy to be around. She was a little stout, but always friendly. She would have come along regardless, because of Ben, but she'd been preserving for decades the food that Ben killed or picked. She'd help us prepare for the winter, something that we'd need to do as soon as we picked a spot to settle.

We wanted to get it right the first time. We'd build on the work we would do each year. If we moved, we would have to start over.

Two very young engineers joined us. I wondered how they were picked as they seemed ill-equipped to deal with the Alaskan wild. I thought they were straight from Silicon Valley. I didn't see any callouses on their hands, like the hardened members of the Community had. Even the twins looked sturdier than our engineers. I had to ask.

"What brought you guys into this?"

"Dude! We co-wrote a paper on power generation in remote Arctic communities when we were finishing our Masters at MIT," the man said with pride. I nodded.

"Em. Eye. Tea. Alright, Mit, but can you put that knowledge to practical use? This is going to be austere, with a capital A." That sounded as sarcastic as I meant it to be. We couldn't carry any dead weight. Everyone here had to take care of themselves and their families. We'd share, but we didn't want another John in our midst. We'd barely survived the first one.

"Mit? My name's Cullen, and he's Shane." The second man tipped his head. "We can build it. We have an idea what survived from the blast, but if we can get outside the EMP zone, then we'll be able to build something better and faster."

"What's that?" I asked as I pointed to a pile of boxes that looked heavy.

"That's our gear," Cullen said matter-of-factly. He stood next to Shane. Ben and Clarisse had a quad and pulled a trailer of dog food. Everyone else had their dog sleds. Cullen and Shane wore hiking boots.

"Who's going to carry that for you?" I pointed at their gear and then to our menagerie of transportation.

They looked around dumbfounded. The residents of Dawson City, there to see us off, started laughing. Mike, the first man we'd met in Canada, came to their rescue.

"Here. Take mine." He pointed to the quad he was leaning against. It was a two-seater but had a long bed. I pulled out my new cell phone and started typing a text.

"You are the man, Mike. What's your phone number?" I asked. Mike gave it to me, and I finished my text and put the phone back in my pocket. Then I fished it back out and put it on airplane mode.

"My buddy Frank will give you a call and we'll buy you a new quad." I held out my hand. We shook firmly.

When I looked back, Shane and Cullen were still standing there. I ambled up to them and waved them to lean in close.

"Gentlemen, if you become a burden, we'll leave you behind. If you become a problem, we'll feed you to the bears. Now load your gear on the quad I just bought for you while we watch." I looked for some kind of acknowledgement, but there was nothing. They looked at each other and back at me.

I shrugged and walked away. It wasn't my call whether they came or not, although I was starting to lean toward leaving them behind. I wanted to check on everyone else.

The twins had a twelve-dog team each, and they beamed. Abigail and Phillip both mushed sixteen-dog teams as they carried Emma, Jo, and Tony, along with towing sleighs loaded with more supplies. Chris, Darren, and Lucas mushed twelve-dog teams, with their partners and children in the sleds. They towed small sleighs loaded almost exclusively with dog food. With our three quads, that made our group. We had a total of twenty-two people and ninety-four dogs.

I was happy we wouldn't have to run under the cover of darkness. Our travel would be tough enough with running the dogs on the roads. I expected we'd have more than one crash and skinned bodies. Colleen had a robust medical kit with her.

I was worried that we were traveling too heavy. Most of us had something electronic with us. How quickly we had gotten used to civilization, but then again, while living at the resort, we had power and running water. The Community had done without for only a brief period. Madison and I had grown used to a wood-burning stove and no electricity for the better part of two years. Then we re-spoiled ourselves with the introduction of the bigger generator.

I also had a satellite phone secreted away within the quad. That was a special treat we'd surprise the others with at a later time. Our benefactor said we had unlimited minutes. I expected that we'd use all of those between the adult members of the group.

When the engineers were finally ready, I figured everyone wanted to hear something motivational. I'd been thinking about what to say ever since we were told that we could return home. So I stepped in front of the people assembled. They quieted down as everyone gave me their attention.

THE JOURNEY BEGINS

"I never thought we'd be going back to our former home," I started, then swallowed as my throat had gone dry. I took a drink from an offered bottle of water.

"What we saw as a wasteland is now more like the wonderland that Jack London saw when he ventured into a wild Alaska over a century ago. Will we have to live as he did? No, we won't. There are homes throughout Alaska that we can borrow, use as we need to, then leave behind if we need to move on. When we've won the diplomatic war to regain Alaska for the United States, then we'll get more support than we'll ever want." I hesitated. This wasn't easy. We'd seen the world change around us, but it wasn't the world that had changed. It was our role in it, how we treated each other, who we'd become.

"I realized that I didn't like the old world after we returned to it. Mercenary. Driven by things. People who'd lost their way. I preferred our world, the one we are returning to. I'm not willing to call a place civilization; that's reserved solely for the people who make it that. When we get back to the interior, we will have civilization once again. Not what we saw in the Lower 48, but what we see here, in our group of friends and family." Everyone's eyes were locked on mine. I had to look away. I didn't know what else there was to say.

"Time to go?" I asked, then added in an old Alaskan joke, "We're burning daylight. The sun will set in another two months, so let's not waste it!" No one cheered. No one clapped. We reached out, touched shoulders, shook hands, and then turned to our own thoughts.

It was something we did well in the Community – introverts hanging out together, not needing to talk to share the experience.

I saw Chris out of the corner of my eye as he pulled the two engineers to the side. After a brief exchange, the young men nodded vigorously. Chris was not a violent man, but he was physically imposing. I would have to find out later what he told the newcomers. So far, I wasn't impressed. I saw them as dead weight, years from making a difference for the Community. In time, we'd see if we needed to feed those two to the bears.

They may have thought I was kidding.

Chris might see something different. We were far stronger than the group that John tore apart years ago. Together, we were better. I wasn't sure that these two made us better, but I'd give them a chance.

I shook my head and made sure that we were ready to go. Just like before, I'd lead the way, but this time, we would get to take the road. The Yukon River was flowing freely and we had to cross it using the bridges. We left heading northwest on Highway 9, also called Top Of The World Highway. It added fifty miles to our journey, but vastly reduced our risk over traveling the back country.

At fifty miles a day, we were only eight to ten days from getting to Fairbanks. We could base out of our old home to start, but couldn't stay long. We wanted to get to the river where we'd have water and fish, a way to irrigate, and the moose that came there to drink. We needed to stock supplies for the winter.

There was much to think about over the next week. I had a small notebook and pen with me. I promised myself that I'd keep good notes as we went, although I had no plans to do anything with them.

As soon as Bill started bellowing at something, I started the quad and worked my way past the dog teams. I headed up the road at a slow pace, letting Abigail fall in behind me. The twins followed her, driving side-by-side for the present. Then Chris and Colleen, with the two other quads behind them. The rest of the dog teams fell in line with Phillip bringing up the rear.

I looked back often as we led the parade, but Madison kept hitting me in the shoulder. I then realized that this road still had traffic. If anyone was coming, we needed to slow the oncoming vehicles down so they didn't run into our people and their dog teams. But arrangements had been made. We were safe.

The mayor of Dawson City put out the word far and wide and the radio station blared our status. We were oblivious to it all, simply being pleasantly surprised that we had the road to ourselves as we crawled forward on the highway. We started later than I wanted. It was ten in the morning when we finally left the Dawson City limits. That meant we had another sixty-six miles to the border. I expected we'd have to camp within Canada on the first day.

Which brought us back to Mike. He said that he'd follow us in his truck and deliver dog food so we didn't have to dig into our supplies while we weren't yet in Alaska.

The excitement of the trip wore off quickly and we settled into the grind. We'd run the dogs for an hour before taking a break. It was too warm for them. We went through a lot of water, but we had access to as much as we needed. Mike would figure prominently if there was a follow-up to my memoirs. In the interim, Frank would pay him well.

Mike didn't ask for any money, but paying him well was the right thing to do. It's what civilized people did.

It's what we were looking forward to on the other side of the border.

WELCOME TO ALASKA, THE GREAT STATE

The second morning out of Dawson City we crossed into Alaska. I was surprised to see border guards securing the border while acting as immigration officers. They seemed to be waiting for us as they waved us down. We presented our passports, and they dutifully stamped our exit from Canada on this day. They looked around, then leaned close and told us to give those Russians hell.

We laughed as we told them our entire goal was to never see a Russian, but to establish a settlement and rebuild civilization.

Rolling across the border, we pulled to the side of the road and waited as the others came to the checkpoint, showed their papers, received their stamps, and continued on. We moved to the Davis Dome Wayside where there was a huge Welcome to Alaska sign. Abigail set up to water her dogs and the others as they arrived.

Everyone went through the checkpoint dutifully and painlessly, except the engineers, who couldn't find their passports.

Once in Alaska, we were able to carry our weapons. I expected we'd see all types of big game as we traveled this road through the mountains, including bear. Darren had a new 300 Winchester Magnum with a healthy stock of ammunition. My 45-70 was in a gun case on the side of the quad and I was happy to put my shoulder holster on containing my trusty M1911 .45 caliber pistol. Chris also carried a weapon; this one he'd purchased in Canada: a .30-06 hunting rifle.

Together, we were well-armed. I pulled the rifle out of its case and walked back to the middle of the road so the flustered engineers could see and feel my displeasure. The two young men cheered when the last bag they checked contained their errant documents. They pumped their fists and smiled, until they saw me not a hundred feet away. I resisted the temptation to aim my rifle at them.

I was no threat to them, but they would be in danger soon enough.

After watering the dogs and giving them a short rest, Abigail suggested we could cover one hundred miles that day, putting us not far outside of Tok. Between Abigail and Phillip, we had two experts watching the dogs, making sure they were safe and healthy.

Phillip had been raised in a kennel and knew dogs. He'd been studying to be a veterinarian, but wouldn't leave the kennel when his parents moved away. We couldn't ask for someone with us who knew more about the animals.

The twins were like sponges, watching everything the dog mushers did. They watched, and they learned. Maybe they wanted to be veterinarians.

Ben and Clarisse were enjoying the ride. This was more like a summer drive for them. For us, too, I had to admit. The two engineers kept to themselves. They'd already failed to fly below the radar. I pointed to my eyes with two fingers and then pointed at them. "I'm watching you," I mouthed.

Madison rolled her eyes. "Stop terrorizing the children," she told me as I climbed into the driver's seat.

"They're going to do something to piss me off, and I'm going to have to take their quad away, make them walk all the way back to Canada," I said with a hint of anger.

"No you're not. You are going to make sure those two assimilate and contribute, even if you have to hold their hands. Remember the part where we have to have a larger settlement whenever the accounting happens? That means we need everyone we have and hundreds more. Now that we're here, no one gets to leave," she said calmly but firmly.

She had a point.

BEARS

We'd been back in Alaska for a total of four hours and we were pushing hard. The mountains would be behind us soon, leaving us an open run down a long valley toward Tok. Once in the open and on a smooth decline, we should be able to make record time, assuming the brakes held up on the wheeled sleds. I squirmed uncomfortably in my seat as the twins mushed by, hanging on for dear life as they were thrown around in the rickety contraptions flying behind the dogs.

Dog tongues lolling, they raced ahead. Clouds filled the sky, and the air cooled. We took care passing the dogs and mushers as we raced ahead. I believed we would make good time.

Until we saw the bears. No mothers on earth want a pack of strangers between them and their babies. This grizzly sow was no exception. As we drove, Abigail not far behind, we glimpsed the bear coming into the road milliseconds before she rammed into our quad. I gunned it when we were thrown up on two wheels.

Our ride was slow to respond. The bear stood and swiped the side of the quad as it came back to the ground. Madison screamed as she tried to throw herself out of the way.

She was belted in and didn't get far. The bear's claws raked her seat, catching her shoulder. I saw her wince as I wrestled with the wheel to turn the quad away from the massive beast. When the wheels hit the ground, they spun, lurching us forward. The edge of the trailer hit the bear's front leg as it powered past. She almost fell into the snow machine, but stayed upright until we were past. I ran the quad forward until I was sure the bear wasn't following, then slammed on the brakes.

"Are you okay?" I asked Madison while trying to pull my rifle from its case.

"No. It burns!" she stammered. I couldn't see the wound from where I was. I unbuckled my seat belt and leaned forward. The tear in her jacket was bad, but the injury itself didn't look deep.

"Wait here," I said, trying to sound calm. Jumping out, I aimed the rifle back up the road, but the bear was gone. I jogged a few steps, breathing quickly, but fully. I ran farther up the road as Abigail tried to slow her dogs, but I waved her on. "Keep going, a bear, but she's gone now," I yelled as her team ran past. The dogs were alert as the bear scent must have been overwhelming, and they started running out of sync.

"Ha!" Abigail yelled, encouraging them to run through it. I stayed at the side of the road, aiming toward the brush where the bear had disappeared. I listened, but could only hear the next team coming, Charles with Aeryn close behind. Next up was Chris and Colleen.

"Madison needs you!" I yelled and Chris immediately responded, trying to slow the dogs down. He wasn't able to stop the wheeled sled until he was fifty yards past the quad. Colleen handed Hermione to Chris as she grabbed her medical kit and ran to see Madison.

I was relieved at the look on Colleen's face. She gave me a thumbs up, *all is well*, as she pulled something from her kit and started dabbing it on the wound.

The other quads arrived. I asked Ben to run ahead and get in front of Abigail. He nodded confidently as he patted his well-used shotgun in the case at his side. That gave me comfort. He was a man who wasn't afraid of what Alaska threw at him.

The engineers wanted to know the whole story. Grabbing Cullen's collar, I pulled his face toward mine. "Get up there and keep an eye on my kids," I snarled. "I'll owe you." I let go and he nodded before racing down the road past our quad and Chris' dog team.

When Phillip went by, I waved to him and told him to keep his eye out for bears. He also carried a hunting rifle. I didn't know what kind, but I was certain his dogs had dined on moose on more than one occasion.

Colleen only had to clean out the wound and apply antiseptic. Between the roll bar, the seatbelt, and the seat itself, the claws hadn't gone more than skin deep. With the injury cleaned, it only looked like a bad scratch, almost a rug burn. I breathed a sigh of relief. After flexing her shoulder and rotating her arm, Madison was happy that the wound was minor. She hung her head toward her lap and became pale. I tried to pull her close to me, but the quad's seats weren't made for that. I held her hand instead. The come-down after an adrenaline rush weighed on her. She shivered, although it wasn't that cold outside.

"Let's go check on the twins, make sure they're okay," I said, trying to give her something else to think about. As with the mother bear, we now had a bunch of people between Madison and her children. Most were family, but Charles and Aeryn would always be our responsibility.

I started the quad, hoping that it wasn't damaged, and listened closely for strange noises as we moved out. There was a squeak in the back, so I stopped and got out, looking around for any sign that the bear had returned.

Chris continued to rock Diane, while they watched us to make sure everything was okay.

I found the trailer hitch was bent. Driving on two wheels while towing a heavy trailer is not recommended. I was sure that was in a user's manual somewhere. I had my "shopping" tools with me and with a few loud adjustments, using the sledgehammer, the bar straightened sufficiently. At our next break, we'd look more closely to see if it needed more attention. I could always hit it a few more times with the sledgehammer.

We do as we have to. I secured my tools, and we waved Chris forward. Once we were moving again, we were able to maintain fifteen miles an hour, the speed of the dogs running downhill. We caught up to the group at a pullout not far from the valley.

TANACROSS

We stayed the second night in Chicken, but we covered seventy-five miles that day. The next day we made it Tok, but it was still early, so we continued the road to Tanacross. We found that the smaller communities were better equipped for long-term survival. They had more canned goods in their cupboards, and their homes were more inclined toward life without electricity or water.

There was tent space enough for all twenty-two in the Community. We rallied at a house with an oversized shed where the dogs would be most comfortable. The dogs were our means of transportation. As we saw with the damage the bear caused to our trailer, it wouldn't take much and we'd be fully dependent on the paws of our furry friends for all of our transportation needs.

It was warm and sunny; welcome to nighttime during an Alaskan summer. We still made a fire, counting on the smoke to chase the mosquitoes away. We'd use it to heat water and rehydrate our travel rations.

Ben looked at them in disgust. He told us that if he could spend a couple hours hunting, we'd have a decent meal.

"Soon, Ben, soon," I said, nodding. "I know and agree, this stuff is garbage. I can't wait until we have some moose on the grill, maybe even salmon. Wild vegetables and rhubarb, birch syrup and berries. There's a whole gourmet out there with our names on it!"

Clarisse grabbed Ben's arm and bobbed in delight. Jo changed places with Colleen, so she could sit next to Clarisse. We'd gone through the introductions many times, but as we got closer to our new home, each of us explored the strengths of our new companions. Jo was the Community's chef and it looked like Clarisse could be an incredible addition to the kitchen as well as filling the role of our stand-in mother. We didn't know if she'd snap a towel at someone who didn't wash their hands before eating, but I was sure that she had some way of enforcing her rules.

Darren and Becca sat on the ground next to Ben and started talking to him about their experience hunting moose. Darren got up and walked away, shortly returning with his 300 Win mag rifle, with the bolt open to show that it was unloaded.

Ben caressed it lovingly, appreciating its clean lines and raw power. He handed it back and shared his shotgun. It looked like an old friend, the wood stock checkered with scratches and stained dark from the sweat of its owner.

The engineers looked on from the other side of the fire. They were unarmed, although they should have carried weapons. We never knew what we might run across or who would have to fight back if wolves showed up. I strolled in their direction, trying not to be obvious that I wanted to talk with them. They'd grow quiet when either Chris or I was around.

I gave up trying to act casually and walked straight at them, taking a knee so I could speak at their level. Looking down on them while I talked wouldn't accomplish what Madison had insisted I do and that was to make them feel like they were equal members of the Community.

"The other day, I asked you guys to watch over the twins while we were dealing with the aftermath of momma bear. I didn't say thank you, and that was wrong. I appreciate you staying close to them." I smiled and they nodded abruptly. "That also tells me you need some kind of weapon. Just in case." I offered my hand. They hesitated before they each took it.

Even the smallest of progress was progress.

"I've never fired a gun," Cullen said. Shane shook his head with an I-don't-know expression on his face.

"We can fix that. We'll find you something you can use, even if you only use it as a noisemaker. You won't need to hunt; we already have plenty of hunters. With this many people and dogs? I think we'll need five or six moose every year, but we'll be the only ones hunting. Ben will make sure we add plenty of fish as well. Do you guys fish?" More shrugs. I could feel my blood pressure rising.

"What's your plan when we get where we're going?" I asked. I hadn't intended to get in their faces, but it wouldn't be long before everyone had jobs to do. I wanted to know how they were going to contribute, and I had yet to get a straight answer.

"We intend to build a power plant. We have designs for geothermal, wind, water, and steam with us. We will build a plant using equipment and materials and should be available to bring power back to a limited grid." They both brightened as Shane described their strategic objective.

"How long will it take you to decide what you can build and then how long do you think it will take you to build it?" I asked, instantly skeptical of their grand plan.

"It won't take long to figure out what we can build as it will depend on what we find of the remaining infrastructure. Wire, transformers, and things like that should still be there, right?" I nodded, and he continued, "Then we'll be able to get right into it. With twenty people, the work should go quickly." That's what I was waiting for.

"No problem at all, I can guarantee that you'll have yourselves as manpower, and then maybe two more to help you each day. It's halfway through the summer and we have to get ready for the winter. Do you know how much provisioning we have to do for this many people and nearly a hundred dogs? I hope we don't have to work too many sixteen-hour days, but I expect that will be the norm from here until the first snow. And then we'll work twelve hours. Look at what we might want to do as winter work – detailed indoor stuff that will be time-consuming. We will have nothing but time when it gets cold." I'd upset their plans, but they were engineers. They'd go back to the drawing board and come up with a new plan.

They'll figure it out or maybe we will have to feed them to the bears, I thought.

THE ACCIDENT

There's nothing like the open road to wear a person down. The dogs kept running. The only problem for them was the heat. With streams paralleling the road, we always had a ready source of water. Knowing that humans hadn't contaminated it over the last four years, we all drank readily from the crystal-clear water. To stay together, we decided to run the quads slowly, barely more than idle speed which was enough to keep pace with the dog teams.

Since I was leading the parade, I had the opportunity to race ahead, scout the road, then drive back. It's exactly what I did on our run out of Alaska in the first place. It worked then so there was no reason to change it.

Although in retrospect, I should have.

As Madison and I were driving back to the group following one of our look-aheads, we were surprised to see that the teams were stopped. We slowly passed the barking dogs. Neither the dog mushers nor their passengers were anywhere to be seen. We continued past the twins' sleds and grew concerned as they weren't with their teams either.

I swung wide around the teams and accelerated, hitting the brakes hard as soon as I rounded the corner. Everyone was together, with some in the ditch working on an overturned quad.

The engineers had gone over the edge.

We slid to a stop, scattering those who were standing on the road, although I don't think it was as close as they thought it was. Chris and Colleen were both in the ditch while Charles held Hermione and Aeryn cooed to the baby to help her calm down.

"They were both talking, but we don't know how they are. Chris is working to get them out and Colleen has her medical kit. Ben is down there, too," Charles said, concern in his voice, but not panic. They shouldn't have been that mature for six-year-olds, but they were.

I crawled over the edge of the ravine, helping Madison down with me. All the men were there along with Colleen.

"What do you need us to do, Chris?" I asked as he stood back, looking from the quad to the trees.

"It's holding them both in as it's wedged between these rocks. We need to lift it up to use the winch on your quad. I was thinking we can throw ropes over these trees here." Chris pointed to one heavy branch overhead and a smaller one to the side. "We hoist it enough to relieve the pressure and get those two out, then drag the quad up the hill, see what we can salvage."

The two young men were yelling hysterically. Cullen seemed to think he was hurt badly judging by the amount of noise he was making. Colleen yelled at him to shut up as they weren't helping. Shane seemed to take that as a challenge and stepped up his screams for help.

"Rope!" I yelled, but they'd already thrown it to us. We tied it off, letting Ben make sure the knots would hold. Then we braced ourselves and started pulling, but it wouldn't move. We dug around underneath and found one of the roll bars wedged into a rock as if it were an anchor. Little Bill bugled something from the road as if he were a cow moose in heat. Becca picked him up and carried him off.

"Hacksaw!" I yelled. It took Clarisse a few moments to dig one out of Ben's supplies. While we waited, I tried to engage the engineers. I didn't think Shane was hurt, but he was panicking and kept yelling for help, despite our assurances that everyone who could help was already there. Chris pulled me back from the opening before I punched the young man. Instead, Chris reached in and grabbed a handful of hair, pulling it until Shane's head was twisted at an awkward angle.

"I think the man asked nicely for you to stop yelling. You need to shut up and let us get you out of there." Chris emphasized his point with an extra tug on Shane's hair. Wide eyes held Chris' for a second, and then he started yelling again. Chris let go, then with a motion too quick to follow, he punched the young engineer in the side of the head.

The screaming stopped. The hacksaw arrived, and I crawled to the side of the quad and started cutting on the roll bar. It was made of sturdy material so we all took turns. Saw for a minute then hand off.

The blade was hot enough to start a fire when we finished. With the last cut, the quad lurched, settling heavier on its top.

We rallied to pull the machine from where it was wedged. The doors were twisted and wouldn't open, but there was room through the windows. We cut away the canvas strapping and while extra hands held Shane in place, we cut his seatbelt. We guided him through the window opening and he was out. Colleen took him aside while we did the same for Cullen. His left arm was clearly broken and would present a problem in working him out the door.

With Shane out of the vehicle, Cullen calmed down and we were able to talk with him. He thought his leg might be broken, too. His chest hurt, and he didn't know why. He couldn't see because of the blood in his eyes from the gash on his head. But he was talking.

"You sound just fine to me," I said while the others braced the quad to keep it from moving. We would all have to help Cullen out through the window. "Welcome to Alaska. In the old days, you'd have to set your break yourself, along with fix everything else and then fight off a bear. We were tougher back then." Despite his injuries, Cullen smiled, then winced.

I started to call Colleen over, but stopped when I saw her push Shane away from her. Chris was there in a heartbeat, putting himself bodily between the two. The young man sat on a rock, covered his face, and wept.

Colleen came to Cullen's side so she could best examine him. The bleeding from his head had mostly stopped, so she cleaned the wound and bandaged it. He blinked his eyes clear. She wanted to put a splint on his arm before we pulled him out of the quad. We each took a position where we could best brace the engineer's arm. Colleen held a rag over his face while I prepared to pull his arm straight out while Ben and Chris held his elbow.

The trick with setting a bone is pulling it hard enough to get the bone spurs past each other. The muscles would pull it back tightly. Without setting it, the bone would never heal. Colleen wouldn't let that happen. It was up to us to get it right. One and done.

At the count of three, I pulled for all I was worth with my legs braced against the rock beneath the quad. Cullen screamed while Chris and Ben pulled the arm away from me.

When I let go, his arm looked straight, although there was great deal of bruising where the bone had broken. At least it wasn't an open fracture where the bone broke the skin. Cullen's arm shook as Colleen put a splint on it and wrapped it tightly. The young man passed out.

We needed his help to get him out, so we had to wait. Within a minute, he was back with us. We'd already cut the webbing away from the window. The only thing left was Cullen's seatbelt. He whimpered and started hyperventilating as Ben's knife hovered, ready to cut.

"Hurry up!" Colleen urged.

Ben sliced it cleanly and dropped his knife to the ground to use both hands to help the young engineer. We kept the man's forearm from touching anything but he had to brace himself with his elbow. That caused him to cry out in pain, but gave us the leverage we needed to pull him free. Colleen was already removing his shirt as we laid him down.

The steering wheel had jammed into his chest, causing an ugly bruise, but Colleen didn't think any of his ribs were broken. His leg also seemed to be only bruised. He was in pain, so much so that he was unable to move.

We used a sleeping bag as a stretcher so we could manhandle him up the hill. We moved him to the side of the road and gave him plenty of water.

We faced my quad toward the ditch and blocked the front tires. It took all of us to coordinate lifting the damaged vehicle using the ropes while the winch dragged it up the hill. Once back in the road and upright, we didn't think we'd have to abandon it. The trailer was a total loss, but we recovered all their gear since it had been packed in metal cases, which were sturdier than the trailer on which they rode.

We distributed the boxes among the dog sleds and repaired the quad to a point where people could ride in it. It started up when we tried it and a quick test drive confirmed that although it pulled to the left, it was drivable. We recovered all our ropes and gear, including Ben's knife, which had fallen between the rocks, and we prepared to leave. This wasn't a good place to camp.

Shane was still in the gulley. Chris climbed back down the hill. Ben drove up the rode with all the dog teams following him, while we waited for Chris. Colleen held their daughter while their twelve-dog team barked and bounced, wondering why they weren't allowed to run after the others. Madison was ready to drive our quad with Cullen as her passenger, and I was behind the wheel of the engineers' quad waiting for Shane. As I thought about it, I'd paid for this quad, so it was mine, too. Odd to think about something like that, but as it turned out, I had nothing else to do for quite a while.

An agonizing amount of time later, Chris led Shane by the hand up the hill and to the quad. Shane hesitated, but Chris guided him in. He covered his face and started to cry again. At least we could go, but I was none too pleased with my weeping passenger. One broken arm between the two of them? We got off easy, and we should have been thankful for that.

Shane had nothing to do with the accident. I could think of no reason for the man to be so traumatized. I'd seen Marines come unhinged in combat, but this wasn't any of that.

I ended up holding his hand as we drove, and that seemed to calm him. I had no more empathy in me. My six-year-olds were up ahead and deserved my attention, not this guy. The seed of mistrust I'd planted earlier was watered and now growing to the size of a redwood. I wanted to get out and tell him to take the quad and get the hell out of my state, but knew Madison would be angry.

I'd tolerate him, but after this, the others better keep him away from me.

THE RECOVERY

We wanted to push on because we had to. Ben took the group another twenty-five miles up the road before finding an area where the Community could bed down. We showed up an hour after the others. Clarisse and Jo were already working their magic to create a meal worthy of the title of "feast."

Hours after the accident, Shane still hadn't said a word. When we pulled in, Colleen checked on Cullen and found him to be in good spirits, even though he was in a fair amount of pain. He had his Alaskan battle wound, so we cheered for him and wished him well.

Colleen pulled Shane aside to check on him, finally announcing that he had a concussion, a bad one. I looked at Chris. He couldn't meet my gaze. It probably wasn't from the punch, but the less Colleen knew, the less she could hold against us. She put him in the shade and gave him cool water to drink. She had no idea how long it would take for him to recover.

As we sat around the fire enjoying the meal and each other's company, the conversation inevitably turned toward the accident. We grew quiet when Cullen prepared to speak. He looked at his incapacitated friend and shook his head.

"I'm sorry," he started, but that wasn't what he really wanted to say. "It's my fault. I fell asleep and drove off the road. There's no excuse for the trouble I've caused, for my own injuries, which don't seem as bad as what Shane is going through. I can't go back and fix it, but I'll take care of him until he's better, even though I only have one arm. We promised that we wouldn't be a burden, but that's all we've been. We'll work double shifts, do what we need to support the Community. We'll turn the power on. I promise all of you that we'll succeed, and we will make you proud," he finished without a flourish and sat down.

Madison looked at me with a broad smile and started clapping. The others joined in, as did I.

I wanted to hate them both, but if this was more than a speech, they might turn out okay.

I got up and walked past Chris, slapping him on the back as I went. He still wouldn't look at me. I knew he had to feel horrible. I also knew that he'd come clean with Colleen, and then there'd be hell to pay. I didn't want to be around for that.

DELTA JUNCTION

We made the run to Delta Junction in less than four hours, arriving before noon. But we stopped short of Fort Greely, south of the city as we didn't want to run headlong through any lingering radiation.

When we left Alaska, we'd skipped past the city and headed inland from the airport located to the north. That wasn't that long ago, only four months.

So we took a reading now. Madison and I moved slowly forward. She drove while I held an improved Geiger counter the government had given me out the window. It clicked and showed levels slightly above normal background radiation. We continued at a crawl as there was debris in the road. The dog sleds would never make it through all of this. As we got closer to where we assumed the blast had been, the debris cleared, probably blown away by the detonation. Much of the city was leveled, but the airport was miles from the gate and that's why it had survived intact.

We drove past Fort Greeley's entrance. The radiation picked up, but it wasn't anything alarming. I was surprised by how little damage was done to the ground itself. I would have thought that a nuclear bomb would leave a massive crater. This one must have been smaller than the one in Fairbanks and most of the detonation must have gone laterally. Maybe this one wasn't even a nuke, but a simpler dirty bomb – a huge amount of high explosives with radioactive isotopes that would scatter with the explosion and subsequent dust and debris.

Four years was enough time to cleanse the earth, especially there in Delta Junction where it was always windy, sometimes with winds of fifty to sixty miles an hour. We traveled through the blast area and along the main road to the north. Debris returned after we cleared the primary blast site, but there was less in the north. We scouted a path through to the turn-off for the airport. We'd made this turn when snow packed the road. Everyone who'd been there before knew the way.

We headed back to meet the teams and did what we could to clear the road south of the Fort Greely main gate. We waited until everyone was there, and at barely faster than a walk, the dog mushers dragged their brakes and kept their dogs from running ahead. It was harder on the dogs to go this slowly, but it was necessary until they got past anything that could tangle their leads or upset the sleds.

Ben took a sharp turn away from us and headed toward the town. I wondered where he was going, figuring something had piqued his interest. I wasn't worried. He'd find his way to the airport. Ben was a person who could take care of himself.

When everyone finished picking their way through the rubble and debris, we sped up and raced past the gate and toward the north side of the city. When we hit the turn to the airport, I looked back and saw plenty of people smiling. We had good memories from this place.

I floored it and we bolted away from the others. We pulled into the parking lot of the hangar, stopping as far to the side as we could go. The second I shut off the engine, we heard a single rifle shot come from the south. I wondered if Ben had bagged dinner.

I was surprised to see that we hadn't shut the door when we left. Animals had gotten in and the place was foul. Or did we leave it that way? Madison and I got out the brooms and started throwing refuse out the door. We were halfway done when Abigail arrived with the twins close behind. We would have put the children to work, but they needed to get their dogs settled. We watched them as they easily controlled their dogs, tying them to nearby trees, watering them, feeding them. Phyllis and Husky jumped off the sleds when they saw us and ran to us, then went into the hangar, probably to make sure it was safe for their humans.

The other teams arrived and did the same thing. When Cullen pulled in with his quad, we waved him over to park closer to the door. When they shut off the engine, I said, "Handicapped parking," and pointed to a sign on the building.

I gave them the thumbs up and returned to the hangar to finish cleaning it.

We had more people to squeeze in around the stripped-down airplane still sitting in the middle of the hangar, but we didn't have the sled dogs inside this time. Our dogs, of course, were with us. Wherever the twins were, Phyllis and Husky were not far behind.

As we were getting everyone settled, Jo decided to start dinner. Since it was warm, we made the fire outside. We heard the quad approaching and it was making a hellacious noise. Everyone gathered around and waited. The dogs started howling. Abigail and Phillip ran into the trees to calm them.

Ben wore a broad grin while Clarisse just shook her head. Tied behind the trailer was a moose on a large piece of sheet metal. Ben had already gutted it and removed the head to cut down on how much weight he had to drag. I was surprised the quad could pull it, even with the reduced weight. That was one big moose.

We joined him at the edge of the parking lot, and the celebration began.

WHAT WILL WE DO WHEN
WE GET THERE?

Nothing like a belly full of lean, rare moose to put a dog into a food coma. Once they were out cold, we sat and enjoyed our freshly cooked, over-sized moose steaks.

Shane showed an interest in something finally. After his first tentative bite, he dug in, finished his quickly, and then went for seconds. Even though he was in pain from his injuries, Cullen helped Shane. It had only been two days since the accident which was just long enough for the young engineer's broken arm and bruises to turn ugly shades of blue and green.

Bill serenaded us with howls of joy at eating moose again after a four-month hiatus. To answer the question often asked, "No," they said, "he doesn't have any other volume." I was reminded of the incident at the resort where someone called him "that little hell spawn." His parents, Becca and Darren were good people, and they were incredible for not getting twisted out of sorts whenever Bill bugled the call of his people. Maybe they were deaf. The jury was still out on that one.

Little Tony was all smiles. For the life he was born into, he should have been miserable. Out of the entire Community, Tony exemplified what we were trying to build. People could be who they wanted to be, work with others to help themselves grow. He was happy as he was unconditionally loved by us all. He received the most attention, although Hermione was quickly gaining in popularity, but Colleen rarely let anyone else hold her.

I was curious how they were going to tell Tony and Hermione that they were siblings, although that was none of my business. Since we were all family, maybe they'd raise the two children who were only a month apart as twins with different parents. They'd be together all the time anyway.

Madison and Amber said they'd set the school back up. That meant extra space to heat, unless one of the homes we were going to establish doubled as a school house. That made the most sense. Logistically, it was going to be all we could do to set ourselves up before winter arrived, let alone have the added burden of heating an extra building.

I hoped, more than anyone else, that we'd find sufficient provisions, canned goods, to fill the void created by our late arrival. One can't plant crops in Alaska in June. The growing season was only another seventy-five days at the most. Without the ability to prepare the ground properly, we wouldn't attempt it. We'd forage, and we'd hunt.

We talked about the next steps once everyone finished eating. Ben said that we may have missed the best time to fish, but he refused to be denied. He wasn't sure we'd get enough for the dogs for the winter, although he would try building a fish wheel as soon as we arrived. That would have been illegal in the State of Alaska, but in the Territory of Alaska where I was the military governor, it was approved as a necessity for our survival.

I already felt the blisters I'd be getting from cutting wood. Everyone worked, even if they had a long title like mine.

All eyes turned toward Cullen as he stood. "I think the best thing for us, Shane and I, is to survey what we have, make notes, and then spend the rest of the time helping the Community get ready for winter. Once winter falls, we'll start with our detail work, make the drawings we'll use to build whatever power generation system will work the best. So, what I'm trying to say is that we will be extra manpower for you this summer, not the other way around as we initially thought. And we want to thank you for taking care of us. I think that steak was the best I've ever had." Cullen looked down at Shane, who nodded. The young man held his head in his hands as the movement had been too much and the pain returned.

"One other thing," Cullen said. "If you would know of any clubs where we might meet some fellow engineers of the female persuasion, we would be awfully grateful." The Community booed him, and someone threw a small rock that hit him in the leg.

We had a good laugh at his expense. It would be a while for the poor youngsters.

NEXT STOP, FAIRBANKS

The rest of our journey was uneventful until we arrived on the outskirts of Fairbanks. When we'd gone through previously, we didn't have good light, but in the daytime, we saw that North Pole was completely intact. The stores, the houses, even Santa's Village. It was far enough away that they would have seen the mushroom cloud, but unfortunately for them, they were downwind from the blast and received the worst of the radiation.

Our new Geiger counter showed the town wasn't hot. The threat from radiation had passed. The weather had carried the worst of it away. Even when we tested the dust inside a building, it came up clean.

We stopped and tied off the dog sleds to the light poles in the parking lot of the Safeway supermarket. It was late in the day, but of course we had light. Looking at the lack of destruction, I thought North Pole might be the best place to stay the first winter. It might not take long to scavenge supplies. Maybe it wouldn't be as hard as I thought.

Chris and Colleen looked sullen as they bedded their dogs for the night. Even Hermione looked sad.

"What's up?" I asked, casually petting the dogs as I walked toward the couple. Neither answered as they looked at each other and then at me. I waited.

"The horses," Colleen whispered. We'd gone through Delta Junction and hadn't asked if they wanted to run down the valley, see if the remaining two horses had survived the winter. I felt like an idiot.

"We'll drop the trailer and you can take our quad. It'll be faster that way. You can make Delta Junction in two hours or less. I don't know what the terrain in the valley looks like without snow. It might be impassable or it could be fine." I could see them thinking about it. They were torn between their loyalty to the Community and their desire to save the horses.

"Go on. If we stay here, we won't be killing ourselves before winter. Let's go in the store first and see if there's anything we can use. If there is, then we'll be able to do without you for a while," I offered. As a group, we went inside through the broken glass of the front doors. The concussion from the blast had reached here.

We saw something we hadn't expected. Dead bodies.

Amber and Lucas turned around with Diane in between them. A two-year-old didn't need to see this. Charles and Aeryn looked as they passed, but didn't fixate on them. Their eyes were focused elsewhere. We continued into the store. What I thought was a ransacking was the damage from the initial blast. A couple registers looked like they'd been broken into, but not all of them. Charles reached for a Snickers bar in a checkout lane.

"Stop!" I yelled, pulling out the Geiger counter. The food within would be safe as long as any contamination from the package didn't get on it. The instrument said that the candy bar wasn't radioactive. "Let me check to make sure," I said as I carefully unwrapped the candy bar and made a show of waving the Geiger counter past it, before shoving half the bar into my mouth.

"Dad!" they yelled together as they dove for the rack, grabbing a replacement bar before I could stop them.

"We're away from this stuff for a week and this is the first thing you want?" I asked. I thought we had weaned them from candy and bad foods.

"Wrong!" Charles stated definitively. "The first thing we wanted was moose, and we had that last night." Aeryn pursed her lips and nodded once in agreement.

"Spread out! Let's take stock of what's here. We need to feed twenty-two people and one hundred dogs for six months." The couples each went their own way down different aisles. Little sunlight reached the interior so we used the wind-up flashlights we'd brought. There was no sense using battery-powered lights as we had no batteries.

Then again, maybe we had more than we thought. The store had flashlights in the exit lanes along with batteries. I took a handful of MagLites and opened them one at a time, putting new batteries in. I was rewarded with the bright light that these flashlights were known for. I yelled for everyone and passed them out. It made our job searching much easier. If we spent any time in here, we'd need to clean out the refrigerators. It looked like Jurassic Park, overgrown with mold and other less savory things. I was surprised that anything was growing after four years. Maybe a scientist would find something less repulsive in this oversized Petri dish, but not me.

We worked our way into the back warehouse where pallets of goods were stacked high, too high to get without a working forklift. If the windows blew out, then the EMP had ripped through here, too. Anything electronic was fried, which meant the forklift was dead.

We could always tip them over. It didn't have to be pretty, only effective.

There was enough food here for all of us for all winter. It was nice to have the "shopping" done so we could get to some real work. There were a thousand things we needed to do, but finding canned goods to survive the first winter was one of the most important.

I shook hands with Chris and wished him well. Madison and Colleen hugged. They left that night for the short trip back to the hangar in Delta Junction. Tomorrow morning, bright and early, they'd head cross-country in an attempt to follow our trail. Whether they found the horses or not, it'd be a while before they returned. I hoped they'd find the horses, for Colleen's sake.

If we went anywhere, we agreed to leave a note on the bulletin board inside Fred's.

With that chapter of our journey closed, the rest of us settled in for the evening.

NOW WHAT?

The inside of Safeway was less than welcoming with the dead bodies, the long-rotted fresh food section, produce, the unworking refrigerators, and a lack of airflow. The destruction here wasn't like anything we'd had to deal with before. The Fred Meyer in Fairbanks had been systematically evacuated, so there weren't any dead and some of the spoilage was hidden under a partially collapsed roof.

There was no way anyone would sleep inside the tomb of Safeway. Once in the fresh air, even though the midnight sun shone brightly, we put up our tents and climbed into our sleeping bags. We slept well. All of us, even Shane and little Bill.

When we crawled out of bed in the morning, the first thing I did was set up an impromptu bathroom facility in the ditch between the store and the highway. It didn't take much and gave everyone a little privacy. The bad news was that it attracted bugs. The good news was that behind us we had an unlimited supply of bug dope, the Alaskan term for bug repellant. The next person to use the facility lit a mosquito coil and put it inside. That made it better for those who followed.

And that led to the second order of business: Where were we going to stay? I called for a group meeting at breakfast. Everyone went into the store to look for favorites. I had to wrestle packages of Twinkies away from the twins. In the end, they settled for protein bars, which probably had enough chemicals in them to last for decades.

Madison and I preferred the moose jerky that Ben had made out of the choicer parts of our left-over feast from two days earlier. We also had a stock of moose meat that was smoked to preserve it for the dogs.

While people were eating, I stood up in the middle of the group. All eyes were on me.

"Now that we're here, we need to find places to stay that have wood-burning stoves, a source for split wood, and access to the river. We also need an idea of what kinds of supplies we have available. Ben, could you head to the river and see if there are any fish? Someone needs to inventory the canned goods, see how many meals we can get." I waited as Clarisse and Jo both waved to volunteer for that duty.

"We need to find a place to stay where we either have a wood-burning stove or can set up to burn wood. Then we need to stock enough firewood for the winter. I think we should try to stick to one or two buildings, have a central place to eat. This first winter won't be pretty, but that's not our goal. We need to survive and then be ready to kick off next year as soon as we see the light, so to speak," I finished, smiling, proud of my pun. No one else seemed to get it.

"We'll take our broken quad and see if we can find a power source. Isn't there a refinery near here?" Cullen asked.

"Right down the road behind us, but it closed about a year before the attack, and even if it hadn't, the full force of the EMP went through here," I answered.

"Doesn't matter about the electronics. Refining is a mechanical and chemical process. The electronics make it markedly safer, but to run the process, you don't need them. You only have to know which valves need to be open and closed. We want to take a look, then find a backup," Cullen said.

"Okay, the rest of us will go house hunting. There's an elementary school nearby, and then the middle school, and finally the high school. There are churches on almost every street corner along with people's private homes. Please remember that unlike what we saw on the western side of Fairbanks, the people here were killed in an ugly way. Every house you go into could have bodies. Be aware. I'm keeping a bandanna over my nose and mouth, keep out the nastiness and hopefully some of the smell."

The others nodded and prepared to go. Abigail and Phillip said they'd take care of all the dogs. I looked at Charles and Aeryn. They inclined their heads toward our temporary kennel off the parking lot. I nodded and waved them away. They raced off before I could change my mind. A few of the dogs had jumped onto the cars and were sitting on the hoods as they warmed under the morning sun.

I looked to each and every person sitting around the circle. Amber and Lucas, Darren and Becca, Jo and Emma, Cullen and Shane, Ben and Clarisse, and Madison. Diane and Tony were there, along with little Bill who was surprisingly quiet. I couldn't help but smile at him. He was destined for great things.

Our children and the dog mushers were doing what they did best, handle the dogs.

Chris and Colleen were off with their daughter in search of the horses that their child had never seen. Which reminded me, Colleen was our only nurse, doctor, and caregiver. "By the way, no one get hurt. Help is a week away, at least."

And we each went our separate ways, everyone to their own affairs. We'd return no later than dinnertime and share our discoveries.

CHRIS AND COLLEEN

Without pulling the trailer and having mostly open road in front of them, the trip to Delta Junction only took an hour. They stopped at the hangar that we'd called home and stayed the night. They left in the morning while most civilized people were still in bed.

The route we'd taken was much different at this time of year. Most of it was overgrown; small streams and ditches had become insurmountable obstacles. They sidetracked and backtracked often, racing ahead through the open areas when they could, always looking for any sign of the two horses.

They figured it was only twenty-five to thirty miles from Delta Junction to where they'd turned the two mares loose. They decided the best way to look would be to find where they'd stashed the saddles and look from there.

The first day, they drove in so many circles that they lost the valley entrance. They drove to the top of a hill to look back toward Delta Junction to get their bearings. Chris reoriented himself and set out to a waypoint he decided would lead them into the valley where Winnifred had died. They held hands as they drove in the open areas. Colleen squeezed hard whenever she saw a dark spot in the grass, thinking that might be her old friend. They'd had no choice and understood that if we hadn't put her out of her misery and abandoned the other two, the little girl held tightly in her lap may not have survived.

Leaving the others was the risk they took. Now was the time to put their lives back on track. Colleen wanted the memories that brought her peace. Her horses embodied much of what she loved about Alaska. Animals that powered through the challenges of weather and the vast open spaces, lived life without remorse.

She thought back to her husband and son. That seemed like a lifetime ago. She released Chris' hand and hugged her baby tightly to her. It was more than time, it was in a different place. She didn't even feel like the same person. But the one thing that was a constant in her life was the horses.

"We have to find them," she said out loud, wearing a determined look on her tear-streaked face.

Chris thought he understood what she was thinking, but he didn't want to ask. Although he hadn't been married before the destruction, he also had lived a different life, one he'd run away from. Whether it was lack of responsibility, fear, or simply his dislike of college that drove him north, now he was taking time to learn more about himself, about what he wanted.

Then everything had changed and his life mattered again. He was important for who he was, and not who other people thought he could become. Colleen never asked what he wanted to do when they were in Canada. His answer would not have changed from when they lived at the resort. He wanted to be with her and their child, help the others, and live.

Was it too much to ask that they simply enjoy life?

Late in the day, they found the campsite where Chris spoke after Winnifred passed away. They dug through the heavy underbrush until they found the saddles. They were dry and cracked. The weather had not been kind, but they loaded them on top of the gas cans in the small bed of the quad. They decided to stay there for the night and resume their search when they awoke.

They hadn't slept well last night and they weren't sleeping well this night either. Too anxious. Too many things running through their minds. Concern that something had happened to the horses after they'd been abandoned.

It never got dark, so they judged the time by the sun's position in the sky. If it was in the north, then it was nighttime. It had swung to the northeast by the time Chris and Colleen found themselves awake but exhausted.

They walked around the campsite, looking for any sign of the horses, but didn't find anything. They drove slowly in the quad as the valley grasses and weeds were high. They didn't want to get into an accident this far from the Community.

It was slow going much of the time. Colleen wanted to race from one point to the next since they could see a long way, look over that hill, then move on. She was anxious and nervous and depressed.

Chris stayed focused throughout the first day, disappointed that they couldn't find any sign of the animals. The valleys and hills were covered with growth and moose roamed throughout. They often thought they saw their mares, only to be disappointed when a moose cow and her calf ambled away.

They circled wide, stopping every couple hours to give Hermione a break outside the vehicle. Exhausted from the search and the lack of sleep, they finally camped on a hillside miles from where they'd released the horses.

The second day, they continued. Then the third. They'd made it nearly all the way back to Delta Junction when Chris suggested they run back to the hangar to get more avgas, refill their containers. Colleen agreed reluctantly, her sour mood bringing them all down.

Hermione cried a lot. Chris second-guessed himself for agreeing to come along. With enough internal reflection, he realized that he had no choice. When your partner is in pain, you do what you have to do, even if that course of action leads to more pain.

He was there for her.

They refueled and searched for a fourth day, ending back at the original camp. They decided to take the trail toward Canada. The horses may have followed them for some way. They agreed that this was their last shot. If they couldn't find the horses in two more days of searching, they'd head back to North Pole and rejoin the Community.

Colleen remained quiet after that. She felt as if she'd given up on her husband and son when she'd waited at home for them. There was nothing she could have done except go into town, expose herself to radiation, and join them in their graves. She looked at Chris, who smiled back at her. She pushed him away and stormed off. Chris hung his head, trying to hold back the tears. He knew that it wasn't him. Colleen wrestled with her demons, and she wasn't winning.

They left early in the morning without a word to each other. They crisscrossed the valley as they drove east for one full day. Without seeing any sign of the horses halfway through the second day, their sixth day of searching, Colleen put her hand on Chris' arm and told him to head back.

Chris took his time turning around, hoping for a glimpse of horse manure, a dark shadow at the edge of the woods. He didn't want to appear that he was ready to return to the others, although he'd hit that point four days ago.

The return was quicker than intended, but they still needed to camp one last time before the final run to Delta Junction and the quick trip to North Pole. They camped where they had released the horses. It was light through the night, but they still made a fire, much bigger than they needed, but the sound and smell of burning wood was soothing. Colleen finally accepted the loss of the last remnants of her former life. With one great sigh, she curled up in Chris' arms and went to sleep.

The sound woke them both. A whinny, the kind that only a horse makes. Carefully getting up so she didn't wake the baby, Colleen bolted into the early morning fog, stopping, listening, and walking.

Then she began to call for them. "Penelope! Sophie!" She walked carefully, the fog clinging to the lower areas of the valley. She walked uphill to get a clearer view.

At the edge of the woods, she saw the two mares, shaggy, but looking healthy. They pranced, not sure of the human as she approached. She stopped and dropped to her knees, breaking down, sobbing uncontrollably. The horses circled away from her briefly and then approached. Their soft muzzles pressed against her head.

She embraced them both as she stood, apologizing over and over. They didn't seem to care. When Chris walked up with Hermione cradled gently in his arms, Colleen looked at him through red and puffy eyes, smiling broadly. He arched his knee beside Penelope so Colleen could use him as a step. She slowly climbed up and sat astride the horse's back, holding tightly to her mane.

"Now, if you were only naked while you were up there, that'd be a sight!" Chris said playfully, and he could not have been happier as joy, in the form of two raggedy-looking mares, returned to their lives.

FINDING A HOME

After our first day, we came together over a magnificent dinner to share what we'd found.

Ben spoke first. "I think the river here will be okay, but I would prefer Nenana because of the confluence of two rivers. We only need fish to supplement a diet heavy in moose. The dogs will eat well this winter, have no doubt, and we will not go hungry. I will build a smoker to preserve the moose meat and racks to dry the fish we'll catch."

Cullen raised his hand to speak next. Many chuckled as the Community usually gave the floor to whomever was ready to talk because they were reluctant to stand. Most of us didn't like getting up in front of the group, even though we considered ourselves family. To me, Cullen just showed that he didn't consider himself part of the family.

"What do you have?" I said as I nodded toward the young engineer.

"We think we can restart the refinery. We can use leftover crude oil in one of tanks, refine it into diesel. Do you know of any diesel trucks or maybe a diesel generator?"

"A diesel generator that hasn't been fried by the EMP?" I asked myself out loud, thinking before answering. "We can try Eielson to the south. I bet they have something there. If we come up with one, what can you do with it?"

Cullen gave me an odd look. "Is that a trick question? We can burn the diesel and generate power."

I smiled and dropped my head. I didn't have the luxury of being snarky. "Sorry, that wasn't a good question. How much electricity and for how long?"

"Diesel engines are made to run a long time and are relatively low maintenance. If we can do regular preventative maintenance on one, a twenty-kilowatt engine can run all the homes we need, five or six of them, without any problem, as long as we don't use the electricity for heat. Without running electric heaters, we'll have plenty of power." Heads nodded as Cullen finished.

"Freezers," I said and looked at Ben. He was thinking the same thing. "Thanks, Cullen. That helps. If we can find one that survived, then we'll need find a big forklift. We get one of those running, we'll be able to move a big generator, split wood, all kinds of good things…" I wasn't talking to the group anymore. I was thinking out loud as I often did. That was a natural result of spending the time alone like we'd done for years.

Abigail stood up. "Wherever we decide to stay, we need shelter for the dogs. A warehouse or oversized shed would work, then we can start adding doghouses. If I can get back to the resort, there are doghouses, chains, everything." She sat down without further discussion.

"I might have an idea. Right across the street, we have the Santa Claus tourist attraction. They used to have reindeer, with a pen and shelter. The reindeer are long gone, but the area is fenced, and it's larger than what you had at the resort," Darren chimed in. Becca nodded while little Bill snoozed.

"I think the best place for the number of people we have is the Mormon Church. If we put wood-burning stoves at each corner, we should be able to heat the whole thing. With a generator, we can use electric heaters, and yes, I heard you, Cullen, but with one single building and one kitchen, we won't stress the system out. We'll set up a single laundry. It'll work, but we have one little issue to resolve before we move in," I said with a grimace.

A couple of the others hung their heads. Amber spoke softly, "In their last days they sought the solace of the church. It's full of dead people, isn't it?"

"No one needs to see that. It can come back to life with us, with the Community. The elementary school is empty, but it would be much harder to make it work because it's a bigger building, drawing more power, harder to heat." I thought my argument was persuasive, but I had no allies.

Amber stood up and smiled. "Sounds like the elementary school will be perfect," she said, using her mayor's voice.

"Once we clean up Jo and Clarisse's excellent dinner, let's take a stroll, all of us, and take a look. Some of you look like you could use some exercise!" A fresh-baked bun flew at my head. Clarisse scolded the thrower, who turned out to be my own son. She'd worked hard to bake those using four-year-old flour and dried eggs.

Clarisse washed dishes as she cooked so it took us no time to clean up the rest; we were using paper plates and plastic ware, which we shoved into a trash bag. I looked at the bag once it was stuffed full. I saw the others looking, too.

"We need to compost our refuse and stop using plastic ware," I stated. The others nodded in agreement. Even the twins saw it as waste. Everywhere we looked, we saw something that needed to be cleaned up and thrown away. We had enough to fill a dump with the debris remaining from the explosion. Maybe we would start clearing the area, but not until we were ready for the winter.

NORTH POLE ELEMENTARY SCHOOL

The unimaginatively named North Pole Elementary School was close to Safeway, close to Santa's Village, and was generally in good repair. We didn't have to fix the roof, repair many broken windows or, and most importantly, remove any dead bodies. We let the engineers determine where best to put the wood burners. It was good to see Shane reengage with the living. He contributed his thoughts to the conversation, generally interested in the topic at hand.

Everyone else looked at the various rooms and then started staking claims. There were five couples with children, including Madison and I. Then there were Ben and Clarisse and Cullen and Shane. We wanted to establish seven or even eight rooms to give everyone their privacy.

We also committed to building two outhouses because that made sense, not for segregation, but because there were too many of us for a single toilet.

Laundry, kitchen, and common area. Much of the furniture had to go, but we also would keep one classroom intact. The small chairs, schoolroom with books, and decorations on the walls were focused toward children's education.

Moving here made the most sense. I was glad that Amber insisted, also glad that we didn't have to remove any bodies. I vowed not to go into any more churches.

With the long days, we took residence in the former school that evening. The next day, we used the quad to shuttle supplies from Safeway. We fabricated a couple of handcarts as well. It was hard work, but nice to have a home and rewarding to see the place come together so quickly. I found that my new lungs were okay, but still felt my limitations. I couldn't keep up with the younger members of our group.

RETURN

They didn't expect me to. The challenge was only what I put on myself, which always earned me a punch in the shoulder from my wife.

Selfishly, we set up the kitchen before we brought beds in. One has to have priorities. Clarisse and Jo made for a dynamic partnership. Little Tony spent most of his waking life in the new kitchen, a space that had once been a faculty break room. But it had everything we needed, including a room next door that we converted to a massive pantry.

We also found a location for two large chest freezers. Despite their size, empty freezers were rather light. We found, dumped, and cleaned a couple big ones and then manhandled them into the school.

We carried mattresses and bedding next. We asked everyone to help as we scoured nearby homes. We left those with bodies in them, but there were plenty other bedrooms that were unoccupied. We slept in our sleeping bags on top of the mattresses until we got the laundry functioning, which wouldn't happen until we had a generator.

Lucas was critical to our success. He was the Community handyman, and despite the damage to his arm, he could still fix things better than the rest of us.

We planned a run to Eielson Air Force Base to look for a generator and a vehicle to move it. Lucas didn't bother putting together a toolbox. We knew that the base would have every tool imaginable. Where else could you find a five-hundred-dollar wrench?

We saw the humor in that as we tried to squeeze three grown men into Ben's quad. Then we all got out as none of us could move. Lucas said he'd ride in the trailer. I let him because he was youngest. We set up a few cushions from someone's lawn furniture so he wouldn't get too damaged on the trip. With a casual wave, Ben spun the tires on gravel, shooting rocks over the trailer. Lucas shouted profanities until we were sure he was okay and then in a more casual manner we headed southeast to Salcha and Eielson Air Force Base.

THE AIR FORCE LIFESTYLE

"Would you look at this?" I asked the others as I pointed into the office of the maintenance shop. To me and my Marine Corps sense of austerity, it looked like an office from Wall Street's top executive. To the others, it looked little better than what you'd see at Jiffy Lube. "Air Force," I mumbled.

We found the forklift first. The Hyster was rated for at least eighty thousand pounds. We couldn't imagine needing more lift than that. It had bigger tires so it should negotiate the thirty-five miles to North Pole without much of a problem. When we tried it, the battery was dead. We couldn't be sure that the electronics weren't dead, too. We needed power, but the battery on the quad wasn't strong enough to jump the big forklift. We removed the massive battery from the piece of equipment and that's why we were in the maintenance shop. We found a battery charger, but it needed electricity.

We headed to the flight line to look for a power unit they'd use for an airplane that we could use to recharge the battery. We found a unit in the middle of the parking apron that looked like it was abandoned. Half the airplanes were still there, but that meant half the airplanes had made it out.

Ben and I were looking the small unit over when Lucas yelled something, but we were too caught up in trying to figure out if we could get the abandoned unit to run. Lucas returned and tapped me on the shoulder. I looked up, a bit perturbed at having my concentration broken. He shrugged and pointed to a hangar not far off.

"The hangar. Is there something in it?" I asked.

"Next to it," he said flatly.

I squinted in the sunlight. "What is that?"

"It's a portable generator and I think it's powerful enough for all of North Pole. We might not need the wood burners if we can keep that monster fueled," he said with a smirk.

Ben stood and walked away without giving the small generator any more of his time. We looked over the portable generator which had a tag reading "CAT 2000kw." That sounded like a good number to us. "You think our engineers can hook this up?" I asked.

They both nodded.

The CAT generator was big, the size of an eighteen-wheeler's trailer. It had its own control room. The unit was labeled clearly with instructions for its use.

We checked the fuel tank by undoing the cap; the seal popped, hissing loudly as hot gas escaped. I took that as a good sign. Being sealed against the elements had kept water and other contaminants out. We tightened the cap and went inside the small control room. The touch panel seemed simple, although there were more steps than I liked, but we had directions to follow, which could be the greatest challenge for three grown men.

The easiest answer was to let Lucas take care of it. The room was too crowded for three people and even a little tight for two, so Ben and I left. Lucas had figured out how to fly an airplane using a single book for instruction. He'd be fine with this, assuming the batteries contained power and that the radioactive dust driven by the winds hadn't caused any permanent damage.

Ben and I had made it twenty feet from the generator when we heard the engine turn over and reluctantly belch to life. It smoked excessively at the start, but quickly smoothed out. Lucas leaned out the door and gave us a hearty thumbs up. "I'll keep it running for a bit and see how it does. Maybe you two can bring me the battery from the forklift and we'll charge it, unless you can find something better to pull this thing with?" He went back inside and shut the door.

"What the hell is he doing in there? He could give us a hand," I suggested as I turned to get him. Ben put a hand on my arm.

"We gave him the job of starting the generator. Just because he was more efficient than we were, doesn't mean that he should then do our jobs for us." Ben blinked slowly as he talked. I clapped him on the back. Of course, he was right.

The battery was already loaded in the trailer of the quad, but we needed the battery charger from the maintenance shop's work bench.

It was industrial strength and took both of us to manhandle it into position next to the battery.

We dropped off the trailer next to the generator and beat on the door until Lucas came out. He looked cold. "Do you have the air conditioner on in there?"

"Well, yeah!" he said defensively. We pointed to the battery and charger as Ben unhooked the trailer in which they sat.

We drove off in search of a vehicle to pull the generator. We needed a semi. So we checked the motor pool.

The forty-five miles between ground zero and the Air Force Base were significant. There were few vehicles parked, either civilian or military. I thought that most were likely taken toward Canada or to their nearby homes. The generator proved that the EMP hadn't reached this far. Ben and I agreed that we needed to spend time here and scavenge more than just the generator.

"Ben, why are we so fixated on building the new Community by Fairbanks? Why not here?" I wondered.

"I'm new to this game, but the way I see it is that we're building in the way they built the city a hundred years ago. It's the crossroads for people traveling the river, driving the roads, even flying. Sure, there's a nice runway here, but nothing else. The real crossroads is Fairbanks. We have to establish our Community there," Ben finished, then stuck a long blade of dead grass into his mouth.

That was what I felt, but hadn't been able to articulate. Ben had clarified it for me, for us all.

"I guess that's it then. We better find a tractor to haul that generator. Otherwise, can you see us trying to drag that thing back to North Pole behind the forklift? The image of monkeys and a football comes to mind," I chuckled as I pointed Ben toward the commissary and the exchange.

We were rewarded by finding a newer tractor still attached to a trailer filled with pallets of what used to be fresh food. We unhooked the trailer, but couldn't move the tractor. It would have to do that itself. The keys were in it, but they were set to the run position. The tank was empty. They'd left it running to keep the refrigeration system functioning, until it ran out of fuel. Maybe there was no one left to turn it off.

That was probably better. Diesel in an unsealed container wouldn't last. It took us an hour to remove the battery and take it to Lucas. He hooked up the new battery, despite protesting that the other one hadn't begun to charge properly.

"We have to use the tractor to tow this thing. The forklift won't do it. It was a good idea until something better came along. And we could use some of the diesel from the generator. What do you think, Ben, thirty gallons?"

"Hey," Lucas continued protesting. "We have a full tank, but we'll burn through that pretty fast!"

"We won't run the generator much until our engineers can confirm they can make diesel or even biodiesel – we can find a lot of vegetable oil! Think of every restaurant and every store," I said.

"Okay. I'll get a hose. I'm sure there are cans around here somewhere." He still looked cold. We considered it a little victory to have him in the sun and heat with us.

While the battery charged and Lucas siphoned out thirty gallons, we scavenged further, finding that the commissary had been mostly cleaned out. Water and prepackaged foods were gone, probably purchased or taken by people going on a road trip, thinking they were heading back to the Lower 48. I wondered what happened to them when they ran into the checkpoint at Tok.

A resettlement camp. There had to be one past Tok. And that reminded me that as soon as I could break free, I had to head to Healy and Denali National Park, see if I could find any people who'd stayed behind, and specifically one worried man's daughter.

We ate a meal that we scrounged up. Ben wrinkled his nose, preferring fresh food. I didn't blame him. We'd be eating enough baked beans when winter came.

We replaced the battery which Lucas said was only charged to fifty percent. Good enough, we thought, for an attempt to start the Kenworth. Lucas shut down the generator and joined us.

We added the diesel, checked the oil, and ended up adding more after "shopping" for a few quarts in the auto shop. We pulled the fuel filter and filled it with diesel. This would help prime the engine and get the fuel flowing again. Running a diesel out of fuel can vapor-lock the fuel system.

I turned the key one notch and pressed the button to let the glow plug pre-heat. I pushed in the clutch and turned the key the rest of the way. There was a little screeching from dry cylinders, but the oil we'd added found its way in soon enough. It turned over and turned over, finally catching and spewing black smoke from its chrome exhaust pipes. I gave it some gas, and the smoke billowed.

I looked over the inside and wasn't exactly sure what I needed to do to drive the thing. I called Lucas over. Of course, he said he could drive it.

I didn't know if he could drive it or not. I expected that he didn't want to ride in the trailer behind the quad, and that was his primary motivation. That being said, I knew that he'd figure it out quickly enough. We didn't need precision. We had the road to ourselves.

Lucas let the engine run for fifteen minutes as he exercised the various systems: power steering, brakes, and the transmission. Even moving slowly, the truck was reluctant to stop. That could have been a big problem hauling a load as heavy as the generator, but the issue resolved itself as the air pressure built back within the braking system. Lucas drove to the flight line and backed up to the generator.

We hooked it up like we'd been doing it our whole lives. Lucas checked the connections and then drove off. We followed him in the quad, pulling our trailer fully loaded with a variety of acquisitions.

We didn't follow the semi too closely, just in case something fell off that wasn't supposed to.

CAST A WIDE NET

The engineers were ecstatic when they saw the generator. They pulled the manuals from the drawer in the control room and disappeared into them. They were in heaven.

We needed diesel and our engineers were the only ones capable of producing it. Although they said it wouldn't be a problem, I still worried. I stopped and took deep breaths. We had months to resolve it before the big beast of a generator needed to run regularly to protect us from the cold and dark of the Alaskan winter.

We did as we always did when something affected everyone; we called a meeting, but this time, we had it in the new common room in the school.

"Things are coming too easily for us, and that scares me," I started. The others booed and someone yelled "dark cloud Nagy" into their hand. It was hard to stay concerned. I'd seen what the Community could overcome when they put their minds to it. Madison was sitting in front, where she stretched out and kicked me in the leg.

"Okay, okay, I get it. I don't like putting all my eggs in one basket, so to speak. So I suggest we put in the wood-burning stoves, just in case. We can stock wood along the side of the building. Now that we know we can find vehicles to help us at Eielson, we'll bring one or two up here. There's plenty of avgas to give them a little spark. That lasted best out of all the fuels." I took a drink from a plastic Safeway-branded water bottle.

"Until we are up and running with electricity, we have to limit our use of the satellite phone. It has a solar recharger, but that takes a while. I suggest we all call one person and let them tell the rest of the family whatever you have to tell them. I'd like to conserve the battery in case of an emergency. Who needs to make a call?" Only three people raised their hands. We hadn't been gone long at this point, just a few weeks. I was happy to see that people weren't clamoring to get on the phone.

Maybe we had left the other world behind.

"I want to share some wisdom that Ben articulated perfectly. We, the new Alaskan settlers, are rebuilding the city that was established over a hundred years ago. It's the crossroads for people traveling the Alaskan interior. The best place to build is where it all started, on the navigable part of the Chena River, where the road, rail, river, and airport meet. It's there that we need to establish our real settlement. And then we help the goods flow. We'll stay here this winter, but since we are already well ahead in preparing, I say that we start laying things out for next year. Let's get ahead there, too."

Heads nodded as people agreed.

"One last thing. As soon as we have the wood-burning stoves installed and Chris and Colleen return, I have to run to Healy, Denali and scout the area. Call it the drawback of a secondary mission." I proceeded to tell them the whole story, our benefactor who'd sent the jet and his continued search for answers related to his daughter. I wasn't looking for volunteers, but Lucas stood up.

"Maybe we can take the plane?" he asked. He quickly twisted away as his wife, Amber, tried to punch him in the groin. The joys of being newlyweds. They'd gotten married in the short time we spent away from Alaska. As the Community, we didn't care, and I expected that they didn't either. They probably did it more for their families than themselves. The commitment to another, especially one that you've gone through a life-or-death trial with, is stronger than any piece of paper.

"You know, that's not a bad idea," I said slowly as I looked at Madison. Her eyes narrowed as her gaze turned into a glare. "Maybe we'll just drive, but we need to find an older vehicle. I researched using old gas and it seems carbureted engines don't care. We need to find us an old beater truck, Lucas." Amber calmed down as did Diane. She started swinging her little fist at her dad's leg, which was not well-received by either of her parents. Children mirror actions. We all decided to stop punching each other in jest, without any of us having to say a word about it.

The twins moved in and took Diane's hands to help settle her down. They were the bridge between the adults and the babies.

Everyone wondered how Chris and Colleen were doing. They'd been gone for a week, living on the road with their four-month-old baby. It had to be hard. We hoped that the risk was worth it.

Jo asked for the phone and then Amber. Madison would call her mother after the other two made their calls. Lucas and I stepped to the side. He was excited about our upcoming trip.

"We can't do anything until we get our quad back. Then we can venture as far as we want to find what we need," I said conspiratorially in a low whisper. It didn't register, so I looked around, made sure no one was close. "Even if we have to go all the way to the resort, if you get my drift." The lights went on and he broke into a toothy grin. "And if you let on that we're considering that, we'll both get kicked in the groin. During my scavenging days, I saw a few trucks in Two Rivers that will probably work. You can fix one, right?"

"Chuck, I was raised to work on old trucks. There's nothing better and we'll put a barrel of gas and a couple spare tires in the bed. It'll be just like camping. It won't be hard since we know people won't be shooting at us!" Lucas was excited. He loved the adventure side of what we were doing.

"I can't guarantee that people won't be shooting at us," I said smoothly, softening it with a smile.

"Yeah. I won't share that with Amber, either." Lucas shrugged and returned to his wife and child. I watched them, thinking about what kind of risk we were taking. I liked the jet rides, but were they worth my life? Of course not, but I could take a look. If things got hot, we'd run. I wasn't too proud. My family liked having me around, plus I liked living.

"What do you think, Ben? Time to go fishing? Maybe bag a big bull on the way back?" Everyone drifted away to their own tasks while Ben and I went fishing. It was almost like being on vacation, except we either had to catch fish or shoot a moose, otherwise we'd be eating baked beans again. With the dogs, we needed to catch and dry some eighteen thousand fish or shoot a moose every two weeks. We hoped for a balance between the two.

We were quiet as we took Ben's quad to his new favorite fishing hole. He grinned when he asked me not to tell anyone where it was.

As I cast into the river and gently reeled the lure through the water, I redid the calculations again. "Eighteen thousand fish, Ben. That's how many we need to catch and dry," I said just above a whisper.

"I know," Ben answered, not taking his eyes from his bobber. He turned the crank a couple times very slowly as he watched, then yanked to set the hook. He had a fighter who weaved back and forth across the water. We didn't have time to play so once he was certain the hook was set, he horsed the fish in and threw it in a big plastic bucket. It flopped around until it resigned itself to its new confines.

A grayling, not the meatiest fish but at least something was biting. He moved further away and cast into a new place. He soon had a second fish on. Then a third, and a fourth. The last two were rainbow trout, which were more substantial and tastier than the grayling.

I finally caught one, pleased with myself when I reeled in a rainbow and added it to the bucket. Ben started describing his fish wheel. He wanted to build it up the river, so we threw our gear into the quad's trailer. Ben and I cleaned the fish quickly, rinsed the bucket in the river, then put the fish fillets back in with the clean water. It was amazing how clear the river ran when there were no people to spoil it. It hadn't rained in a while either so no silt flowed.

It was a beautiful day to scour the riverbank looking for the perfect place to put a fish wheel. It would be built between floats and could be put anywhere on the river, but to maximize its usefulness, Ben had to guide the fish toward and through it. He described how the fans would rotate with the water flow, catching the fish as they swam upriver. There was an angled exit chute that dumped the fish into a holding area that Ben intended to make from a double layer of fish net. He had a good plan and when he described everything, he wasn't talking to me. Ben didn't need anyone to put his plan into action.

He looked forward to doing it, especially since fish wheels had been illegal in the rivers he'd worked for his entire adult life. That made me wonder how he knew so much about them. I didn't ask, but I had to ask a different question.

"Do you think eighteen thousand fish is possible, Ben?"

"No. A quarter of that, maybe. For every thousand fish we get, it saves a moose. The fish are good for the dogs' coats and their digestion.

They are the only thing we can count on. We can't put our faith in that generator or any of these vehicles. The dogs? We can trust them. All we have to do is take care of them," Ben said firmly.

"I couldn't agree more. Have you been spending too much time with Abigail and Phillip?" It sounded like them, but it also sounded like me. I appreciated the quad as a means of transportation, but the dogs could be the difference between life and death.

If it were winter, Lucas and I would mush to Healy. The summer gave us the opportunity to drive. Hopefully the destruction along the road was limited. There'd been forest fires in the previous four years. We had no idea how far they'd ranged or what they'd damaged. Lucas and I would find out, for what it was worth. If it didn't hold us up, then it didn't matter.

CHUCK AND LUCAS UNLEASHED!

Ten days after their departure, Chris and Colleen still had not returned. We were beginning to worry, but we also had things to do. The wood-burning stoves were in place where the engineers told us to put them, but we hadn't moved any firewood. We identified stocks of split firewood within a mile of the school that would last us the entire winter, so there was no rush. We wanted to wait until the weather got cooler and we could slide the wood over the snow. Filling the trailers and pulling them with a quad was too much wear and tear on the vehicle even without moving that much wood.

That freed Lucas and I to go truck "shopping." We used Ben's quad as he was engrossed in building the fish wheel and wouldn't need it for a few days.

We headed out of North Pole on Nordale Road. It looked far different than the last time we took it. It had been dark then. We now drove in the middle of a summer day, where the foliage was trying to reestablish dominance. We had to slow and climb over vines and through weeds, but it was clear enough that we made it to Chena Hot Springs Road in forty-five minutes. I stopped at the intersection and looked at Lucas. To the left, our home was close by. We needed to turn right to go to Two Rivers, another fourteen miles up the road. The resort was only fifty miles away. We had plenty of gas and the quad was running without a problem. Our tool kit was in the back; the trailer remained in North Pole. This was a scouting run, not a scavenger hunt, but we also hoped to drive a truck back with us.

Lucas nodded his head to the right. I jammed the gas and we peeled through the corner and raced up the road. Next stop, Chena Hot Springs Resort.

Once we arrived, the giddiness we felt disappeared as we saw the destruction of our former home in the broad daylight. We'd spent four years of our lives here and it was disconcerting to see it like this. A tear crawled down Lucas' face.

"You go check on the airplane. I'll look and see if there's anything here," I said without looking at him. He wasn't the only one with tears in his eyes. He took the quad, speeding away to put distance between him and the destruction.

I walked around the main area of the resort. My last impression from before, under the fleeting lights of the snow machine, was of everything destroyed. It was different in the daytime. The main lodge was leveled, and the building with the restaurant and kitchen was gone, too. The Ice Museum was cut in half, all the ice gone. There was a small puddle above the inlet at the bottom of the outside rock pool. The hot spring was alive, but needed power to return to its former glory.

I dug through the rubble of the destroyed lodge, looking for something personal that we could take back, give to its former owner. But things didn't matter as much. The people. That was important. No one cared if they didn't save the hard drive with all the movies. It would be nice once we had electricity, but we didn't need it.

Which was convenient because I couldn't find it, although I searched. I personally liked watching a movie before going to sleep. *No one else needs this, you big baby,* I thought to myself.

"That's it then," I said with finality. "I think this will be the last time we see you. Thank you. You took good care of us. You will be fondly remembered and sorely missed. Maybe one day…" I looked around to make sure Lucas didn't hear me talking to the rubble. With jaw set, I strode briskly for where we'd stored the airplane.

Lucas was elbow-deep in the engine, but he was making happy sounds. He talked to each part as he checked it, then moved on. Talking to inanimate objects is a habit one picks up when living alone for too long.

"Lucas!" I shouted as I approached. He jumped, but then settled back into what he'd been doing.

"I don't see why we can't take this baby for a ride today!" he said from within the engine cowling. "I know what you're thinking, but for the last three years, I did the PMs, the preventive maintenance on this plane every month. It hasn't received any love the past five, but otherwise, it's in the same shape as the last time we flew."

It had been years since our trip. Despite Lucas' assurances, I had no confidence that the plane was airworthy. The avgas was old, but it had been sealed. I checked it while he continued his work. No sheen on the top and no standing water. I took the hand pump out of the airplane and topped off its tanks.

Lucas extracted himself from the engine after hooking up the battery. He asked me to exercise the controls slowly, working the flap, ailerons, and the vertical stabilizer. When he gave me the thumbs up, I tried to start the engine. It cranked slowly, but coughed to life, sending out more black smoke than I was comfortable with, but Lucas beamed with joy. I contorted my body to climb into the copilot's seat as Lucas pushed me out of the pilot's seat. He took his place, put on the headset, and started to taxi.

I was aghast. "What are you doing?"

"We're going for a ride! We're pretty sure no one is going to shoot at us, right?" He grinned as he worked the controls.

"You mean somebody besides our wives, the people closest to us who we promised that we wouldn't do exactly what you're doing? Does there need to be anyone else?" I tried to make my case, but we continued taxiing to the end of the runway. Lucas turned the Cessna into the wind.

"Yeah. I meant beside them. I'll stay to the north and low so they can't see or hear us. Want to run to Denali?"

"No. We're not going all the way down there, but I do want to look at the road, Parks Highway. What kind of problems will we find when we drive it?" He nodded and gunned the engine. We built speed and slowly lifted into the air. He leveled off at five hundred feet, flying above the road to Fairbanks.

NOT SURE WE COULD'VE SCREWED UP MORE...

We flew over Madison's and my old house. It was comforting to see it standing there, as if we could walk right in, be as comfortable as we were before.

Continuing past, we flew over the northern edge of the city. The destruction was bad, but not complete. Much of the city had survived. I was surprised at how much. It became clear what had happened to all the people as we followed the Parks Highway south out of town. Broken-down vehicles lay dead in the road, but a lane of travel remained open. Maybe someone drove a bulldozer to clear their own way. More and more vehicles were abandoned the further we got from Fairbanks. Dead cars choked the road as we approached Nenana. We looped around the city. There were too many vehicles parked within.

I had no doubt bodies filled the town. We continued past Nenana, following the road that gently curved toward Denali, the Great One, the tallest mountain in North America.

With a great cough, the engine hesitated. We dropped fifty feet before the engine caught again, but it was running roughly, as if only half the cylinders were firing. My heart leapt into my threat. Lucas looked worried. With a final sputter, the engine seized and the propeller ground to a halt. Vehicles filled the tree-lined road. I panicked. There was nowhere to land.

Lucas eased into a shallow turn and headed for the river. We were losing altitude too fast. He banked briefly, letting the wind hit the underside of the wings, bouncing us a little higher. The plane leveled, then started descending again. *C'mon little fella, you can make it,* I pleaded in my head with the plane. I cringed as a tree stood tall in front of us; its top branches were just below the propeller as we shot over it. We didn't hit. That relief was short-lived as the river zoomed up to meet us.

The wheels dug into the water, throwing the plane forward. The propeller hit and we crashed to a halt. Lucas and I both slammed against our restraints.

The plane was sinking. I was dazed from the violence of the impact, but I'd protected my head. Nothing was broken, but I was sure the belts had left bruises across my chest. Lucas looked dazed.

"Get out!" I yelled as I undid the central buckle of the cross harness. Lucas clumsily popped his, then shook his head to clear it. We opened our doors just in time to let the water rush in. I pulled myself against the flow of cold water, getting my head out before the cabin went under water. The airplane twisted as it was pulled downstream by the current.

I went hand-over-hand, using the wire antenna along the spine of the fuselage to move myself to the tail of the airplane. Halfway there, I looked back. I saw one hand flopping lazily out of the water. I dove forward, slamming hard against the roof over the cabin. I held the wire with one hand while grabbing a handful of Lucas' shirt to pull him out.

He came into the water readily as he pushed himself out with the last of his energy. He gulped a deep breath as I held him in my arms, trying to stand on the airplane as it sank beneath us.

Soon, I was treading water for both of us. The airplane was gone. I kept Lucas on his back as I side-stroked toward the western shore. The current pulled us downstream, farther away from Nenana with every stroke. Lucas started kicking his feet to help me. Slowly, we made progress. Finally, my foot touched the bottom. I pushed hard to gain a foothold and then crawled onto the shore. Lucas rolled over and puked. I felt like joining him, but I didn't have the energy. I lay there panting.

"I think we made a big mistake," was all I managed to get out between my shallow gulps of air.

Lucas closed his eyes and held his head in his hands.

WHERE IS EVERYONE?

When we didn't return by dinner, people weren't too surprised. When we didn't return by bedtime, Madison and Amber started to get anxious. When we hadn't returned by dinner the next day, they wanted to form a hunting party and go after us.

The engineer's quad wasn't safe. Ben's quad was at the resort. Chris and Colleen had our quad and they hadn't returned. Then the crying began. The two women were inconsolable. They were angry and sad and scared, but they weren't alone. The Community decided that finding us was the new priority. The engineers dropped everything they were doing to fix their quad so that it could be used for the search. It took scavenging an oxy-acetylene welder to touch up some of the support bracing and a full day of tinkering to get it where it would drive straight.

The group looked at Amber, Madison, and Diane as they prepared to leave. Jo and Emma held the twins close. They had an entire Community to watch them while their parents were away.

With one last wave, the two women drove away, heading for Nordale Road and the way from North Pole to our old house.

They saw where we'd driven over foliage encroaching on the road. Nordale intersected Chena Hot Springs Road near the bottom between two hills. To the left, our house. To the right, Two Rivers and Chena Hot Springs Resort. The tire marks where I'd slid around the corner were clearly visible. Amber turned to the right and followed. They didn't find anything to tell them which road we'd taken into Two Rivers, but they followed them, one by one, honking and hoping that we'd be close. They shut off the engine often to listen.

"You don't think...?" Madison started to ask.

"Of course they did. They went to the Resort!" Amber snorted. She spun out more quickly than she intended, which jostled Diane. She slowed and regained control. Once on the main road, she sped up. It was only another thirty-five miles to the resort.

Soon, they were sitting on the runway, looking at the quad sitting next to an empty spot where the plane used to be.

"If he isn't dead, I'm going to kill him!" Madison vowed angrily. Amber hung her head.

"Was there ever a doubt? When those two are together, they get weird. It's like they think they can conquer the world through their shared force of will. I thought they might come here. I hoped they wouldn't, but I knew better," Amber finished in a whisper.

"But they shouldn't have! They lied to us," Madison insisted.

"Maybe they didn't intend to take it when they first came out here. Lucas had been keeping the plane ready to fly. He didn't think I knew, but I did. Why are we trying to make them something that they aren't? In some ways they're like little kids. In other ways, there's no one else I want around. They kept us comfortable, even when we had nothing," Amber said, watching a raven flying in the distance. "They are who they are and we married them because of that. Now we don't like something that they would have always done? Shame on us. When they get home, and I mean when, not if, maybe you can watch Diane while Lucas and I take a couple days for a lover's retreat. And there he'll get the spanking he so richly deserves." She smiled devilishly.

Madison didn't know what to say. She had to think about it. They were comfortable. Lucas and I hadn't left them to fend for themselves. They had plenty to eat, good shelter, and an endless supply of drinking water. There was time before anything else needed to happen.

"I'll drive the other quad. Let's stop by my old house. I'd like to bring a family picture with us to the new place." Amber nodded as they belted Diane in. It wasn't optimal for a two-year-old, but they didn't have a child's car seat.

Madison looked at the gun case, seeing that the 45-70 was still there. She looked in the back. All our tools and gear were still on the quad. She shook her head, knowing that we'd flown without taking any equipment.

The two quads turned and headed down the road, leaving Amber and Madison to their thoughts as the wind and trees rushed by.

CHRIS AND COLLEEN

Colleen rode Penelope as they walked slowly on the road to North Pole. It took a couple days to get the horses used to human company again. The saddles were in sorry shape, so they had to scavenge Delta Junction to find a cream that they could work into the leather to soften it.

Taking it easy was Colleen's idea. Chris thought that she wanted the time to daydream and relive an old life that was comfortable. He knew she missed it, but he couldn't help any of that. All he could do was give her time to reconcile herself with today and what that meant.

She let her horse walk casually. Chris couldn't talk with her because he had to keep the quad away from the horses. He didn't want to spook them. So they traveled in silence. They could have made the trip in a single day, but it extended to three days. When they were a few miles from North Pole, Colleen waved Chris ahead and yelled to let the others know that they'd be there soon. She smiled at him as she hadn't in a long time.

He smiled back at her and waved. Hermione slept peacefully in her carrier buckled into the passenger seat. They'd found it when they were looking for saddle soap. Chris took the carrier and put it to good use. He felt better with the baby protected, and she seemed happier, too.

And now they were all happy. He grinned as he let the quad run up the straightaway toward their new home.

He pulled in to find the other two quads gone and only a couple of people around. The engineers were at the refinery. Amber and Madison were searching for their husbands who had disappeared two days previously. Abigail and Phillip were exercising the dogs as they prepared to go in search of the search party. Jo and Emma watched the twins, their Tony, and little Bill. Becca and Darren had taken a dog team moose hunting. Clarisse was in the kitchen and Ben was trying to get his fish wheel working.

Outside of that, everything was normal. Chris parked the quad, hoping that they had running water, which they did not. There was a hand pump to fill a portable gravity shower that fed into a large hole they'd dug in the sand of the playground. This made up their outhouse, septic, and wastewater disposal area.

It would do. He stripped and washed, using a towel to cover himself to go into the school and dig out new clothes. They'd been gone for eleven days. It was nice to finally have a shower, even if it was lukewarm.

He was clean and refreshed when Colleen rode in on Penelope, leading Sophie. The few people there cheered as she held her hands above her head as if she'd just won an Olympic gold medal. With Chris' help, she climbed down and greeted everyone warmly. They walked as a group to a fenced-in field a few blocks away. They told her how Lucas and I were going to scout the area, find an old truck that would be fine with the gas we had, fix it, and then return. Once Chris and Colleen arrived, they'd go to Healy, and see if they could find any sign of people, and specifically, the lost daughter.

After removing the saddles, they put the horses into the small pasture. The grass was thick and the horses started grazing. Although they were shaggy-looking, Colleen had brushed them whenever they stopped on their return journey. They looked more respectable. The pasture didn't have a water source. Chris said he'd take care of that and he headed back to the school.

Colleen couldn't believe that she was reunited with her horses. Maybe God was smiling down on her. She'd come to grips with her new life and she liked it. She liked her previous life as well, but that was a world and a lifetime away.

The group slowly walked back to their new home. Bill held Jo's hand as he walked, yelling at this or that when they passed anything that interested him. The twins rolled their eyes every time he opened his mouth. When he was older, I expected we'd see some fireworks and a major throw down between him and the twins. Until then, we had a marginal truce.

As the group approached the school, they could hear a quad in the distance. They waited until it approached, only to see that there were two quads, the engineers' and Ben's, but there was no sign of us. Amber and

Madison drove up and stopped next to the vehicle Chris had parked in front of the school. They shook their heads as they got out. Everyone wanted to know what happened and where we were.

"They took the airplane," Amber said as she turned her back on the group and carried Diane inside. Madison nodded to the twins with a look of reservation.

As usual, they had complete confidence in me, their father. They weren't worried. They shrugged and headed for the kennel to see their dogs.

NENANA

Lucas and I stayed at an abandoned cabin by the river. There were three cans of green beans and nothing else. We ate those and drank lots of water to help our bruised muscles. After two days, we had to start moving, find food, and a means of transportation.

"Besides not telling our wives, nothing else has changed," I said. "Sure, we wanted to wait until Chris and Colleen were back, but since we're halfway to Healy, maybe we can find a truck down here. Fix it, get it going, and drive the rest of the way. Take a look and then go home. Then we won't have to go away again. I'm not sure I want to drive this road twice."

"All we have to do is find a vehicle. Do you think the restaurant in Nenana has a drive thru? I'm pretty hungry," Lucas said in a tired voice.

"I'm sure it does, my man. Let's go see what we can find." We walked to the highway and then turned north. We avoided looking at the cars at first because of the dead bodies, but then the realization hit us that these people may have packed food for their trip.

We looked into back seats, hoping to see beef jerky or anything in a sealed package. The insides of the windows were covered with a nasty film caused by the decomposing bodies. We looked for vehicles without people, but all of them were covered with pollen, ash, and dirt from sitting outside for four years. We used our sleeves for a quick clean of the back-door window. Peer inside, and move on. The first one that held promise was empty of people. I tried smashing it with a rock, but it crumbled when I drove it into the window.

"You have got to be kidding me." I looked at Lucas and he started laughing. We looked around, finally settling on a metal fencepost in the ditch. I dragged it into the road and both of us used it like a battering ram to run it through the window. Lucas reached his good arm inside and pulled on the door handle. It popped open and we dug through the boxes of goods in the back seat. Spam, Vienna sausages, and canned bread. The spam and Vienna sausages had lids that opened with a pull tab. But we needed a can opener, or at least a sturdy knife to open the bread. Using our battering ram, we broke through the back windows of ten different vehicles. We used rags from the first car to cover our faces and hands while digging through the back seats.

We found everything we needed, but wanted to wash it all off before we touched anything further. So we used bottled water – almost every car had a few. We drank and ate until we couldn't move. We decided that once you scraped the weird jelly from the spam, it tasted good.

We hacked down two small trees using an axe that someone thought to bring along, and tied T-shirts to them to make what the Indians would call a travois, which made it easier to drag our supplies up the road. I thought we only had ten or fifteen miles to go to get back to town. When we passed a road sign, it said twelve miles to go. At our pace, that was six hours of walking before we could rest. We both wanted to get home.

Never keep your better half waiting.

It was amazing how we were able to keep going with food in our system. We made the walk in five hours, but we were tired when we arrived. We looked for a home that was unoccupied, finding a small cabin on the outskirts of town. We set up a temporary home as we looked for a vehicle to fix and drive away. We didn't stray far from the cabin the rest of that day. Our feet hurt and we were tired and bruised.

We used bug dope from inside to douse ourselves before lounging outside. We lit a mosquito coil, then a second that we put to box ourselves in. I fell asleep sitting in the chair. Lucas lay on the ground and was out cold. I don't know what time it was when we awoke, but I had a hard time standing. My legs were stiff from too much exercise, but at least my chest had stopped hurting.

Lucas got up and stretched. He didn't look or act sore. That was the advantage of being twenty years younger. We didn't appear like we'd crashed a plane three days earlier, but we had. We were walking and that was testament enough to our transgression.

I wanted to find a ride quickly and get this over with. How long would it take to get to Healy and search for the missing woman? I had no idea, but had no intention of letting it drag out any longer than necessary. Either she was alive and willing to be found or she wasn't.

A SINGULAR FOCUS

Lucas and I found a truck not far away. It was parked in the driveway as if they had just returned from the store. It was older, we thought a late 1960s Chevy truck with a small block V8. Lucas was in heaven. He tore into the engine with reckless abandon. I felt useless except to hand him tools from the owner's garage. I then excused myself to go "shopping" for more food.

I kept a rag wrapped around my face as I went from house to house. Many were unlocked, making it easy to take a look inside. I towed a four-wheeled garden wagon behind me. I had already added my normal shopping tools: a pry bar, a sledgehammer, bolt cutters, and an axe. I found six unopened quarts of oil. I'm sure we could find more if needed. The truck used at least that much.

The best find that I made were two hunting rifles. Both were .308 caliber and there was ammunition with them. We didn't know what we'd run across by Denali National Park, whether Russians or the grizzly bears. Being well-armed was the best hedge against the unknown.

I circled back to meet up with Lucas. He had the hood closed and was wiping his hands.

"I think she's good to go, but the battery's dead," he said without preamble.

"I don't know if we can find a good battery, but I'll start looking. There has to be a garage or gas station where you can buy a battery. We won't be paying, of course." I laughed at my own joke.

"No need, Chuck! I topped off the water in the battery. Once we get it started, it can charge itself," he said. I looked at him oddly, reminded of the chicken and the egg philosophical debate. "It's a stick," he added.

Finally it registered. We could push start it, pop the clutch and get it running. I started to climb in to the driver's seat, but Lucas held me back.

"Come on, Chuck. This is my baby!" He looked confident.

"The last time you kicked me out of the driver's seat, we ended up in the river, swimming. You push." I gently removed his hand from my shoulder and got in. I tipped my head toward the back of the truck.

"Fair enough, but once we get going, I drive."

"Once we get going, we load up everything we need, then you drive," I made my point firmly. Last time we flew off without any of our stuff, but then again, if we had, it would all be at the bottom of the river.

I pumped the brakes until I felt pressure. I released the emergency brake, the foot pedal type, and waited for the truck to start rolling. I heard Lucas in the back grunting as he pushed. Something snapped and it started rolling forward. I took my foot off the clutch while it was in first gear and it stopped on a dime. I heard Lucas yell.

"What the hell, Chuck!" He was holding his bleeding lip where his face smashed into the tailgate when the truck stopped so abruptly.

"Sorry about that, Lucas. Brakes must have been rusted. I was hoping we'd get it to turn over sooner rather than later." Lucas wiped his mouth and spit blood on the ground.

"Wait until you're going a little faster this time," Lucas counseled me. I nodded and waved an arm out the window.

I pushed in the clutch, and this time the truck rolled more freely. Lucas pushed it on the level, quickly building speed. I almost lost sight of what I was doing and narrowly avoided hitting a parked car. I swerved and popped the clutch at the same time. The engine barked once and the wheels chirped on the pavement. It didn't catch. I stopped.

Lucas jogged up, breathing heavily and started pushing again. We were starting to run out of room. At the end of the street, I popped the clutch again and it barked, coughed, sputtered, and quit. Lucas was bent over with his hands on his knees. I parked the truck and got out.

I pointed to the cab with my thumb. Lucas didn't seem as tired when he jogged forward and jumped in. I pushed the truck forward and around in a circle. We were pointed back the way we'd come. I started pushing. After two steps, Lucas let up on the clutch. I hadn't built any momentum, so I didn't smash into the tailgate. I stood up straight and met his eyes in the rearview mirror.

"Age and deceit over youth and ability any day, my good man. Any day. Now let's get this beast started and get on the road!" I put my shoulder into it, happy with how well the truck rolled. Halfway down the street, Lucas popped the clutch and the engine roared to life. After the first few belches of blue-black smoke, it settled down. Lucas grinned and waved at me to get in.

We drove down the street, stopping at the truck's home so we could liberate the toolbox from the garage. This went into the truck bed, along with the garden cart and everything in it. We drove to the cabin and loaded up our food. In just the neighboring houses there was enough canned food to feed us for months. Food wasn't the problem in Nenana during the exodus from Fairbanks. It was the radiation and the panic.

"How much gas do you think we need?"

"Ten gallons would be good, twenty would be better." We stopped at every house that had a garage or a shed, until we had our gasoline. We also took some T-shirts to use as filters when we poured the gas. More oil, too, just in case the old gas was hard on the cylinders.

Lucas had the window cranked down as he kicked it past first gear, settling to travel in second gear because of the jumble of vehicles on the road. First ten, then twenty, and thirty miles of dead vehicles in the road, but there was a clear lane of travel, almost as if someone had moved vehicles out of the way. Although we'd walked the road for five hours, we hadn't thought about it until we saw it through the windshield.

GETTING READY FOR WINTER

Darren and Becca were successful in killing a moose but soon discovered that a twelve-dog team can't pull seven hundred and fifty pounds of meat, unless the humans pushed, too. Which they did, making for a very long and tiring trip home. They figured they were ten miles away when they shot the big bull. Then they ran about nine and a half miles, pushing the wheeled sled and trailer while the dogs labored to keep it moving. Abigail and Phillip found the hunters when they were almost back home.

Abigail and Phillip were pleased with the kill, although they suggested next time take a sixteen-dog team or one of the quads. Becca and Darren looked surprised and then ecstatic that the quads were back, until they learned what Amber and Madison had found at the resort. But Chris and Colleen had returned with the two mares. The Community had machine power, horsepower, and dog power. If the engineers had any success at the refinery, then they'd have electrical power, too.

Despite the victories, our absence cast a dark shadow over everyone.

When you get depressed, there's nothing like work to bring you back to the land of the living, at least that's what Ben told everyone. He needed help getting his fish wheel into the water and then he'd show everyone how to clean the fish and hang them on racks to dry.

"The racks will be downwind, won't they," Emma asked Jo out the side of her mouth.

"I sure hope so. The outhouse is bad enough," she answered as they handed Tony back and forth while they walked. It was part of a game that he enjoyed. As soon as he hugged one of his mothers, he'd hold out his hands to go to the other.

The sheer size of the fish wheel was impressive. Huge scoops were built around a central hub, held in place by two long poles. Once the wheel was in the water, Ben could use the poles to push it further into the current or pull it closer to shore. The poles also kept the contraption from being pulled downstream. It took four people to lift the fish wheel and carefully move it to the water's edge. They lifted on the poles while the others on shore pushed toward the water.

Emma let go with a yelp and started biting her hand. A splinter. The others let the fish wheel down into the water. It settled into the current and started slowly turning. A chute ran from the top of the poles to a collection net. While it was in the water, someone would have to monitor it to remove the fish before the net filled and they escaped.

It had only been in the water for twenty seconds when the first fish rode the wheel upward and slid out the opening in the scoop and into the chute. Everyone watched the fish drop into the net and splash around.

"I'll be damned," Ben said with a toothy grin. He looked at Clarisse, and she smiled back in her matronly way.

Another fish and another. They stood on the shore and cheered, even Madison and Amber. They would have cheered louder if we'd been there as we would have high-fived the others and run around like idiots. We would have called it dancing, of course, because that's how we rolled.

As the fish gathered in the net, Ben made everyone get knives for cleaning. They threw the guts and heads into a barrel that Ben would dump downstream. He didn't want to scare the fish or pollute the water at this point.

When the fish wheel dropped its five hundredth fish, Ben was beside himself. He'd never expected these numbers. Maybe they would get half of what they needed to feed the dogs. It cut down on how many moose they needed, which would help keep the moose population growing.

Ben felt good about doing his part for the Community. He saw how hard everyone worked. He couldn't believe his luck in joining such a group of people. He said a prayer as he'd found a good home for Clarisse and himself.

Clarisse watched her husband revel in the success of the fish wheel, seeing his face change as he looked at the people cleaning the fish and having fun doing it. She saw pride, his pride in the group. Clarisse was happy to be here, too. It was what they'd practiced their entire lives for.

THE ENGINEERS

Shane talked constantly when he was with Cullen, but when he was with the group, he kept his mouth shut. Cullen told him that we were all good people, but something held him back.

Colleen checked him out after her return and declared him to be past the worst of his concussion. She watched his body language change when Chris was around. It was more than fear. It bordered on terror. When Colleen confronted Chris, he decided to come clean.

"Remember when he wouldn't stop screaming?" She nodded. "I punched him in the head so we could get him out of there. Chuck was going to do it, but I wouldn't let him. Chuck does all the crap jobs. It was my turn to shoulder the load," he said with no hint of remorse.

"I see," she said coldly.

"I've tried talking with him, but he shuts down completely. I can only say I'm sorry so many times." Chris shrugged, waiting for his verbal beat-down. Instead, Colleen pulled him into a hug.

"Sometimes, you just have to do what needs to be done. Maybe he'll come to realize that. Neither of you were wrong, but we're too close here. You two will have to make peace at some point. When that time comes, make it happen," she told him.

He held her head in his hands and looked deep into her eyes. "I don't deserve you," he whispered.

"I know," she answered, playfully pushing him away. He'd never been happier.

Unlike the engineers, who had extreme highs, followed by crushing depression. No one could tell if they were happy or not. They surveyed the refinery and determined that they could use the fractional distillation process to produce diesel fuel for their generator. The problem came when they had to reroute some piping systems. They had no way to clear the pipes of residual hydrocarbons, that is, flammable material.

That meant that they couldn't cut the old pipe without risking a fire or explosion.

They only had the one facility. After two days of tinkering, they decided the best solution was to build a new system. Refining oil was as simple as boiling the oil and capturing the steam at different heights based on its weight. They had to build a still. Although simple, it was dangerous as everything within the system was sensitive to fire.

They had a tank they could use to heat the fuel oil. They could build a tree on top that captured the different vapors from the process, and then they needed additional tanks for the distillates, the separated liquids condensed from the oil-steam.

Shane calculated that they needed fifty gallons an hour to feed the big generator. They weren't using it to capacity, but if they wanted to use electrical heat, it would pull a heavier load, although still far short of its capacity. That meant twelve hundred gallons a day or the staggering amount of two hundred and sixteen thousand gallons for the entire winter. They didn't have enough crude oil. If they couldn't distill a sufficient amount, then there'd be hours where they couldn't run the generator.

The engineers found this disconcerting. Their job was to provide power and they had the equipment, but were stymied by a lack of natural resources. How much wood had to be burned to boil the oil? That would probably cause a shortage, too.

They looked for alternatives. The river froze in the winter so hydro-power generation wouldn't work. The wind was inconsistent. Solar power worked well in the summer, but without massive storage capacity, the sun couldn't generate enough electricity during a winter day to power a cell phone.

"We need to change some of the variables," Cullen said as they sat in an office at the refinery. "How can we trim the usage rate?"

"The absolute minimum usage on that beast is forty gallons an hour. If we ran it only six hours a day, that's two hundred forty gallons and six months comes to forty-three thousand two hundred gallons. We can do that." Shane said, setting his jaw firmly, and nodded.

"But that's not good enough," Shane started to say as Cullen looked at him through narrowed eyes. "We need a smaller generator or we need one that burns fuel oil. Almost everyone around here has a fuel oil tank outside their house. One of these tanks here has fuel oil, too. I think the variable we need to change is what fuel we burn."

Cullen thought about it. They hadn't invested too much time in the refinery, although what they proposed was another shortcut. They knew what I'd say. It's living for today, planning for tomorrow. In the other world someone would call it outside-the-box thinking. That metaphor only worked if you believed in boxes.

"We need to talk to the others. I think we can sell them on the idea," Cullen said. Shane crossed his arms and dropped his head, assuming a self-protective posture. "Dude! They may have treated us like crap when we started this adventure, but hell, look at everything they've done for us? What have we given back? Not a damn thing. Not yet, anyway. We're living down to Chuck's and Chris' expectations, but they've given us space, even apologized to us. I don't think we've earned that. I know we haven't. Let's go in there, with our heads held high, naked in front of them all, and show them what we can do. I, for one, would like electricity for more than six hours a day. We're going to provide that power, and we're going to enjoy it." Cullen slapped Shane on the shoulder as they walked out.

After another fabulous dinner provided by Jo and Clarisse, Cullen and Shane moved to the middle of their small dining room. Cullen opened his mouth to speak, but stopped as he watched Shane take off his shirt, then his pants. As he prepared to pull down his underwear, Cullen grabbed his arm.

"Dude! What the hell?"

"You said that we'd be naked in front of everyone. You said…" Shane looked around at the group as people snickered. The twins laughed out loud.

"Euphemistically, but I like your motivation. You might want to get dressed," Cullen told his friend. Shane turned a bright shade of red as he made to leave. "Where are you going?" Shane stammered an unintelligible response to Cullen's question. "Stay here, dude. They've already seen the worst of it, and we have something to say." Shane nodded once and pulled his clothes back on. As he buttoned his shirt, Cullen spoke to the group.

"The big generator isn't going to work. Sure, it runs fine, but it burns too much diesel. We can convert it so it'll burn fuel oil, but it still burns way too much for what we need. Two things. We have to find a smaller generator, probably in the range of ten to twenty kilowatts, and we will convert it to burn fuel oil. That means we'll have to scavenge what's left in the home storage tanks for this whole area, filter it, and build a large storage tank to hold it all. And we have about two months to get all that done so we have electricity 24/7 for the entire winter." Cullen took a deep breath, expecting questions or a counter proposal. He thought they might even attack them for coming up with a plan that required the others to do more work.

Chris stood and started clapping. The others joined in. All they'd ever wanted from the engineers was a sound plan to get them through the winter. Cullen and Shane had failed to articulate what they were going to do until now.

"Just tell us what you need us to do," Chris said as he shook Cullen's hand and then Shane's. Shane started to shy away and then turned back, stood tall, and awkwardly slapped Chris on the shoulder. Chris pulled the frail-looking young man to him and gave him a one-armed man hug. "We're here for you and we'll get it done. Two months? No problem, as long as we find ourselves a generator that will work. First thing tomorrow, we drive."

Colleen watched Chris with amusement. She hadn't expected the issue to resolve itself so quickly. She was pleased that it did and ready for the Community to move on. There was always something else that needed doing and not enough time to do it. She shook her head as she thought about how many more fish they'd need to clean and dry.

HEALY

After forty miles, we passed the convoy from Two Rivers. They'd departed less than a week after the initial explosion, which put them toward the front of this traffic jam. We stopped at the top of an incline, in case the battery hadn't charged.

I walked along the vehicles, wiping the windows as I went and looking in. They were all empty.

"Where did they go?" I asked, not expecting an answer. We topped off our truck's tank using a gas can from one of the Two Rivers' trucks. I was hesitant to check the dog boxes, but they were empty. I was glad that the dogs got out, but the sleds were still on the top of the vehicles. They hadn't mushed the dogs away. It looked like they'd been released to fend for themselves.

"Do you think there was a formal evacuation of some sort? Maybe there were buses, and that's why they kept this lane open. I'm pretty sure they didn't bring a military convoy to Fairbanks. I have to believe that we would have heard or seen something like that," I said quietly, not really sure what to believe. "Lucas, when's the last time someone used this road?"

"I don't know. Fairly recently? We just drove on Nordale a week ago, and we know that hadn't been traveled in years because of the weeds and trees. Compared to that? This has seen some traffic. Who would be here? And with a vehicle?"

The hair stood up on the back of my neck. "What do you say we keep the rifles close?" I put my hand over the comfortable shape of my .45 in my shoulder holster. Most of the time, I forgot it was there. I was glad to have it. I had no idea what we were getting ourselves into, but maybe the unknown vehicle driving this road held a couple people just like us, trying to survive until tomorrow.

We continued toward Healy, driving slowly as we approached. There were hotels and other places for tourists in the ten miles north of town.

When we passed these, the presence of others become more obvious. Vehicles had been recently broken into. Weeds were crushed on the pavement.

"I think I understand what happened. When the Russians bombed us? They did that as they were pulling out, at least that's what I heard at the Pentagon. People around here must have remained hidden until the Russians left and now they are into scavenging, where before, they probably lived like cavemen in the hills, not risking getting caught. That had to be tough. Denali is known for its grizzly bears and wolves."

"So what do we do?" Lucas asked, absentmindedly stroking the sling of his rifle.

"Let's see if we can find where they're staying. Maybe we can meet them without getting shot. I'm a big fan of not getting shot. I still have the scars on my head from the shotgun blast when I made contact with the wrong people. Yeah, not a fan at all."

We hopped back in the truck and drove to the resort town of Healy, Alaska, where the only coal mine was, along with the entrance to Denali National Park. I wondered if it was still considered a national park since the government sold us out under threat of a nuclear attack on the Lower 48? I didn't spend much time thinking about that as it didn't matter.

Smoke from a chimney told us that someone was staying at the Denali Touch of Wilderness, a bed and breakfast hotel. I couldn't blame them. We had stayed in the nicest rooms at Chena Hot Springs Resort. When you survived the end of the world, you took certain liberties, without remorse, like hunting when you needed food, regardless of the season.

"Moment of truth, Lucas," I said as we pulled into the parking lot. "First, turn the truck around and leave it running, so if we have to, we can make a quick escape. That was a hard lesson learned, by the way. Be ready to get us out of here if I come running like an idiot. Give the horn a couple honks and let's see what's next." I opened my door and slowly exited. My body seemed to fight me. The muscle memory of getting shot was strong. I took a few steps away from the truck and put my hands up.

A shaggy-looking man jumped onto the porch, looking at us with jerky movements. He waved a rifle, but it looked rusted and old. "Get out! Don't make me shoot you!" he yelled, almost hysterically.

"We're not here to hurt anyone or get into your business. We're looking for someone, a young lady named Tanya Bezos. Would you have seen her?" I projected using my Marine Corps voice.

The door opened and another man walked out. "Put that gun away, Bob, before you hurt yourself again." They wrestled briefly before the second man took the gun away, and Bob went back inside. The second man opened the breach to show that it was unloaded and leaned it against the wall of the lodge.

"We let Bob keep that so he's less afraid. He's had a rough time, and we kind of take care of him. I'm Randy, Randy Silvers, by the way." The young man strode forward without hesitation, hand out. I met him halfway, and we shook.

"Chuck Nagy, and this is Lucas. We're from outside Fairbanks." Lucas joined us and they shook. "I think we have a lot to talk about. First, do you know of any other survivors around here? We're looking for a Tanya Bezos."

He shrugged.

As we were heading inside, I waved Lucas back, telling him to stay outside, just in case it was a trap. My Military Intelligence paranoia was working overtime.

Once inside, I saw Bob curled up in a corner on a dog bed. An older woman was cooking something on the wood-burning stove. She waved and introduced herself as Agnes.

"Yeah, there are other people scattered around the hills," Randy said as he handed me a glass of water and set the stage for his story. "When the Russians showed up, we didn't know what to do, but then they started herding people onto buses. They set up a camp just down the road, but the conditions. Man! It was November, and all we had were tents. People died, froze to death in their sleep. I'd never seen a dead body before that. Then I woke up next to one." He hesitated and took a long drink of water. I waved out the door at Lucas to join us.

"I was one of the stupid ones who went with them. Some people fought back. That didn't last long. Others ran for it. Others gave up and once they in the camp, they tried to fight back. It wasn't pretty, but it gave some of us the chance to escape. We ran for it; ten of us made it out. Two of us survived that first winter, me and Bob, there." He pointed.

Agnes brought each of us a small bowl of stew. I stood to take it from her and thanked her. It smelled perfect. Lucas thanked her as well. I noted that Randy took it without acknowledging Agnes' existence. She didn't seem to notice. We ate small bites; it was hot.

"You've seen Bob. He hasn't been the same since he saw his girlfriend eaten by a bear. That happened right in front of him. I don't know how he got away. He got a nasty scar out of it. I'd ask him to show you, but when he's calm, we leave him be."

"The Russians. They pulled out six months ago, didn't they?" I asked.

"Most of them left long before that, maybe three years, but they'd still harass us. The soldiers would show up, conduct a sweep, and then disappear again. It was often enough that we never felt safe. But six months ago it all stopped. We haven't seen any sign of them since. Hell, we only moved in here a month ago when we realized they weren't coming back."

He looked finished, so I told him what I knew, our survival, our run through the winter to get to Canada, and then our return. We talked about the charter, the mandate to settle Alaska once again, establish a new legitimacy where the UN would recognize who owned the state. We wanted it to be us.

Randy and Agnes were excited. They were lifelong Alaskans and didn't want to leave.

"You don't have to. Establish a settlement. Get yourselves set for the coming winter, and I think next year will be a big year to consolidate and start building again. I believe that within a couple years, you'll see the return of commerce, trade, everything that makes for a civilization. The infrastructure is still mostly in place except for the big cities and military bases; those were all nuked or bombed in some way. But we can build around that. I didn't like Anchorage anyway," I said to see if he was listening. He gave me a closed-mouth smile. Maybe he lost family in Anchorage.

"I'm sorry. A lot of people died down there. I didn't mean to make light of that. Or Fairbanks, or Delta Junction. A lot of people died. The government heard from a few of the native villages, because of satellite phones. I'd like to think that most, if not all, are okay. So what's that leave us, twenty to thirty thousand people still here? Everything else was turned into a resettlement camp until it was evacuated, like Valdez, Bethel, Nome, Homer. I still can't believe the magnitude of it all," I stopped. I had thought about it, but here they were in front of me. Three people. No one was in Nenana. I wondered how many people were still in Circle?

"It's okay, Chuck. I like what you said. We're going to rebuild. Maybe I can be the Mayor of Healy? Ha! What do you think of that, Agnes?" Chortling, he slapped the table. Agnes smiled and returned to her needlework.

"Let us clean that up for you, Agnes. It's the least we can do to show our appreciation for your hospitality." We picked up all the bowls and headed for the door to what we suspected was the kitchen. Agnes brightened immensely. Randy looked angry. I ignored him as Agnes followed us into the kitchen carrying a kettle that had been on the stove. A jug of clean-looking water sat on the sink. We mixed the two and did the dishes for her. It took us less than ten minutes start to finish.

When we returned, Randy was standing with his hands on his hips. "You're going to ruin it!" he spit out.

"What are you talking about?" I asked, surprised, but not at his demeanor. This young man had put himself in charge. He was probably part of the reason Bob was still a basket case.

"We have a good thing here and you're ruining it. Agnes takes care of everything for us, and that's how we like it." He finished by thrusting out his chest and standing close so he could loom over me. My expression didn't change as he put his hands on my shoulders, but Lucas snickered. When Randy looked at him, I kneed the younger, larger man in the groin as hard as I could. He came off the ground and crashed through a chair on his way to the floor.

"Agnes! Grab your stuff if you want to go with us," Lucas told her. She shuffled away, returning after two minutes with one bag.

"That's it?" I asked.

"Yes, dear, I don't need much," she smiled as she tottered out the door. Lucas followed her to the truck. I stayed behind.

I pulled out my pistol and made a show of racking the slide, which was just a show. There was already a round in the chamber, so I only went part of the way to avoid ejecting one of my precious rounds.

I kneeled sideways beside him to limit his target had he chosen to lash out. He wisely whimpered and held himself. I forced the barrel between his lips. "If I ever see you do anything like that again, I will kill you," I hissed at him. "Here's what you're going to do. You will clean this place up and prepare it to receive visitors. You're going to figure out how to get running water back in here. And you are going to build yourself a smoker so you can stock some meat and other supplies. Do you understand me?"

He nodded slightly. I stood and slowly backed away, keeping my pistol aimed at his head. His eyes were slits as he glared at me. I mouthed the word "boom" at him and backed out the door. I jogged to the truck, grabbing the rusty rifle on my way past.

"Does he have a gun, Agnes, or a vehicle?"

"That's the only one. I told them to take better care of it. And that truck over there is running, but just barely." She pointed to a newer truck. The old gas probably didn't agree with the fuel injection system.

"You want to grab that and we can drop it a few miles down the road?" I nodded toward Lucas. He hopped out and ran to it. It fired up, but coughed and smoked. I let him lead the way in case the truck broke down. We both spun our tires as we sped from the parking lot.

"How about that, Agnes? A real jailbreak!"

She laughed as she cranked the window down on her side of the truck, letting the wind pull her hair behind her.

"Where did the others go, Agnes? I need to find this woman Tanya if she's out there somewhere. Can you point the way?" I pleaded with her. I expected there was a great deal she knew but hadn't shared with Randy.

"Keep going this way and then there's a Jeep track. I think we'll be able to take it, even if it's overgrown a little. We'll need to drive it all the way to the end which is well inside the park. There are cabins out that way with people staying there," she said slowly.

"Don't be afraid, Agnes. I think you'll like our group and we'll be happy to have you. We have all types and we have one type. The one thing we insist is that everyone works to make the Community better. After that, you do your own thing. We have a number of children, from a few months old to our six-year-old twins."

She bobbed her head in rhythm with the bouncing truck. I waved my arm out the window at Lucas, and he pulled to the side. "There might be some survivors in the hills, but we'll have to take an overgrown Jeep path. You up for that?" I asked.

Of course, he was. He told me to lead the way and then pull aside when we were at the turn-off. He had no problem abusing the truck we'd just stolen.

When we reached the so-called road, I waved Lucas ahead. Even he stopped and looked sideways at it. Overgrown didn't begin to cover it. I thought we were looking at the entrance to Jurassic Park. Agnes nodded and pointed. The truck protested as Lucas engaged the four-wheel drive and powered into the brush.

THE COST OF POWER

The engineers and Chris and Colleen took two of the quads in search of the elusive right-sized generator. They knew the most likely candidates would be found at the Air Force Base. Chris had been there before and led the way. The quads raced down the highway. Sometimes it was nice to feel the speed of the machine, but only on the straightaways. No one wanted to deal with another rollover, least of all the engineers.

They pulled past the abandoned guard shack and through the open gate. The engineers asked if Chris knew where the buildings were that might need auxiliary power in case of an outage, places like a hospital, clinic, or headquarters. Chris shrugged. The base wasn't that big. They split it into two pieces, the hangars and everything else.

Chris and Colleen drove to the flight line. The planes were arrayed across the tarmac as if waiting for the crew to show up and fly them away.

There were hangars and other support facilities that lined the parking apron. At the end of the runway, a second taxiway led to an area where fighter jets could be parked along with infrastructure suited for the smaller planes.

They took a businesslike approach and started with the first hangar, a massive structure where the biggest airplanes could be serviced. The building-sized doors were closed, but the normal door built into the larger retracting walls was unlocked. They went through and into the musty darkness.

Chris had to return to the quad and get their flashlights. In the beams of their lights they saw equipment lining the walls, leaving the central area open. Colleen went one way and Chris went the other. They didn't know what most of the equipment did and the going was slow as they checked tags, looking for a label telling them more about the equipment. Halfway down one wall, Colleen yelled for Chris.

"I know what I'm looking for but I don't know what I'm looking at. Can you make heads or tails of these tags! What is this stuff and what does it do?" Exasperated, she leaned against a small tractor used to move aircraft around. Chris laughed.

"Thank God! I thought it was just me. I bet there's something here they can use. Let's go find our young adventurers and tell them about this place. We can check out other things, see what we can use. I think we might need to make a major 'shopping' run here." They held hands as they walked out of the building. Driving slowly, they listened for the other quad until they caught sight of the engineers.

After a brief update, the two excited young men headed straight for the large hangar. Chris and Colleen went to the exchange to pick up cans of spray paint so they could tag places they wanted to come back to. And then they started the unsavory task of going through people's homes, looking for canned goods. They collected enough to fill the trailer, then consolidated more into a few houses where they spray painted fluorescent lines on the doors. They were happy that they didn't find any bodies, but also surprised. They wondered where the people had gone.

They finished with as much personal housing as they could stomach before exploring from the quad. There was a tank farm at the far end of the base. Chris thought about climbing an outside ladder on one of the tanks, but Colleen stopped him by pointing to a small building to where all the pipes led.

The manifold building controlled the distribution of the fluids. Chris wanted to know what flowed through there. Inside, he was rewarded to find the pipes were clearly labeled. Jet fuel in six of the tanks and diesel in the last one. They didn't know how much was in each tank, but Chris thought he could rig a rope with an anchor and conduct manual measurements. Five more tanks were across the road with piping leading to a second manifold building and pumping station.

Before they did anything else, they wanted to talk with the engineers and devise a plan to go after the right resources in the right way.

They drove onto the taxiway and followed it to where the engineers' quad was parked. They stopped and yelled. They tried the first hangar, but no one was there. Then the second, and then a smaller third one. They were nowhere to be found.

Chris went one direction and Colleen the other, both calling for Cullen and Shane. They looped around the buildings and met back at the quad nearly an hour later. There was still no sign of the engineers.

"What do we do now?" Chris asked, torn between being angry and concerned.

"We have to find them. When did we last see them?" Colleen's eyes pleaded with Chris. She was concerned and afraid.

"A couple hours, maybe? And that's before spending the last hour looking. You go where I went, and I'll retrace your steps. Maybe you'll see something that I missed. Did they get into something they shouldn't have?" They ran in opposite directions, quickly disappearing into the hangars.

It only took ten minutes before Chris heard Colleen screaming for him. He broke into a sprint and nearly ran Colleen over as they reached the hangar door at the same time.

"I found them, but can't get to them!" she said as she took off at a dead run. Chris easily kept pace while preparing himself for the worst. They ran to the hangar that they'd first gone into, the one he'd gone through by himself an hour ago. Colleen ran across the open floor to a misshapen mountain of supplies and equipment in the back covered by a large canvas tarp. Some careless individual had covered certain chemicals and supplies that shouldn't have been in the hangar to begin with. One corner of the tarp was pulled up.

He hadn't thought to look under there. He started mentally kicking himself. Colleen waved him to the other side and she grabbed a handful of tarp. He mirrored her action. Together they rolled it back, the smell of an industrial chemical attacked his sinuses, burning with each breath. He almost lost his grip, but turned his head away and exhaled sharply before gulping a breath of fresher air to the side. They kept rolling the tarp back until the two young men were lying in the open.

Colleen took a couple steps toward them, then coughed and retreated, holding her shirt over her mouth.

Chris pointed her away from the area, toward the open floor. He leaned to the side and took a deep breath. He ran to Cullen, grasped under his arms, and dragged him backwards out of the area. Chris' chest heaved with the effort to take his first breath once in the open.

He panted and then took in another big breath before going after Shane. When he dropped Shane next to Cullen, he watched as Colleen performed CPR, which made him check Shane's pulse. He had one, but was blue and barely breathing.

Chris thought he remembered seeing an oxy-acetylene welding rig. He shone his flashlight along the walls until he found it, and he ran for it. It was on a cart which made pushing it back easy. He unhooked the oxygen line and secured it on the top of the tank, turning the valve to let the oxygen flow, but not at full pressure. He took off his shirt and made a tent over Shane's face, blowing the oxygen into the small area.

Colleen continued performing CPR, but she was getting tired. Chris took over so she could examine Shane. Her skills were needed more on the living than the dead. When Chris gave Cullen a breath, he knew. The young man's face was cold.

He'd been dead for a while. Chris stopped what he was doing and carefully lifted the man by his armpits and dragged him toward the door. He walked back to Colleen, feeling tired and very old.

THE SURVIVORS

Lucas revved the engine on occasion to keep it running while delivering extra power as he drove through dense bushes and over small trees. He backed up every now and then to get a run at the foliage that failed to give way under the slow approach. He could see enough to stay on the track and was happy when they finally broke into an open valley. He followed the old track across the valley as his engine temperature rose. He figured he'd punched a hole in the radiator, but didn't care as long as he could plow the way for me in our other truck.

We didn't want our ride home to take the beating he was delivering to the stolen truck. And Lucas enjoyed every minute of it. We could hear him whooping and hollering with each new victory over nature. Agnes and I marveled at how his whole body bounced into the air as he negotiated ruts and small sinkholes.

When the heat gauge redlined and the engine started sputtering, Lucas surged to a small open spot to the side and let the truck die. He jumped out, then used the classic hitchhiking pose to wave us down.

"Going my way, mister?" Lucas waved to Agnes as he drawled his question.

"Why don't you walk ahead and scout the best route. We can't afford to lose this truck, too." I was all business. I wanted to know if Tanya lived here, and then I wanted to go home.

Agnes and I crawled after Lucas, but it made the drive much easier on us and the truck. The truck cleared the brush, and a stand of trees spread apart before we entered an open meadow around which a number of cabins stood. I stopped the truck, but before I could get out, the windshield shattered as a bullet tore through it, whizzing past my head and out the back window. I ducked to the right as Agnes dodged to her left and our heads cracked together like two melons hitting the floor. Agnes grunted and I shoved her underneath me as I used my body to protect her as a second shot sent the remaining glass over us.

RETURN

Lucas yelled at someone to stop firing while he scrambled to get behind a tree. He was unarmed and couldn't shoot back. I had my pistol and both rifles in the front seat with me, but was hesitant to expose myself outside the truck. Then again, if they shot the engine, we'd be trapped up here. I put it in reverse and backed away, fast, weaving as I did so. A shot missed the truck and then another as I drove backward erratically toward the path down the hill.

Lucas was yelling at me to wait, but there was no stopping, I could barely see and my foot was jammed sideways against the brake pedal. Until I could sit up straight, the truck would continue downhill. I sat up just before we missed our path through the woods, yanking violently on the steering wheel while mashing the brakes.

The truck slid sideways, stopped, then eased backward down the trail and into the brush. I stopped out of sight of the cabins. Agnes sat up and brushed the glass from her hair.

"I'm sorry. I probably should have told you they are kind of wary of strangers," Agnes apologized. She opened her door

"Where are you going?"

"They know me, dear. Let me smooth things over, and then you can come up." She patted my leg as she got out of the truck and walked up the hill, yelling as she went.

"It's just me, old Agnes!" She walked with her hands up. I feared that I would hear the angry retort of a rifle, but it didn't come. I got out of the truck and followed part of the way, staying behind branches and bushes as I neared the opening in the brush. I peeked between the leaves as Agnes walked past where Lucas hid. She talked with him briefly before continuing.

I thought about getting a rifle, but that wouldn't get us what we wanted, which was information.

A number of women materialized from behind cover. They all carried hunting rifles, and they looked too thin. Life in the hills around Denali must have been hard. Agnes greeted them warmly, but they didn't seem happy. They looked warily in our direction. The conversation lasted far longer than it should have before Agnes waved us forward. I walked out of the brush with my hands up. Lucas joined me once I was even with him. He held his hands up, too. Prudence demanded humility.

"That's close enough!" one of the women shouted, leveling her rifle at us. I froze. Lucas started to say something until she pointed the rifle at him. He stopped.

We stood there so long that my arms started to hurt. The rifle started shaking as the woman struggled to maintain her aim. "Somebody has to do something," I said. She turned the rifle on me. "I'm going to put my arms down, and I would greatly appreciate it if you didn't shoot me. My wife will thank you later. And his wife won't kill me if I can bring him home in one piece."

She finally let the rifle barrel drop toward the ground. I don't think it was as much our pleas as it was she just couldn't hold it anymore. They were probably weak from hunger. Not weaklings and not defenseless, but not up for any extended displays of physical prowess.

"We are here for one reason only. I promised Mr. Bezos that I would look for his daughter. He is very concerned. Understand that I'm not here for money or anything else. I'm here because I couldn't look a father in the eye and tell him that even though I was the only one in a position to help him, I wouldn't. So here I am. Once I get the answer, we'll be on our way. Our wives are probably worried sick as we've been gone too long. I'm sure our kids miss us, too." I wanted to establish that we were family men. Their fear of us was real, but only because we were men.

I couldn't imagine what they'd gone through to become like this.

"You've talked with my father? When?" a voice spoke from the back of the now large group of women and small children, the oldest no more than three.

"Tanya? I talked with your dad maybe two months ago. He'll be relieved to find out that you're alive, to say the least." The women started talking excitedly among themselves. I couldn't hear what they were saying. When Tanya stepped forward, she held the hand of a blue-eyed, blond boy about two years old. I looked from him to her. "We've been Outside and only recently returned as part of the effort to resettle Alaska, take it back from the Russians through building and establishing a new colony."

An older woman stepped forward and looked closely at me. I stood still as if getting sniffed by a bear, watching her without moving my head.

"I think he's telling the truth," she said as she stepped back. They waved us toward one of the cabins. Although I was considered truthful, I noticed that two women followed us at a short distance, their rifles at the ready.

The pain they carried must have been immense.

We were shown chairs at a small dining table and given water. I hadn't realized how much I'd sweated, but that came from the tense few minutes where I wondered if I was going to live or not. I still wondered what they'd do with us.

We told our story first, ending with the bombing six months ago and our run from Alaska. Then our short stay outside and the government's offer for us to return. I went into detail about why we couldn't stay out there, how life here was better with our Community.

Tanya hovered nearby, but deferred to Terri, the apparent leader of the group. When Terri started speaking, no one moved. She spoke in a hostile voice, angry at the world. She talked of how the women were separated and then passed among the Russian men.

I hung my head, tears welling in my eyes. I'd never felt so helpless. They were here the whole time we were living at the Resort, without a care in the world. And they were tortured by men for the simple reason that they were women.

"We escaped one night when others rushed the guards. We went into the Park, way into the Park, but there are too many grizzlies and wolves. Ten of us died that first month. We couldn't protect ourselves; we were too weak. We finally made our way here, found the rifles and ammunition and a place that we could defend. We've been here for almost a year now."

"We have a nice Community, all couples, plenty of children, same age as these little guys. We have a school, too. There are only twenty-two of us total, but we have skills, survival skills. We've got a good place and we'll continue to grow, build a new society, fair, peaceful. We already have a community that we're proud of. That's what we want to see for a new Alaska. You can join us or stay here. It is all your choice, but we're going to leave. We want to get back to our families. Tanya, what do you want me to tell your father?" I wanted to leave right then, but Terri grabbed my arm with her skeletal hand. I looked down at her fingers as they turned white with the strength of her grip.

I put my hand over hers, and she flinched. "I just want you to let go, that's all." She released the pressure and mumbled something that I couldn't hear.

"You can talk with my father? You have a radio that works?" Tanya stammered.

"We have a satellite phone that your father gave me so I could call him when I knew something. It's available for anyone to use, but it's back where we're staying in North Pole. We can get it and return, but I don't know how long that will be, and I sure as hell don't want to drive back up that road to get here."

They all started talking at once and even with Terri yelling, it was chaos. I started to stand and Terri clamped down on my arm once again. I grabbed her wrist and ripped her fingers from me. Her eyes blazed in fury as she tried to pull her rifle into her shoulder.

"Listen!" I bellowed with everything I had. "I'm not threatening you, and I demand that you don't try to hurt me. Do you understand? I'm not your enemy! We're leaving and if anyone tries to stop us, I will shoot back." I threw the table out of the way and stormed out the door.

"Wait," a lone voice cried from within. "Wait." Tanya ran out the door, trailed by her two-year-old.

"I want to go with you. We want to go with you," she said, taking her son's hand and leading him up to us.

"Get your stuff. Bus leaves in ten minutes," I said coldly. She picked up the little boy and jogged toward a distant cabin.

"Wait," a second voice said from the doorway. "I'm sorry. Will you give us time to talk about this? Some more may want to come along. As you can see, we don't eat real well here." Terri hung her head after speaking, turned, and went back inside.

Lucas look at me and then the cabin. His gaze drifted away into the trees. "I can't imagine what they went through. Do you think we could have done anything if we came here when they being held? Could we have broken them out earlier?"

"No. There's nothing we could have done. They were being held by real military. Scumbags, but real military with real weapons. We wouldn't have stood a chance. The only thing we can do is treat them with respect now. It's the only thing we can do for anyone, whether we know them or not. They have our trust unless they show that they can't be trusted. And if they come, they'll be equal members of the Community, just like the rest of us," I talked softly, unsure of what I wanted. It would be easy if we could just drive away. I couldn't do that, even as hostile as they were. I couldn't let them die out here.

"We'll protect them, too, Chuck. They probably haven't had a good night's rest in years. Always hearing noises, living in fear," he whispered, before squeezing my shoulder. "Once again, Chuck, you save the day. What if they all come?"

"We make do. How many do you think are here? Twenty, thirty?"

"Standing room only in the bed of the truck. We need bigger wheels," Lucas said, watching the cabin door open and the women emerge, Terri in front, Agnes at her side.

"We will all come along," Terri stated in a loud and clear voice. There was a small cheer from the others. Just like Lucas had predicted.

"We welcome you to the Community. How many is 'all,' by the way?"

"Thirty-seven. Eighteen adults and nineteen children."

I whistled through pursed lips. It was roughly ten miles downhill to the highway outside Healy. From there, it was about one hundred fifty miles to North Pole, further since we had to drive the long way around Fairbanks. They could walk ten miles downhill if we carried all their stuff in the truck and then in the massive parking lot of vehicles, I knew we'd find one that would run. We had our truck to jumpstart another vehicle, and then another, as many as we needed, as many we could find that would run.

We had a plan, but it was too late in the day to execute it. Lucas and I insisted on sleeping in our truck, which gave the women extra time to get ready. We didn't have much food with us, but we gave it all to the group. We could go without for a day. We knew where there was more in Nenana, only fifty miles away.

"We leave first thing in the morning," I said to Terri. She offered her hand, and we shook. Neither of us smiled.

SHANE

Colleen kept the oxygen tent over Shane's mouth until his color improved. Together, they carried him outside where the air was fresher, although Chris returned for the oxygen tank, just in case. Shane was groggy and couldn't seem to wake up. They put him in the quad. Colleen took the driver's seat. Chris said that he'd take care of things and be along shortly.

She slowly drove away, looking back once before speeding up and disappearing around the building.

Chris took a small tarp from a pallet of material. He wrapped Cullen's body and hefted the bundle over his shoulder. He put Cullen in the back of the engineer's quad and took it to the small clinic that serviced the base. He broke in and then broke a series of doors before finding a room that looked like the morgue. It only had two places for bodies and both of those were taken. Chris gagged and returned to the vehicle. He carried Cullen back in and dropped him in the corner of the tiny room. Chris didn't know what to say, so he didn't say anything.

On his way out, he saw oxygen bottles. He took these along with a few bags of IV solution. They were old, but there was no alternative. He took the needles, too. Colleen would have to establish a clinic in one of the spare rooms of the elementary school. They could get most of their supplies from here. It would be a return trip that Chris didn't look forward to.

He left the clinic and since the engineers' trailer wasn't full, he went back to the houses with the painted stripe and emptied them. He drove off carefully. They'd already had enough tragedy for the day.

He made it to North Pole without incident and parked next to the quad Colleen had driven. They hadn't emptied the trailer yet. He took three grocery bags in each hand and waddled to the door, pushing his way through to the inside. He staged the canned goods outside the pantry and went in search of Colleen. She was easy to find as everyone was huddled outside Cullen and Shane's room. Chris ran back outside and brought in one of the small oxygen battles with valve, tubing, and a nose piece. He handed it through the crowd to Colleen, who thanked him and put it on Shane, turning the valve fully open.

She was trying to flush his lungs clean, but she feared that some of the damage would be permanent. There was nothing else she could do, so she chased people away to let Shane rest.

Madison, with the help of the twins, corralled the children and headed back to the classroom. She had to talk with Colleen about giving classes in first aid to the youngest among them. With the way everyone worked, you never knew who would be there when something happened. Everyone needed to know how to stop the bleeding at a minimum. CPR would come later, as even Charles and Aeryn didn't have enough body weight to perform chest compressions on an adult.

Colleen looked once more at the young man, closing the door gently on her way out. She saw Chris carrying more bags in and joined him to clean out the trailer. Once everything was inside, they turned over the stacking to Jo, who was alone in the kitchen. She and Clarisse had a system and woe be to anyone who messed it up.

Clarisse was with Ben at the fish wheel as were Becca and Darren.

Colleen asked what was available. Jo gave her some fresh bread along with a can of Chef-Boyardee spaghetti and meatballs. Jo empathized and didn't prod Colleen for the story. Chris sat next to her, eating his bread and moose jerky, while drinking bottle after bottle of water. He couldn't get the taste of the morgue out of his mouth.

He and Colleen ate in silence. At some point they'd rehash what happened, but not now. Since arriving in North Pole, the Community had lost three people, or so they thought. At least Charles and Aeryn had confidence in their old man and his sidekick.

TRAVELING HOME

The bed of our truck was filled with personal items as we headed downhill. I used the rifle barrel to clean off the remainder of the glass and a rag to wipe most of it out of the cab. I looked in the rearview through the shattered remains of the back window as the women and children followed us, walking with a purpose.

We sped up when we could. Our uphill trip had cleared enough foliage that it took us less than hour to get down to the highway. That meant we had time before the others arrived, maybe three more hours to find a vehicle. We raced north, looking for anything that could burn the old gas better.

I wanted to check on the vehicles from Two Rivers. There were a couple of motorhomes, rather substantial beasts. I wanted to fit everyone into one vehicle. I didn't want a circus train of barely running vehicles.

Sometimes we don't always get what we want.

We found the convoy from Two Rivers and, despite our best efforts, we couldn't get the big engines of the motorhomes to turn over. We had to look somewhere else and we were running out of time.

We headed back toward Healy. As we passed older trucks, we'd stop, check the engine, clean the fuel filter, hook up the jumper cables and give it a shot. Two of the trucks started and ran, roughly, but they ran. Lucas jumped in one and I looked to Agnes to take the other.

"Oh, I don't drive," she said with a smile.

"I don't care if you don't have a license. Just get in. Gear shift, brake, and gas. That's all you need to know. Turn the wheel a little bit to keep from running into things." She was hesitant but she gave it a try.

And promptly rammed the truck full speed into the vehicle to its front. She hit her face on the steering wheel upon impact. She got out, a little shaken, bleeding from a cut on her forehead. Once I was sure she was okay, I started laughing. She looked at me questioningly.

"You weren't kidding, were you? You really can't drive!" She shrugged disarmingly.

Lucas and I continued down the road in our two old vehicles until we passed a truck with dual rear tires hauling a fifth-wheel trailer.

We both stopped at the same time. I wondered why we hadn't given this one a try on the first pass. If we could get that beast cranked up, it would solve our problems. Lucas broke the window and unceremoniously dumped the body of the driver on the pavement.

"Keys," I told Lucas. He pulled the set from the ignition and threw them to me. I unlocked the trailer and went in. There was enough room, especially if they put four adults and two or three children in the cab. Cramped in a trailer was far better than walking.

I checked the gas and felt certain it was empty. I put in the contents of one gas can. Five gallons would get this rig twenty-five miles up the road. If it didn't run, we'd just wasted the gas. We cleaned the fuel filter and hooked up the jumper cables. Lucas shut everything off so the heavy-duty battery wasn't powering anything besides the starter. It took ten minutes of charging before we tried it. It turned over slowly, but we stayed on it as long as we could. It took a while to pump the gas back into the engine with a dry fuel line.

Ten minutes more and it belched, choked, coughed, and sputtered to life. It sounded like two of the eight cylinders were working. The oil we added took a while to get to the valves and the cylinders, but once there, it ran a little rough, but it ran. This wasn't a new truck, but it had fuel injection, so we poured another five gallons in, straining it through four different layers of material. If we only had avgas to perk it up.

Clear Airport was about twenty miles up the road.

"Can you drive this rig?" I asked. Lucas' only response was to look at me like I was stupid. We parked the extra truck off the side of the road. We could pick it up on the way as long as we salvaged enough gas. But we had to pick up our survivors first. "Tally ho!" I shouted and drove slowly past Lucas. He angled the truck sharply then smoothed out the corner to get it and the trailer out of the line of traffic.

The women and children were standing by the side of the road when we arrived. Lucas drove past and used a motel's parking lot to turn around. He slowly pulled up and called "All aboard!"

Terri looked at the vehicles and organized everyone. It took two minutes to get loaded up. I'd never seen such efficiency from a group so large. Once buttoned up, she twirled her finger in the air and we drove away.

We found avgas at Clear Airport, but not in a tank. Those were all empty. We siphoned it from two small airplanes abandoned on the tarmac. The big truck appreciated the extra spark the high-octane gas provided. We didn't waste any more time than we had to, so we pulled out with every intention of stopping for lunch in Nenana.

We made it to the middle of the small town, parking in the shade, scavenging what food and cooking gear we could find before building a fire to prepare a feast. By the time we actually ate, it was close to dinnertime. We talked it over with Terri and decided to remain overnight there in Nenana. First thing tomorrow, we'd get on the road and we wouldn't stop until we were home. I couldn't wait. I decided to go fishing as that would help me relax so I could get to sleep.

Of course, that meant more scavenging, but I barely noticed what I was doing. I took the best rod from a house next to the river and even helped myself to a four-year-old warm beer. It was bad, but seemed to fit the moment. I even caught a fish, but released him. I cast and reeled, cast and reeled. I wished that I had my music with me.

Terri joined me. I pointed to the house and told her to get herself some gear. She returned shortly with a jig and a bobber attached to a child's pole. She punched in the thumb button and cast straight into the shore. We both chuckled as she kept trying.

"I'd offer you a drink, but it's really bad. And warm. Warm and bad is no way to drink a beer."

She took it regardless and helped herself to a big swig. She coughed and smacked her lips.

"You weren't kidding. That is horrible," she said with her mind clearly on something else. I didn't interrupt her thoughts as I cast my lure back into the river. "Thanks for waiting for us, Chuck. And you'll have to keep waiting. We'll require a lot of patience."

"When you see what we have, what little we have, you'll find the only thing we can really give you is our promise to help. We have food, enough for all of us. And you'll get the chance to work, too. There's always something that needs doing. But the work will be on your terms. Now if you don't mind, I'm trying to do some fishing here," I said in my most stodgy voice.

"Is that what you call it?" she said with a smile as she took her pole to the house, putting it back where she'd found it.

She's going to fit in just fine, I thought.

POWER

Shane woke up after a full day in bed and was able to walk himself to the outhouse. He refused to talk with anyone, but they'd seen that before as his way to cope. The Community was rocked by the tragedy, especially as the engineers were coming into their own as full members.

Chris spent his breaks and spare time with Shane. Although the young man seemed unresponsive, Chris talked to him anyway. He shared stories of himself, of the Community, of what they did and what they meant to each other. Of the tragedies we'd all seen. Felicia's death, my fight with the hostile strangers, and how we overcame it all to escape, only to return after a few short months.

The twins seemed the least affected. They kept Phyllis and Husky close, never straying far from the dogs. Madison did not worry that they were being taken care of, either children or dogs. They all knew to ask for help when they needed it, and they weren't afraid to. They also had no doubt that Lucas and I weren't dead. They were fearless and unperturbed. They spent half their days in school and the other half helping Abigail and Phillip at the kennels or at the pasture where Penelope and Sophie ran free.

Chris found an antique hand scythe and worked three overgrown fields outside the town. His job was to lay in enough feed for the horses for the winter. He was incrementally filling a shed that had previously been a machine shop. He was working eighteen hours a day, straining himself to do more than anyone else.

He had gone through the hangar and missed finding their injured comrades. His failure meant they'd spent an extra hour breathing toxic air. Colleen told him that it could happen to anyone. In this new world, accidents would happen, and they tended to be deadly. The rest had to accept it and move on.

But Chris worked himself to the point of passing out. Only then could he sleep.

After class one day, Charles stopped to visit Shane to ask a question about a bridge that he'd seen in his schoolbook. "How could something that looks that weak support something so heavy as a train?" he asked in his small voice and waited patiently. "Shane! Shane? Do you know?" Charles' small calloused hand nudged Shane's shoulder. And the child waited longer.

Shane turned his head and focused on Charles' face. "A train?" he asked in a scratchy voice. He cleared his throat. "The forces are redirected along interconnected beams. By directing the weight along the axis of the beam, we maximize its ability to hold weight."

"I knew it! I have to tell Aeryn I was right." The boy beamed and bolted off.

Shane laughed to himself. *Life goes on, doesn't it,* he thought. *Because I wasn't strong enough to tell Cullen not to check out the barrels under the tarp, there's only me to bring power to the Community. Without electricity, we'll spend the winter cold and in the dark. These people are still counting on me.*

Shane got up and dressed. There was a lot of work to do and the first thing was to go back to Eielson and secure the generator they'd found. He needed to find Chris as soon as he got something to eat. He was ravenous.

THE TRIUMPHANT RETURN

Having refueled with avgas and restocked with oil, just in case, our caravan of two vehicles left Nenana, heading to Fairbanks. Lucas drove slowly at first, but sped up over time. We stopped after each hour to make sure everyone was okay and give everyone a relief break.

That was mostly for me. We'd found coffee and I was drinking too much of it, which necessitated frequent breaks. And I was happy as can be. We continued to the outskirts of Fairbanks, turning off short of the city to take the roads that led around the north side. We had to take Goldstream. After nearly four years, I wondered if the bodies of the two men I'd killed would still be there.

I was happy to see that they weren't. One snow machine sat there, a monument to a battle fought long ago, a life and death struggle best left behind.

We continued to Steese, then Chena Hot Springs Road. I pointed to the street that led to our house as we passed. Agnes nodded as we kept going. I started to get excited when we made the slow turn onto Nordale Road. If anything happened from here on out, we could walk the rest of the way.

But nothing happened to hold us up. When we entered the outskirts of North Pole, I laid into the horn and Lucas quickly followed: Then mine froze and blasted a continuous, annoying tone. Lucas stuck his hand out the window, reaching past the wide mirrors to give me the finger. I stuck both my hands out the door to show that I wasn't holding it down. He changed it to a thumbs up and we found ourselves back on Steese for a brief drive to the exit for the school. Lucas turned off, followed the road, rolled past the school, and parked on the street.

Amber raced from the building, almost knocking Lucas over as he walked toward her. He lifted her and swung her around in a circle as the other survivors exited and gathered around.

I stopped, opened the hood, and ripped the wire from the horn before running toward the school. Madison jogged toward me.

"I'm so sorry," I cried into her hair as I hugged her to me. I could feel her sobbing in my arms. She pushed me away with a smile, wiping her tears on her sleeve.

"Don't ever do that again," she said, sniffling. "Looks like you brought company."

"Hi there, I'm Agnes and we are so happy to be here. I expect you're Madison?" My wife nodded. "I just want to tell you that he saved us. He saved us all."

Madison looked at the number of women and children standing around. "Of course he did. It's not the first time, you know. Maybe you can introduce us?"

People started haphazardly delivering introductions. It was just after noon and most of the Community were working. The only other adults were Jo and Clarisse. The small children were there, but the twins were not, although we expected them shortly as the kennel was close. There was no way they'd missed the honking horns.

I stood on a step and called for everyone's attention.

"For those of you who just arrived, welcome to the Community. The most important thing is that we make you feel welcome. There's plenty of work to do, but I think the first thing we need is to eat and then get your rooms ready. There's nothing like a full belly and a warm bed. Welcome home."

The twins had arrived with Abigail and Phillip. They looked surprised and relieved. For some reason, they saw the humor in the number of people that we'd brought with us.

"Hey, Dad," was all my children said as they went to their mother to ask about the new people.

Abigail stifled a laugh, turning it into a snort. "They never doubt Superman, do they?"

"No, they don't," I said proudly. Then leaned close, speaking conspiratorially, "and they'll have nothing to worry about as I think I'll be grounded for the next ten years."

AND BILL BELLOWED

The first thing we did after eating was hand Tanya the satellite phone. She looked at it and apologized that she didn't know her father's phone number. Madison and I both heard her say "don't know" as opposed to "don't remember." There was a world of difference between those two phrases.

"It's programmed into the phone," I said as I scrolled through the phone's address book. I saw that most of the other members of the Community had added listings. I wasn't surprised. Technology was a drug that we found too difficult to shake off. "Ready?" I asked and she responded with a terse nod.

I pressed the button and the phone started dialing. Madison and I excused ourselves, even though we were in our room. Tanya deserved privacy.

We shut the door carefully as she was saying "Daddy?" We didn't want to interrupt, but our good intentions were ruined when Bill let out one of his trademarked glass-shaking cries. I almost jumped out of my skin. The little hell-spawn was standing right behind us.

"God! Would you lose the bullhorn already!" I said a little too sharply. He started bawling and ran off howling. I looked at Madison only to see her scowling at me. I held up my hands in surrender. We walked away to check on the others.

Settling the newcomers was easier than I imagined. Once Terri got the lay of the land, she brought the adults together for a brief powwow. The orders were issued and off they went.

Ben and Colleen ran into a couple of the new women as they were raiding a house looking for mattresses.

"People," Colleen said while pointing. The women waved and continued on their mission.

"Maybe that's what the honking was all about. It looks like we have visitors," Ben answered as he waved back. He'd only been a settler for a couple of months. Strangers weren't new to him. They continued on their way to the school without another word.

The impressive truck and fifth wheel were parked prominently on the road in front of the school. The first thing they heard was Bill expressing his displeasure about something. Then they saw the children and the women. "You were right, Ben. We have guests."

Madison and I were heading out the door when we ran into Ben and Colleen.

"You're alive!" Ben exclaimed. "Sorry, never doubted it. Hey! You'll like how the fish wheel turned out. Wanna go see it?" He received the look that Madison had given me moments before. As good men do, he withered and stammered something about having to talk to Clarisse. He smiled at me as he patted my chest.

"Me, too, Ben," I told him.

"Newcomers," Colleen started. "This was all your doing, I expect."

"Guilty! But we couldn't leave them. They were starving. They made a break about a year ago from the Russian camp," I said easily, but then got choked up.

"They'd been abused, that's where the kids came from." I couldn't say the word "rape." It tore me up inside to think about it, let alone say it. I wanted to help them past that chapter in their lives. Everyone deserved to be happy. This was our chance to build that very society, one where people were safe. "I couldn't leave them there," I said barely above a whisper.

Colleen read my body language well and understood. "You wouldn't be you if you left them. Did you have to kill anyone?"

I perked up. "No!" I said with a half-smile, "but he won't be walking upright for quite some time." I hadn't told Madison about breaking Agnes out of the bed and breakfast. I wasn't trying to hide anything, but we'd talked more about the airplane crash and the survivors themselves.

We were still outside talking when Tanya came through the door and handed me the satellite phone. Her eyes were puffy from crying, but she looked happy. She mumbled, looking for the words.

"No need," I said. "It's just the way we do things here. By the way, what's your little boy's name?"

"Mark, after my grandfather." The boy held on to his mother's leg. Madison led them back inside to show Mark where he would be going to school. My wife wasn't ready for full classes, but she hoped the increase in numbers would help the others to socialize. With the new children's ages from three months to three years, there was variety for all.

"I'll just wait out here until Bill is done doing what he does," I said to the door as everyone else had gone.

JUST DO WHAT NEEDS DOING

Shane found Chris in the field, soaked with sweat as he swung the scythe, harvesting the grasses for the horses' feed. Shane waved, wearing a closed-mouth smile as he drove the quad into the field. Chris dropped the scythe were he stood and wiped his hands on his pants as he walked toward the engineer. Shane reached out from the driver's seat and they shook, warmly, as friends do.

Chris made to speak and Shane stopped him with a gesture.

"Thank you for everything," he started, speaking slowly. "I heard you when you talked with me. I heard it all, but I held myself hostage. I need to leave that behind. I've never been counted on before, and all of you have shown me that it isn't about leaning on other people. It's about just doing what needs to be done. I'm here, and I need your help. The right-sized generator is at Eielson. Let's unhook the trailer and go get it." Shane wasn't trying to convince Chris of anything except that something needed done and they were the ones to do it.

Chris put his shirt on, grabbed his water bottle, unhooked the trailer, and climbed in. Shane drove without excess, maintaining a steady speed. He was probably their slowest driver and for good reason.

Chris didn't mind. The drive was therapy for them both. For Chris, he could only think about Cullen's body rotting away in the morgue. For Shane, he couldn't remember anything beyond joining Cullen under the tarp to check one last thing. He hadn't gone very far in when the fumes hit them. That saved his life. Cullen was too close for too long.

But that was a completely different world. Shane saw today as his rebirth. There were new challenges, like how to get the generator out of the hangar.

Chris didn't have any ideas, but he wasn't worried either. He knew they'd get it out, because they had to. They'd do what needed to be done.

Eielson looked the same. The hangar looked the same. When they turned off the quad, it sounded the same, too. Chris hesitated before going through the door. Shane shrugged and went in, stopping two steps within to let his eyes adjust. Chris joined him. They turned on their flashlights and Shane walked directly to a piece of equipment and pointed at it when they stood before it.

"Twenty kilowatts," he said proudly. "Should be enough to run that whole school. We'll have power for all the good stuff and maybe even a little heat. I'm thinking a burn rate of seven gallons an hour under a full load, maybe one hundred fifty gallons a day for thirty-thousand gallons. That's running all out 24/7. If we don't use that much electricity, we'll give ourselves a reserve. So, two things. How do we get this out of here, and you were saying you think there's a storage tank of fuel nearby? If they stored it correctly, then we should be able to use it. Just need a little water separation filter and we're home free!"

Chris' funk over being where Cullen had died was short-lived. Shane's excitement was infectious. First thing they had to do was get the big door open.

It was a really big door. It needed electricity for the drive wheels to move the door sections, of which there were three on each side of the center. Without power, Shane hoped the door drives didn't failsafe by locking onto the track. There had to be a manual release. He searched the edges carefully and found what looked like a bottle jack pump. He inserted the lever stored conveniently next to it and started pumping. He felt it build pressure and it became harder and harder to pump. He asked if Chris could muscle it.

Chris looked at a manual switch above the contraption. It was rotated to the right to the "close" setting. He flipped the switch to the left until it pointed to "open." "Now try it," Chris said, giving way to Shane. The engineer chuckled as he worked the handle with fresh energy. The door creaked and there was one pop as one of the wheels broke free from its rust. The door opened, agonizingly slowly. They changed positions twice before the door was open far enough to get the quad through.

The rest was easy. They hooked up the generator and drove carefully away. Without the standard trailer hook-ups, the only brakes they had were those on the quad, and the generator probably weighed as much as their vehicle. It would be a long, slow drive home, but well worth it.

Shane checked the manifold buildings and suggested he could rig the generator to pump the fuel out of the tank and into a tanker truck. There were a few of those on the flight line. They'd dump the avgas, if they had any, and refill them with diesel from the tank. He checked and was pleased to find that it was full. That meant less oxidation and less algae buildup.

They had their truck that they'd used to haul the big generator. They'd bring it back and hook up the fuel truck.

They had a good plan, but it required some tools and another day. Chris took the wheel as Shane directed him where to put the generator. Shane intended to hardwire the pump for the diesel fuel and run it using a manual switch. Chris chocked the tires, unhooked it, and they drove off. Shane was lost making a list of what he needed and running through a few calculations on a pad of paper that he carried.

Without the generator, Chris made short work of their trip home and got quite the surprise when they pulled up to find two trucks and a fifth-wheel trailer parked out front. Women and small children seemed to be everywhere. Some carried mattresses, others carried bedding and clothes. The children were under the watchful eye of an elder woman who kindly waved at them before returning her attention to the little ones.

"Would you look at that?" Shane said simply.

A NEW DAY

A week later, we saw how much could change. Shane worked a miracle in setting up the new generator and staging a fuel truck with enough diesel to last the winter. It would require constant monitoring to ensure the fuel stayed dry, and he shunted the exhaust from the generator back toward the fuel truck to keep the diesel fuel warmer than ambient temperature.

It was nice to have lights and working appliances. We had chest freezers, but they were empty. Berry-picking time approached as did the prime hunting season.

Everyone had worked shifts at the fish wheel, even the new people. And everyone was tired of cleaning and drying fish. The only ones not tired of the fishing routine were the dogs. After the ten thousandth fish, Ben declared victory, and a team of workers pulled the fish wheel onto the shore, where it was braced and stored.

Chris kept working in the fields, but Terri assigned him one of the women each day to help. The newcomers weren't afraid of work because they knew they'd get a good meal, and they had a secure place to sleep. The women were starting to gain weight and get color back to their skin. Jo and Clarisse's more rounded diet worked wonders for the group.

Which led to the next crisis, or maybe it was an old crisis in a new way. We didn't have enough food. The horses did and the dogs did, assuming we were able to bag a moose every few weeks. But canned vegetables we lacked. We were able to do no gardening or farming this year because of our late arrival. That was a huge drawback.

The massive scavenge campaign resulted in our first, second, and third cases of botulism. One of the women and her two children, ages three and one, got sick quickly, but Colleen knew what it was. Induced vomiting and enemas were the only treatment she could think of, then lots of fluids.

Botulism was hard on the victims. They suffered extreme weakness and had trouble talking. Clostridium botulinum was a neurotoxin. After Colleen explained it, I internalized my understanding by relating it to nerve gas, except that the microbes continued to pump out the toxin as long as they were in the person's body.

The victims were in a bad way, but Colleen kept them as comfortable as possible. Terri was angry and shared that with everyone. She saw two fewer adults to work: the woman who had eaten something poorly canned and Colleen, who had to take care of her.

Colleen saw it as an excuse to open a clinic. She started building a list of medical needs, hoping that an outside resupply could take place sometime. She asked me if I would talk with Mr. Bezos and leverage his joy at finding his daughter into meeting us at the border with a load of supplies.

I don't know why I hesitated. There was no doubt that we needed help. What happened when the scavenged supplies ran out? What would we do if we had no success growing food for our fifty-eight people? Would I let them starve to prove we could make it on our own?

No. My real plan was to help us survive until civilization could be reintroduced, trade reestablished, and supplies brought in. I was willing to work, but wanted a shining light at the end of the day without having to light a fire to get it.

I was a child of the modern era and would always embrace the conveniences that technology provided. I took Colleen's list and, at dinner, I asked the whole group if I were to make a call, what did we absolutely have to have.

WINTER PREPARATIONS

Before we added thirty-seven people, we were mostly prepared for winter. All of a sudden, we were short of everything. Something as simple as outhouses. We needed more. We needed more washing machines. We needed more dishes. We needed more food, more water, more wood.

We filled the school, not to overflowing, but there was little empty space with all the classrooms becoming people's new homes, so Abigail and Phillip moved to a small building by the kennel. The twins wanted to go, too, but we made them stay, telling them that they had to attend school first and visit in the afternoon as they always did.

Charles and Aeryn helped Madison and Amber run the school. They provided the example for learning as well as corralled the younger students when they grew rambunctious. Two of the women joined Amber and Madison as teachers, giving them four adults for the twenty-five children. With the twins helping, it was manageable. Having them all in one room was not.

We needed some structure and leadership.

The catalyst in the turnaround at the Community of Chena Hot Springs had been the mayor, not in the traditional sense of a politician who sat in her office and issued edicts. The mayor had to be everywhere, know everything, and lead by doing.

I nominated Terri for the job as she'd softened her approach immensely since our arrival. She started trusting men again. I wanted to think that our group represented the way people should treat each other. We tolerated nothing else. Those behaviors then became our habits.

Our society was growing and our new additions started to embrace the way we acted. Propriety, dignity, integrity – those were our words and our way.

RETURN

We knew we'd reached an extreme level of comfort when I walked into the laundry to find two naked women running the wash machines. They waved and went back to keeping their kids from touching things they shouldn't.

I left because there weren't any wash machines open.

Terri reluctantly agreed to be the mayor as long as I would be co-mayor. I suggested Chris as the better choice, but she politely refused. I asked Chris to talk with her, but he slapped me on the back and told me it was my turn as the Grand Old Man of the Community.

I asked him not to be so hurtful in calling people names. He saw the humor as he walked away. I wasn't kidding. I really wanted him to be the mayor.

I've parroted the phrase that if you have the ability to act, you have the responsibility. I lived that way, too, within reason. Madison tolerated it. I was still grounded because of my disappearing act, and Amber and Madison colluded to keep Lucas and I from leaving the building together.

Sometimes people can't appreciate that the best adventures aren't planned. I still reveled in the fact that we didn't die in the plane crash. Lucas felt he owed me for pulling him out before the plane went under.

Madison wanted me to be the co-mayor as it would keep my adventurism to a minimum. I admit that being able to breathe was an added bonus, even though I couldn't keep up with any of the younger people. I could breathe better, but I would never be at one hundred percent. So I agreed and then Terri and I dug into the cold logistics. Her idea of how much food we needed was half of what I wanted to see.

They'd survived on almost nothing. No one was going to get fat on what I proposed, but at least we wouldn't lose weight over the winter. So we compromised and put a minimum and maximum. We wanted closer to my number but would accept anything above her number.

That meant hunting parties. Some of the women were expert marksmen. I was thankful they weren't the ones shooting at me when we drove up to their camp outside Healy. Becca and Darren took two dog sleds and headed out to get something we could smoke, freeze, or eat fresh. The newcomers couldn't drive dog sleds, so we sent the twins to drive their teams, taking one adult each. No one went out alone.

Ben took the final hunter with him in his quad. They scattered in different directions with supplies for two days. They'd overnight if they had to, but everyone was to return no later than the next day.

The two days came and went. Not a single team returned. The twins were supposed to travel together so there should have been four people telling each other it was time to go back.

We took the other quads and our old beater truck and went in search of our people at first light on the third day. Abigail and Phillip took their dog teams out, too. The rest of the Community took buckets in search of berries. It was August and they were ripe. We had no choice but to keep working while we looked for the members of our family, our Community.

THE TWINS, WYNONA
AND ANGIE

Charles and Aeryn argued hard for sixteen-dog teams, but Abigail wouldn't let them. They took their twelve-dog teams, which were strong and well-rested. They'd been exercised, but a two-day run would be good for them. It was getting cooler and that would keep the dogs from overheating. They planned on heading south then northeast to the edge of the foothills where they hoped to find game. They would follow a stream in the area so they'd have water.

It was a good plan that ended as soon as they saw the bull moose with three cows. The animals bolted to the south and kept running. Charles followed the path the moose had taken, slowly as it was over rougher terrain, while Aeryn drove along the roads in a wide sweep to get in front of them and set Wynona up for a shot.

Once they thought they were in place, Wynona jumped out and Aeryn mushed the dog team out of sight where she watered them and let them rest.

They waited, and waited, and neither the moose nor Charles appeared. Wynona waved at Aeryn, who hooked the team back up. She mushed to Wynona's position and pulled the dogs to a halt.

"What do you think we should do?" Wynona asked. Aeryn was mature for her age but she was still only six years old. Aeryn shrugged. She wanted to find her brother. Even with the adults who carried rifles, this world could be a dangerous place. Wynona agreed. She called off the hunt and they went in search of the other team.

Aeryn wanted to go straight into the woods and drive until they were found, but Wynona insisted that they go back to where they'd lost them and follow their trail. They would eventually catch up. By heading into the woods, they might miss them and get lost themselves.

They circled the team and headed back on the roads as fast as the dogs could run, which made for a wild ride. The wheeled carriages were shaky at the best of times. It was no surprise that they tipped over when Aeryn tried to make the corner to Charles' track too quickly. Wynona went face first across the weed-covered pavement. Her rifle hit hard, bending the scope on top. Aeryn tucked and rolled, coming back up on her feet, yelling for the dogs to hold. She was able to right the sled herself as Wynona dusted herself off and started yelling.

Aeryn was six. I wasn't pleased when they told me this story. There was only one adult present, and she wasn't carrying her weight.

Wynona climbed aboard and, with tears streaming down Aeryn's face, they slowly followed the other sled's tracks.

Once in the woods, the tracks made a sharp turn and headed into a shallow area, then up over the next hill. Wynona jumped out and helped Aeryn manhandle the cart and the dogs through this area. They didn't see any footprints. Aeryn brightened.

"Charles is a better musher than me. He made it through here with Angie riding." Wynona hadn't noticed, but appreciated the observation. She also took the time to apologize to the little girl. Then they were off again on a wild downhill ride. Even with Aeryn standing on the brake, they didn't slow down. When they hit the bottom, they kept going straight even though Charles' track turned left.

The dogs ran straight into heavy brush and got tangled up. They had to get out and physically realign the dogs and the cart. Every second they were stopped was that much farther her brother and Angie got from them. Aeryn begged Wynona to hurry. Along the small valley, the foliage was high, but the ground was firm. Plus, the track had been broken by the other team.

They mushed fast and felt like they were gaining. Wynona started yelling for Charles and Angie. Aeryn stayed true to the trail. The dogs started slowing. They needed a break but she encouraged them to keep going. It was cool in the shade of the wood, and they pushed on.

Finally they stopped. Aeryn's lead dogs hung their heads. She quickly broke out the water and let them all drink. Wynona helped, doing as Aeryn told her since she had no experience with a dog team.

"Wait! Did you hear that?" Aeryn asked. Wynona shook her head. Aeryn had been raised in a non-technological world. Her ears were better than those of people inundated with noise. "Dogs. I hear dogs!" she yelled and started running. Wynona quickly caught up to her and stopped her, telling her to stay with her team, and that Wynona would run ahead.

The woman started yelling and running. She'd been riding most of the time, and despite being tense, she wasn't tired. She ran, looking back to keep her bearings, and the barking dogs grew closer. She stopped and yelled for all she was worth. The dogs responded and headed toward her. When they ran into view, they were dragging their rigging and tow line but not a cart. She held the rig of the lead dog and she turned back the way she'd come.

Wynona quickly found out how hard it was to drag a team of twelve dogs behind you while hunched over holding a wire rig. She stopped often to catch her breath and yell at the dogs. She was tired and hungry and knew that the dogs would be, too.

She summoned all the energy she had remaining, but it wasn't enough. She found a small pond and took the dogs there. They drank heartily of the mostly clear water. She assumed it was better than nothing, although decided not to drink it herself. She pulled the dogs to her, not unhooking them as she fell asleep.

Aeryn waited until she couldn't stand it. Then she set out on the track that Wynona had made. Aeryn was scared. It was late in the day. They'd managed to get separated from Charles, and now she was alone and lost in the woods. She traveled slowly, holding the dogs up as they wanted to run. She was afraid and almost incapable of mushing the team forward. The dogs weren't intimidated by the dark of the forest, or the sounds of the unknown.

She was relieved to finally see the track go from that of a lone person jogging through the brush to the wholesale weed trampling of a dog team. They turned to her left and she decided to follow, not knowing if that was Wynona returning or if it was where the dogs ran in front of her. She could turn around if she didn't find anything.

Aeryn was happy to hear dogs nearby barking as they heard her team approach. She mushed them into the clearing and called a halt, as Wynona shook her head, trying to clear the fog of sleep.

"Where's my brother?" Aeryn spit at the older woman.

"I don't know; the dogs were running with just the rigging. I never saw the sled or the others. I'm sorry I fell asleep. It was so hard dragging the team. I was exhausted," Wynona pleaded with the child.

"We need to find my brother! Don't try to lead the team, that's the lead dog's job. Let them pull you. Yell 'Ha' to go, 'left,' 'right,' and 'hold' to stop. That's all you need to know. Now, let's go. My brother and Angie are out there, and they might be hurt!"

Their only plan was to backtrack the dogs, see where they might have lost the sled. So they let the lead dogs take them back the way they'd come on a journey through the woods.

The cart was obvious when they came to it. It was wedged between two trees and half-destroyed. No wonder the rigging had come lose. They yelled and waited, then yelled some more. There were no footprints, no blood, no anything that suggested the people were in the sled when it crashed. They made their way around the obstruction and continued backwards along the track.

Finally it got too late, so they spent the night. They were exhausted but didn't sleep. They were up with the sun and off, backtracking their way out of the forest. It was slow going because Wynona walked and jogged as she could, but it wasn't anything like when the dogs pulled a wheeled cart over the open ground. When they broke out of the forest Aeryn was disappointed. She'd hoped to see her brother.

They continued to the road and took a right to go back where they'd originally circled around the woods. As they mushed up the pavement, two figures stood out of the grass, one tall and one much shorter. Aeryn waved and Charles waved back.

BEN AND MAGGIE

Ben took the long route. He wanted to go north where he figured the moose would just be coming out of the higher mountains. His target hunting area was about one hundred miles away. They took off and drove, spending half the day to get there. They set up a camp and then started hunting on foot.

Ben saw signs of moose, but not the animals themselves. He and Maggie waited through the late dusk, but saw no movement. Ben spotted a flock of ptarmigan and shot two of them with his twelve-gauge. He was happy to clean them for dinner and roast them over an open fire on an improvised spit.

"What makes you a good hunter?" Ben asked, not in a way that would make her defensive, but because he wanted to know what her edge was. Ben was always learning. He was comfortable that he could hunt, but was open to new and better ways of doing anything.

"I could gut the animal and clean it without gagging," Maggie laughed. Ben saw the wisdom in the approach. He nodded thoughtfully.

"That would be good. Can you shoot?"

"I learned. Out of necessity, I learned. I think I can shoot okay, but I like to be close. It helps to get a head shot. Makes the cleaning easier without losing any of the meat," she said in a businesslike tone.

"I see. Welcome to the Community." Ben breathed deeply of the smells of the fire and the roasting ptarmigan. "They remind me of the village where I grew up, without any of the big problems. No one drinks. Everyone works. Everyone has a purpose. I'm glad they invited Clarisse and me along. I hope that we can build on what we have, while keeping what we have, if you understand what I mean."

"Sure, the friends who are family. It's like us. A bunch of escapees who survived. And we took our children with us, even though none of us planned on motherhood. That happens under those conditions. I don't think the Russians intended to stay as long as they did. I think they might have been trapped, just like we were. But there were more of them and they had the guns. Then we broke out and they didn't have enough soldiers to search for us, so they gave up quickly." She finished by taking a drink of water. She stared into the fire as it popped while Ben turned the spit.

"I'm glad you found us. I don't know how much fight we had left. Things were pretty grim."

"We won't let anything happen to you. We're one family now, one tribe as it may be. It's us against nature, not each other now that our enemy is gone. Even if they come back, we'll fight them. All of us will fight them together," Ben said matter-of-factly as he declared the ptarmigan ready to eat. Maggie enjoyed it and rolled her sleeping bag out in the back of the trailer. Ben slept on the ground under the stars where he was most comfortable.

Until he was kicked by a moose that walked straight through their camp. Maggie woke with a start at Ben's cry of pain. In the light of the false dawn she shot the big cow from a range of twenty feet. She didn't even try to look through the scope. The moose jumped and ran five or ten steps before falling to the ground, unable to get back up. Maggie climbed out of her bag and put the animal out of its misery.

Ben was in a heap. She tried to wake him, but he was out cold, a nasty bump on the side of his head showing where he'd been kicked. She didn't know what to do. She guessed that more blood to his brain would increase the swelling, so she rolled her sleeping bag to put under his shoulder and his sleeping bag to put under his head. His pulse seemed strong and he was breathing. She dribbled some water on his lips and tongue. She couldn't think of anything else to do except make sure that the moose didn't go to waste.

She started cleaning it as she checked on Ben every five seconds. After ten minutes, she'd barely made any progress and he was still unconscious. She started working, wanting to get the moose ready to go as soon as Ben woke up. She didn't want to think about it if he didn't wake up. With a burst of adrenaline, she worked through the moose, cleaning it and cutting the meat into smaller, manageable sizes. She bagged each chunk and threw them into the trailer one by one.

She took a break and drank sparingly of her water. They were running low already. They'd planned to refill at a stream, but hadn't gotten to it yet. She checked on Ben as she had been doing, and his eyes were open, but unfocused.

"Ben! Ben! Can you hear me?" she cried. He leaned to the side and threw up, breathing heavily and holding his head as he tried to sit up. Maggie helped him.

"What happened," he slurred.

"You got kicked by a moose," she told him.

"Figures. We chase it for half a day when all we had to do was lie here and wait. Damn, my head hurts." His speech was already improving, but he said that he couldn't stand. She tried to help him, but he wasn't moving.

"I guess we're staying here for a while, and we need water," Maggie said, suddenly feeling very tired.

"Go get some. There's a stream down that way." He pointed in a general direction. "Do I smell blood?"

"We got our moose and the trailer is full! Maybe seven hundred pounds of meat. We're ready to go whenever you can manage."

Ben shook his head slowly. "Give me my gun, and then unhook the trailer so you can get us some water. I think a moose steak cooked on an open fire will taste pretty good." His head swam, but he was hungry. There was nothing left in his stomach, and the wave of nausea had passed.

With a full load in the trailer, Maggie was hard-pressed in unhooking it. She managed it, but knew that she wouldn't be able to hook it back up without Ben's help. There was nothing she could do until he felt better.

She drove in the direction Ben indicated, hoping the stream wasn't too far. She wasn't comfortable driving the quad in the rough terrain.

BECCA AND DARREN

Becca and Darren followed moose tracks through a small woods. When they were clear through the forest, they found a herd of caribou grazing in the valley beyond.

They mushed their dog teams in opposite directions, hoping to trap the caribou between them, setting up for a few good shots. Becca picked a spot and tied up her dog team. Darren rounded the opposite side and flushed the caribou, then stopped. He didn't want them running past Becca at full speed.

She carried a 300 Winchester Magnum, just like he did. That eliminated mismatched ammunition. Although the round was a little bigger than what they needed for caribou, there was no excuse for not getting a kill.

Which is exactly what Becca got with her first shot. The second shot was at a running animal and she knocked it down, but didn't kill it. The herd turned and ran away from her at an angle that would bring them closer to Darren. He set the brake and hopped off the wheeled cart that served as the summer dogsled.

He didn't like to shoot while standing as he wasn't steady in the offhand position, but the grasses were too high for him to kneel. He aimed his best and tried to put his reticle just in front of the shoulder. When the rifle bucked, he thought his aim was true. He misjudged how far he had to lead the caribou, but the end result was the same. The bullet went through just in front of the heart, but took out the lungs, and the animal quickly collapsed.

Becca jogged down the hill to dispatch the wounded caribou. She would have normally cut its throat to save ammunition, but it had horns and was thrashing its head about. She took the easy route to put it out of its misery. She looked across where Darren stood and thrust her rifle in the air. He did the same thing, then they each started the cleaning process. When he finished with his, he estimated he had a hundred and twenty-five pounds of meat. He loaded it into his sled and took the team to where Becca had already started on her second kill. They finished it together and headed further up the hill to find a nice place to spend the evening.

They hung the meat in a tree and took the dogs fifty yards away where they set up a camp with a single bed under the stars. They missed Bill but they appreciated the peace and quiet. They knew he would be well taken care of in their absence. They made love long into the night and fell asleep exhausted.

They awoke when the dogs started barking furiously. A mammoth grizzly bear was standing on his back feet and pawing at a bag of caribou. Darren pulled his rifle out and, while standing naked before God and the world, put a bullet through the bear's head. He cycled the bolt to load another round, expecting to shoot again, but the bear was dead where it dropped. Next to him, Amber stood also without clothes, holding her rifle steady as she aimed.

He never took his eyes from the curves of her body as he carefully put his rifle down. She watched him with a smile as he reached for her. "Don't make me shoot you," she said slyly.

"I am the luckiest man on earth."

"You keep saying things like that and you will be. Shouldn't we clean that bear first?"

His answer was muffled as he buried his face into her neck and hair.

THE RESCUE PARTIES

Lucas started to get in the truck with me, and that's when the screaming started. Both Amber and Madison were coming unhinged and running toward us. I was ready to gun it, but Lucas caved and got out. He jumped in the quad with Chris, and Terri climbed in the passenger seat next to me. Then Madison chased her out and joined me instead, and Phyllis and Husky climbed over her and filled the remainder of the bench seat. She shut the door and we were ready to go.

With musical chairs concluded, we headed south, the direction the twins had gone. Chris went north after Ben, and Abigail and Phillip went east where we thought Darren and Becca might be. We simply went south on the highway, driving slower than I wanted, but we were looking for any signs that the dog sleds had gone from the road. It would have been much more obvious in the winter as the wheeled carts didn't leave as clear a trail.

After a very long hour, we'd gone less than twenty miles, but that was all we needed. Our children and the two adults were standing at an intersection. They only had one sled, but they still had both dog teams. They cheered when they saw us. We stopped and Phyllis and Husky almost bowled Madison over as they raced from the truck to see all their buddies, the twins and the two teams.

There was a great deal of barking.

We hooked all the dogs together. Charles took the reins of the super team, twenty-four dogs, but it was a level straightaway. Aeryn insisted on riding along. That meant she wanted her turn mushing the big team. We loaded the others into the truck. I sat in the bed with the dogs and Madison drove as we followed the twins the rest of the way home.

Abigail and Phillip followed Becca and Darren's dog team tracks unerringly. They trailed them as they entered the woods and continued to the valley on the other side. When they got there, they watched as the two dog teams struggled with immense loads on the carts and towed trailers.

"You're a sight for sore eyes. We couldn't leave it and we couldn't move," Darren said as they approached. Abigail looked wide-eyed at the mounds of meat filling the sleds and trailers.

"What did you get?" she asked, surprise on her face.

"Three caribou and one rather large grizzly bear," Becca said with a smile.

"Shot him offhand, buck naked!" Darren blurted out, grinning, only to get punched by Becca.

Phillip chuckled while Abigail feigned shock.

The two groups spent the next hour rearranging the loads, splitting the weight as much as possible. With all four sleds loaded heavy, they rolled downhill, trying to keep their speed under control so they didn't run over their own dogs.

Chris and Lucas followed Nordale to Chena Hot Springs Road to Steese and turned north when it met the Dalton Highway. They had extra gas as they didn't know how far they needed to go. Ben had said something about one hundred miles. Chris was afraid they wouldn't find where he'd turned off. Lucas planned to drive one hundred twenty-five miles up the road, then slowly backtrack. He didn't expect to drive off the main road. Alaska was a big place. They didn't need to be the next casualties.

Lucas was happy to get Chris talking about the engineers and the "incident" at Eielson as they'd taken to calling it. Chris was able to talk about it without breaking down. And Lucas wanted to know. He didn't want an accident like that to happen to anyone else.

They drove farther than they thought Ben had gone, then returned south. They saw no sign of where Ben and Maggie had turned off. They took four hours driving back and forth between the eighty- to one-hundred-twenty-mile markers. Seeing nothing, they left for home, hoping that the hunters had gotten behind them and were already on their way.

When Chris and Lucas arrived late in the evening, everyone else was there, except for Ben and Maggie. Clarisse met them at the door. Lucas shook his head.

"We'll go back out tomorrow," Chris stated before hugging the older woman.

JUST A FLESH WOUND

After two full nights of rest, Ben felt immensely better. He could stand without the world spinning. Maggie was a wreck. Ben had both sleeping bags so he could sit upright. She also felt she had to stay awake all night to protect the moose meat. She catnapped and that wasn't enough.

Ben watched her during one of the brief periods where she slept, not wanting to shake her awake with the rifle braced across her lap. He waited, feeling refreshed, smelling the cool air of the late summer. The fall weather was starting to settle in. He loved this time of year. It meant hunting and berry picking, followed by a feverish rush to put everything up before the snow fell.

He and Clarisse would then relax over the winter, reading and doing detail work with leather and wood. The hunting vest he wore was the one he'd made twenty years prior. He touched up the intricate designs on it each winter, adding a little something new to the worn panels of a never-ending story. The leather was supple, almost as soft as flannel.

Ben started the fire, hoping to make a cup of coffee, but Maggie had drank it all. He hoped she'd awaken soon so they could go home, back to the schoolhouse where they'd spend the winter. The moose in the trailer would go a long way toward filling the freezer. They'd get more when they needed it.

He felt guilty, but he couldn't wait any more. He walked carefully toward Maggie and then grabbed the barrel of her rifle, shaking it gently.

She was startled awake and reflexively pulled the trigger. The shot rang in their ears as the round went somewhere toward the mountains.

"Easy!" Ben said loudly, without trying to yell. His head started hurting again.

"Sorry, sorry," she mumbled, putting a hand to her head, then rubbing her eyes. "Ben, you're standing up."

"Not for too much longer. I think it's time to go home, don't you?"

Maggie stood and stuffed her rifle into the back of the quad. She kicked dirt over the small fire and took a drink of water. Together they hooked up the trailer, although it was rough on Ben. She climbed in the driver's seat as Ben walked around to the other side. Once in, she spared no time driving back toward the Dalton Highway. She went as fast as she dared, but soon the drone of the quad's motor made her eyelids droop.

Ben smacked her arm, and she woke up. He kept his eye on her but found it hard to keep himself awake as his headache returned. It felt like his head was twice its normal size.

They finally pulled over when she dropped off and started to veer off the road. They pulled over near a stream that ran alongside.

"Give me some privacy, please. I'm going to take a quick bath, wake myself up. I want to be back home as much as you. My little girl is waiting for me, and she's probably worried sick."

Ben nodded and walked downstream until he found a spot where the water pooled. He took off his clothes and eased himself in, the cold water shocking to his system. He didn't stay long, but used a little sand along the shore to scrub himself clean. He found the berry bushes as he was climbing out. He was hungry for something besides moose, so he started picking and eating. And he kept picking and eating, savoring the season's best blueberries until he heard Maggie shout his name.

"Here, I found blueberries!" he yelled as he kept eating.

"Ben!" came the cry from the road. At that point, he realized his clothes were still hanging on the bush, so he eased himself back into the water. He dressed while she retrieved the quad. They picked and ate more berries, then headed down the road greatly refreshed.

RUNNING FAST AND GETTING SOMEWHERE

Chris and I were ready to take another trip up the Dalton Highway to look for Ben and Maggie when we heard the quad approaching. We waited as it drove in, not too fast as it pulled a trailer filled with moose.

I held out my hands in the traditional "what the hell?" Ben put up his hands, while Maggie nodded and high-fived us as she walked toward the school.

"Would you believe that we hunted the moose just until it found us?" Ben smiled. "I got kicked in the head for our troubles, but the moose got butchered and loaded into our trailer." He looked tired. The knot on the side of his head was alarming in size. Chris took one of Ben's arms to help him out of his quad, then escorted him inside to Colleen's new clinic.

I drove the quad around back where we could get the meat to the kitchen for processing without dripping blood through the hallways. We were having a hard time keeping the hallways cleaned. Too many people running in and out leaving their shoes on. That was a good problem to have, since it seemed we were successful in heading off our food shortage.

August was a great time for berry picking in the interior of Alaska, but North Pole wasn't the best area for it. We needed some elevation, so we fired up the convoy and loaded every single person, along with Phyllis and Husky, for a day trip of berry picking and anything else that might supplement our diet of moose, fish, and aged canned goods.

Terri thought there would be nothing better than a day of the whole Community picking berries. Children too young to walk were strapped to their parents while the toddlers ate more than they put in the buckets. People compared purple and red fingers as a sign of hard work. We filled a great number of buckets that day. We returned as a very sore bunch of people.

In the business world, companies would have paid a small fortune to conduct the team-building event we went through, but for us, it was our shared understanding that our very survival was at stake. Everyone carried their own weight and a little extra for the person beside them.

Some of the children fought. That was to be expected, but the conflicts were managed, and people grew closer.

Shane's contributions were significant. Cullen's death led to the young engineer's awakening. His revelation was that he didn't say anything when he should have. He beat himself up over that, but understood that to move forward all he had to do was speak up. He was still an introvert, but able to manage the social side of a life when too many people were in a confined space. He found plenty to do outside the school, but would still smile and talk with the others when he was indoors.

Tanya took a special interest in him and soon they were often seen together.

As August gave way to September, we had our supply run set up. We planned to drive the Alaskan Highway, a straight shot for two hundred sixty miles. We'd take both of our trucks, burning a mix of strained old gas and avgas. I was driving our old beater truck; Lucas had changed the oil and tuned it up specially for this drive, the same thing he'd done on the big truck. We'd also replaced the windshield with one we found in a junkyard.

Tanya was coming, along with her son, Mark. She asked Shane to join us. They sat holding hands in the back seat while Lucas drove and Amber rode up front with Diane between them.

I wondered who was going to ride with me, until Colleen climbed in. Madison didn't want to leave the twins or the school for what could be a long and boring ride. We'd meet at the border. Stay there for a brief time, most importantly for Tanya to spend time with her dad, but also for Colleen to check the medical supplies, then drive back home. We were leaving in the dark and we'd probably return in the dark. I looked forward to the trip, but not the drive.

We requested a pizza as we expected to get there around lunchtime. If they didn't have pizza, then tacos, heavy on the cheese. We didn't have flour or cheese, so these were delicacies in our book. But we didn't want to gorge on goodies while the others had been without for so long. That being said, if they showed up with pizza and tacos, we couldn't let them go to waste, could we?

THE SUPPLY RUN

We'd already driven from Tok and knew the road was in good condition, except for where we had to pick our way through the backroads of Delta Junction. That delayed us, but we made up time on the road to Tok. Without regular traffic, the only thing we had to deal with was debris and foliage that had been blown onto the road.

When we reached Tok, we found the checkpoint that had been set up. We stopped for a relief break while Lucas and I reminisced.

"It looked a lot different when people were shooting at us," I said, seeing the garbage that had been left behind and the tent which was shredded and lying on the ground. "Malicious compliance, my friend. I'm glad they didn't try to shoot us down. Would any of us be here if they had?"

"No. But the Community would still be at Chena Hot Springs because the Russians would have never known we were there. We led them back. We saved our lives, but it cost Felicia hers," Lucas said, staring blankly into the distance.

"Years later when they pulled out. Maybe they knew we were there all along, but couldn't risk flying over the DMZ until they had nothing left to lose. And I'm not making excuses to stroke my own ego. If we'd been shot down, things would be far different. How many of the women from Healy would have lived through this coming winter? Sometimes it costs lives to save lives, a hard lesson from the Marine Corps. And you know what? It still sucks a whole lot. Felicia didn't do anything to them. Neither did the people of Fairbanks, or Delta Junction, or the women trapped in Healy. If we get this right, Lucas, then we get our state back. I feel more alive now than ever before. I'm not sure what else we need. I don't need the government to come back and start regulating again. Maybe we can keep things as they are." I kicked at the dirt and looked around for the others.

It was time to get going. Next stop, the Badger border crossing.

Unfortunately, we had to stop three times to cut trees that had fallen across the road. We didn't have a chain saw, but we had two axes. At least the trees were smaller. We used a chain on the big truck to drag more trees out of the way. We took blind corners at a crawl, not wanting to hit something waiting for us just around the bend.

Overall, it was a pleasant drive and the return trip would go much faster.

The highway widened and the road was in perfect condition for the last few dozen miles to the border. We had the windows rolled down as we cruised through the cool mountain air. The weather was perfect for this time of year. We were upbeat, which made me start to worry. When I felt like this, bad things soon happened.

This time, I was wrong. We pulled to the border station and stopped. There was a large parking area to help us turn around, because we needed to hook up the trailer that Tanya's father had brought. We hadn't been expecting that, only a few crates of supplies. That wasn't the important reason we were here, just an added bonus.

We stopped and Tanya was the first one out. She helped her two-year-old son out of the truck and waited for Shane, who was hesitant to get out. She smiled at him, then walked across the border to where her father vibrated in anticipation.

Shane followed closely behind, holding little Mark's small hand as Tanya and her father embraced. I had to look away as the man who was little older than me sobbed uncontrollably. Colleen was all business as she walked to another person standing by the truck and the trailer. They shook hands and he opened the back for her.

"Holy cow!" she exclaimed. They had to move a few things to get to the medical supplies. She started to inventory what would soon stock her clinic. She couldn't have been happier, although she turned down some of the supplies as unnecessary. Flu vaccine only mattered if you were exposed to the strain. We had no such exposure. She accepted the pneumonia vaccine instead. She turned down more drugs. They also removed a few cases of baby formula. She insisted that we didn't need any of that as the babies would breastfeed until they were old enough for hard food. Baby formula was a twentieth-century creation to take the place of a working mother. We didn't have that restriction either, although she took a breast pump instead.

I left her to it. I couldn't follow what she was saying anyway. She had good reasons for every decision that were hers alone to make.

Lucas and Amber were on the phone inside the border control building. That left me to myself. There was another vehicle, a suburban with darkened windows. The driver waved me over. I thought that vehicle had been for Tanya's father. When I climbed in, I learned differently.

The general was there. He was the one I was supposed to report to. I'd called once since we'd returned and hung up on him when he'd asked too many stupid questions. I wondered if he was miffed about that.

"Hey, General, glad to see you," I said with as much joy as I could muster, holding out my hand. He reluctantly took it. "Had I known you were coming, I would have dressed up, although I did shave!" I held up my chin for him to see.

He started to laugh. "You're a pain in the ass. You know you couldn't tell me about this little unsanctioned side trip, since we can provide no assistance. And Canada can't either. I'll tell you, strictly off the record, that I am personally pleased that you're getting this stuff."

I nodded. "Off the record," he said. That was the bureaucratic idiocy that I was happy to not have in my life. I looked forward to walking back across the border.

"Why are you really here?" I asked, already tired of playing the game. The general didn't seem to want to be here either.

"The Russians are moving. They've landed a group outside Anchorage and they're heading north in a convoy. They have vehicles and a supply train, all illegal under the treaty, but nonetheless, they're heading north. We think they might be coming to Fairbanks."

"Military?" I asked, giving him my undivided attention.

"We think many of the forty are military, but believe their goal is to establish a settlement so they can contest our claim before the UN, who's going to make the determination next year after they conduct a survey."

I thought about it. Forty military. We'd be vulnerable. We were in a fixed position, without vehicles, with few shooters and only two with any military training. I exhaled and rubbed my temples. Another change and an unhappy one.

"What do you want us to do about it?" I finally asked, afraid of what the answer might be.

"We want you to get some pictures of them using prohibited equipment. We don't want you to engage them in any way, not even a dialogue. We think they went with those numbers knowing that you went in with twenty-two. But with the survivors from Healy, your group outnumbers them by a good measure. By the way, well done on the rescue of the women and children. You'd get a medal if I liked you, but I don't, so you'll have to accept something else. In the trailer, we've stashed some extra ammunition for your .45, 45-70, and 300 Win mag. Those are your weapons of choice, aren't they?" The general sat there with a smug look on his face.

"For not liking me, you seem to be my creepiest stalker, but I appreciate the ammunition. More is better. I have my phone and can take pictures with that. Will that work?"

"Yes. Download a copy to this," he said, handing me a thumb drive with a lightning connector for my iPhone, "and give it to the UN representative when they arrive. If you can get a copy to us ahead of that time, then we would be most appreciative."

I was going to ask him how I did that, but he didn't care how far I traveled or how dangerous it was. He only wanted the pictures to solidify his own position. I nodded once without offering to shake his hand again and I got out. I leaned back in. "For the record, I don't like you either." I don't know why I felt compelled to say that. It didn't make me feel any better. I closed the door without slamming it and walked boldly back toward the border.

Tanya and her dad stopped me before I crossed. He wanted to shake my hand, thank the person who'd brought his daughter back from the dead. He held his grandson in his other arm. His eyes were still red, but all of them looked happy. Their reconciliation was long past due. It was good to see them embrace today, plan for tomorrow. Shane stood nearby, looking far more comfortable.

RETURN

I thanked the man for the supplies. Inevitably, something in there would be used to save a life. There were drugs for the people still suffering from botulism. The three had survived, but their recovery was glacially slow. The medicines would speed up their return to health.

There was something for everyone, from spices to the parts most likely to fail on our generator. There was flour, cheese, and eggs, enough for a few meals. These were to celebrate the newcomers, the survivors from Healy. They'd been deprived for a long time and deserved a special treat.

We'd discover what else was there when we unloaded back at the school. It would be like Christmas, except better.

The last two things he did before we departed was to top off our gas tanks with fresh gasoline and hand us hot food: fifteen boxes of pizzas and a couple bags of tacos. The only place the pizzas would fit was in the bed of my beater truck. Mr. Bezos took off his jacket and wrapped the pizza boxes in it and then wrapped them in a second layer using a blanket from his vehicle. It wouldn't be warm when we got home, but it would be the best pizza any of the survivors had had in years.

WINTER

We saw the first snowfall at the end of September. The second through tenth snowfalls were at the beginning of October. By Halloween we had four feet on the ground. On the first of November, temperatures plummeted and stayed that way through December when the snow started again.

I was happy to fire up my snow machine and take it for a spin. With three feet of cold snow on the roadways, we could make great time anywhere we went. I made it to Delta Junction in just over thirty minutes. I didn't tell Madison that part. I don't know why I drove the snow machine so fast, but maybe it was just how they were meant to run.

Not a typical Alaskan winter but close enough. We were mostly ready. Our arrangements with the outhouses turned out to be woefully inadequate. People would wait until the very last minute, then race outside to do their business, returning two minutes later half-frozen.

Erecting a temporary building in the middle of winter was a challenge in and of itself. At least we didn't have anything else to do. With the snow and the temperatures, everything was ten times more difficult. A dozen of us worked together in acquiring the wood, which consisted of dismantling a nearby shed and rebuilding it on a skid that would sit above the holes we'd dug for the outhouses.

We built stalls and insulated it all. We put in an electric heater that worked great until someone accidentally left a few squares of toilet paper too close to it. After our temporary building burned down, we built a better one the second time around, putting the heater into the ceiling, insulated and grounded to prevent another accidental fire.

Clarisse and Jo managed the kitchen duties. Everyone took their turn as prep cooks and clean-up crew. There were too many people to eat in one shift, so we split into two groups, rotating members so that people got to the chance to see all of our Community members at some point during the week. We wanted to keep things fresh.

Then one day we realized that Bill was no longer yelling. We asked Darren and Becca what was wrong. They said that he'd finally grown out of the bellowing stage, but it also may have had to do with something else. Becca was pregnant again and it seemed the baby was sensitive to loud noises. When Bill howled, the baby would start kicking and wouldn't stop until it was quiet again.

I would have never thought that. I suspected we'd get another howler. We could not have been happier for them because they were happy.

The members of the Community grew closer with each day. That included all of us, new and old. Shane and Tanya decided to get married. This caused a full deliberation between Terri and me. As mayors, we didn't have the authority to marry people. As the military governor, I thought I could, just like the captain of a ship. In the end, we realized that we didn't care if it was legal by someone else's laws. It was their decision. The formal ceremony would be for their benefit. No one here cared if anyone had a piece of paper with a governmental stamp approving their relationship.

So we gathered everyone together in the cold gymnasium and said a bunch of good things about the happy couple. They committed to each other and that was that. We removed the tables from the dining room so we could all fit for the banquet. It made for a tight squeeze so we filled the wide hallways, too.

I hadn't checked on the Russians. I started calling the general once a month to let him know our headcount, food, and fuel status, that we had no problems. He seemed to like those reports. I thought they were ridiculous. The most important thing I had to report was that another month had passed and no one died.

We had a huge bash at Christmas. We offered no presents as we didn't want people "shopping" with the weather so extreme. We didn't have much room for things, so we settled on telling each other what we liked about them and the group. It was different, but the men all had plenty of help in expressing their feelings. We were outnumbered six to one. At the end of the day, we retreated to our rooms with our spouses, happy with the world we'd created.

In January, I couldn't hold the general off any longer. The Russians had set up on the south side of Fairbanks, at the far end of the airport along the Chena River in an area we'd scouted and determined was perfect for our first fields and long-term home.

That threw a wrench in our plans. We'd done initial work with the ground to get it ready for planting in the coming season. It wasn't much, but enough that it would have allowed us to get the most out of our growing season.

We had looked around, but once we found the spot, we didn't look further. We had no backup plan, no secondary fields, and we couldn't look now. The only thing we could do was hope for an early thaw. As I always said, hope is a lousy plan.

That irked me enough that I wanted to go see them, spy on them, take pictures, and do all the things that would get them in trouble. Being in trouble with the UN wasn't like really being in trouble. It was closer to being unhappy with a distant relative you never had any contact with.

If the UN deemed us the better settlers, whatever that meant, then the Russians would have to leave. That was supposed to carry political weight, but what if they didn't want to leave? This is where the UN had no teeth, and the United States had already demonstrated that it wouldn't fight for Alaska, except in the realm of diplomacy.

It was up to me.

No, that wasn't right. It was up to us, the Community to decide what we wanted to do about it.

THE RUSSIANS

I asked Terri and we broached it at a group meeting of all the adults, which meant everyone attended. The only place big enough was the gym. So we set up a box to stand on and Terri and I stood in our parkas and stocking caps, waving our gloved hands for silence.

"The Russians have taken the area we were going to plant next spring. They've moved in at the south end of the airport. I think they wanted that place so they could hide their vehicles and supplies. They have forty people, or so I've heard, who are trying to prove to the UN that they are better to settle this land than us."

A number of women in the crowd yelled angrily that we should go kill all the Russians. I wasn't opposed to fighting, but didn't want to start something we couldn't win. Terri shut down the hostility of the crowd by speaking softly, but forcefully.

"These aren't those Russians. If they were, then we'd take them into custody and execute them for crimes against humanity." There were cheers. I froze in place, not from the cold, but I didn't know where she was going with her speech. I didn't want her to commit us to a tragic course of action.

"These aren't those Russians. These are people just like us, living for today, planning for tomorrow. If they weren't, why did they take the most fertile land we'd found? It's where we should have been, but we hesitated because we were comfortable here. We were going to move there eventually, right? You snooze, you lose! When the snow melts and the ground thaws, we're going to find a better place and we're going to grow enough food for all of us and then some. When the UN comes next summer, they'll find the people who can stand on their own feet right here. They're going to look at us and see us doing what we do best, taking care of each other, raising our families. We're better than they are. We've always been better than them," she ended with a harsh tone.

Silence greeted the end of her speech. A small child starting crying, stopping when his mother picked him up. I wondered what else they wanted. They looked at me, expecting me to say something.

"We've been here all along, in our state, our country. I'm going to go down there and introduce myself, see what they're up to and let them know that they don't have a chance. Even if they're from Siberia, they're not ready to survive here."

It wasn't as impactful as I intended, but it was heartfelt. People in the crowd started murmuring. I couldn't hear anything specific until Lucas shouted, "And I'm going with you!"

Most of the people snorted and chortled as Madison and Amber started yelling at both of us. Terri pushed me and I almost fell off our soap box.

Ben asked if he could speak, and of course, anyone was welcome. I gave him a hand as he joined me on our impromptu stage.

"My people have lived here for generations. We've lived off this land, thrived because of what it has to offer. I was ashamed when we left during the war, ashamed for all of my people. Coming back was the second happiest day of my life." He nodded to his wife and then continued, "I carried the Raven on my shoulder back to this country. I claim it on behalf of all those who've gone before us and all those who will follow. We are Alaskans and there's no way I'm going to let the Russians drive me from this land again. I'm going with you!" he declared with a shout and a fist pump.

"Ben and I will go, and we'll talk with them. Terri will go, too, to put to rest your fears that these are the Russian criminals. They are not. These are settlers, not soldiers," I lied. There was nothing else to say. The fate of the Community was in our hands. If we screwed this up, then we might start a new war.

No pressure at all.

THE SETTLERS

Travel in the winter was so much easier than in the summer. From North Pole to the Fairbanks Airport it was about eight miles straight up the Tanana River. We had to take dog sleds because we weren't supposed to have any technology. I made sure my cell phone was charged so I could take pictures.

No technology? We'd heard what the Russians brought. At least we'd scavenged our generator and most of what we had, although we did import our engineer. If anyone had watched us build our improved outhouse, both versions one and two, they probably would have laughed themselves into a fit. We were far from the well-oiled machine I expected to see in the Russian camp.

We mushed our two dog teams up the river and through a hole in the airport's perimeter fence. We continued across the runways and taxiways straight to the hangar the Russians were using. It was obvious as they had armed guards. I slowed the dog team I was driving. I hadn't anticipated that they would be carrying weapons. When it was apparent we'd been spotted, one of the two ran inside the hangar. An older gentleman came outside and waved to us, beckoning.

Once we arrived, I was glad we weren't them. In the hangar they'd chosen, forty cots were arranged in neat rows. Temperatures inside were the same as outside. That meant it was a balmy ten degrees below zero Fahrenheit. This is where they lived.

On the far side within the hangar, their convoy was parked in rows, supplies clearly sorted and stacked. I heard a generator, but couldn't see where it was. They weren't using it for heat.

I wondered where they hid their outhouse. I wasn't a fan of dropping trousers when it was below freezing, let alone below zero. I thought about all of this as we approached. I had my .45 in my shoulder holster as usual. Ben's shotgun rode in the sled as Ben drove the team. I hadn't known that he was an accomplished dog musher, but I wasn't surprised. Ben was a true Alaskan.

The older gentleman plowed through the snow to meet us. As he approached he stopped to pet each dog. The dogs seemed to like him. I knew that I should be wary, but anyone who greets dogs before people is probably the right kind of person. I wanted to hate him but couldn't. He hadn't even said his name yet and I was all smiles.

Ben lightened as well, seeing the Russian treat the dogs with kindness.

"Dobro pozhalovat'," the man said in Russian. "Welcome."

"Dobriy den'. Menya zavut Chuck, i vot Terri, i Ben," I pointed to each as I introduced them.

"Ah, you speak Russian, my friend. Very nice. I am Sergei Sergeevich Kashirin. What brings you to our home, and where did you come from?" He switched to English quicker than I expected.

"We have a thriving Community just up the river. I'm sure you've seen our smoke on clear days."

"Yes, we wondered. We do not yet have such fine animals as these, so we are forced to spend more time here than getting to know our neighbors. We have snowshoes, yes, but they are not quite the same as a good dog team." I nodded and removed my glove. He looked at it then did the same. His hand felt warm compared to mine. Maybe he had better gloves than I had. His grip was strong.

I was certain he was military or had been until recently.

"Vashi voiska…" I started to say. "Your forces…" He stopped me with a raised hand.

"Not troops, no. We are pilgrims. This is the right word, is it not? We are here to find a new home. We've left Russia behind to seek a new way of life." He smiled as he talked. He was starting to sound like a politician. This helped nurture my dislike for what he stood for.

That was easy, but the man was still pleasant. The armed guards had moved off, never pointing their weapons at us.

"Why do you have armed guards?" I asked, hoping to put the matter to rest.

"Bears. On the way here we encountered more than one. If a bear got into our camp or into our food, we would have a hard time. We barely have enough to get us through this winter. I expect we'll all lose some weight by spring."

"I doubt you'll see any bears in this area, but that's just me. We never used to post guards, but maybe we'll start." My threat wasn't so subtle. Ben bristled and Terri tried to look farther into the hangar to see more of the men's faces.

"Maybe it's time for us to retire our guards. You are right. We have seen no bears or bear tracks in this area. Although there used to be plenty of moose," he grinned. Moose meat for all. There was no finer cut in all Alaska. I liked how he countered my statement. If it was his intention to win me over with kindness, he was doing a great job at it.

Sergei turned and motioned for us to follow. We went through the hangar and into an area that was enclosed in the back. It was heated and the rest of his people were in there. Terri looked deliberately from face to face. When she finished, we made eye contact and she shook her head slightly to let me know that she didn't recognize any of the people.

That was a huge relief. I didn't want to call someone out, but the thought of what the others had done made me angry. I took a deep breath and nodded a greeting to each of the Russian faces. It looked like a perfect split between men and women. Leave it to the Russians to issue women with husbands or vice versa. I doubt any of them had a choice besides saying "yes" that they would go.

How they partnered after that was irrelevant. I didn't see anyone that looked pregnant, not that I was judging, but wouldn't the UN have to consider all the children we had with us and an established school in which to teach them?

Sergei stepped aside and looked at me as if I was there to talk to them about how they could get cheaper car insurance. I would try not to disappoint him. I worked my way to an open space in the middle of the room.

"Dobro pozhalovat' v Fairbanks!" I held up my hands and turned in a circle so I could see them all. Some nodded, no one spoke. It was going to be a tough crowd. "Welcome to Fairbanks. We haven't seen the coldest weather yet, but if you've lived in Siberia, you understand. If not, you'll learn. Come February, it'll start to warm up, and by March, it will be pleasant in comparison.

"I hope you are all enjoying the northern lights! We've been having some great shows this winter. The sky isn't spoiled by pollution, not any longer anyway. We wish you all the best for the remainder of this winter and, come spring, maybe we can have a barbecue where you can meet the rest of us and we can get to know each other a little better. Thank you." I looked for a place to sit but there weren't any free chairs.

Ben and Terri both looked unhappy. I worked my way back toward the flap leading to the unheated part of the hangar. "Sergei, thanks for your hospitality. We just wanted to check on you and see how you were doing. The weather can be harsh. We'll be on our way, if you don't mind," I said, not waiting for an answer as the others went ahead. Sergei stayed with me, giving me no opportunity to take a picture of their equipment. I wasn't going to push it. There'd be opportunities later.

I wasn't a fan of tearing the other guy down to prove that I was the better person. The cots showed a military mentality, not a settler one. Settlers would find a way to be more comfortable, make it more like a home than a barracks.

We returned to our sleds and teams. The guards were there, playing with our dogs. Their weapons had disappeared sometime during our absence. Ben looked alarmed until he saw his trusty old shotgun right where he'd left it.

The dogs seemed happy. Maybe the Russians were lonely. Forty of them thrown together without a worthwhile diversion. Which made me ask the question, "Sergei, what do you guys do for fun?"

"That is a good question, my friend, a very good question indeed." He nodded as if I was supposed to understand everything from his ambiguous statement. I had to admit that it was a very Russian answer. I nodded back knowingly, having no idea what he meant.

We loaded up, lifted our snow hooks and mushed the dogs around in a wide circle to head back home. I hoped the Russians didn't come for a surprise visit like we'd just done to them. Our people would probably be less welcoming.

AN EARLY SPRING

The melt started in early March with an unseasonably warm streak. Our six feet of snow dwindled to three in a week, which left lakes everywhere we went. The poor dogs were miserable as the kennel was almost completely underwater. Areas in the direct sunlight melted even faster.

We realized we were going to have problems when the Tanana River ice buckled, letting the flowing water break through and run over the top of the ice. It streamed down river, running up on the river banks, melting snow piles which added to the quantity of water heading downstream. The ice jumped and churned.

It was too early for break up, but the entire Tanana River was a mess. We wondered if the Chena River on the other side of the city was in the same shape. We stayed mostly inside. There was too much water and too much mud. The gym was warm enough for the children to play, which they did, to everyone's delight. They were finally tired out after a long winter trapped in a too-small space.

I couldn't wait for it to dry out.

This was the in-between period where there wasn't enough snow to ride the snow machine, and it wasn't clear enough to take the quad. I felt trapped.

So I put on my rubber boots and went walking. I took Phyllis and Husky with me. Neither of them cared about the water. We could dry them off when we returned. There were plenty of towels. They splashed and swam as we hiked to the highway. It wasn't far, maybe a quarter-mile, but it took us a while because the dogs were easily distracted. I gave up trying to herd them in the direction of the road and simply walked. It was nice to stretch my legs.

One of my boots leaked and I didn't care, although the water was just above freezing. I'd have to go back soon. I could tell the dogs were cold as well. It was warm out for March, but far too cold to be walking around wet. We climbed the on-ramp and walked back to the bridge over the road.

I looked in the direction of the airport and saw what looked like smoke, black smoke billowing into the bright morning sky. It was too wet for anything to casually burn. The fire causing those flames could not have been intentionally set.

The Russians were in trouble.

DESTRUCTION!

"Hey! Hey!" I yelled as I ran back into the school with two soaked dogs running past me. "The Russian camp is on fire!" I kept running around the school looking at people. The survivors from Healy shrugged as I passed. I understood why, and if I were them, I'd feel the same way. We rallied everyone from the Community of Chena Hot Springs. Terri joined us and just a few of the women who had been close by.

"I saw the smoke. Something is wrong and I bet they need help. We have to go, see what we can do and we need to go now," I said quickly, looking for agreement. Head nods, but no one spoke out loud, not even Chris. Then Terri leaned in.

"Why?" was all she asked.

"Because they are human beings and there aren't too many of us around here. I could have said the same thing when somebody shot out the front window of the truck when we tried to talk with you. How many of your people would be dead now if you hadn't come along?"

Terri clenched her jaw and closed her eyes as she struggled within herself. Then she opened her eyes and nodded tersely. She looked back and said, "You three, come with us. The rest of you, take care of the kids."

"Trucks out front in five!" Chris yelled beside my ear. There was a moment where everyone stood, then the scrambling began. Ten minutes later, two trucks with the fifth wheel behind pulled into the standing water, fording toward the highway.

We had to drive the long way around. Eight miles as the raven flew or forty miles skirting the destruction in the city. The roads were clear enough to maintain a steady speed, but snowdrifts and other obstacles slowed us down. It took us over an hour before we arrived at the airport. The Russians had left a gate open so we drove through.

The hangar roof was collapsed and smoke continued rolling from within the wreckage. People were lying out front, others trying to help them. We pulled up and parked. Colleen was first out and looked at the injuries as she walked between the rows of people. She looked at her surroundings, then started setting up for triage. She determined the fifth wheel was for the patients in the worst condition.

The walking wounded moved to one side as Colleen issued a stream of commands. Heavy burn victims right here. Others there. Bring the medical kit from the truck. Put this over there. Put pressure on this. Clean the debris from the wound.

Everyone did as they were told. Madison walked with Colleen and translated the commands into Russian for those who couldn't understand English.

Ben and I found Sergei among the walking wounded. He was trying to rally his people, but was having no success. When he tried to speak, he broke into a racking cough.

"Just breathe, my friend. Is this all your people?" He shook his head.

"Are the others inside?" He nodded vigorously and started to cough again. "Ben, put us together an entry team. I think we'll be going in – we need tools…" He was off before I could finish.

"Any alive inside?" He nodded.

"Where?" I asked. He tried to speak and coughed, choked and almost fell over. I held him upright as he wheezed and let me support him. "Are they in the back, where you had the heater?" He shook his head.

"By your convoy, your trucks?" He nodded.

"Any up front?" He shrugged. He didn't know. I helped him to the ground and let him lie down. We had an oxygen tank with us, but there were too many suffering from smoke inhalation.

Ben returned with Lucas, Shane, Tanya, Terri, and Jo. I waved at them to follow and we jogged to the front of the hangar. Once there, we needed a plan so we stood in a circle as I talked them through it.

"Shane, we need you to see if it's sound enough for us to enter and then where the safest entry will be. We are heading for the area of the convoy, located rear center. It looks to be next to the worst of the roof collapse. Sergei said there wasn't anyone alive in the back. We'll take his word on that. I expect that's where the fire started. He didn't know if anyone was up front. If we can do it safely, look through the cots. See if anyone is still there. Only the living. If we find someone dead, we leave them and move on. Pull their coat or something over their face to let others know that they've been checked. Everyone ready? Shane, you've got point."

He looked at me. He'd never served or even watched war movies it seemed. "You lead. Find us the safest way in," I corrected.

The hangar doors had fallen askew and he shook his head as he walked past those and jogged around the side. There was a door that he opened, and he looked inside. There was some smoke, but the fire was on the opposite side of the building. We put our faces inside our coats, under our shirts to filter the air somewhat, but oxygen would be lacking. I stopped everyone.

"If the smoke gets too bad, we leave. No one dies! Tanya and Shane, stay together and watch each other. Terri and Ben, together. Lucas, Jo, and I are the last team. No exceptions!" I nodded to Shane and he led us in.

We went through a side room that had been set up as an office of some sort. The exit door led into a hallway that dumped into the hangar. Once inside the hangar itself, we could see why so many were injured. It was chaos and destruction. I waved Terri and Ben toward the sleeping area to check for survivors.

The rest of us weaved through the debris toward the vehicles and the area where the smoke was heavier. We walked in a crouch to stay close to better air. Shane waved us far to the side. He noticed something overhead that he didn't like. We followed him. We came to the lead vehicle and found nothing. We worked our way carefully down the line of trucks until we came to an arm sticking out from under one of them. Jo checked the pulse and nodded. We pulled out a young woman. She didn't appear to be injured, but was unconscious. Two other people were under there as well, both alive.

I told Jo and Lucas to stay with them. Lucas shook his head and pointed forward. I tried to take a breath, but the smoke was starting to get to me. I waved Lucas ahead and I stayed behind with Jo. We started dragging the survivors toward the front of the convoy, having to stop often to rest. Jo looked at me, then told me to stay as she went back for the third person. I saw Jo stop ahead and look forward. The others appeared out of the smoke and crawled the last few feet to her. She dragged the last survivor to me. I stood the smaller woman against the fender of the last truck, then let her drop over my shoulder so I could carry her. Lucas and Shane each took a survivor. Jo led us out, avoiding the area that Shane had pointed to earlier. Tanya stayed behind Shane, holding his shirt and making sure no one was left behind.

When we got outside, we put the three people on the ground as we all gasped for air. It took ten minutes before we could carry the Russians to Colleen's triage area.

Ben and Terri were already there. They'd found seven people, but only two were alive.

While we were inside, Sergei succumbed to smoke inhalation. He stopped breathing and died right where I had put him down. In total, twenty-five Russians were still alive. Colleen needed more oxygen. She pleaded with me. I looked at Lucas, then Madison.

"Go. If anyone can find some, it's you two," she said softly and turned back to the patients.

We bolted for the truck, Lucas faster than me having already recovered his breath from our foray into the hangar. He jumped in the driver seat. We rolled down the taxiway to the other side of the terminal. The first hangar we came to had a rack of green cylinders just outside the door. Lucas screeched to a halt. The tanks didn't say empty so I assumed they were still full, or at least they were full when stored here long ago. We muscled the tanks one by one into the truck bed, piling them like cordwood. In a different world, that might have been considered unsafe.

"Do not wreck us on the way back!" I stated, emphasizing each word. Lucas nodded, eyes wide as he took a painfully slow turn and accelerated deliberately. We followed the taxiway to the end and turned toward our truck and fifth wheel. We pulled close and parked.

People lined up behind the truck as we dropped the gate and carefully pulled the tanks out. I looked at Lucas. We didn't have any hoses to connect to the tanks. "Wait!" I yelled. "Lay the people with their heads together in a circle, and make a mini oxygen tent. Crack the valve, but don't point it at anyone. It's too high pressure. You'll get a lot of oxygen. If you can sit people up, back to back, the oxygen will concentrate around their heads. The carbon dioxide will sink lower. Got it? Go!" We continued to hand out the tanks. We had more than we needed as these were the two-hundred-fifty-pound versions.

The helpers set people up in ten pairs. Colleen must have been with the other five in the fifth-wheel trailer. We'd try to wrestle a bottle inside if she wanted it. Chris took a bottle by himself and carried it to the furthest pair of victims. They used coats, blankets, and even a small tarp to set up the oxygen tents around the people.

After that, we waited. Chris went to the trailer, then came back to pick up another oxygen bottle. Lucas helped him carry it inside. Then they came back for a second. I was sharing the biggest oxygen tent as I'd gotten light-headed after putting the bottles in the truck. I wasn't quite recovered from the trip into the hangar. I was out of the game for a while.

An hour passed. The Russians started standing and offering to help their friends. Two more Russians passed away in that time.

Ten were back on their feet, and eight were coherent and would soon join them. Five more were still being treated. Two of the survivors had been hit by shrapnel when the generator exploded and caught fire. Three were injured by falling debris. The rest of the survivors suffered from smoke inhalation. They'd lost their leader, half their people, and all their food.

As soon as Colleen had the most severely injured stabilized, we loaded everyone into the fifth wheel and the trucks. We slowly started the long drive back to the school. What took an hour to get there took two going home. I had oxygen bottles in the back of my truck. I was happy that we'd decided to replace the windshield on it after we returned from Healy, but we didn't do a very good job and it leaked when I splashed through the bigger puddles.

Maybe later we could find caulking and fix it the rest of the way. The old beater truck had become my stalwart companion. I kept my thoughts on the trivial things that made me happy because when thinking about the extra people, the only conclusion I could come to was that we would run out of food very soon.

JUST ONE MORE DAY

We set the Russians up in the gym. The best we could do were blankets on the ground. If we went back to the hangar, we could probably recover most of the cots, but they'd smell like smoke.

Becca and Darren were successful in bagging a moose although they had to bring it home in two trips because of the mud. We'd eat more meat and less of everything else until something changed.

The first thing to change was the weather. It turned markedly colder after a healthy snow fall. We took dog teams along the river bank where the shallow water had refrozen. Once they were sure we had solid ice, I took my snow machine, hooked up a sleigh behind it and returned to the hangar. The fire had burned itself out. With the roof caved in and the doors hanging crooked, there was enough air flow to clear out the remaining smoke.

We recovered ten cots with sleeping bags on our first trip. I made it there and back in thirty minutes. Chris made a trip, then Lucas. We rotated until we recovered as much as we could. We had cots for everyone and smoky sleeping bags. Lucas found some food and filled the sleigh. I didn't ask how he got it. I didn't want anyone to take unnecessary risks, but the food was sorely needed. Any food.

When the snow melted, we made a scavenging run to Salcha, outside the Air Force Base. We broke into every single home. I made a note that in case of the apocalypse, leave your door unlocked. No one is going to take your pictures of Aunt Margaret. All they want is food and anything to help them survive.

Salcha wasn't a big town, but it was big enough and the people were typical Alaskans, well-stocked with canned food.

Just like when the Community returned from the scavenging run to Fred Meyer all those years ago, we pulled in, honking the big truck's horn as I hadn't bothered to fix mine. Everyone stood and cheered. Our Russian additions insisted on unloading the trailer we'd gotten from Tanya's dad. They weren't afraid of hard work and did everything they could to fit in.

No one could say they weren't appreciative. Even Terri grudgingly admitted that this group was made up of good people. Unfortunately, the Russian accents still caused many of the women to wince and cower. There was nothing we could do except keep them apart. Forcing the former victims to integrate would be too traumatic. Terri spent time with them. None of us were psychologists or had any idea how to deal with Post-Traumatic Stress. We did our best to reduce the triggers and then to show them a different side to the new people.

When we were comfortable that we finally had enough food thanks to a hunting frenzy by Ben, Darren, Becca, and Maggie, there was more than enough meat for all, including the dogs in the kennel and their new puppies, which we gave to the Russians.

They finally got the dogs they'd longed for, and they were happy. Abigail and Phillip mentored them in training dog teams. It would be a long road, but they'd get there. Most importantly, they loved the dogs.

I knew that I had to call the general, but I was dreading it. The weather had broken again and this time, we thought it was for real. Spring was on its way.

I went outside wearing a light jacket and walked around until I couldn't avoid it any longer. I dialed the number and the general answered on the first ring.

"I wondered when you were going to call. Satellites showed something very interesting. Was that your handiwork?" he asked.

"If you're talking about the rescue of twenty-three Russians, yes, I'll claim some credit. Their generator exploded. It brought the house down around them. We didn't get there for a long time, but when we did, we only managed to save just over half of them. We have their survivors here with us." I waited for the inevitable tirade.

The general surprised me, although his position was self-serving. "I expect you had no choice and it was the right thing to do. As far as the UN, I think you've made it clear who should lead the resettlement efforts. Well done!" I didn't answer for so long that the general asked if I was still there.

"You're trying to trick me," I finally said. "You're never happy and you never give compliments."

"Don't be the nut job that everyone else here thinks you are. Of course I'm happy. Your group is now around one hundred people and the Russians are at zero. We win!"

I win, is what you really mean, I thought. It was clear to me why he was happy. I was here and he'd take all the credit, probably earning another star. But that wasn't my world. Everything around me now constituted the sum total of all that we were.

A Community where you could be yourself and where you could help others, not because you had to, but because you wanted to.

Madison stood in the doorway and watched me, knowing that I was checking in with Washington, D.C. She was always there to support me, knowing how these calls upset me. I smiled at her and gave her the thumbs up. She nodded and continued to watch. She would wait for me to hang up to be sure that I was okay. The twins burst out the door with Phyllis and Husky close behind. They waved as they ran past, heading toward the kennels.

And the general confirmed that we were staying. I breathed deeply, taking in the cool air of the Alaskan spring. The sky was clear, and the ground was drying out.

We'd won and I didn't know how to feel. I turned slowly, looking at a broken-down city with people breathing new life into it. It was going to be a good year.

End of Book Three

GLOSSARY OF TERMS

Alaskan Term Definition

Break up   Spring thaw in Alaska where the ice breaks apart on
               the rivers. During this transition, most snow is melted
               but much remains in the shaded areas. The mud is
               horrendous as the ground beneath is still frozen.

Generator   Backup power source; burns gasoline to generate a
               limited amount of electricity

Green Up   When the tree blossoms bud – usually happens in a
               single day, turning the wilderness from the brown of
               winter to the green of spring

Dog team   Consists of two lead dogs, two swing dogs, six team
               dogs, and two wheel dogs. The lead dogs are the smart
               ones. They pick out the trail and they set the pace. They
               lead the dog team. The two swing dogs are trained to
               form an arc around a corner. If the dogs just followed
               the lead dogs, then they'd dive off the trail. Everything
               has to be done smoothly. A good team flows behind
               the lead dogs, taking the weight of the sled with them,
               allowing the leaders to focus on the trail ahead. The
               team dogs are the work horses, pulling the majority of
               the weight. The wheel dogs are the strongest as they
               have to deal with the constant jerking of the sled. They
               are responsible for getting the sled moving. They pick
               up the tension if the sled pulls back. The wheel dogs are
               calmer. They have to be.

Mush   To drive a dog team

Musher   The one who drives the dog team

Pellet Stove   A stove designed to burn pellet fuel versus cut firewood,
               but used in the same manner as a wood-burning stove.
               Note: You cannot cook on a pellet stove.

Permafrost	That part of the ground that never thaws. There are places in Alaska where the ground is frozen to one thousand feet deep.
Quad	An All-Terrain Vehicle (ATV)
Rigging	Attaches dogs to sleigh. Includes tug lines, tow line.
Sled	A snowmobile
Sleigh	A trailer towed behind a snowmobile
Snow Machine	A snowmobile

ACKNOWLEDGMENTS

First and foremost, I'd like to thank my wife Wendy for continuing her work as a University Professor without pause, which allowed me to delve into writing. My mother-in-law Mary Whitehead has been very supportive. She's always a good one to call and talk with.

My best friend Bill Rough and his better half Linda were stalwart through many phases of my life and were the first ones to read this book and provide feedback. I'm honored to call them friends.

Monique Happy became the editor for this series through a serendipitous online author/editor exchange. She helped breathe new life into the book that used to be It's Not Enough To Just Exist – my first book. I added some 70,000 words to that story and then we broke it into a trilogy. I am quite pleased with the end result. My readers of It's Not Enough were begging for a sequel – they now have that. And those who've chanced to read this are asking for another sequel. We shall see…

I want to thank some readers by name as they are the ones who we look to when we're feeling a little down. Diane Velasquez and her sister Dorene Johnson are powerhouse readers, ready for anything I throw at them and always willing to give feedback. Norman Meredith is a new addition to the team and has provided valuable input to me and my process. They have also been very kind with their comments. Chris Rolfe, Cathy Cauthan Northrup, Monique Lewis Happy (also one of my editors), Joyce Stokley, and so many more. You great people help make every day that much sunnier.

ABOUT THE AUTHOR

Craig is a successful author, on track to publish ten books in 2016. He's taken his more than twenty years of experience in the Marine Corps, his legal education, and his business consulting career to write believable characters living in a real world.

Although Craig has written in multiple genres, what he believes most compelling are in-depth characters dealing with real-world issues. Just like Star Trek, the original series used a backdrop of space, the themes related to modern day America. Life lessons of a great story can be applied now or fifty years in the future. Some things are universal.

Craig believes that evil exists. Some people are driven differently and cannot be allowed access to our world. Good people will rise to the occasion. Good will always challenge evil, sometimes before a crisis, many times after, but will good triumph?

Some writers who've influenced Craig? Robert E. Howard (the original Conan), JRR Tolkien, Andre Norton, Robert Heinlein, Lin Carter, Brian Aldiss, Margaret Weis, Tracy Hickman, Anne McCaffrey, and of late, James Axler, Raymond Weil, Jonathan Brazee, Mark E. Cooper, and David Weber. Craig learned something from each of these authors, story line, compelling issue, characters that you can relate to, the beauty of the prose, unique tendrils weaving through the book's theme. Craig's writing has been compared to that of Andre Norton and Craig's Free Trader characters to those of McCaffrey's Dragonriders, the Rick Banik Thrillers to the works of Robert Ludlum.

Through a bizarre series of events, Craig ended up in Fairbanks, Alaska. They love it there. It is off the beaten path. He and his wife watch the northern lights from their driveway. Temperatures can reach forty below zero. They have from three and a half hours of daylight in the winter to twenty-four hours in the summer.

It's all part of the give and take of life. If they didn't have those extremes, then everyone would live there.

Website: http://www.craigmartelle.com/
Facebook: https://www.facebook.com/AuthorCraigMartelle/
Twitter: https://twitter.com/rick_banik

Other Books by Craig Martelle

Free Trader Series:
Free Trader Series Book 1 – The Free Trader of Warren Deep
Free Trader Series Book 2 – The Free Trader of Planet Vii
Free Trader Series Book 3 – Adventures on RV Traveler
Free Trader Series Book 4 – The Battle for the Amazon (est. Aug 2016)

Rick Banik Thrillers:
People Raged and the Sky Was on Fire

PERMUTED
PRESS
needs **you** to help

SPREAD (THE)
INFECTION

FOLLOW US!

ｆ | Facebook.com/PermutedPress

🐦 | Twitter.com/PermutedPress

REVIEW US!

Wherever you buy our book, they can be
reviewed! We want to know what you like!

GET INFECTED!

Sign up for our mailing list at
PermutedPress.com

PERMUTED
PRESS

KING ARTHUR AND THE KNIGHTS OF THE ROUND TABLE HAVE BEEN REBORN TO SAVE THE WORLD FROM THE CLUTCHES OF MORGANA WHILE SHE PROPELS OUR MODERN WORLD INTO THE MIDDLE AGES.

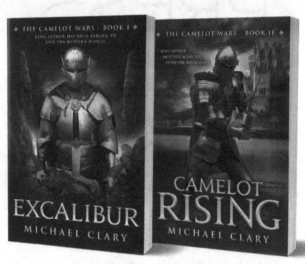

EAN 9781618685018 $15.99   EAN 9781682611562 $15.99

Morgana's first attack came in a red fog that wiped out all modern technology. The entire planet was pushed back into the middle ages. The world descended into chaos.

But hope is not yet lost— King Arthur, Merlin, and the Knights of the Round Table have been reborn.

PERMUTED PRESS

THE ULTIMATE PREPPER'S ADVENTURE.
THE JOURNEY BEGINS HERE!

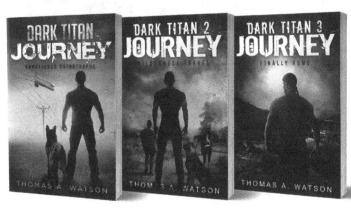

EAN 9781682611654 $9.99   EAN 9781618687371 $9.99   EAN 9781618687395 $9.99

The long-predicted Coronal Mass Ejection has finally hit the Earth, virtually destroying civilization. Nathan Owens has been prepping for a disaster like this for years, but now he's a thousand miles away from his family and his refuge. He'll have to employ all his hard-won survivalist skills to save his current community, before he begins his long journey through doomsday to get back home.

THE MORNINGSTAR STRAIN HAS BEEN LET LOOSE—IS THERE ANY WAY TO STOP IT?

An industrial accident unleashes some of the Morningstar Strain. The

doctor who discovered the strain and her assistant will have to fight their way through Sprinters and Shamblers to save themselves, the vaccine, and the base. Then they discover that it wasn't an accident at all—somebody inside the facility did it on purpose. The war with the RSA and the infected is far from over.

This is the fourth book in Z.A. Recht's The Morningstar Strain series, written by Brad Munson.

PERMUTED
PRESS

GATHERED TOGETHER AT LAST, THREE TALES OF FANTASY CENTERING AROUND THE MYSTERIOUS CITY OF SHADOWS...ALSO KNOWN AS CHICAGO.

EAN 9781682612286 $9.99   **EAN** 9781618684639 $5.99   **EAN** 9781618684899 $5.99

From *The New York Times* and *USA Today* bestselling author Richard A. Knaak comes three tales from Chicago, the City of Shadows. Enter the world of the Grey—the creatures that live at the edge of our imagination and seek to be real. Follow the quest of a wizard seeking escape from the centuries-long haunting of a gargoyle. Behold the coming of the end of the world as the Dutchman arrives.

Enter the City of Shadows.

PERMUTED
PRESS